WAITING FOR WYATT

A RED DIRT NOVEL

S. D. HENDRICKSON

This is a work of fiction. The names, characters, places, and incidents are products of the author's imagination or have been used fictitiously. Any resemblance to actual persons, living or dead, events, or locales, is entirely coincidental.

Waiting for Wyatt © 2016 by Stacy Dawn Hendrickson

Copyediting by Curiouser Editing
Cover Design by The Cover Lure
Design Layout by Champagne Formats

ISBN-13: 978-1518742996
ISBN-10: 1518742998

For the dogs, sitting in cages, waiting to be adopted.
And the wonderful volunteers who run the shelters.
Your kindness makes the world a better place.

Part 1

Emma

CHAPTER 1

Emma

I SMASHED MYSELF AGAINST THE APARTMENT WALL, CLUTCHING Charlie to my chest. His erratic heartbeat fluttered under my fingers. Blood dripped off the wound on the side of his head, soaking into my favorite yellow tank top. The little dog let out a noise that was a cross between a whimper and a bark.

"Shh." I put my fingers around his muzzle. The giant brown ears flattened against his gray speckled back. Craning my neck, I peered toward the front window located in the kitchen. A large bearded face smashed against the glass, looking inside my apartment. Flipping around the corner, I glued my body tight to the wall. I couldn't move. I couldn't even dart to another room. The window gave a full view of our entire living area.

I was going to kill my sister for not shutting the curtains. I told Blaire every day not to leave them open, but she wanted to see her food with natural light as she cooked it. She could *see* it just fine without the curtains open.

A loud banging came from the door. "Emma Sawyer. I saw you run in there with my damn dog. Open the door."

I knew that crazy man would snatch him right out of my hands if I opened the door. Charlie wasn't technically mine. I had rescued him from our abusive landlord.

"If you don't open this door, I'm coming in with a key. I've got rights, you know. And you've got none. Not when you stole that piece-of-shit dog."

Taking my chances, I ran into the living room, sliding open the back window. I crawled outside onto the tiny ledge, balancing Charlie with one arm. My nails clawed the glass back down. Little prickles of fear slipped down my back. Blowing a blonde curl out of my eye, I chose not to look at the rocky area below our apartment. The ledge wasn't meant for people. It was more of a cement decorative area that ran along the top floor. I moved, one foot at a time, one breath at a time, over to the next window.

Tapping lightly, I waited for Mr. Hughes. He was an elderly man who lived next door. I did his weekly grocery shopping and cooked him dinner a few times a week. The curtain moved slightly, revealing an old face that slipped into a toothless grin. He pulled up the glass with his crooked fingers.

"Emma, what are—"

"Hold him." I transferred Charlie over to Mr. Hughes. Crawling inside his living room, I shut the window behind me and covered the glass with the thick, blue curtains. The adrenaline coursed through my blood, making my hands shake.

"You finally did it," he said with an excited gleam in his eye.

"Yes. And he saw me. I thought I had enough time to get in and out of his office." I took Charlie back into my arms. His little body shivered in fear. I doubt he'd ever experienced much of anything besides terror from Kurt. That man was incompetent as a landlord and borderline psychotic when it came to animals.

Yesterday, when I came home from my shift at the nursing home, I'd heard terrible sounds coming from the manager's office. His voice, shouting and screaming, followed by the repeated squeals of a tortured animal.

"Where are you going to take him? You know he can't stay here."

"I don't know. Maybe my parents'? I'll call them." Pulling the phone from the pocket of my tight denim shorts, I pressed the auto dial for my mother. I sat down on the couch, waiting for her voice.

"Emma?"

"Hey, I have a favor."

"Oh, honey. What have you done now?" Her voice flowed with a hint of a drawl.

"It's not that bad. I rescued a little dog. But he can't stay here at my apartment. I have to find him a place. Will you take him?"

"I'm sure he's a very nice dog. But I just can't bear to have another after Rolly died. It's too soon."

"It's been five years, Mom."

"I know, but I still can't shake that image, Emma. You weren't there. Just the thought of it makes me sick to my stomach." My parents got Rolly when I was ten. A few years ago, he was hit by a car.

"It's okay. I just thought maybe you were ready. I'll think of something else."

"You just need to talk to your sister. I know she doesn't like dogs, but maybe you can entice her. Work that Emma magic on Blaire."

I rolled my eyes even though my mother couldn't see me. "It's not Blaire. It's my landlord. You met the guy. He's not the world's kindest person. I just need to get the dog out of here before Kurt finds him."

"I would love to. But I really can't, honey. I'm sure you will find it a home. You are so good at that kind of stuff." I pictured her face with that wide smile as she fawned over me with her flowery words. "Are you coming to dinner Thursday night? I missed seeing your sweet face last week."

"I'm sorry." The guilt flowed in my chest, hearing the sadness in her voice. She was good at that too. "I had to cover for a girl at work. I'll make sure I come this week."

"You know how important our weekly dinner is to me."

"I know, Mom. It won't happen again. I promise."

"Okay. Well, I have to go, Emma. I'm working in the flower bed today. I need to get it done before I burn up out here. Good luck with your dog."

"Thanks. See you Thursday." Clicking the end button, I watched Mr. Hughes come back into the living room, leaning heavy on his walker, carrying a duffle bag. I needed to speak with Kurt about transferring him to an apartment on the first floor. He'd struggled getting up and down the stairs the last few months. I guess that conversation would have to wait until Kurt forgot about the Charlie incident.

"She said no?"

"Yeah, she wishes me luck." I frowned. "So I guess we need another option."

"I was thinking. It's Saturday, right? Today is Saturday?"

"Yes, it's Saturday." I nodded my head, feeling a little sad. Over the last few months, I'd noticed other signs of his fuzzy thoughts. I guess that's what happens when you stay in an apartment seven days a week.

"That pet store. You know, the one in that outdoor mall thing? There used to be a shelter place in front of it on Saturdays."

I vaguely remembered the little cages next door to the shoe store. I grinned at him. "That actually might work."

"Here's you a bag. Go wrap him up in a towel and zip him up in the bag. You'll have to make a run for the car."

"Okay," I said, holding Charlie tight to my chest as I got up from the couch.

I found an old towel under the bathroom sink. Wrapping it

tight around his body, I felt a surge of emotion, seeing his terrified eyes peering out of the duffle bag. I didn't know what kind of dog had features like Charlie's. He was the strangest little animal. Almost like the giant ears of a brown rabbit were yanked off and placed on the body of a gray and black dog. He was one of a kind.

"Hey, little guy. You are almost home free. Just one more trip." I zipped the top closed and put the black straps over my shoulder. The weight of the twenty-pound animal cut tight into my skin. I patted Mr. Hughes on the arm. "Thank you for the help."

"Anytime—and good luck."

Unlatching the door, I pushed it open an inch, checking the walkway for my landlord. My eyes followed the stairs from the second floor down to the parking lot and over to my car. I didn't see the six-foot bearded man anywhere. Maybe he went back inside the manager's office. Charlie whined from deep inside the canvas. Nerves fluttered under my skin. It was now or never.

I fished my keys from my pocket. Taking off in a sprint, I felt a sharp twist in my knee. *Seriously?* My knee had to act up today of all days. But I knew better than to be running in flip-flops. The pain came in burning stabs through my leg. Taking the stairs two at a time, I got to the parking lot without seeing Kurt. I glanced to my left toward the manager's office before running in the direction of my car. The white Fusion was roughly half a building away.

My leg jerked again, sending pain right through my kneecap. The muscles curdled into complete mush. I lost my balance and flew forward. I cried out as I hit the ground. My arm scraped across the cement. I came to a stop, feeling every ounce of pain as the bag with Charlie slid across the parking lot.

No, no, no. I scrambled to my feet, limping over to the black duffle bag. Charlie whined from deep inside. "Sorry, little guy."

I grabbed the straps and ran the final few yards to my car

door. Putting the bag in the passenger's seat, I started the motor and threw the car into reverse. My heart beat a hundred miles an hour as I left the apartment complex with the face of the bearded man in my rearview mirror.

CHAPTER 2

Emma

I DROVE TO THE PET STORE IN STILLWATER. THE RED DIRT CLAWS rescue had roughly fifteen cages set up out front. I carried Charlie in my arms. His eyes held a wild gleam as I set the little dog down in front of the older woman. She seemed like a reasonable person in a T-shirt bearing the name of the rescue. Her long black hair was pulled up in a youthful ponytail on the back of her head that showed off a gray streak across the front. She resembled a skunk, which made me want to laugh.

"I need to find him a place," I pleaded with her. "He was in a bad situation, and I got him out. But I can't keep him."

"I'm sorry, but we can't take anymore. The rescue is full." Her kind, blue eyes trailed over the stains on my yellow shirt and back to Charlie. "I've got an idea. I think Wyatt might take him. He usually has space. I would try him. I doubt he'd say no to you."

"Where is this Wyatt?"

"You know Marshal Road on the west side of town?"

"Yeah."

"It turns into County Road 3210. Take that about thirteen

miles. Turn left at the blue barn. Go another five miles. It's a silver gate. Can't miss it."

"Okay. You have any info flyers on this kennel?"

Her lips curled up on the sides like they possessed a secret. "It's not that kind of place. But you should go out there. He'll take good care of that little guy."

"Okay. Thank you." I didn't have much choice. Picking Charlie up from the cement, I held the scared dog tightly against my chest. His head tucked slightly under my chin. He was getting used to me now. My heart filled with sadness. I wanted to keep him. I wanted to give the battered dog the home he'd never had with evil Kurt.

My little white car bounced over the ruts in the road, covering the outside with a layer of red dirt. I searched for a blue barn as the weeds grew taller in the ditch.

I reached over to pat Charlie on the head. His nose stayed glued to the window, making a wet spot. The little dog seemed to love car rides. I grinned, seeing the first sign of something besides fear coming from those terrified eyes.

At the blue crumbling landmark, I made a wide turn in the dirt road, sending a cloud of dust behind the car. The silver gate came into view with old cow skulls hanging from the fence poles next to it.

Pulling off the road, I parked in the grassy entrance. The place seemed so abandoned and desolate. I opened the door and walked to the gate. Climbing on the rungs, I peered out into the distance, seeing a few buildings. A black bird landed next to one of the boney heads on the pole. Its yellow eyes glowed against its dark feathers. I cringed, looking back out across the tall grass to the buildings. *I guess this must be the place.*

I unlatched the gate, which lacked any type of lock. Climbing back inside my car, I held Charlie in my lap as I drove over the semi-visible path, hearing the tall weeds scrape the underside of my car. I paused in the dirt clearing, taking in a view of the area.

On the north side, a single-wide trailer sat propped up on cinder blocks. The kennel resembled a large metal shop building with outdoor pens attached to the sides, making an indoor-outdoor run for the dogs. Charlie jumped out of my lap and went crazy against the window.

I parked close to the kennel. The sound of dogs echoed even before I got out of the car. I looked around for signs of people, but the place seemed vacant. I lifted Charlie out of the passenger's seat, tucking him against my chest. He latched tight to my shoulder.

"Hello?" I yelled, looking at the buildings. "Anybody here?"

I walked toward the kennel entrance, trying not to sneak up on this Wyatt. I got a little nervous. This was a stupid idea, coming out here by myself. I knew nothing about the lady at the rescue or this person she sent me to find in the middle of nowhere.

Wyatt might be some crazy, old man with a sling blade. It's not like I could even outrun someone. My knee was a complete mess after the fall in the parking lot. Scary man with a knife would equal a few quick sprints and then another face-plant out in the middle of the pasture—stab, stab, and then lots of blood, followed by dead. *Great!* Now I sounded like my sister.

"Hello? Anyone here?"

I pulled open the door, peering inside the entrance of the building. A blast of cool air hit my face. I didn't go inside. I thought it best not to go poking around without an invite. The dogs ran from the outside kennels through the little flap doors. Each face pressed against the inside gates with another round of barking. Still no sign of Wyatt.

The mysterious man was either hiding out in the trees with a gun or he was away. The lady at the shelter didn't give me a phone number for the place. She didn't even suggest it. *Great! I came all the way out here, and he's gone.* I turned around to go back to the car.

"Oh my gosh!" I jumped and almost dropped Charlie. My stomach fell right out of my skin. "You scared me."

A guy watched me from the cement steps of the single-wide trailer. He didn't smile. He didn't move. This did not seem promising. I put on a brave smile and walked toward him, getting a better look at the mysterious man.

He was younger with short brown hair. My eyes slipped down the rest of him. Nothing fancy or out of the ordinary about his clothes. The guy wore a simple white T-shirt and jeans with a pair of brown work boots. He was attractive in a brooding sort of way, like that old poster of James Dean that hung in the Cinemark. I glanced back up to his piercing face. He watched back with an unhappy snarl.

"Hey, I . . . well . . . um. So this lady at the rescue said you might be able to help me." I paused, but he still didn't say a word. His face stayed in that unfriendly, bewildered look of surprise and anger. The longer I waited for him to respond, the more his lips flattened into a thin line. He wasn't happy that I was here.

I smiled again as my nerves fired under my skin. "I'm sorry. Th-this is Charlie. Can you help me? I can leave if you can't. That's okay. I'm sorry. I mean, you look busy. You're busy. I'm sorry for just stopping in. She didn't give me a phone number. I would have called. I-I'm sorry. I can go. We can just go. Yeah, I will get out of here. Sorry to have bothered you."

I walked away. *Awkward. Awkward. Awkward.* I wanted to get right back in my car and drive away from this unfriendly guy. Maybe he had been asleep and I'd woken him up. That had to be it. He'd been asleep and I'd ripped him right out of some dream and he just wasn't awake yet. Or maybe he was just an angry, terrible person and I needed to get in my car as quickly as possible. Yes, I bet that was it. My feet moved faster across the dirt.

"What lady?"

Startled again, I turned around to the sound of his deep, raspy voice. The guy's soft lips pressed into a hard line. He slipped back into that unfriendly gaze, which made me nervous all over again. Mr. James Dean sure had a way with intimidation.

"I-I'm sorry. I didn't get her name. She was at the pet store over in Stillwater. The Red Dirt Claws rescue was set up in front. She said they couldn't take Charlie. But she thought a guy named Wyatt who ran this place would take him. Are you Wyatt? I'm sorry for just dropping by. She said to just come out here."

"She did?" His tone said he didn't believe me, like I was making the whole thing up.

"Yes."

"What did she look like?"

"Oh, um. She had black hair with a little white piece in front."

"I see," he muttered.

"She seemed to think it would be okay. I'm really sorry for just showing up without calling."

"What's wrong with him?"

"I don't know. I'm sorry. I should know the answer to that question. I guess it's just his foot and, well, his face too. I . . ." My voice trailed off. I couldn't tell this guy I'd technically stolen Charlie. I'm sure some rule or law existed with this sort of thing. Can't take stolen jewelry to a pawnshop. Can't take stolen dogs to a rescue.

"I found him all beat up. I think it's just an infected cut. Almost like he got it tangled up in something. Then he chewed it. And he got kicked. But not by me. I wouldn't do something like that. But someone kicked him. I just don't know who." I paused, seeing his jaw grit up tight. "I'm sorry. I guess you didn't need to know all of that."

He let out an annoyed breath loud enough for me to hear. "Let me see him."

Leaving his spot on the steps, the strange guy came over to me. He was a whole foot taller than my blonde head. His hands reached for Charlie but didn't take him, almost like he was afraid to accidentally touch me. I held Charlie out, and he picked him up. The guy went toward the building with the kennels. His boots kicked up small dust clouds in the dry dirt path.

I followed Mr. James Dean even though I'd not been invited inside the kennel. I walked through the door, feeling the cool air on my skin. Goosebumps pricked up on my legs. A little office sat on the right side just inside the door. He put Charlie on the table and unwrapped my makeshift bandage I'd tacked on in the car.

"He's all bones. I don't think he's been given much to eat by the owner." I knew for a fact that Kurt didn't feed him. Charlie had lost weight since that jerk brought him to the apartment complex. "Or maybe he was on the run. Like I said, I . . . um . . . found him."

Mr. James Dean didn't say anything as his fingers ran over the area with the cuts on Charlie's leg. Very meticulous. Very precise. They moved up to his little face, slipping inside the flap of his mouth. They examined the area where Kurt had whacked Charlie in the head with the heel of his boot.

I fidgeted, trying to stand still. The silence was making me uncomfortable. "I . . . um . . . really did want to keep him. I can't have pets in my apartment."

The lie slipped off my tongue a little easier this time. It was also technically true. I couldn't have Charlie because I would get caught, harboring my stolen dog. My leg twisted around again, feeling the aching pain from my fall, which had caused my old knee injury to flare up again. "I just want you to know. I'm not like one of those people."

His gaze lifted up in a burning glare. I stopped twisting around as the green eyes narrowed and my words dropped off. "I'm sorry," I muttered, flashing a faint smile.

"Why do you keep apologizing?" His deep voice was a little softer this time.

"Because I . . . um . . . don't know." His stare made my words disappear.

"Don't apologize. You haven't done anything wrong. Okay?"

"Okay," I muttered.

He wrapped Charlie back up. The dog's pink tongue reached out, catching the guy on the cheek. A brief smile popped up on his lips. *Dimples.* I saw a flash of dimples, and my breath caught in my throat. They made his whole face light up. The harshness melted as the dimples shined on each cheek. He was cute and sexy and troubled. Deeply troubled. That part hung around even with the dimples. His green eyes shifted back over to me. The dimples disappeared into a cold stare.

"I've got a spot for Charlie."

"Thank you." I nodded back at him, feeling a flood of relief. If this didn't work out, I wasn't sure where else to take the dog. I gazed back at the strange guy. Even though his lips flattened tight again, I liked how he'd remembered Charlie's name. The one I'd muttered only once after Mr. James Dean had sneaked up and scared the crap out of me.

He lifted Charlie off the table and transferred his little body back over to me. Once again, he did his best not to touch me. Not even an accidental hand graze. I cuddled the little furry head under my chin and followed the stranger deeper into the kennel, past the rows and rows of dogs.

Knowing he couldn't see me, I examined every piece of him. In my whole life, I'd never met a person who made an impression like this guy without a name. His silent face, absent of a smile. I wanted to know why he was so unhappy. Such an odd thought about a person I didn't know at all. Maybe he was just simply a jerk. Sometimes a bruised apple was just a rotten apple with nothing good inside.

Then I remembered the dimples. They were just as real as the soft lips that went with them. I wanted to know why he didn't flash those dimples to the world. I wanted to know why he sat out here alone with his closed-off, hateful frown when every girl in town would walk miles just to see those dimples and kiss those lips.

I continued with my inspection of the stranger, letting my eyes linger on his backside. Mr. James Dean had a nice one. Cute dimples and a tight butt. He glanced over his shoulder, feeling the probing gaze from my eyes. I smiled in embarrassment. His lips tilted into a snarl, letting me know once again, he didn't like me being here and he *really* didn't like me staring at his butt.

The sooner we got Charlie settled, the sooner I would be out of his hair. Whether he was a good apple or bad apple, it didn't matter. I didn't need to be thinking about him like there was something to be figured out. He was odd, and my life was a little scattered right now.

I was still trying to figure out my future since I didn't go to college with my sister. Over the last couple of years, I didn't do all the things I'd imagined when I'd graduated high school. I didn't make glamorous new friends and go to fun parties. I didn't date much. Not that I was thinking about dating this strange guy. I cringed. This wasn't the kind of guy someone contemplated dating. He was strange. He made weird people seem normal. But what right did I have to call anyone strange? My friends consisted of my *weird* sister and the old man who lived next door.

"This is what I got." He stopped next to the only empty pen. "You can put Charlie in there."

I bent down, prying the tiny paws from my shirt. His little body seemed dwarfed in the large indoor pen. A little bed sat in the corner. I looked into the brown eyes of my new friend.

"Bye, Charlie." I scratched his gray and black fur one last time. A tear fell out of my left eye. Good thing I'd piled on the waterproof today. Standing up, I shuffled out of the way. Charlie jumped against the metal cage, watching me with his sad eyes. I needed to get out of there immediately, or it wasn't going to end well. I would take that little dog back with me. And that couldn't happen.

Charlie flipped his ears up, begging me not to leave. Those eyes. Those ears. I needed to get out of here. "He likes car rides. You might mention that to whoever looks at him," I muttered before spinning around.

Charlie whimpered as I left him behind. He yelped, but I kept on walking. The single yelp turned into a string of wails. The desperation in his voice tugged and pulled and twisted up my insides.

The kennel came alive with the sounds of the other residents. They barked as I moved faster, hearing my flip-flops click with each step. I didn't look at their faces this time. The sad animals were just too much.

This place was a home for the neglected and the forgotten, just like Charlie. Another tear fell down my cheek. I flicked it away before I could offend Mr. James Dean with my girly emotions. I glanced over in his direction, but he wasn't there. I turned back around, and the scene grabbed me a little in the chest.

The unfriendly stranger was bent over, talking to Charlie. His voice was lost in the sounds of the kennel, but I saw his lips moving. Words. Lots and lots of words, strung together in sentences that he couldn't seem to manage to say to me. He smiled, letting the dimples settle into place. I saw them all the way across the room. They pulled at my heart as he calmed the poor little dog.

After a few moments, he stood and walked slowly in my direction. I wanted to ask what he said in his private conversion with Charlie. I wanted to ask, but I knew he wouldn't answer, even if I threw out a hundred questions.

He stopped just a few feet away, tucking his hands in the front pockets of his tight jeans. The green eyes stayed upright and blinked in silence. They never dipped down to take a peek at my body. He never followed the outline of my curves in the cutoff shorts. He never looked at me like other guys. This silent stranger was different.

I smiled faintly. He should talk. It was his turn to say at least *something*. I'm a guest at his place, but that's the catch. He wasn't going to mutter a word because I was the uninvited guest. The awkward vibe in the air got even thicker.

"How long do you think it will take?" I asked, breaking the uncomfortable silence.

"For what?"

"To find a family. I mean, some of them seem like they've been here awhile."

"They have."

It was all I got from the strange guy, but at least he was talking. "Do you advertise them? I'm guessing not many people find their way out here by accident."

"I . . . uh . . . " He stumbled for the first time. "I don't really have visitors out here."

"Oh."

"Diana takes them to town. At least, the ones she thinks she can get matched up. Some of them are going to stay here and live out the rest of their lives. They're too old or hurt to be adopted out. She gives them food and a good place for the end."

I think he just broke a record on the most words strung together. I waited, watching his face. It betrayed nothing but more secrets. "Who's Diana?"

"She owns the place."

"Oh. So it's not your place?"

"No."

"Do you work for her?"

"Something like that."

He watched me again. No elaboration. No smile. Nothing.

Feeling like I'd officially worn out my welcome, I glanced toward my car.

"Well, I guess I should go." He didn't respond, making it even more awkward. "Thank you, I guess. You know, for taking Charlie."

He nodded. I thought I might see a smile. I hoped for one last glimpse of those dimples as a parting gesture. No such luck. I left the building and walked to my red dirt-covered car. The flip-flops aggravated my leg, making my butt twist a little as I limped.

"You could come back. You know, to check on Charlie."

What the . . . I stopped cold in my tracks as he startled me with his deep, raspy voice. I turned around, seeing a strained look on his face like he wished to take back those words. Well, he wasn't going to get that option. I wanted to see Charlie again. And I wanted to know more about . . . *him.*

The idea pulled tighter in my chest, tugging at that place in my heart that always got me in trouble. I wanted to know why he didn't talk. Why he seemed so angry. Why the guy with the dimples was so *sad.* My life might be a bit of a mess right now, but he was far worse off than me.

Closing the gap between us, I forced the guy to stare down at me. The summer heat burned into his skin, making the glare from his eyes reflect with a scorching twist. I wouldn't let him look away. I tried to see what I was missing.

I probed deeper into the eyes of the stranger. This guy was hurting something fierce. He fought an internal battle. He fought something awful, but I pushed back. He didn't want me here. Not really, but something made him do it. Something made him spit out those words and invite me back.

The green eyes flashed with deep pain, and then his jaw clenched, breaking our locked stare and sealing up his emotions. The stranger had stopped me from seeing the broken pieces that existed beneath the hateful mask he broadcasted to the world.

And I had to remember he was just that to me. *A stranger.* But I knew at least one thing I could fix in this moment.

"If I'm going to be coming back, I think I should at least know who you are." Even though I felt the jittery nerves from our impromptu staring contest, I stuck out a hand to the guy who towered over me. "I'm Emma. Emma Sawyer."

He peered down at my fingers for a few seconds before taking them in his big hand. He gripped tight, but not to the point he crushed my bones. His hand felt warm and soft and hard, just like the glimpse he'd shown me of his heart.

He muttered in his deep voice. "Wyatt."

"Wyatt?"

"Caulfield." The last syllable came out like he swallowed razors. The grit of his jaw went to an extreme level of intensity, grinding his teeth against the sides of his mouth. Our hands melded together in the fiery warmth until Wyatt suddenly let go.

Taking a step back, his right hand gripped tight into a fist, the same hand that had just touched mine. I waited for Wyatt to ask or say or do something, but he shuffled back another step, putting more distance between us.

"Thursday? That work for you?" I asked quickly, trying to rein his attention back to the original question. I did everything I could to act like this wasn't affecting me. I was practically shaking from the strange undertone pulling me toward him as he pushed me away.

"Huh?"

"You said I should come back."

"Oh. I guess Thursday's fine."

"Okay. Oh, wait." I fished my cell phone from the pocket of my denim shorts. I held it, trying to act normal. "Give me your number. You know, in case something comes up. I won't drive all the way out here and you be gone or something."

"I'll be here."

"What if something happens? You might have to—"

"It won't." He cut me off.

This was getting weird between us. "Well, okay . . . um . . . let me give you mine."

His lips clamped down even tighter in a thin line and the color disappeared. I worried for a moment Wyatt would pull back his offer. I'd pushed too hard, too fast. It was just a dang phone number, but he seemed to have a problem with it. This was a normal question, I reminded myself. Normal people exchanged phone numbers all the time. But this guy was far from normal.

"I don't have a phone," he muttered, sticking his hands down inside the pockets of his jeans.

"Wait. What? You don't have a phone?"

"I don't have a phone."

"How do you not have a phone? I mean. You live all the way out here. How do you talk to people? Meet up with people? Find people? Call people? How do you—"

"I don't. Have. A phone."

He said it again so firmly my mouth stayed slightly open. I knew from the tone it was by choice and not because of money. That made it all the more bewildering and confusing.

"I'm sorry for . . . wait—no. I didn't mean to say sorry." I was rattled, and Wyatt just kept twisting me up even more with his strange behavior.

"Thursday. Come at four," he muttered. "I'll be here."

"Okay. I'll see you Thursday, Wyatt Caulfield." I held his gaze for a moment and then walked quickly to the car.

As I drove through the tall grass, I looked over at the towel I'd used to wrap Charlie up in the seat, but my thoughts stayed on the guy who was caring for him. Wyatt Caulfield just might be the strangest and most haunting person I'd ever met.

CHAPTER 3

Emma

BEFORE I GOT BACK TO THE APARTMENT COMPLEX, I STOPPED at McDonald's. I found a T-shirt in the trunk and replaced my bloody, paw-print-covered tank top. I removed all the evidence of Charlie from my car, stuffing each item in a trash can outside the fast food restaurant. Goodbye, favorite shirt. I wiped the blood and dirt from the seat and door. I needed to be prepared if I expected this little plan to work at my apartment complex.

Driving back home, I hesitated before pulling into the parking lot. Part of me hoped to get this over quickly. Kurt came out of the manager's office before I even killed the engine. I mentally braced for the confrontation. He was a very intimidating man at six-foot-two, three hundred pounds with about twenty of that being a long, wispy beard.

I would tell my next lie of the day. I would tell that worthless piece of trash that I knew nothing about his dog. Opening my car door, his large head blocked the late evening sun from my view.

"Where's my dog?" he growled.

"Oh. You still haven't found him?"

"Don't play dumb. I searched your apartment. Didn't find him. So where did you stash the little bastard?"

A vile feeling settled in the pit of my stomach, imagining Kurt standing in my bedroom as he searched for Charlie. I had left my bras hanging up to dry all over the room after I hand-washed the delicate fabric this morning.

If I wasn't locked into our lease for another year, I would pack up and leave immediately. I hated this place, but we couldn't afford to pay the cost to break the contract. Another reason I needed to yell at my sister. She'd insisted on signing that stupid two-year agreement because it knocked a hundred bucks off a month. I steadied myself and put on the performance of a lifetime.

"I saw the dog running by my apartment. I tried to catch him, but I've got a bad knee." I pointed at my right leg. The ugly swelling and scrapes were still present around my kneecap.

"Hmm," he grunted.

"Yeah, I tried to get him in my apartment, but he ran off in that direction." I pointed to the wooded area behind the complex. "I'm sorry."

"Is that so?" His face moved a bit, but the wiry hairs around his lips blocked most of the expression. I wished Kurt would get so angry he released us from the lease, but I knew that man was too vindictive and devious to let that happen. Our landlord would force us to stay to the bitter end.

His gaze lingered on my face, then drifted to a brazen stare at my breasts. The brown eyes grew a deeper hue. Images of Kurt rifling through my drawers flashed in my head. He was the type who would get the most from his visit inside my apartment. Even in the heat of the summer, my skin got clammy as the beady eyes returned to my face. I think Kurt half-believed me, but I wasn't sure.

"Yeah. I wish I could've saved him." I took a few steps backward. "Coyote will probably get him out there."

"Probably so. He's a worthless little bastard, but I gotta find him. That pup already belongs to someone else."

"Well, if I see Ch—the puppy again, I'll try to catch him." My backward steps had me within three feet of the stairs. "I have to run."

With a quick spin, I sprinted up the wooden steps, ignoring the stabbing pain in my knee. It would be a night of freezing ice wrapped around my leg. I pulled my keys from the pocket of my shorts, but my sister had the door open before I could use them. She slammed it behind me, turning both locks on the frame.

"I was afraid he was going to drag you into the office and not let you come out." Her eyes flashed wide from behind her glasses. Blaire pushed the center piece back straight on her nose.

"Kurt might be a dog abuser, but he's not going to kidnap me."

"You don't know that. He's got shit for brains." My identical face stared back at me. That's the thing about being the Sawyer twins. We were completely the same yet different like two sides of the same coin.

In a huffy turn, Blaire went into the living room, falling down on the couch, knocking over her giant tuba case. It clanked against the coffee table before hitting the carpet. "You just had to take that damn dog. Now we are going to be stuck with Kurt crawling up our ass."

"How did you know?"

"Mr. Hughes told me. Really, Emma? You climbed out on the *ledge*? Are you that stupid?" Her eyes squinted from behind her glasses in disapproval. I wore contacts. She refused after reading some story about the Loa Loa worm that had grown to five inches in a man's eye.

"He almost killed Charlie yesterday. I wasn't going to just sit in here while that man murdered him."

"That dog has a name now? What am I thinking? Of course you gave him a name. You are just too nice. It gets *exhausting* sometimes. Charlie and Mr. Hughes and all those people at that nursing home. Wonderful Emma. Sweet Emma. Blah, blah, blah. But you need to think sometimes. We have to live here. Unless you've got some idea of how to get us out of the lease."

"You need to figure that one out. It's your fault we still live here."

"Oh, please. Don't try to pin that on me." She rolled her eyes behind the wide lenses.

Blaire and I had shared a room growing up. As we got older and moved out of the house, it had never occurred to either of us to seek out someone else as a roommate. Not even when she'd gone to college and I technically didn't.

Blaire and I were born as mirror image twins. I'm right-handed. She's left-handed. We came from the same sack in the uterus. Doctors still liked to brag about that one in our little town. Apparently, it's pretty rare.

"You met someone this afternoon." Her voice came with a dry clip.

"I don't know what you mean. I was busy finding Charlie a place at a rescue. Not meeting people."

"That's not all you did this afternoon." Her brown eyes widened. "Unless you met someone there. I was giving Aaron his tuba lesson, and I felt it right here." Her polish-free hand rested against the front of her T-shirt. "All bubbly and happy. And I knew because Aaron plays like shit. And is always going to play like shit. Sounds like a cross between a farting cat and someone running over its tail. But I cash his parents' checks anyway. So what made you *sooo* happy while I was trapped listening to cats dying so we can have rent money?"

I stared at her and she stared back. That's how I'd perfected the look I'd used on Wyatt. Blaire got my super glare of death almost every day. And well, she could use it back just the same way. I let out a deep breath.

I already knew she would ask when I got home. We didn't talk about it much, but Blaire and I had this connection. It came across weird and slightly demonic if we shared it in front of the wrong people. My sister and I just knew things about each other, like when we got sad or really happy or scared. Our little secret.

"I don't know what you felt. I didn't *meet* anyone. So stop making dramatic accusations. And you know you like giving tuba lessons."

"I don't believe you." She brushed a trickle of sweat off her forehead. Blaire's hair was piled on top of her head in a ratty mess.

"*Fine.* There was this guy when I dropped off Charlie." I plopped down next to her on the old, flowery couch. I flipped my soft blonde curls back off my sweaty neck. The air-conditioning was on the brink again, which showed another sign of Kurt's incompetency as a landlord.

"I knew it. So who is this guy? What's he like?"

"I don't know. Intense, I guess. I think he lives with the dogs at the kennel. It's really sad. He's out there all alone."

"He's like some crazy, recluse dog hoarder? Really, Emma!" Her eyes grew huge. "You've sunk to that?"

"I've sunk to nothing. We met. That's it."

"Emma?" She twirled a strand of stringy hair around her finger. It ratted up in a ball as she peered at me from the next cushion.

"What?"

"That's not it."

"Fine. I'm going back there on Thursday," I muttered.

"Alone? You don't know anything about him. Typical Emma. You are so freaking clueless. This guy could be dangerous. He lives out there all by himself in some compound. Who does that?

Killers. That's who."

Blaire would have a breakdown if she actually saw where Wyatt lived and that unfriendly glare coming from his green eyes. But she didn't see him the way I did today. I don't know what piece got stuck with me more on the drive home: those poor dogs in the cages or the guy locked in the mental one.

I wish I could say everything to Blaire, but I just couldn't explain what happened today. She wouldn't understand why I had to go back there. Normal social things were difficult for her. She wasn't like me when it came to other people. Complicated issues that involved compassion and emotion were hard for her to comprehend.

"It's not like I'm dating him. I'm just getting to know someone. And I think it makes Wyatt interesting."

"He's *interesting*? That's what girls say right before they get the shit knocked out of them and stuffed in a fucking trunk."

"*Blaire!*"

"What?" Blaire leaned back against the cushions, tucking her knees against her chest.

"Wyatt's not gonna hurt anyone." I leaned over, slipping my arms around my sister's little body. She hated it when I went for an unsolicited hug. She bristled up like I was squeezing a cactus, but I did it anyway, as a distraction to her current fit. "I watched him with Charlie. He was so meticulous and kind."

"How old is he, anyway?"

"I don't know. He's around our age, I guess. And he's got dimples, Blaire. They just came out of nowhere." *And then they were gone.*

"Emma. You really are crazy." She pushed me away and went back into interrogation mode. "You can't base him being safe on dimples. You are a terrible judge of character. You'd let strangers stay on our couch if I didn't say no."

"Not that again. You know Couchsurfing is a legitimate website and we could make a lot of money during the university football games."

"The answer is still no. And I think the answer to this one should be no too. I can't believe you're attracted to some weirdo in the woods. You have lost your damn mind."

"But you don't understand. You didn't see him. The way he looked. There's something . . . " *Going on with him. I think he may need help.* "There's just something about Wyatt. I want to see him again. Spend some time with him. I think he could use a friend."

"Friend? Hmm."

"And the dogs. It was terrible, Blaire. They looked like those awful commercials."

"I'm sure it was very sad. The dogs and *the guy*. But this has nothing to do with you, Emma. Not that any of them ever do, but let this one go."

"I need to do this. I can't just ignore what I saw today."

"Fine. But don't call me when this *Wyatt* guy has you tied up in his trunk. I'm not coming to get your stupid ass."

I smiled at my sister's joke. She didn't get out much. Not that I had attended a large amount of wild, raging college parties. But Blaire was a social recluse because she chose to be that way, and I think her personality scared people.

She didn't even drive. It's not that she physically couldn't get behind the wheel. Blaire just chose not to learn. According to my sister, she didn't want to be responsible for a thousand-pound vehicle, hurling down the road like a shotgun bullet. She had a whole list of death facts to go along with her reasoning. I'm surprised she even rode in the car with me.

But that was my sister. Even with all her quirks, I loved her more than any person in the whole world. How could I not? Blaire was literally the other half of me.

CHAPTER 4

Emma

On Thursday, I returned down the red dirt road to see Wyatt and Charlie. As I turned off the motor, he walked out of the kennel building, wearing the exact same outfit as last time with the exception of his shirt. Today it was brown.

He didn't seem happy. He didn't seem happy at all. I didn't really expect Wyatt to come running out and sweep me up in a big hug. A smile would've been courteous with the dimples being a bonus. Instead, Wyatt had a glare of uncertainty. He still regretted inviting me back.

I got out of the car, wearing cutoff shorts and a tiny V-neck T-shirt. My hair fell down in blonde, shiny curls I'd styled with my curling iron. As I walked over to where he was standing, his piercing eyes never looked me over. If Wyatt had a choice, I think he would've shoved me back in the car and pointed it toward the silver gate. Yet his grouchy attitude didn't make me nervous like it did the first time.

"Hi, Wyatt." I smiled up at him. His eyes squinted a bit without a response. I was too close, and he had to look down to see me. "I came back."

"So you did."

"Ok. So . . . do you want me to just go see Charlie or did you want me to do something else?"

"Like what?"

"You tell me. You need help with anything?"

"No." He shuffled back a few steps, putting more distance between us.

"You sure? I could help you . . ." I trailed off, not sure what to suggest. I smiled up at his hard face and shrugged.

"I don't need your help. Just go see Charlie. That's why you came. Then you can go."

"Okay then." Ignoring the sting of his dismissal, I walked past him inside the kennel. Slower this time so I could take in each animal. Some of the dogs pressed against the gates with open mouths and tongues, hanging out like they were smiling.

I stopped next to a medium-sized, brown dog. Bending closer to the ground, I scratched his face through the gate. My heart felt something awful inside as I noticed his ears were cut to the scalp, jagged and uneven, almost like a dull knife had sawed into the skin. And the scars. They were everywhere. The gray scars wrapped around and around his mouth like a person . . . no way. That couldn't be possible.

"That's Chewy." I heard Wyatt's voice behind me. I waited to see if he continued, but he didn't say another word.

Glancing over my shoulder, I saw his tight, sealed lips. So this is how it was going to be with him. "And?" I prompted.

He let out a loud breath. "Chewy had his mouth wired shut when Diana found him on the side of the road. He could open his mouth just enough to get a sip of water. The more he tried to work it free, the deeper it embedded into his skin."

I swallowed hard, running my fingers over the raised scars.

"Why would someone do that?"

"Why does anyone do any of this stuff?" His hand gestured out toward the other dogs.

I got up from my spot and walked slowly past the next few kennels. I was speechless. Each animal peered out with big eyes, grabbing me like a fist inside my chest. Each had some form of brutal injury that marred them for life. Each had the remnants of torture; a product of some selfish desire to own what couldn't be owned. So they broke them physically until the poor animal had no choice. The whole place was ten times worse than Charlie. I froze, feeling the burn in the back of my throat.

"I had the same reaction the first time." His voice was soft and scratchy. I looked over toward Wyatt. His arm was resting on the metal gate. Our eyes held for a moment before he looked at the ground. He seemed more relaxed than when I'd first arrived today. I wanted to ask him questions. Hundreds of them flew through my head all at once. But he was talking and he seemed to work better if I allowed it to happen on his own terms.

"So I guess that means it gets easier seeing them?"

"Yeah. Sometimes I still have to remind myself the scars are there, but nobody's hurting them anymore. We are giving them a better life than where they came from." His face twisted up as the deep words floated between us. They came from a person who was filled with more on the inside than the mask he wore on the outside. He was a good apple, just a bruised one full of compassion for his animals.

The invisible pull was there again. The invisible fingers tugged at my hands, my heart, and my feet. I moved closer to where Wyatt stood by the next kennel. His body visibly tensed, but I didn't let it affect me.

"What about that one?" I pointed to the rat terrier with a pink scar shooting across his back hip instead of a leg. He bounced around on tripod feet.

"Ricky Bobby." Wyatt reached over the kennel fence, scratching behind the dog's ears. He smiled faintly as the rat terrier licked the palm of his hand. The animals seemed to melt the granite wall, surrounding this broken guy. I saw it every time he touched one.

"What's his story?" I whispered.

Wyatt glanced at me as the smile lingered on his lips. "This guy thinks he can outrace cars. Got hit by one. His owner wanted to put him down instead of amputate. The vet called Diana, and he came here."

"Why would someone just put him down for that?"

"You shouldn't ask why in this place. There is no why for them. Some people are just selfish bastards." His eyes lifted up, catching mine for a brief moment.

"I'm sorry. I didn't mean to ask it that way."

"I told you. You don't have anything to be sorry for."

"That's not what I meant. I know I rescued Charlie, but I haven't seen a place like this before. There's so many of them."

Wyatt didn't respond that time. I let out a deep breath, moving toward the next pen, but it appeared empty. Looking toward the back, I saw a black shape huddled in the corner. The more I looked, the more it pressed back as far as it could get from the gate.

"That's Cye." His voice grated on the words. "He's a little timid. And he's only got one eye. I think it scares him, not being able to see everything clearly."

"What happened?"

Wyatt didn't answer, and his jaw gritted up. He came over and stood just a few inches away, which surprised me. We both studied the sad creature in the back of the pen. Then he started to talk again. "The vet thinks he was beat with a hammer. It's taking awhile for him to trust people."

"Not even you?"

"No, and I'm not sure if he ever will."

"How long has Cye been here?" I whispered.

"A year. I touched him the night he arrived. Diana had the poor guy sedated. Cye hasn't let anyone touch him since."

"I don't know how someone could do that to an animal." My throat burned as the scared eyes watched me from the back corner. The more I invaded his space, the more he hunkered to the floor. It felt wrong to even look at Cye. "Does he ever go outside to the other part of the kennel?"

"He's like a ghost. I know he goes outside because I scoop it out of the grass. But I never see him do it though."

"How do you do this, Wyatt?" I looked up at his face. "It's just so sad.

His green eyes stayed guarded even though mine were close to tears from hearing the stories. Wyatt's jaw tightened as he swallowed hard. "Some of their stories are worse than others. But I do my best to make it better for them."

"Oh," I whispered. "You're like the keeper of the island of misfit toys."

"The what?" He frowned.

"You know, from Rudolf—the movie?"

"Hmm," he grunted.

The longer I stood in his personal space, the more I felt his hidden pain, weaving back and forth between us. I wanted to step even closer. I wanted to let him know that whatever was tearing him up inside would be okay.

Wyatt got fidgety and rubbed the side of his neck. I got a whiff of his scent. It wasn't cologne. Not that I expected any. Wyatt didn't seem like the type to wear something fancy. Instead he just smelled clean, like he'd rubbed dryer sheets into his skin.

"How long have you been doing this?" I let the question slip out.

"Awhile." He squinted with that pained look again.

"Do you work here full time or do you go to school too?" I knew better, but I said it anyway. His face clamped down and he shuffled not one, but three steps away.

"Why don't you just get Charlie? There's a fenced area in the back. Take him out there."

With that grand announcement, Wyatt ignored my question and walked back to his office. I went to the kennel that held my little dog. When I opened the gate, Charlie lunged toward my face, covering me with slobber. Just a few days away, but it must have felt like years for someone like him.

I carried Charlie down the aisle of sad eyes. I wanted to take each of them with me. Maybe I would later and Wyatt could just deal with it.

Charlie and I played for a good thirty minutes before I noticed Wyatt's presence. He watched us safely in the shade to the side of the fenced area with his shoulder propped up against a storage shed. I thought Wyatt would leave once his cover was blown, but he didn't. He stayed. He stared. He intrigued me even more by the minute.

I wanted more than anything to figure out Wyatt Caulfield. Hot and cold. Withdrawn and angry, and then a flash of dimples and compassion for his dogs, followed by pain. The poor guy needed someone or something. I looked back over to where he stood in the shade. Slowly. I had to remind myself to approach him slowly.

"Why don't you come in here?" I yelled over in his direction. He didn't say anything. He didn't join us in the pen, but he didn't leave either.

I left Charlie inside the fenced-in play area. My knee cramped as I returned to the kennel room. It had always held twinges of pain since my accident, but the fall this week opened up a whole new level of intensity. Every step gripped my leg as my shoes clicked against my heels. I chose to ignore it as much as possible.

Trailing down the long row, I stopped in front of Chewy. My chest tightened, seeing the wire scars around his mouth. The brown dog was bigger than Charlie so I looked around until I found a leash. I carefully opened his gate and latched it to his collar. His brown eyes lit up bright. I think he actually pranced down the aisle past the rest of the dogs.

Once again, I felt a sadness reach inside my body and wrap around my heart. It was a happy place. It was a heartbreaking place. Being here was a dose of reality. My problems felt insignificant compared to those of a creature who had survived the lashes of a hammer or had his voice taken away by a piece of wire.

Wyatt was still leaning against the shed when I came back out to the play area. The irritation flashed all the way over to where I stood with Chewy. Opening the gate of the fence, I released the latch on the leash. Chewy ran straight to Charlie. My stomach caught for a moment, imaging a giant fight of teeth and blood. But the two dogs ran around, chasing each other. It made me smile. Charlie wasn't even close to the animal Kurt had tortured in his office.

"Chewy's a good one for Charlie."

"Huh?" I jumped at the sound of his deep voice, coming from behind me. "Do you have to keep doing that? Don't sneak up."

"Sorry." A faint smile flashed on his lips like he enjoyed it. Wyatt had so many pieces of strange to his personality.

"I thought Chewy would be good too. There's just something about him in there. He might become one of my favorites. Do you have favorites?"

"I try not to, but it happens," his gruff voice answered. "Some of them are lifers, so yeah. I have some that are favorites. I guess."

"Lifers?" I glanced over to him again. Wyatt tucked his hands inside the front pockets of his jeans. I wasn't sure if that was a defensive move or just habit.

"They won't get adopted. Many of them will live the rest of their lives here."

"Is Chewy a lifer?"

"I don't know. The scars bother people when they see them."

"Really? He's not even bleeding."

"I think it makes them sad or they see him as deformed. That's just the way most people are about this kind of stuff. Actually, I figured you would be too."

"Why would you think that?"

He shrugged. "You seem the type."

"The type?"

He shrugged again without explaining the odd statement.

"I'm in school to be a nurse." I paused, shifting my weight off my bad leg. I thought talking about me would make this easier for him. "Well, I guess that's not exactly true. I'm behind. I'm still trying to get all the prerequisites finished before I can start the program. I don't go to school full time so it's taking awhile."

His eyes slipped over to me and then back out to the fenced-in area with the dogs. I waited for Wyatt to respond, but he stayed silent. Talking about me wasn't any better than talking about him. We watched Charlie and Chewy play for a while longer.

Blowing a curl out of my eye, I plunged in with the question that I needed to run past him. "Wyatt, I know you don't really like me here. But I would like to come back."

"You want to come back?" He voice seemed raw with an edge of pain. He said it with no trace of a smile.

"I like it out here. I want to help."

"I don't need your help."

"Not you. The dogs. There's so many of them. I could volunteer or something. I've got a couple of jobs right now. I work at the nursing home and the bookstore. But I could find some time to come out here. I want to help them." *And yes, I want to help you too.*

"I don't think it's a good idea for you to come back." He seemed frazzled and agitated again. His full lips flattened into a thin line. His boots shuffled a few steps away like he was ready to bolt.

"Wyatt, please don't leave." Turning to go after him, my shoe slipped across the grass. I winced, sucking in a deep breath. The pain shot down my leg into my foot. I needed to go to the doctor. I'd ignored the problem and hoped it would go away, but I knew it was a delicate situation even before the fall this week.

"What's wrong with your leg?"

"I . . . um?" I stared back at him. Wyatt surprised me with both the question and the level of compassion in his voice.

"The leg? You limp a little. And I saw the scar."

"Oh." My eyes popped open wide at his observation when he appeared to ignore everything about me. I looked down out of reflex at the scar across the top of my calf that rested just below my swollen kneecap. "Well, my leg thinks it needs knee surgery. I've told it no."

"Should you be wearing those shoes?"

"Probably not, but it's summer so I wear them." I bent my knee up and down, feeling the pain loosen a bit. "So back to my question."

"Why do you ask so many questions?" He frowned again.

"What do you mean?"

"You just ask a lot."

"I want to learn about this place and you don't exactly volunteer information. How else am I supposed to get to know you?"

"You can see Charlie without knowing anything about me."

"So does that mean I can come back? Like on a regular schedule or something?"

"Emma . . . I don't know." He paused, gazing down at me, but all I heard was the sound of that gruff voice saying my name. He said it for the first time and it was almost sweet. Almost human compared to his block-of-ice personality.

"Is that a yes or no?"

"You can come back, but keep it simple, you know. We don't have to stand around talking and shit. You come do your thing. Then go."

"I'm not going to come back and pretend you're not here. That's weird and strange. You obviously live here. If you don't want me to come back again, then I won't. I'll say goodbye to Charlie. I won't bother you again."

"Wait. Don't." His hand grabbed my arm, softly, almost like a reflex. The warmth of his fingers burned into my skin. Wyatt seemed to realize he was touching me, and let go. "Look, I'm a little rusty."

"Rusty at what? People? Acting like a normal human being? Not being an antisocial jerk?"

"Yes." His face scrunched up with that pained expression again.

"Oh," I whispered. "I didn't really expect you to admit that."

"I don't see too many people out here."

"Really." I faint laugh escaped my lips. "I couldn't tell. So do you act like this when you go into town too or just out here?"

"No, well, not really. Look, Emma. Things with me. They're complicated."

"Like how? I understand complicated more than you realize. Why don't you explain it to me?"

"I can't. It's the kind of complicated where I really shouldn't even have you out here. But I know you want to come back . . . and I don't know. Maybe I don't want to stop you."

"You don't?" His words caught me off guard, making small tingles flutter under my skin.

"No." That twisty invisible pull surfaced between us again. It tugged me closer and closer to his sadness as his raspy voice spoke softly. "You should spend time with Charlie. I shouldn't be the reason you don't come back."

My flip-flops crunched in the grass as I slowly closed the space between us. Charlie and Chewy tumbled around in the pen barking. I ignored them as Wyatt tilted his chin down to see me. I captured his eyes with mine. They opened wide in surprise. He didn't even try to block me out this time. My heart beat with a rapid pulse in the veins under my skin. I stared into his green eyes until I saw him crack, just a little, and then it splintered.

Pain. The raw, knock-you-down-in-the-mud, rip-out-your-heart-and-beat-it-with-a-stick kind of pain. It flowed out around him in a wild, savage agony, consuming every cell in his body. As our eyes stayed in a locked stare with his misery pulling me closer even though my feet never left the ground.

My breathing got heavy. My stomach dropped right to my knees, causing my skin to tingle and my thoughts to swirl around in my head. I wanted to reach out and touch this stranger. I wanted to close the remaining gap. I needed to close the gap. I needed to touch his skin. I needed to touch the pain. In my entire life, no one had ever affected me in this way.

"What happened to you, Wyatt Caulfield?" I asked softly. The feelings rushed through my whole body. I was falling. I was falling fast through the open crack he allowed me to see in this moment. I wanted to know why he was broken, not for myself, but for him. I now knew what existed on the inside of the apple. His soul was crushed to a pulp and all I wanted to do was fix it. I wanted to make it better.

"You don't want to go there, Emma," he whispered.

"Please, Wyatt." I mouthed the words. "I want to know your story. You told me theirs. So tell me yours."

"Maybe I don't want you to know my story."

"I get it. You don't know me. I don't know you. But I want to know you. Let me."

"So you can do what, Emma? Hit me with a bunch a questions and try to fix whatever you find out? Well, I don't like people prying into my life. It's complicated, and I don't like questions."

"I-I'm sorry. I didn't mean to pry. I just—"

"Then don't," he snapped. "Come see Charlie. I want you to. But that's it. Okay?"

"I . . . um . . . okay."

"No questions." His face hardened as the last piece of our connection shriveled up and died.

I nodded. The sudden bite to his mood caused my breath to vanish from my lips. Turning away, I watched Charlie and Chewy. My fingers gripped the metal of the fence. I felt my pulse as it hammered away inside my body. The sun burned sharp in the sky, causing sweat to soak my clothes.

Behind me, heavy footsteps crunched the grass. I turned, seeing his broad shoulders slip away. His body moved in ridged steps. I'd pushed too hard and made him angry. His boots stomped up the stairs to his trailer.

Wyatt looked back in my direction before he opened the door. His eyes burned all the way across the yard. They pulled and pushed. Holding onto the fence, my stomach caught the way it did when I drove too fast over the hill going into Beckett. He had let me see something today. He had let me see inside his tormented soul, and it had broken every piece of my heart.

CHAPTER 5

Emma

When I returned on Saturday, I never saw Wyatt, but I knew he was at the kennel, hiding in his trailer. I just knew. Wyatt was too meticulous and careful to leave me alone at his place. His micromanagement tendencies placed him somewhere within a few yards of every item of his that I touched. Plus, I saw the thick curtain move in the trailer every time I spun around.

I went to the doctor on Monday. The pain and swelling had continued to get worse around my kneecap. Once again, Dr. Westbrook said surgery was imminent after looking at the x-rays. The longer I put off the procedure, the greater the chance of doing more damage. When I refused, he ordered another round of physical therapy to see if that would help the pain.

I didn't want the surgery. I didn't want the physical therapy. All of it just reminded me of why I was in this situation and the setbacks it had caused in my life. I'm sure everyone was frustrated with me, including my doctor. I just didn't want to deal with it.

Since I was already off work for my appointment, I went

back out to the kennel. I took a bag of dog biscuits, which served as an intricate piece of my new plan to get Cye out of his pen. I stayed for two hours but never saw Wyatt. Just like last time, the brown curtain moved whenever I glanced over in his direction. I guess Wyatt really was serious about us not speaking when I came to see Charlie.

The less I saw of Wyatt, the more I thought about him. I thought about him every day and every night as I drifted off to sleep. His smile. His dimples. His sadness. I needed to get Wyatt out of his trailer. I needed a plan for him too.

On Thursday, I pulled on a pair of denim shorts and thumbed through my shirts, looking for the perfect one. I thought about my last date, which had been about four months ago and a setup by a coworker at the bookstore. I think his name was Cory. He had taken me to hear a country band play at the Tumbleweed, but he spent the whole show talking about winning some beer-pong tournament the night before. When I didn't seem interested in going to his apartment afterward, I'd never heard from him again.

The blatant dismissal by Cory really didn't faze me. We were at different places in our lives. I took a class here and there, but mostly I worked at the bookstore and the nursing home. And usually after my shifts, I stayed for a few hours and visited with the residents. They were sweet, especially Vera. She loved to gossip, which always made me laugh.

"What are you doing?" Blaire stood in my doorway with her arms crossed over a faded red shirt. She never cared much for clothes. Most of the time, she pulled on whatever reached her hand first, not caring if the fabric had holes or matched anything else she wore.

"I'm getting dressed." The answer came out muffled as I pulled a white tank top over my lacy bra. "What does it look like

I'm doing?"

"Where are you going? You don't have to work today."

Tugging at the bottom of the shirt, I situated the hem over my shorts. "I'm aware of my work schedule. You don't need to remind me. I'm just going to run an errand this afternoon."

"It's Thursday, which is dinner with Mom and Dad tonight. You have to be here to pick me up on time this week. You know I don't like being late."

"You know Mom doesn't care if we are late as long as she sees us. But I'll leave earlier this time so you don't have a panic attack." My sister was rigid with her schedule to the point of almost being creepy.

"Leave earlier from where?"

"Just some stuff I've got to do." I shrugged, not wanting to start one of her interrogation conversations.

"You're gonna see *him* again." Her sarcastic drawl pulled on the word. "That's why you are wearing that shirt."

"There's nothing wrong with this shirt. It's a normal shirt I bought at Old Navy." If only Blaire were normal, we could swap items and only buy half the amount of clothes, which would save money.

"Doesn't it scare you, Emma? You know nothing about him and he lives in the middle of nowhere. He could have bodies out there. And that shirt. I don't know. It says stab me."

"Stop being dramatic. Wyatt isn't a serial killer and this isn't a stab-me shirt. It's just a white tank top. It's not even that tight." I rolled my eyes, pulling the sides out a bit. "See? There's lots of space."

"Stop joking. You really don't know anything about him. You don't know what he is or isn't."

Her words did have a slight truth to them. But over the last week, Wyatt had become a borderline obsession in my mind. Instead of focusing on myself, I had daydreamed about all the different scenarios that had turned him into the broken guy who hid behind the curtains.

My sister didn't need to know this bit of information, even though I was pretty sure Blaire could feel it from me. I went over to where she stood in the doorway, placing a hand on each of her shoulders. "I promise. I know what I'm doing."

"I don't think you actually do," she spat. Blaire had this natural gift to turn everything into some catastrophic event. "You are always so busy being nice to everyone in the world that you don't see people for who they really are."

She was right about this little fact, but I couldn't turn away at this point. I wanted to help him. I wanted to figure out what forced Wyatt into this life of solitude. He wasn't any better off than one of his dogs. I knew that now. He was like Cye, hurting in the corner, hiding from the world, hoping nobody took notice.

"Blaire, he's fine. Wyatt is just a very complicated guy who is maybe a little misunderstood. He likes his space. That's all." I smiled to myself. Now I sounded like Wyatt.

"Complicated. Misunderstood. Hides in the woods. Sounds like an unsub profile."

"I told you to stop watching that show. It gives you too many ideas." Blaire was obsessed with *Criminal Minds*. Last year, she was convinced our mailman was an *unsub* of some investigation by the FBI because of a scar across his right cheek. She said it was the kind placed when a person violated gang rules. Blaire seemed to forget we lived in Stillwater, *Oklahoma*.

I walked over to the dresser and applied a layer of summer pink lipstick. I dabbed a tissue to remove the excess and then smiled at my sister. "How do I look?"

"The neckline of your sexy shirt gives just enough space for Wyatt to slide his fingers around your throat."

"Stop worrying so much. And I thought this was a slash-me shirt. Not a strangle-me one."

"Emma . . . don't joke about this shit."

"Don't have a panic attack." I grabbed her for a quick hug. Tightening my grip, I waited for her to squeal, but she just stood there in the doorway.

"I want to meet him sometime."

"Twins buried alive." I joked, trying to lighten her mood. "You think they will send the *Criminal Minds* team? Or the CSI team? Or maybe both? And the FBI? Definitely the FBI."

"I'm serious. I want to meet him." Blaire pushed herself out of my arms.

"Okay. Just not today. It would be better not to spring it on him. I don't think he would like a surprise."

"You're not helping yourself right now."

Ignoring her flippant remark, I grabbed my keys. "Want me to drop you off at the library so you don't have to ride your bike?"

"Sure. Just don't forget to pick me up." Her eyes squinted, causing the glasses to slip a bit on her nose. Absently, she pushed them back up with her finger.

"It was one time, Blaire. And if you drove, stuff like that wouldn't happen."

"I don't need to drive."

"Come on. The car is half yours too."

"I ride in my half of it all the time."

"You are graduating in less than a year. What are you going to do? I can't drive you around forever." I opened the apartment door, holding it wide as she came out behind me with the giant backpack. It must be awful to try to balance that thing on her bicycle.

"I'm not discussing this shit today."

"We have to at some point. I could teach you. And you would get used to it. I promise."

"I'm not letting someone with four speeding tickets teach me how to use a car. You are a terrible driver."

“I drive perfectly fine.” As we reached the bottom of the steps, I glanced over to the manager’s office. Kurt stood in the doorway with crossed arms. His eyes followed both of us as we walked to the car.

“I think he’s hiding something,” she whispered. “He fits the profile.”

“If you don’t stop watching *Criminal Minds*, I’m going to cancel the cable.” I opened my car door, feeling his stare on my backside. The vile feeling returned in the pit of my stomach. Blaire might be half right this time.

CHAPTER 6

Emma

I DROPPED MY SISTER OFF AT THE LIBRARY AND THEN STOPPED AT Sonic Drive-In. I got two large Cherry Cokes. Hopefully, the ice wouldn't melt before I got out to the kennel.

I pulled up close to the trailer. I didn't see Wyatt anywhere outside. He didn't know my schedule of dropping by each time, but the long pasture driveway had always given him plenty of notice to dodge inside his home.

I walked up the trailer steps with both Cherry Cokes. Balancing one against my chest, I knocked on the door. I knocked hard and loud five times, then waited. It was an old trailer. Paint flecked on the plastic shutters that outlined each window. I think they were red at one point, but the sun had faded them to a pink color. The tan siding was in the same shape.

I beat my fist against the door for a second time. The cheap aluminum rattled in the frame. I reached forward with my fist again, but the door opened, showing his familiar, hard face.

"I brought you a drink. It's Cherry Coke." I held out the cup for him to take from my hand.

Wyatt watched me with an odd expression. His T-shirt choice of the day appeared to be white again. And well, Wyatt's hair only did one thing. The short pieces fell all natural on top of his head.

I bet his hair would feel soft if I touched it. I bet it would brush across my skin, making my neck feel tingly. I bet those soft lips would feel nice too. Except they smashed down into that thin line again as he stared at the Styrofoam cup. I shook the drink in his direction.

"Are you going to take it or what?"

He clasped the cup in his hand, brushing my fingers as I let go. A jolt shot up through my arm from the contact. I took a drink of mine, watching his bewildered expression. My peace offering caused a bit of confusion. Wyatt hesitated, looking at the red straw and then back at me.

I rolled my eyes. "Of course you hate Cherry Coke. I took a guess and I thought everyone likes cherry."

"I like cherry," he muttered in his raspy voice.

"Then what are you doing? It doesn't mean anything. I was just being nice. You know, a thank-you for letting me come back out here."

"Oh. Thank you, Emma." And then he smiled. *A real one.* The first real one ever tossed in my direction. His pink lips stretched out with a flash of white teeth. The dimples fell right into place.

I froze. Wyatt Caulfield was incredibly good-looking when he allowed his face to open up and be seen by the world. So breathtaking and mysterious with the sadness still engrained in the creases around his eyes. He put the straw between those perfect lips. A look passed over his face. One of deep intensity and I think, pleasure? I felt like I was invading a private moment.

"Do you want me to leave you alone with that?" I laughed and took another drink of mine. My chest fluttered a little, watching him swallow.

"I was just thirsty. It's been a while since—never mind." He smiled faintly. The dimples came and went again, but not my attraction. It came in small tugs, pulling me to the damaged person who was hiding behind the frowns and broken smiles, pulling me closer and filling my head full of questions, filling my body with feelings that I pretended didn't exist.

He took another drink and eyed me cautiously from the doorway. I looked past his wide shoulders to the secrets hidden inside the trailer. I didn't expect to be invited in when I'd originally knocked on the door. But now, I was so close. I wanted to see inside the cave of the bear. *Great!* Now I was daydreaming about going inside his house. I needed to get out of here before I did something stupid to ruin my progress.

"Well, I'm going to see Charlie." I turned to walk away. The door clicked shut, but his boots pounded down the steps. I smiled to myself. My idea of bringing him something nice seemed to work. I got him out of the trailer.

I walked toward the kennel, feeling his presence just a few feet behind me. I was curious. Did he watch me as I was walking? He knew I couldn't see him. Glancing over my shoulder, his face betrayed nothing.

Once inside, I went straight to Cye. He stayed in that pathetic, hunkered-down pose in the far back corner. My heart lurched every time I looked at him. I felt angry, so very angry at the evil person who had done this to him. Only a monster would beat a dog with a hammer. A horrible, evil monster that should be locked in a cell with another evil monster that was conveniently slipped a hammer.

On my last two trips to the kennel, I brought something special for Cye. I'd put a little bone inside by the gate before I took Charlie out to the play area. When I came back, it was always gone. The ghost dog did venture out more than just at night. I had a plan for Mr. Cye too. By the end of summer, he would let me pet him. Slowly. I would have to use patience. I would have to wait until he was ready.

I opened the gate, crawling on my hands and knees inside the kennel. I placed his bone on the cement, a little closer than last time.

"It's not gonna work." I heard the raspy, deep voice and looked over my shoulder, seeing Wyatt leaned back against the gate on the other side. He watched me crawl backward out of the pen. He seemed slightly amused too. That was a new one.

"We will see." I smiled at him.

"You don't think I haven't tried that one?"

I blew a blonde curl out of my eye as I stood up to face him. "Maybe he'll take better to a girl."

"Maybe." He closed those puckered lips around the straw. Wyatt got that look again as he took another swig. I never thought a guy drinking a Coke would constitute as something sexy, but I grew mesmerized by the way he sucked on the straw. I shook off the feeling before turning around to the next pen. I stopped dead in my tracks.

"What? Where's Chewy?" I spat it out. Terrible thoughts flashed through my head with all the horrible images I'd imagined since visiting this place. "What happened to him, Wyatt?"

"Calm down. Nothing bad. Diana got him yesterday. She found a home for him."

"So he's, like, just gone? I didn't get to say goodbye."

"It doesn't always work like that here, Emma." His faced softened a little.

"Where'd he go?"

"Retired military guy. He lost a leg in Iraq. The scars on Chewy didn't bother him." He came over next to me. "That's Daisy and Gatsby."

I was so distraught over Chewy I'd failed to see the new occupants of the pen. Two old chocolate labs lay on the cement with their bodies intertwined together as they kept their heads down.

"Did you come up with those names?" I slipped a look in his direction, but he stayed focused on the brown dogs in front of us.

"Yes."

"Did you name the others too?"

"Some." He glanced over at me with that answer. "And yes, I like Will Ferrell."

"What? I didn't ask about Will Ferrell."

"I assumed with all the questions that would be your next one. Did I name the car-chasing dog Ricky Bobby because I like Will Ferrell?"

"No." I tried to frown at him, hiding the smile I got because he'd volunteered something without my asking.

"Really?" He studied me for a moment, then turned back to the pen in front of us. He took another drink and remained silent.

"So Daisy and Gatsby. What's their story?"

He didn't respond immediately. I braced myself, waiting for his deep voice to share another tale filled with heartbreaking details. "Well, the owner just died. The family didn't want them either. They left the dogs in the house for three weeks before the neighbors figured it out."

"They just left them?"

"Yes, and went back to Arkansas."

"What did they think would happen to the dogs locked up in the house? It doesn't make sense. That's just . . . just so *wrong*."

"I know." His eyes softened with compassion toward my anger. "Some people are just selfish bastards, and it's the animals who pay the price."

I focused on the two dogs that morphed into one pile of chocolate fur. Each face was covered in gray hair that reflected their age. They seemed lost. They seemed alone. They seemed confused as to why they were left behind by the only person who had ever loved them.

Daisy and Gatsby asked why in a place where the question

was forbidden. I closed my eyes for a moment. Each time his gruff voice told me a story, it never got any easier. Yet I continued to ask questions, knowing each answer came with heartbreaking consequences.

"Come on." Wyatt touched my shoulder briefly and my eyes flew open. I saw a flash of tenderness before he shut it down. "Get Charlie out. I'll get Gus."

"Gus?"

Wyatt didn't reply and left toward the exit, carrying his Styrofoam cup. I went to the end of the aisle and Charlie jumped so high he fell over backward. I opened the gate and the spotted dog flew into my arms. As I carried him outside, Charlie did his best to lick the carefully applied makeup off my face. Wyatt came out the front door of his trailer, clutching a white and brown Jack Russell.

I froze right in place. He was good at making the reaction happen, confusing me to the point that he rendered me speechless. And Wyatt did just that as he got closer and closer to where I stood with Charlie.

He was so incredibly cute when he allowed it to show. Wyatt seemed like a different person in this very moment. He seemed almost normal with the little dog tucked under his arm and the cup in the other hand.

I swallowed hard, trying to calm the feelings. I wanted to help him. I wanted to peel back every layer until I knew everything about him. But now I felt those other complicated thoughts. The slow burn of attraction flickered inside of me.

Taking a deep breath, I did my best to push it aside as he joined me on the path to the fenced-in play area. "So that's Gus?"

"Yes."

"What's his story? He seems normal." As normal as you right now, I wanted to add.

"Things are not always what they seem." Wyatt scratched the

dog under the chin, leaving my question unanswered.

We placed both of the little animals in the play area. Charlie pounced at Gus. They took off in a blur, around and around through the grass. I laughed, watching Charlie. He loved everyone. Diana would find him a home soon. It shouldn't take much to get him adopted. I wondered if she tried or if Wyatt asked her to keep Charlie longer for me.

I sneaked a glance in his direction. He had a faint smile on his face and yet the sadness still radiated off his cheeks. It stayed just a little on the surface even on a day like today. This strange and rare day he'd opened up a few of his layers.

"Hold my drink." I shoved it toward Wyatt. He took the white cup from my hand as I went running inside the pen. I chased the two dogs in circles. Laughing, I let them attack me down to the grass. They made me happier than I'd been in a long time. The adrenaline rush of doing something good was almost as intoxicating as the one I used to get while running. With the knee problems, I hadn't been able to do that in a really long time.

As I rested in the grass, Gus attacked my hair, tugging it softly. I pulled him in a bear hug as Charlie jumped on top of me. I glanced over at Wyatt. A faint grin lingered on his lips. I crawled back to a standing position and chased the two little dogs to the other side of the pen.

I slipped another look over at Wyatt. He followed me with his green eyes. I knew he did the whole time as I acted like a complete idiot in the pen. It made those feelings happen again. I craved his attention. In this moment, with mysterious Wyatt, it felt special because I doubt he tossed much of anything out to the world. I doubt he gave many people the look he was giving me.

"Come in here with us." I gave him a soft grin.

"Nah." He shook his head.

He stayed firm in his spot. I got up and went back out to stand next to him. It was driving me crazy not to ask him questions. He gave an inch, and I wanted to run across the dang county with it. Slowly. I had to approach him slowly even though I really wanted to touch him. I wanted to touch his warm skin. I wanted to wrap myself around his body.

The truth is, I still knew virtually nothing about him. My feelings had progressed from questions to craving a full-blown physical attack. I needed to slow back down.

"How old are you?" The question slipped out.

Wyatt tilted his green eyes down in my direction, but he didn't answer. He looked back inside the play area where Gus had Charlie tackled to the ground. He muttered in his raspy voice, "How old are you?"

"Twenty-one."

"You don't look that old."

"We both get that a lot."

"*We?*" He looked down at me again. I didn't think about how I'd phrased that answer. I was so used to Blaire and I practically being the same person.

"Oh. I guess I haven't mentioned it before. I have a twin sister."

"There's two of you?"

"I guess you could say that. We look alike, but we are *very* different."

"Does she ask as many annoying personal questions as you?"

"Annoying personal questions? *Really?*" A flash of anger got the best of me, and I couldn't stop the thoughts from coming out as actual words. "I'm not asking unreasonable things, Wyatt. I just asked how old you are. I didn't ask if you have a girlfriend like the crazy kind that will show up at my apartment because I talked to you. Or if your life is complicated because you have, like, cancer or something and you're hiding out in the woods from everyone. How old are you? It's a simple, reasonable question. Waiters in restaurants even ask it when you order a drink."

I regretted my outburst the moment the second word jumped off my lips. This wasn't how I'd planned for our conversation to go today. Wyatt had made my thoughts flow out like verbal diarrhea, killing all the progress I'd made with the guy.

His lips fell into that familiar thin line. His eyes went back to being razor sharp. Wyatt's body morphed into a stiff and unfriendly lump of coal, ready to burn everything around him.

"I'm sorry." I took a step back, giving him some space. "I didn't mean to attack you. I'm really sorry."

Wyatt glanced toward the kennel building for a moment, then back at me. He was contemplating storming off from our conversation. I read the idea written across his angry face.

"I'm twenty-two." The words scratched from his lips like he'd swallowed one of those swords at the circus and had to cough it back up. "No girlfriend. No cancer."

The expression on his face spoke to my very heart, beating fast in my chest. Those simple words seemed to break him.

I wanted to touch him. I wanted to comfort him. I wanted to pull his hard body into my arms. It was a strange mix of compassion and hardcore lust. Instead of touching Wyatt, I took another physical step backward, giving the beat-down man his space.

"I'm glad you don't have cancer."

"Emma, you don't have a very good pokerface."

"What do you mean?"

He let out a deep breath. "Look, if you're gonna keep coming here, I'm just saying this upfront: don't go home dreaming up any ideas. We are not getting involved with each other. And you're not here to fix me."

"So now you're self-confident enough to think that I'm pining away for you as I fall sleep every night. We just met, Wyatt. I'm just trying to be nice."

"Your face is transparent as hell, okay? I'm just warning

you. I am not available for something like that. My life is really complicated. I'm just trying to make sure you understand before feelings get hurt and there's crying and shit."

"I get it, okay? Complicated. No personal questions. I'm not going home and writing your name in hearts or anything." I smiled at him, trying to salvage the afternoon, trying to recover the damage, trying to pretend his stupid comments didn't bother me. "I could just be your friend, you know. Could you do that much?"

"I don't know, Emma." His raspy voice hung on my name again.

"You know what I think? I think your heart is too big for your own good. That's why you get like this. You're overanalyzing it all. We can be friends, Wyatt."

"You don't know anything. Don't be twisting shit up in your head and making me into something I'm not. I just want to be left alone."

"I don't have to twist things up. I see it. You don't have the pokerface you think you have either. And no one likes to be alone. You like it that I'm here. Just admit it."

"You are here because you won't stay away. You show up here, knocking on my door, making me feel guilty. Girls like you are used to *always* getting their way. No one ever tells you no. It doesn't work that way with me."

"I'm here because you invited me back, you jerk!" I spat at him. "You think hurting my feelings will make me leave?"

"I hurt your *feelings*? You rebound faster than Charlie, running around here, sticking your nose into things, no matter how many times I tell you to mind your own damn business."

"Why are you such an awful person?"

"Do you think asking a hundred annoying questions will make me finally answer one?" He glared back at me as we slipped into a competitive stare.

"Yes."

"The answer is no. There are things you don't know about me. And I don't want you to know them. I am not some do-gooder here who takes care of a bunch of mutts. I'm the bad guy. You need to get that through your blonde head. And . . . I'm taking back my invite."

"You can't take it back."

"I can, and I just did. Go home, Emma." His voice bit hard on my name.

"Wyatt, come on."

"Go say goodbye to Charlie. Then get your shit and leave. We're done here. Don't come back."

With that, Wyatt opened the play area and Gus came trotting out. I stood frozen in place, watching the backside of the most complicated and irritating person I'd ever met. He was no bruised or rotten apple. Wyatt was an onion; the nasty purple kind that ruined everything.

I pulled Charlie out and carried him toward the kennel. His giant ears stood alert, looking for Gus. Hugging him tighter to my chest, I felt sad and angry. I couldn't say goodbye to Charlie forever. Not yet anyway, and not because Wyatt had decided to have a temper tantrum.

"Charlie. Don't listen to him." I scratched behind his brown ears and then under the gray chin. His sweet eyes watched me talk. "I'll be back to see you again."

Closing the gate, my flip-flops clicked as I walked over to his trailer. Pain twisted under my knee, but I ignored each stabbing jolt through my leg.

I knew he watched my every move from behind the thick curtains. Stomping all the way up the steps, I came to a halt in front of the aluminum door. I wanted to snatch the handle and barge into his cave. Let him react to that kind of probing into his life.

"You can't get rid of me that easy, Wyatt Caulfield," I shouted loud at his presence just on the other side of the thin wall. "I know you can hear me. I'm coming back."

CHAPTER 7

Emma

STILL FUMING MAD, I PULLED IN FRONT OF THE LIBRARY TO GET Blaire. She climbed into the passenger's seat, wearing her blue crocheted wool hat in the hundred-degree heat. Her dirty-blonde strands stuck out the bottom like long pieces of straw. My identical brown eyes stared back from her face. "So the unsub's pissed at you."

"Don't start that again." I pulled out before she got the latch buckled on her seat belt.

"Slow the hell down," she shrieked.

"I'm going the speed limit."

"You are not. I can see the damn numbers."

"You don't even drive. You know nothing about what the limit is on this road." I took the corner, hearing the tires screech.

"Shit!" Blaire yelled when I floored the gas through the yel-low—well, red light. A car honked as I cleared the intersection.

Wyatt plagued every confusing thought on the twenty-minute drive to our hometown of Beckett. He took back my invite. Who takes back invites? *People don't take back invites!* Once the words left your lips, you had to grin and bear it. Every word said better come out as a good one because you had to pay the price for them.

I pushed the gas down to the floor as I topped the hill on the outskirts of town, feeling the tires lift slightly off the pavement. My stomach caught in my throat, and Blaire gasped. "Shit, Emma. Stop messing around."

I ignored her words. Wyatt and his complicated issues wrapped through my head. I didn't know how long he'd been barricaded up in that trailer. The socially awkward recluse spent way too much time by himself. Whatever had pushed him to shut down had pushed him good. All a big, guarded mystery behind his closed-off mind that he refused to share with me.

I parked in front of my parents' house. It wasn't a big one. Average I guess, for Beckett. Our mother worked as a teller at a bank while our father worked at the car dealership over in Stillwater. He'd been employed there in some capacity since high school. After we were born, he'd moved up to a sales position. And he'd bought us the Fusion for our eighteenth birthday.

In the world of parents, they were good ones. Loving. Caring. Encouraging and very involved in our lives. They were standing faithfully at the track meet on the worst day of my life. The day my running career ended. Even though I was cursed with the short legs of a Smurf, I had placed second in the state track meet my junior year. My coach said I may be little, but I had Hulk-size determination, beating in the heart of a cross-country runner. He said I was guaranteed a scholarship as long as my performance continued.

But my senior year, I fell in the middle of the season. It was just a regular track meet. Nothing special. My knee had been acting up. I had iced it the night before, which was the usual protocol. During the tenth mile, I hit the ground just right, twisting my knee, causing splintered pieces of bone to burst right through the skin in a bloody mess. I had surgery and drain tubes for a week, followed by four weeks bound in plaster and another four weeks trapped in a horrendous boot.

The accident had devastated me. I loved to run. I needed to run. My body craved the euphoric moment that happened like clockwork. I missed it every single day.

Losing the ability to run wasn't technically the worst part of my fall. I had counted on the scholarship for school. After the accident, I didn't have many options. My sister went to college, and I had followed along with her as she moved closer to campus. And now, she was going to graduate with a double major in business and music education while I had a few credits that *might* get me into nursing school one day.

"Emma? Are you getting out of the car or going to Talladega for a qualifying round?" Blaire looked at me from the driveway. My mother's newly planted yellow flowers glowed like happy beacons from the flower bed behind her. Opening the car door, I stepped out in the driveway, feeling my knee jerk at the weight required to lift my body from the seat.

"Can you just cut me some slack? I've had a rough day."

She studied me for a moment. Worried creases outlined her puffy lips. They were the same as mine, like someone had shot three pumps of collagen into each one. "Fine. Let's do this girly shit. Why do you like him so much? There's lots of guys out there with way less problems."

"I didn't say I liked him."

"But you do. I feel it. And something happened today."

I let out a deep breath, sitting down on the front steps of the porch before going inside the house. "Wyatt told me not to come back."

"Why? Did he see you drive?"

"*Blaire*." My voice shot her a warning.

"Okay, okay. So I guess you got into a fight." She sat down on the front steps beside me. "What happened?"

"I said some things that upset him. I pushed, and he didn't like it very much." I frowned, remembering all the words I'd spat at Wyatt. None of the angry words were *that* horrible, but for a guy who refused to come out of his trailer, I might as well have flung the whole book at him.

"Like what?"

"I yelled some things about Wyatt having cancer."

"He has cancer!" Her eyes got big. The *serial killer* had suddenly become human in her robot-functioning mind.

"No, he doesn't have cancer. I asked if he *had* cancer. And I may not have exactly asked. I may have yelled it at him as more of an accusation."

She snorted a laugh. "Wow. You really know how to help people. Don't look into being a counselor."

"It's not funny. The guy has problems." I frowned at my sister thinking, *So do you.* "I just can't figure out how to help him."

"Maybe you should listen to him and just leave him alone."

"I can't." I couldn't possibly leave him alone at this point. "He needs me."

"Emma. You can't help people who don't want it. Whatever shit is going on with him, maybe you should just let it go and not get involved."

"It's too late. I'm already involved. And I'm going back tomorrow."

"Really? After he threw you out?"

"Yes. I screwed up. He needs help. And I have to keep trying. I have to fix this."

"Maybe you can't fix him, Emma. Some shit can't be fixed. Maybe he's just a jackass. And there's nothing actually wrong with him."

I leaned my head against the shoulder of my eccentric sister. She just didn't get it. "I wish it was simple, but it's not. At least, not anymore."

"So I guess that means you are ready to admit that you *like* like the jackass too?"

I contemplated her question even though I already knew the answer. He was so awful at times, but something changed when he talked about his dogs. His voice came alive with compassion and understanding. There was a good person hiding behind the pain and anger. And maybe I was attracted to that person.

Maybe. Just a little.

But that wasn't my motivation.

"It's not what you think," I whispered.

"Hmm. I don't think you are supposed to fall for the people you are trying to help. That's like a classic textbook violation or something."

"I know. That's why I'm not getting involved with him."

"You are such a liar."

I decided not to argue with her. We sat on the steps for a few more minutes as I thought about Wyatt. I thought about him and the dogs. His lonely existence. I thought about where I went wrong. What I could do differently. I pushed too much and too fast. I pictured his sad face, and it pulled at my heart.

Wyatt had never said that his life was filled with nothing. He had never said it was a life of solitude. He had never shared that part with me. But I just knew. I felt it. Something in my gut said, *Don't give up.*

Everyone deserved to have someone think about them, and I wasn't sure anyone thought about Wyatt. So I thought about him. I thought about his soft lips. I thought about his dimples. I thought about his sadness. It drew me in and twisted up my insides.

I created all sorts of backstories in my head. Maybe he was ex-military. Maybe the time away had screwed with his brain, and he was out there, spending time with his dogs until it felt right again. Maybe he'd lost someone. The girl he loved. Maybe it was a little of both. Maybe he cheated on her. Maybe she cheated on him while he was away and he went crazy when he returned home. Maybe she died. Maybe she was the one who had cancer.

Either way, I wanted to save him from the depths of whatever was making Wyatt this way. I wanted to pull him from the dark pit that made his eyes ache in pain. The guy needed me whether he wanted to admit it or not.

I rubbed my forehead as the thoughts tumbled around inside my head. I jumped up from the steps, holding out a hand to pull my sister to her feet. "Come on. Let's go in the house."

It did me no good, sitting around thinking up a hundred different stories because none of them were *his* story.

CHAPTER 8

Emma

On Friday, I went back to visit Wyatt. I knew the soft approach wouldn't work again. Once inside the fence, I mashed the Fusion's gas pedal to the ground. The grass exploded under the car as I drove fast and reckless. The back tires fishtailed over the ruts. I skidded to a stop in the dirt parking area in front of his trailer.

Wyatt ran out of the kennel room. Jumping from the driver's seat, I headed straight toward the building's door. I'd caught him off guard. Good. He needed a nice rattling.

"I'm back." I walked straight past him, never making eye contact. My flat lips spat out the words. "And don't worry. I didn't bring any peace offerings to offend you."

Entering the kennel, I heard footsteps, following close to my own tennis shoes. I'd pulled my hair into a ponytail today. I knew it was my imagination, but I swore I felt his breath steaming down my bare neck.

I stopped at Cye's gate, trying to compose myself before I sent the wrong message to my scared friend. Closing my eyes, I took a deep breath and hummed a little song. My shoulders relaxed and my eyes opened clear, with a purpose.

Once I was calm and collected, I lifted the metal handle and crawled on my hands and knees inside the entrance. His single eye watched from the corner. I went a few inches further than the last time and put the bone on the cement. I scooted out backward and stood up.

I felt his presence a few feet away. Waiting until I had Cye's gate closed, I turned around to confront Wyatt.

"You not trust me now? Going to watch everything I do? Are you afraid I'll set them all free? Steal them? Whisper bad things about you in their ears? Really, Wyatt? Just go back to your trailer."

He seemed confused at the huffy outburst. I stormed past Wyatt to the wall with the leashes. I removed two and crossed back in front of him. I pulled Charlie out and latched him to the end of the black one. I opened the kennel that held Ricky Bobby. I attached the rat terrier to the red leash. Wyatt followed my every step with his bewildered eyes.

"We are going on a run," I said matter-of-factly. "Please get out of our way since you insist on standing here watching me."

"Should you do that with your leg?"

"My leg is none of your business."

Our eyes caught for a split second, then I pulled away. I left at a small trot out the front entrance. Charlie was happy to be free of the kennel. Ricky Bobby bounced along on three legs. I hobbled on my two, feeling the pain in my knee. It hurt, but I kept going. I wanted to fly fast across the open space. I wanted to feel the wind in my face.

I picked up the pace. Each step over the rough grass vibrated the cells of my skin. The rush started in the pit of my stomach. I tilted my head back, feeling the smile on my lips. I was no longer just running through the open field—I was part of the blades of grass. I was one of them. Suddenly, my body got all tingly and warm as I transcended into sweet oblivion. I floated across the ground, savoring the release.

It was better than being drunk on tequila or having sex. Not that I'd had any real experience to use as a comparison. I'd gotten drunk a couple of times after work with some of the girls from the bookstore. It wasn't that glamorous. As for the sex part, people said it was better than running, but I'd yet to find out. Maybe one day the right guy would prove me wrong.

Kicking it up a notch, I kept going faster and faster, stumbling along the uneven ground. The air felt hot in my lungs. It was too early in the afternoon for a run, but I didn't care. I kept going, farther and farther away from the kennel.

The pain gripped tighter around my calf. It rolled over my knee and into my thigh. I kicked my leg forward, and then I went down. I face-planted, leaving a trail of scrapes on my arms and legs.

"You have got to be kidding me," I muttered to myself. Grabbing the leashes, I held tight to the dogs. I tried to get up, but it was too much. It hurt. It hurt *really* bad this time.

The words of the doctor haunted me as I rolled over on my back, staring up at the sun as it beat down from the sky. Ricky Bobby licked my nose. Charlie licked my hand. I stretched my leg up into the air, flexing the muscles.

"Are you happy now?"

I jumped at the sound of his voice. "Do you have to keep doing that? Don't sneak up on people."

"You okay?"

I glared at Wyatt. "I'm fine."

"Come on. Let's go back and look at the damage. " He reached down, scooping me up in his arms.

"What are you doing!" I struggled to get free. "Put me down."

"Just relax, Emma." My name flowed softly off his tongue. "Let go of the leashes. They'll follow us back."

Wyatt carried me across the meadow with one arm under my legs and the other around my back. I felt small against his large body as he touched me in a hundred different places. His smell came from everywhere.

I relaxed into his chest, feeling the firm muscles under his shirt. My eyes followed the curve of his neck to his face to his lips. They were soft and full today. *Wyatt's a good kisser.* I contemplated the thought. I could only imagine how those lips would feel against mine—all angry and soft.

He glanced down at me, then quickly looked away. "Don't go there, Emma," he muttered.

"What?"

"You know what." The edge of his jaw grew tight like he'd read those thoughts I'd had about kissing him.

We reached the kennel, but he kept on walking until the trailer door came into view. With little effort, Wyatt opened the door and balanced me at the same time. I scrambled to look at everything in his trailer as he placed me on the couch. I was finally inside his cave.

"I'll take them back to the kennel. You just sit there a minute."

He turned around and shut the door. The dark-brown curtains blocked the hot sun from inside the trailer. My eyes scanned the room. Everything screamed simple and organized. The living room was almost bare except for a large bookcase where most people would put an entertainment center.

I looked around, taking in the whole living room and kitchen area. Wyatt had no television, radio, gaming system, or computer. The guy had nothing of the kind in any corner—just a giant bookshelf of paperbacks and a few hardcovers on the top row.

His furniture wasn't anything fancy. The couch was covered in itchy red burlap, and a worn-out leather chair sat in the corner. Besides the little coffee table, Wyatt had no other furniture in the trailer—not even in the kitchen.

The door opened back up, and Wyatt came through the bright doorway. He studied me for a moment, shoving his hands down inside his jean pockets. He didn't seem to know what to do with me now that I was inside his trailer.

He finally let out a deep breath and sat down at the end of my feet. "Does it hurt all the time or just today?"

"Sometimes. It's worse when I run. I'm not really supposed to do that right now."

"I figured as much."

"It's hard, you know. I ran a lot before it happened." I shrugged. "I was a cross-country runner back in high school."

"Hmm. Well, sometimes it helps if you work the muscles. Not with those tools they use in therapy. But just with your fingers. Works out the kinks."

"Like this?" I smashed with my hands as the pain clutched around my knee. "I've tried when it gets tight, but I'm not very good. I usually make it worse."

His conflicted green eyes tilted up to mine, then flashed back down. He did it again before his hand reached forward, touching my leg. The contact burned all the way to the bone. I froze. Just like all the other times he'd surprised me to being speechless.

Wyatt had wanted me to leave and he hated my being within a fifty-yard radius of his presence. But now he held my leg between the palms of his hand. His fingers worked the muscles around my knee and then down under my calf.

"The doctor has me in therapy again." I concentrated on breathing normal. Wyatt was touching me and everything seemed so surreal. "I've skipped it some. I don't like what they do. It's all barbaric and painful."

"You shouldn't skip," he muttered.

"I know," I whispered, staring at Wyatt as he worked down around my ankle. He untied the lace on my shoe and slipped it off, rubbing below the arch of my foot.

I watched completely entranced. My eyes followed up his wrists to the muscles in his arms to the wide shoulders and the hard face. Deep thoughts twisted around in his head. Deep thoughts that intrigued my curiosity and pulled me closer.

His hands made another pass down my leg. They glided softly over my skin, rubbing and touching, inch by inch as I focused on breathing. The warmth flowed along my calf to my knee and across my thighs and settled somewhere around my belly button. The intense sensation shot back down through my stomach.

If Wyatt wanted me to *not* become enamored with him, this was the completely wrong thing to do to me. I wanted to close my eyes and lie back against the cushions. I wanted to melt and disappear into the feel of this complicated guy, *choosing* to touch my skin. His green eyes glanced up to my face before darting quickly away.

"How do you know so much about messed-up knees?" My words slipped out as one of his dreaded personal questions.

"I broke my leg once." He worked his finger underneath my calf muscles again. "How long ago did you get the cast off?"

"The place with the scar isn't recent. I broke my leg back in high school. It busted through right there. But my knee has never been quite the same. I've got a flimsy meniscus and I'm pretty sure the ACL is going to bust at some point. I fell the day I brought Charlie out here, which caused it all to flare up again. Now the doctor wants to do surgery."

Wyatt touched the top of my knee and frowned. His fingers examined my leg with the same meticulous scrutiny he'd given Charlie the first day.

My breath caught, feeling each place he touched on my thigh and ankle. Wyatt moved my leg around in a few positions, watching the kneecap bend in ways it shouldn't on a person. "You should have the surgery."

"Maybe I don't want to have surgery."

His green eyes looked back over to me with a slew of unasked questions. They swirled around under that hard face. They plagued him, but he didn't ask, and I didn't volunteer an answer. Let *Wyatt* have the anxiety of wanting to know more about a person but be denied the chance.

"Emma, I . . . um." His fingers stopped moving and rested on my leg. "I'm sorry about the other day. All that shit I said to you. I didn't mean it, you know. I wanted to—"

"Push me away?"

"Yes."

"You still want to do that?"

"I should, you know. For your own good." His fingers tightened on my leg. "But I don't know. Maybe we can try this friend thing."

The questions swirled around in my head at the meaning behind his words. I smiled back at his rigid face.

"Wyatt?" I whispered. "'I'm sorry. I don't mean to ask all the questions. But I just see you here and I want to do something. And I don't know what to do. So I say things and ask things. I know I shouldn't ask them. But I think if I don't ask them, who's going to ask them?"

"I know."

"You seem so alone. Do you have anyone, Wyatt? Anyone who knows if you even come home at night?"

His hand gripped the skin of my leg. It gripped tight and warm into my flesh as his soft lips dipped into a sad frown. The lines full of pain returned next to his eyes.

"You can tell me." I smiled at him. "It's okay. I'm tougher than I look."

"It's got nothing to do with you, Emma."

"You've told me that. But it doesn't change what I see when I look at you."

"Emma . . ." His words came out quiet with a raspy edge. "I think you always see the good even when you look at the bad."

"Why do you think you're so bad?" My eyes pleaded with him to share those tormented thoughts. "Are you dangerous?"

He let out a slow breath. "Some people think so."

"I don't believe that about you."

"You don't really know me."

"Then let me," I whispered.

Our eyes morphed into a tangled stare, mixed with questions, but no answers. He let go of my leg and stood up. My skin went cold. My time with him was over. I felt the hardness seep back into the room. The glimpse into the broken guy came to an end.

"See if you can stand."

He wanted to get me out of his trailer. I looked up at his tall body towering over me as I sat on the red burlap couch. He frowned, handing back my shoe. This time, Wyatt didn't touch my leg to place my shoe back on my foot.

I shook my head. "Don't go back to doing that to me."

"What?"

I stared at him. "If you want to be friends, you can't act like that anymore."

"Emma, just come on." He reached out one of his large hands, pulling me up from the couch.

"It's better." I moved my leg up and down, bending at the knee. "Thank you."

"The bathroom is right over there. You can wash the dirt off your arms."

"Okay."

Limping across the carpet, I went toward the direction of the bathroom. This required going through the kitchen. Nothing sat on the countertop except a coffee pot and a large red container of Folgers. I hobbled along, glancing through the next doorway. Gus lifted his head up from the old blue comforter on the bed.

Interesting. The little Jack Russell lived in his trailer.

His bedroom had absolutely nothing on the walls—not a picture or a poster or even a clock. Three pairs of work boots and a pair of old tennis shoes lined the floor next to the bed. A beat-up nightstand was on the other side. I turned back to check Wyatt's reaction. His jaw clenched tight, but he didn't stop me from invading his personal space.

I stepped into the bathroom and shut the door. Nothing sat on the small countertop. I peeked around the white shower curtain. The old tub appeared to be scrubbed spotless. Two bottles of some generic shampoo and conditioner occupied the little shelf.

Turning on the sink faucet, I washed the dirt off my arms, feeling the sting of the cuts. I wanted to open his drawers. Smiling to myself, I could only imagine what he stashed inside, but I kept his trust and left his private items alone. Wyatt was sitting in the old chair when I came back into the living room.

"I'm gonna go. I'll let you get back to work." I smiled at his uneasy face. He pulled himself up, making the muscles in his thighs work under the dirty jeans. The old boots stepped over to where I stood on the dark-brown carpet.

"You got plans on Saturday, Emma?"

"You mean tomorrow?" I smiled at him again.

"Right." He was nervous in a twitchy sort of way. "The days get a little mixed up out here. I was thinking you might come early. I mean, if you got nothing going on."

"I've got to do some grocery shopping before I go to work, but I could come out here for a while in the morning."

"Good. Okay." His lips curled up in a half smile. "Wear something you can get wet. It's bath day. I could use some help."

"Bath day. That should be interesting."

"You could say that."

"You . . . um . . ." He stumbled and cleared his throat. "Could you be here by seven thirty?"

"Yes."

"Not too early for you?"

"Nope."

"Didn't see you as a morning kind of girl." My heart picked up, seeing the faint dimples almost slide into place. So close. So very close to getting that layer of Wyatt to surface as he attempted this friend thing with me.

"You don't really know me either. I might surprise you. You might actually like me."

Wyatt swallowed hard. He got a little twitchy again. "I'll see you in the morning, Emma."

He stepped away and opened the trailer door. I followed, taking it easy down the cement steps. Wyatt didn't move. Leaning against the door frame, he waited with crossed arms as I made my way to the car.

As I thought about him watching me, my body got a little tingly. I looked back over in his direction, seeing him in the exact same spot with his eyes still fixated on me.

CHAPTER 9

Emma

I ARRIVED AT EXACTLY 7:20 ON SATURDAY. THE EARLY-MORNING air felt sticky in the Oklahoma summer heat. I was exhausted after twisting around half the night, thinking about Wyatt. The idea of returning made me nervous. What if I screwed this up? What if I pushed too hard?

I'd made progress, but it might disappear in a snap. Our new *friendship* was held together with Scotch tape and not the heavy gray kind. And he needed the heavy kind if he was going to get any better.

The trailer door opened as I got out of my car. Wyatt wore a blue T-shirt with a clean pair of jeans and the dirty work boots. He stared at me for a moment. I stared back, feeling that pull to him. A jittery vibe danced between us as his jaw stayed loose and his lips held their softness. Wyatt's sexy lips turned into a faint grin. In that moment, all my worries vanished.

"Hi." I smiled at him.

"Hi." Wyatt smiled, letting the dimples settle on the corners. He seemed good today. Actually, he seemed *really* good as he took a sip from an orange mug. "You want some coffee?"

"Sure." I followed him back through the doorway. An identical orange mug sat on the counter next to the coffee pot, waiting for me. The thought made my skin get a little warm. Stupid, really, but I liked the idea that he'd actually planned for me to return.

"I don't have anything fancy to put in it. Just some plain milk."

"That's fine."

He poured the coffee in the cup, and I topped it off with the milk. We sipped from the mugs for a few minutes in silence.

"How does this bath thing work?"

"There's a tub out by the storage shed. We'll take them out one at a time, soap them up, and rinse."

"Doesn't sound too bad."

"We will see." He grinned a little and took another sip from his mug.

"Sure. Oh, I have to leave by eleven though."

"Okay." His eyes were full of questions I knew Wyatt wouldn't ask me. To ask required him to answer those of my own, but I let him off the hook today.

"I need to go to the grocery store for my neighbor Mr. Hughes. He can't get himself there anymore. And I usually make lunch for him when I drop his stuff off."

"Do you help him a lot?"

"Some. He wasn't this bad when we first moved in to our apartment. His daughter lives in Nebraska. She comes down to see him a few times a year, but he refuses to move there. Says he loves Stillwater too much. So I help him when I can."

His jaw clenched for a moment as I talked of my elderly neighbor. Wyatt took a few sips of his coffee, trying to push back whatever I'd triggered in him. "That's nice of you."

"He's a good person. He spent his whole life teaching other people and helping them become something in the world. He deserves to have someone be there for him, even if it's just a few little things a week."

"Is he a college professor?"

"No, actually, Mr. Hughes was a high school teacher. Sweet man, but cutthroat when it comes to playing checkers."

"So you help this Mr. Hughes and play checkers with him. And you also work at the nursing home. I assume you play checkers with those people too?"

"Yes, except Vera. We drink tea together."

His green eyes flashed a hint of something I couldn't read. "And you rescued Charlie. Anything else I should know about?"

"I don't understand?"

"Like in your free time, do you knit scarves for blind kids in Somalia?"

My nose wrinkled up as I absorbed the words. "Are you making fun of me?"

"No." His voice got soft, almost like he felt guilty for even saying it. "That was just my bad attempt at a joke. You are the real deal, Emma Sawyer. One of the good guys."

"And what do you call the guy who devotes all of his time to rescuing dogs?"

Ignoring my question, Wyatt ran a hand through his brown hair before shuffling his boots to the other side of the kitchen. "We better get out there. This takes awhile."

He washed his cup out in the sink and then dried the inside with a towel. Turning to me, Wyatt reached for my mug. I chugged the last sip and handed it over. He cleaned the second one the same way with meticulous care. He placed both orange mugs back inside the cabinet.

His lips curled up in a faint grin. "Ready?"

"Yeah. Let's go have some fun."

"If you think tasting soapy dirt is fun." He laughed as his dimples hooked on the corners of his cheeks.

Wyatt was really adorable and sexy today. I wanted to touch those dimples with my fingers, with my lips. He glanced at me, seeing those transparent thoughts tumbling through my head. I felt my face turn bright pink, but he didn't say anything.

Looking away, Wyatt picked up a stack of towels from the couch before leaving out the trailer door. I followed behind him on a small trail in the grass that ended at the large shed.

In all my visits, I'd never ventured over in that area. The front of the shed was open, containing a riding lawnmower and other maintenance items. The side of the building cast a nice shade over an old bathtub. The white porcelain tub sat propped up on cinder blocks with a little wooden ramp leading up to the top.

"I run water in from the hose over there. We'll scrub them down with soap and then rinse. We might need to stop up the bottom and give some of the dogs a flea dip. I'll have to check them and see."

"Okay."

"You okay getting wet?" He muttered, never looking at my clothes.

"I doubt I'll melt." This morning, I'd decided to wear a yellow bikini top with a pair of cutoff, frayed jeans shorts and a cropped white tank top.

"You want to get Charlie first?"

"Sure."

Walking inside the kennel, I felt the pull around my knee. I'd worn flip-flops today because of the water. They slapped my heels as I made my way to Charlie's kennel.

As I opened the gate, the little dog flew into my arms. I carried Charlie outside to the bath area. Placing him down in the porcelain tub, I held his body tight as Wyatt ran the cold water over his fur. I scrubbed the soap, trying to keep him still so he wouldn't shake it off in my face.

"His leg's doing better," Wyatt said, running his fingers over the scabs. "He's almost ready."

"Ready?"

"For Diana to start looking." His eyes locked onto mine as his gruff voice spoke the words. My muscles clenched tight with the catastrophic news he'd slipped into the moment of fun and bubbles.

"You knew it would happen, Emma. It's why you brought him out here."

"I-I know." I pulled Charlie from the tub. He clung to my shoulder, making the water soak my shirt and skin.

"I thought you'd want me to tell you. You know, after Chewy was adopted while you were gone."

Wyatt stared at me while I let the water flow out on the ground. The news of Charlie getting adopted had come with a devastating punch in the gut.

"Please don't let it happen that way, okay?" I clasped Charlie tight to my chest, making him whimper. "Don't let him just be gone one day."

"I won't, Emma. I'll make sure you get to see him before Diana takes him." His raspy voice trailed off. Looking away, Wyatt turned the knob on the hydrant. "Grab a towel and take Charlie inside."

I pulled an old red one from the pile. Stains and holes plagued most of the fabric. Wrapping Charlie up tight, I carried him back inside the kennel. His brown eyes watched back in loyal submission after his dunk in the tub.

I wanted to keep him, but Charlie needed a home—a *real* home and not the fence and bars that came with this place. He never was mine.

Wyatt and I didn't say much over the next couple of hours. We laughed a few times as the dogs shook in the tub, plastering our faces with soapy water. The sun moved higher in the sky and the temperature kicked up with the summer heat.

By the time Daisy and Gatsby got a turn, I was close to being wetter than the animals coming out of the tub. The pathetic duo arrived together. I latched Daisy's leash on the side while Gatsby walked the plank into the tub. He turned his head and watched Daisy on the side lines. He never moved or twitched as the suds filled his old, brown hair.

When Wyatt switched them out, I dried while he washed Daisy by himself with her head turned, ever so slightly, never letting Gatsby leave her sight.

"I don't know if this is making me depressed or happy," I said to Wyatt.

"What do you mean?"

"They are so attached to each other. It's sweet. But then I see them. Sad and lost. Do they want each other? Or do they stay together because everything else in their world disappeared and they cling to the familiar?"

"It doesn't really matter, I guess. They have each other, which is more than the rest of them do."

"I guess." I studied them for a few moments after the gate closed. The two old dogs morphed into a single pile of brown fur on the concrete floor. Daisy and Gatsby needed someone to adopt them. They deserved to live the last few years in a house next to a fireplace eating bones.

"Let's grab Lola next." Wyatt's voice came from the other side of the building. In my visits, I'd walked past "pit row," but had never stopped to look inside the pens. He pulled a solid, white female from her kennel. Lola pranced down the aisle to me.

"Wyatt . . ." I took a few steps back.

"Don't be scared of her. She's not going to hurt you."

Kneeling down, I stuck out a hand in the direction of the pit bull. She lunged forward, clamping her wide mouth down over my whole hand. I let out a gasp.

Fear shot through my stomach, and then I smiled as the white dog tasted my fingers with her tongue. My skin felt the gumminess of her mouth. Pulling my hand out of her lips, I scratched behind her ears.

"Sorry. She doesn't have a lot of manners," Wyatt muttered.

"And she doesn't have any teeth either." Lola came forward and licked my face. She rubbed her square body all over me until I tipped sideways. I fell over on the cement laughing.

"She wouldn't hurt you even if she had a whole mouth full of teeth."

I glanced up at Wyatt as Lola mauled me. He was laughing. The sound of his deep voice floated out into the kennel.

My hand went still, seeing a bit of happiness on his gorgeous face. The rare and beautiful sight gripped my heart. His eyes caught mine. The surreal feeling was electrifying. And then Lola got a lick in across my mouth. I squealed as her large tongue left a trail of drool.

"Come on, Lola." He pulled her off my body.

I wiped my mouth against my right arm. Sitting back up, I patted the white pit across her wide head. "Sorry, girl. I don't know you well enough for that kind of relationship."

He smiled at my comment. Bending down next to her, Wyatt rubbed the soft fur under her neck. The white dog smashed herself tight to his side. He leaned over, giving Lola a quick kiss next to her ear.

The action had come from reflex. Something he must do on a regular basis. Wyatt shuffled around, trying to pretend I didn't witness the brief moment of vulnerability. "Let's get her in the tub."

As I climbed up from the ground, a sharp stab went under my kneecap as I lifted myself up from the cement. I needed to spend the evening with an ice wrap. I didn't know how much longer I could ignore the inevitable.

I followed Wyatt out the door, trying not to show a visible

limp. He led Lola up the steps and into the tub. As I ran water over her body, I touched the permanent marks etched onto her skin.

"How'd she get them?"

"Doesn't it bother you to hear this stuff?" His jaw tightened a bit without looking in my direction.

"Yes, but I gotta know. I can't just do this and not care what happened to them."

"Okay. Fine." He let out a deep breath. "Most of the pits we got here are bait dog survivors from fight training."

"Like dog fight rings?"

"Yeah, illegal dog fight rings. Those bastards toughen them up by setting mock training fights. They pick out the softies. They take away anything that might give the dog a little bit of a fighting edge. Like Lola here. They pulled out her teeth with pliers. They cut marks in her skin to get the blood flowing. It gives the other dogs a taste of what they're going for in the ring. The stripes on her thighs are from being cut up."

I got sick. Not in the actual throw-up-on-the-ground kind of sick. But the heart-crushing kind that stopped the breath in my chest. I got sick because it wasn't one cut.

Lola had scars from knife slices all the way up and down her thighs; short ones, long ones, deep ones that healed in large, chunky, raised hunks. Marks like a bear had grabbed the dog between his paws and tried to swallow her in one gulp—except it wasn't a bear, but a human who had tortured for the sheer fun of it.

"How did she survive?" I asked, massaging the soap into her hair. My fingers felt every scar over her body, every place some demented sicko had ripped into her soft, white skin.

I felt rage in a way I'd never experienced in my life. I thought Kurt was evil by kicking Charlie. This was a whole other level of planned abuse. It wasn't a flippant kick to the face out of irritation. The marks on her body were an act of planned and deliberate exploitation.

"There's some known dumping sites. But they rotate around so it's hard to know. People toss the dead or half-dead animals in the ditch. If someone finds them in time, some dogs actually survive."

I took Lola out of the tub, rubbing an old blue towel over her body. It dried away the water, but the scars remained. They stayed as a reminder of surviving a house of horrors by people who should be in jail.

The rage continued to burn under my skin as Lola's happy face watched with her red tongue sticking out of her toothless wide mouth.

"Someone should go to prison for this," I muttered, looking up at Wyatt.

"I know." His eyes flickered, and he got a little twitchy.

"I don't understand why monsters that hurt something so innocent are allowed to just walk down the street and be out with everyone else in the world. They should be arrested."

"Sometimes the law is not always fair." His lips almost went flat. Wyatt took the leash from my hand. "I'll take her back. It's almost eleven."

"Okay," I replied, not sure what I said that agitated him. His dismissal was evident in the tone of his words.

I turned the hose on at the faucet. My legs had mud streaks from ankle to thigh. Bending over, I washed the dirt off my skin. I stood up and scrubbed my arms. Pulling the shirt over my head, I wore just my yellow bikini top and shorts.

I dipped my hand under the cool water and washed the dirt off my stomach from where it had crept under the edges. Hearing a noise, I looked over by the tub.

Wyatt stood completely still. His chest moved up and down under his wet T-shirt. It clung to his skin, showing off a solid chest. His green eyes held my brown ones in a twisty stare. And then my breath caught in my throat.

Wyatt allowed his eyes to leave my face and continue to drift downward. They lingered over the wet bikini clinging to my breasts.

I was held captive by his stare, feeling him trace each piece of my exposed body. I was afraid to breathe. I was afraid to do something to push him away. The longer he watched, a slow, agonizing burn developed under my skin. It was an achy physical pain. I didn't know it was possible to be this attracted to someone. He set my skin on fire with just the brush of his eyes.

I swallowed hard, and the green eyes jumped back to my face. Fear flashed across his cheeks, but the reaction only amplified his real feelings. Wyatt wanted me. He wanted me bad, and that desire scared him.

The hose stayed in my hand, causing a steady stream to run out all over the place. Turning to the side, I grabbed the faucet, shutting off the water. I looked over my shoulder. He stayed in the same spot. With my back to him, I pulled my wet shirt over my head. I took a few deep breaths to steady myself before turning around to face him.

I wasn't sure if I should just leave or say something. In a normal world, I think Wyatt would make the first move, but nothing about us was normal. Nothing about him resembled a normal guy, which is the part that pulled me to him. It's the reason I was here.

I took a few steps in his direction, stopping close enough that his head was forced to tilt down to see me. "I'm . . . um . . . leaving."

"Okay," he mumbled.

"Um, thanks for letting me come back. I had a good time."

"Me too."

"Okay. Well. I'm going." But my feet stayed planted in

the dirt. The invisible pull between us came out stronger as it pushed me toward Wyatt.

"You missed some." Wyatt touched my cheek. Or rather, he rubbed my skin with his thumb on a splotch of mud. A burning jolt traveled through my body, feeling him work at the dirt. Wyatt had his fingers on my skin. He was touching me on purpose. His hand stayed on my cheek, then suddenly dropped like my face had caught on fire. "Sorry. I think it's still on there."

"That's okay. You . . . um, mind if . . . I . . . um, I brought stuff to change? Could I use your bathroom?"

"Oh, yeah, sure," Wyatt mumbled.

"Okay. Well, bye, I guess." I stumbled through my parting words for a second time.

"Bye." He took a step backward and then another. The distance got larger, but the electric pull remained the same. I wanted to touch him so bad my muscles started to clench up under my skin. "You can let yourself in. I'm just going to stay out here and keep going so I can get finished."

"Okay."

"Hey, Emma. I guess I'll see you Monday or Tuesday?"

I nodded in his direction. The humid air grew hotter the longer I looked at him. "I work those days, but I'll see what I can do. You'll be here?"

"Yes," he muttered in his raspy voice. "I'll be here."

I walked in a daze toward my car. A smile slipped on my face as I thought about what finally had transpired between us. Looking over my shoulder, I saw him watching my backside as I walked away. My heart flipped a little, and I fell deeper for Wyatt Caulfield, the mysterious guy who said he was dangerous and bad.

I saw what bad people did out in the world. They tied puppies up in wire and pulled their teeth out with pliers and shredded their skin with knives. Dangerous guys didn't scrub them in porcelain tubs and wrap their little bodies in towels. Bad guys didn't undress me from five feet away and then let me go.

CHAPTER 10

Emma

THE GROCERY STORE LINE WAS LONG ON SATURDAY MORNING, which caused me not to get home until almost one. Getting the bags out of the car, I heard a noise and spun around to find Kurt practically touching my butt. I sidestepped, moving away from him. My nose pulled in a whiff of sweaty body odor. The man oozed disgusting in the way a sewer flowed with trash.

His black T-shirt fit snug over the barbwire tattoo on his large bicep. Instead of fixing things in our apartment like the dishwasher that quit a month ago, Kurt spent his time lifting weights in the manager's office.

"I'm just curious." He reached out, running a large finger down the side of my car. "Where does the dirt come from?"

I looked at the clump of red he shoved in front of me. "Why do you care if my car is dirty?"

"I don't give two shits that your car is dirty. I'm just curious about where you go that makes it covered in that damn dirt. Every couple of days, you pull in here with a fresh layer of this shit."

Kurt rubbed the dirt between his fingers before dusting it off on his jeans.

My backside pressed against the trunk of my car, trying to get farther away. Something wasn't right with his questions. They were strange and pointed. Kurt usually didn't care about my comings and goings. Ever since Charlie had disappeared, his causal obsession had turned into borderline stalking. He watched me every time I came outside on the second-floor landing like a bell had alerted him of my movements.

His eyes drifted over my skin to my breasts. I'd changed into a sundress in Wyatt's bathroom before I'd left his place. I stepped out of Kurt's way, feeling the violation of his groping eyes. A repulsive gag lingered in the back of my throat. Grabbing the bags, I took another shuffled step in the direction of my apartment. "It's getting late. I've got to make Mr. Hughes some lunch."

"Tell that old man he's not getting a different apartment. He's just gonna have to stay up there and rot. Nothing on the bottom floor is opening up until next year."

"Well, thanks for checking." I cringed at his harsh words. Racing up the steps, I ignored the pain. My knee hurt something awful as I let myself into my neighbor's apartment. I took a deep breath, trying to shake the nasty feeling of Kurt. Dusting the dirt off the back of my dress, I faced my neighbor.

"Hi, Mr. Hughes." I greeted the elderly man. He was sitting in a recliner, watching some hunting show on television.

"Emma, what are you all dressed up for?"

"You, of course."

"Aren't you the sweetest." He balanced against his walker, pulling himself out of the chair. I paused for a moment to make sure he got all the way to standing. He moved at a slow pace into the kitchen as I unloaded the bags on the counter.

"What do you want for lunch?" I always made Mr. Hughes something to eat when I dropped off his groceries.

"You get potatoes?"

"I always do."

"I want some of them fried potatoes you make." Mr. Hughes pulled out a kitchen chair and studied it for a moment.

"Okay, but you need something else besides potatoes. I got you a bottle of ranch dressing. You want a salad?"

"I guess I would eat one if it was on my plate." He grinned at me, showing his gums.

"Before you get all comfy in here, go put in your teeth. I'll have it done in a few minutes."

I could easily go get his teeth. He always left them sitting in a glass by the lamp in the living room. But I wasn't sure how much moving he did these days. Mr. Hughes needed to get the blood flowing around in his body before it turned to sludge.

"Will do. Be back in a jiff." He leaned against the walker, going at a slow pace into the living room. "Oh, and don't forget the potatoes. They always remind me of the time Priscilla and I were down in Biloxi."

"I won't." I smiled. He always liked to tell stories about his wife Priscilla. While she was alive, they seemed to have a wonderful life, traveling all over the United States.

Taking out a knife, I chopped a few potatoes. The skillet was hot as I dropped the wet chunks into the oil. Splatters hit my arms, causing a few burns. I'd just finished the salad when Mr. Hughes pushed his walker back into the kitchen. He leaned heavily on the metal handles as he eyed the bowl of leafy greens.

"So where did you go this morning? I saw your car leave when I was having my coffee. Pretty early. Even for you."

"It's not that exciting." I dumped the potatoes onto his plate and piled a heap of salad on the other side. Mr. Hughes examined the chair for a moment before lowering himself down on the wooden seat. I sat down across from him, putting salad on my plate. "You want some ketchup?"

"Nah. That stuff just hides the taste of the grease, and that's the best part. So tell me about this boy."

"How do you know there's a boy?"

"Well, a girl only gets herself out that early on a Saturday for a boy."

"He's not exactly a boy." I grinned at Mr. Hughes. The flutter picked up in my stomach as I thought about Wyatt. He stopped being a boy a very long time ago and had turned into an attractive, very lonely guy.

"Well, you're too young to be spending all your time with old people like me." His crooked fingers grasped the fork, pushing the salad away from the potatoes.

"His name is Wyatt."

"So tell me about Wyatt. He must be pretty interesting to catch your attention."

"Yes. He's interesting."

An image of Wyatt flooded my mind. A warm feeling trickled through my body as I remembered that Wyatt had looked at me today. It was the kind of look that ingrained in a girl's head forever, making her imagination run wild. I grabbed my cup, taking a drink so Mr. Hughes didn't notice the pink on my cheeks.

CHAPTER 11

Emma

AT THE STOPLIGHT, I CLOSED MY EYES, RUBBING MY FOREHEAD, thinking about Wyatt. Almost a whole week had slipped away since bath day. The last couple of days had been long and tedious. The bookstore had lost an employee. I covered as usual, knowing we would eventually hire another student who possessed the same concept of being responsible. They would either show up late with bloodshot eyes and hungover, or they just wouldn't show up at all. My manager had a strict policy. No show, no job, which caused our high turnover rate.

And that's why he loved me. I was the longest running, most reliable employee he'd had at the store. The guy had offered to make me assistant manager on more than one occasion. I always said no because it interfered with my second job.

I loved working at the nursing home. I loved seeing their little old faces as they smiled when I walked in the room. It was rough at times. And not just in the sense of dirty beds and sweaty bodies. It was rough because I would get close to a patient, only to come back a few days later and find them gone.

Those moments were heart-wrenching and bittersweet. Death was inevitable at a nursing home, but I tried to stay positive in the time I spent there. Some residents were lucky. They had families who stopped by every week. And some were royalty. They had visitors every day. But most only got a quick chat around the holidays.

And that's why I put on my scrubs for each shift. I was the granddaughter they'd never had out there in the world. I played cards and checkers. And as I'd mentioned to Wyatt, I also learned to drink herbal tea while listening to gossip about the other residents.

I knew all about Vera's grandson with the stuck-up wife who was just spending all of his money. They all thought Mr. Rollings was the most handsome man at the nursing home. And Karla liked to tell me stories, while the other ladies thought she liked to tell fibs—especially about the time she'd met Robert Redford.

The car behind me laid their fist into the horn, making me jump in my seat. I pressed my foot on the gas pedal. Just one more turn, and I would be on the dirt road headed out of town. I would see Wyatt.

I'd worried about him every day that I'd been gone, and I'd thought about him every night as I drifted off to sleep. His face always hovered just beyond my closed eyes. He had consumed me. I knew it wasn't good to let Wyatt have that type of hold on my thoughts. But I didn't know how to shut it off or how to shut him out. Something pulled me to him. My heart said he needed me. And I might have developed a bit of a need for him too.

As I reached the kennel, my eyes darted around, looking for his familiar face. We had left things on a strange and heated note after washing the dogs. Getting out of my car, I looked around, not seeing Wyatt. I hoped his absence wasn't some form of a setback with him.

I went inside the kennel, but I didn't find him with the dogs either. Walking the dusty trail to his trailer, I went up the little steps. I knocked on the aluminum door and waited, hearing nothing from the other side. He might get upset, but I turned the knob, opening the door. The living room was empty. Gus came trotting out of the bedroom, stretching across the carpet.

"Wyatt?" I yelled. Hearing no response, I shut the door and went back around the kennel to where the old porcelain tub sat next to the shed. Wyatt wasn't anywhere. I breathed in the heavy scent of summer rain. The sky was full of clouds today.

I spun around a few times, looking in every direction, and then I noticed the contents of the shed. Tucked in the back corner, I saw something covered with a blue tarp. I crawled around a lawnmower, snagging my shorts against the side of a pile of wire. The metal ends ripped a hunk out of the fabric. I breathed a sigh of relief that it didn't grab my skin.

Tugging at the edge of the plastic, I exposed a motorcycle. It appeared to be a fairly nice antique one, with a large amount of shiny chrome. My fingers trailed over the cool metal. Wyatt had a motorcycle. I smiled faintly, imagining him riding down the highway. I bet it felt amazing on the back of it. I bet he *looked* amazing.

"What are you doing?" His voice came from behind, and I jumped, letting out a small squeal.

"Stop doing that." My nerves sparked under my skin from Wyatt scaring me once again. "I was looking for you. You have a bike?"

"I do." His agitation matched the darkness of the cloudy sky. I knew better than to touch his things, but my curiosity had gotten the best of me. The motorcycle was now a piece of the larger puzzle.

"It looks nice. Why do you have it stuck in the back of your shed?"

"I don't do much riding anymore." He took a deep breath. "Could you please cover it back up?"

I noticed the shovel he gripped tight in his hand. His knuckles turned white against the wood. I wanted to ask more about the bike, but he didn't seem to want to talk about it. "I'm sorry. I-I didn't mean to get into your stuff."

"Don't apologize, Emma." My name came with a gravely sweetness from his lips. Every time he said it, I craved for him to mutter it again.

I tucked the blue tarp back over the shiny motorcycle, feeling more confused toward Wyatt. He had his secrets. Lots of them. He didn't move until I had the bike situated back to the way I found it. Crawling over the lawnmower, I tried to avoid the wire.

"Be careful," he muttered.

"Too late. It got me on the way in here." I got around unscathed and stood in front of him. "What are you doing with the shovel?"

His jaw twitched. "I'm not sure you want to know, but I'll show you anyway."

Wyatt went inside the shed to hang the shovel on the wall with the other equipment. Crusty red dirt covered his jeans. They fit tight over his thighs, showing off the muscles in his legs. I think he had runner legs. They bulged in all the places of someone who ran miles and miles. Wyatt turned around and caught me looking at him. He frowned for a moment. "Come on."

I followed beside him into the pasture, navigating through the tall grass and weeds. We walked for a few minutes in silence. This visit was very different than the last one. Something was bothering Wyatt. It twisted him up more than usual, if that was even possible.

As we continued through the grass, a fenced-in area came into view. The image filled my heart with dread. Everything slipped into place. The ground inside was covered with little white crosses. Fear slowly creeped under my skin. "It's a pet cemetery?"

"Yes." He opened the gate, and I followed behind, seeing the little names etched on each piece of wood. Wyatt stopped in front of a fresh mound of dirt.

"Which one?" I was afraid. I was afraid to find out which of the sad dogs didn't survive. I didn't live out here like Wyatt, but my attachment to those poor souls grew stronger every day. They each came from such a miserable existence, only to land here in the end. They deserved better than to die behind bars without finding a family to love them.

"Daisy. She didn't wake up this morning." His words came out clipped. "I'll have to make her a marker."

The sad fingers of time crawled up my skin. It wasn't choking me over Daisy, but reminding me of her companion. "What's going to happen to Gatsby?"

"I don't know," he muttered. "When everyone in your world is gone, sometimes your will to live just disappears too."

I turned so I was standing in front of Wyatt. He looked down at me, his eyes cloaked in pain. I wondered how many times he'd done this. How many of these little white crosses were placed by Wyatt? He rescued them, cared for them, and then buried them.

I wanted to touch him, throw my arms around his slumped shoulders, but I was afraid of his reaction. "Are you okay?" I whispered.

He let out a deep breath. "Let's get her a marker up and figure out what to do with Gatsby."

"Okay."

He held the gate open as I walked through. We returned to the shed without speaking. He opened a container in the corner and pulled out a white cross identical to those in the pet cemetery. I watched in a trance as he whittled her name into the wood. His arms tightened. His body moved and flexed as he used the tools.

I felt that electric pull to Wyatt. As my throat tightened with emotion, I felt that overwhelming need to comfort him as he carved her name into the wood with meticulous detail. He looked up, catching my gaze. The powerful sadness echoed in the depths of his green eyes. It called to me. It beckoned my heart.

Wyatt didn't say anything and went back to work. He seemed worse today than in my other visits. Maybe he blamed himself, but this was out of his control. "This isn't your fault, you know."

He looked up again, his lips thinning as he listened to my words. He swallowed hard. "She wouldn't eat last night. I should have checked on her again, but I didn't."

"She was old and sad."

"And I should've checked on her. It's my job. The only one I got." His voice cracked on the words. He paused for a moment and then went back to the wood, making sure it was perfect.

Wyatt handed his creation over to me. I held the cross, tracing the letters with my fingers. He had made something so simple seem so very beautiful.

"Can you put it out there?" he muttered, not looking me in the eye. "I'll meet you in the kennel."

"Okay." I left the shed and went toward the pet cemetery. The weeds scratched against my legs. Placing the white cross by the fresh dirt, I looked at her spot. I knew pets were not the same as humans, but it was still sad to think of her final days.

Daisy had lost her owner and was left to die in a house. Because of that, she'd ended up here. Maybe Wyatt was right. This place may not be a home, but it still was better than where they had come from out in the terrible world.

I left the cemetery and went back to the kennel. I found Wyatt inside the pen with Gatsby. His jaw was clenched tight as the held the old dog in his arms. "Wyatt?"

"Oh, hey." His eyes drifted up to where I stood next to the kennel gate. The sadness broke my heart into tiny slivers. Something was eating away at his insides, something deeper than just Daisy.

I sat down next to him on the floor, careful not to touch his body. Staying just a few inches away, I was close but not enough to cause some unwanted reaction from him. "I'm sorry. It must be a hard job dealing with this side of it."

He didn't say anything. Wyatt's hand continued to pet Gatsby as he stared at the cracks in the wall. I reached over, touching the old dog behind the ears. Wyatt accidentally bumped my hand. He jerked a little and looked over at me. Our eyes locked on each other. His hand stopped moving as he stared at my face.

I felt that pull into his overwhelming sadness. It was aching. It was seductive. Slowly, I inched my fingers across Gatsby until they touched his skin. I saw his breath suck in a bit. He was unsure. He was fighting this obvious connection between us.

"It's ok," I whispered as my hand clasped around his. And then sparks flew under my skin as he squeezed my hand back. Wyatt slipped his fingers between mine. It wasn't much of anything, just holding hands. But I knew in my gut, Wyatt Caulfield didn't hold hands.

"You can talk to me, you know," I whispered, begging him to let me inside his thoughts.

"Maybe I don't want a girl like you to know those things about me. Some things shouldn't be talked about."

I wanted to push. I wanted to push it right out of him. His pain was a cancer, eating up the inside of his soul. The longer it remained, the more his body disappeared into the all-consuming rot.

I ran my thumb over the side of his palm. They were about twice the size of my hands and a little rough from calluses. He tensed a bit, but I kept touching him, rubbing my fingers across his skin. I needed to find some way to distract him from this pain since he wasn't willing to discuss it.

"Tell me about the books in your trailer. You've got a whole wall of them." It was a simple, open-ended question that allowed Wyatt to control the answer. He could say something important or simple. I wasn't sure if he would take the bait.

He watched me for a second before letting out a deep breath. "I like to read."

I stopped moving my thumb over his hand. My lips curved up at the corners. "I think that's pretty obvious. Any book in particular?"

"No."

"Favorite author?"

"I guess Stephen King. But I'll read anything. I think there's a few hundred books in the trailer now." As Wyatt talked, the tight muscles in his shoulders seemed to relax just a bit. His sad eyes lifted to mine. "Sometimes I come out here and, um . . . I read to them."

"To the dogs?"

"Yes," he whispered. "I bet you didn't expect that one."

My heart beat faster as I saw the slight change in him as he revealed one of his secrets. "You read to them, like, out loud?"

"Yes." A faint grin touched his lips. "I come out here at night. I think it calms them down, hearing someone's voice. Some of the dogs come from homes. They are used to being around people. And the rest. Well, they never got that kind of life so I give it to them."

"You read Stephen King to them?"

"Not usually. I change it up some. Horror, classics, and some of the popular stuff."

"Like what?"

He chuckled. "You really want to hear what books a grown man reads to dogs?"

"Yes."

He let out a deep breath. "Lola really liked it when I read *Tom Sawyer*. Maybe it's the way it sounds, coming from me. I don't know. I've read them *Moby Dick*, *Lord of the Flies*, *The Hobbit*, *Treasure Island*, and um, *Werewolf in Paris*. Now that was a little weird, reading it in here. Then I got a few other ones. *Girl with the Dragon Tattoo*, *Gone Girl*, and *Interview with a Vampire*, which just made me want to read *Dracula*, but I haven't yet. I had a Steinbeck phase. I can't remember them all. I've lost track now."

"Is that why you named them Daisy and Gatsby?"

He clenched my fingers, consuming my whole hand inside his larger one. "Yes. I had just finished that book a few days before they got here. Something about it just felt so familiar when I got these two. The family had left them to rot in that house. The neighbors didn't even know their names. They were so defeated and sad. But this guy here. He wouldn't leave the girl. She moved. He moved. Very Gatsby. And now he lost his Daisy. He's all alone. His beacon of light is gone."

"Is that what happened to you, Wyatt?" The words slipped out before I could stop the sentence. Anxiety flashed through my heart as I waited for his reaction.

"No." His jaw gritted tight. I had touched a big nerve in his weakness. His breathing got more intense and a wild look flickered beneath his green eyes. "You keep trying, over and over again. Have you ever considered that I might be a lost cause?"

My fingers tightened against his hand. "I don't believe anyone is a lost cause."

"I know you like to help people and you keep coming back here, trying to help me," he muttered. "But you should just give up. I'm the worst possible guy you could find."

The air from his spoken words brushed across my skin. He was so close, but so far away in his mental anguish. "I don't think that's true. When I look at you? I don't see a bad person."

"I know."

"You can trust me. I hope you realize that by now."

"I do trust you, Emma." His breath touched my skin as he talked. "It's myself that I don't trust."

"But I trust you," I whispered.

"I know," he whispered back in that gravelly voice. "I see the trust in your eyes. And it scares me."

Hearing his painful admission, I wanted to touch more than just his hand. This thing between us grew stronger with each breath, pulling me closer. His eyes grazed over my lips and then jerked back up. It was there again, the guilty look of desire. He was ashamed of having those thoughts.

I wanted him to know it wasn't wrong. I wanted to kiss him. I wanted to feel his soft lips against mine. *Maybe I should just lean forward and make it happen.* Make that connection between us real. Make him feel something other than the pain. I closed the few inches between us. Wyatt turned his head right before we touched.

"Don't," he growled.

"I-I don't understand. I thought—" I stopped as his face twisted up again and he let go of my hand.

"If a guy wants to kiss you, he will. So don't force it."

"So you don't want to kiss me," I whispered.

"I didn't say that."

"I don't understand."

Wyatt looked at me as the internal struggle danced around in his troubled soul. "I shouldn't want to kiss you."

"So you *do* want to kiss me?" I asked, seeing the pain etched in permanent lines around his eyes. A burning pain that was now burning me. It burned inside my chest, drawing me closer to his body. His breathing got a little stronger. I didn't need to see his chest going up and down to know how much this was affecting him.

"You think you want to know all about me. You don't, Emma." His emotions grated on the words. "And if I told you the truth? You wouldn't like the fact that I wanted to kiss you."

"I doubt that." I reached up, touching the side of his face. Wyatt's eyes closed for a moment as my fingers trailed over his cheeks, tracing those lines of pain.

He was haunting. He was beautiful, pulling me down into the pit of his broken heart. I felt something strong and powerful, holding onto my soul.

My fingers traced his jaw. I stopped on the spot where his hidden dimples stayed just beneath the surface. I was drawn to him like a Band-Aid to a cut. I wanted to touch him, fix him, and make him better.

As if my thoughts were spoken out loud, Wyatt's green eyes flipped open. He grabbed my hand, removing it from his skin. His complicated thoughts swirled around on his face as he clutched my fingers tight in his palm. Wyatt was fighting some internal battle. He was fighting, and the demons were winning.

"Let's get out of here for a while." I felt the rush as I asked him to run away with me. "Go somewhere. Anywhere. Come with me?"

His fingers stilled on my hand. Wyatt refused to look in my direction as he muttered the words. "I . . . um. That's not a good idea right now."

"Okay. Then I'll stay with you."

"No."

"Why not?"

"When you leave here"—his eyes grew a little sad as the words slipped from his lips—"where do you go?"

"It depends. Today is Thursday. So I'm picking my sister up and we are having dinner at my parents' house over in Beckett."

He let out a deep breath. "Do you have a nice family?"

"They're not perfect. My sister is . . . um . . . odd. But yes. I have a nice family."

"Do you have dinner with them every Thursday? Like a family thing?"

"Yes," I answered. "And you can come if you want."

He flinched at the suggestion and continued with his questions. "Your twin sister. Does she worry about you coming here?"

"She does," I muttered.

"Then you need to go back home to them. It might not be a perfect family, but I'm sure they love you. You need to go have dinner with them and leave me alone."

"But I don't think I should leave you alone right now."

"You're going to skip a family thing for some strange guy who lives in the woods with fifty dogs. This place is not normal. *I'm not normal.* Don't you understand that by now?" He pleaded in desperation. "Please just leave, Emma. Go home to your family."

"No. Don't say that, Wyatt. I don't—"

"You're in over your head and you're too naïve to know it."

"I'm twenty-one, Wyatt. A grownup. I work two jobs. I pay my own rent. I buy my own clothes. You act like I'm some innocent girl who can't make decisions."

"I think we have different definitions of innocent. You should leave. Forget about this. Forget about me."

"How can I forget about you? I-I've never felt something like this before. And I know you feel it too."

He dropped my hand when I said it. Fear came in waves over his cheeks as my words scared him to the core.

Looking down at Gatsby, the dog remained in some catatonic trance across his lap. Wyatt scooped him up under his arms. The brown animal must have weighed at least eighty pounds, but he balanced the dog with little effort as he stood up in the kennel. I'd waited this whole conversation for Wyatt to storm off to the trailer. Then he left through the building with Gatsby in his arms.

I sat inside the kennel for a moment, trying to gather my thoughts. This thing with Wyatt was deep and strange and intense. Something beyond my control had decided I was the person who should help Wyatt Caulfield. Something bigger than either of us. And I couldn't give up on him.

Standing up, I walked down the aisle of sad faces. They barked and whined as I passed the kennels. This place required a heart of steel in order to walk away, and mine was all mush. I found Wyatt, struggling with the door handle of his trailer. Just seeing him again melted my heart right on the spot.

"Let me get it." Hearing my words, he gave me an angry glare. "Don't be like this. Just let me get the door for you."

His nostrils flared up a bit before he moved off the cement steps. Wyatt flattened his lips into a thin line as I helped him inside the trailer.

"There's a blanket in the closet by the bathroom," his gravelly voice muttered.

I found an old plaid blanket on the top shelf. I struggled to reach it with my short arms. Jumping up, I snagged the edge, pulling it down on top of my head. I dug myself out from the giant plaid quilt. Turning around, I saw a faint smile on Wyatt's lips as he watched me. A faint smile that was racked in guilt. Why did he feel so awful about having feelings for me?

I walked over in front of his bookcase, making a pallet on the floor. He put Gatsby down. The dog's sad eyes never even looked up at us.

"Maybe he'll do better in here," I said.

"Maybe."

Gus came into the living room and stopped in front of Gatsby. They sniffed each other before Gus curled up next to the old dog. My throat got a little achy with emotion. "Did you know he would do that?"

"Yes," he whispered. "It's why Gus is here."

"For them or for you?"

His throat moved as he swallowed. It bothered him. The question was too close. He didn't need to respond. I already knew the answer. Maybe I just wanted to hear him say it. Wyatt walked over to the door and opened it. "Goodbye, Emma."

I refused to give in to his dismissal. My flip-flops clicked as I made my exit, but I stopped right in front of Wyatt before I left.

"I'll see you in a few days."

His chin titled down a bit to look into my eyes. "Okay."

The sparks picked up between us, pulling me to Wyatt. I studied his lips, so soft and pink. He would kiss me one day. He would kiss me, and my body would melt from the feel of those lips.

"Monday, okay?" I waited to see if he would protest again. "It might be later in the evening after I get off work."

"That's fine," he grumbled. "I'll be here."

"I know." I let out a deep breath. Leaving the trailer, I walked toward my car, feeling the faint touch of summer rain as it fell from the sky. Each drop sizzled in the hot air before reaching the ground. The heavy scent lingered without a downpour of rain. A promise of what never happened.

I looked over my shoulder, knowing Wyatt would still be standing in the doorway. His guilty stare followed me all the way to my white car.

CHAPTER 12

Emma

IT WAS WEDNESDAY BEFORE I COULD GET BACK OUT TO THE kennel. I'd ended up working a double shift at the bookstore on both Monday and Tuesday. Then today, I stayed ten hours at the nursing home. I'd planned to cut out right after my shift, but Vera begged me to try the passion fruit tea she'd received from her granddaughter. I'd stayed for several hours, making it after eight by the time I got to Wyatt's trailer.

As I pulled through the silver gate, the old cow skulls glowed eerily under the moonlight. I'd worried about him. I swear, I'd worried about him every second of every day while I was eating and in the shower and sipping tea at the nursing home.

As I walked up the cement steps, my nerves sparked a little, remembering my last visit. Wyatt had been so troubled with his eyes cloaked in broken shadows. And just as he allowed me to get a little closer, he had tried to push me away again.

One of these days, Wyatt might just throw me out for good. And I wasn't sure if I could take it. I was invested in him. I was haunted by him. I had feelings for the most unattainable person alive. Somewhere along the way, his broken eyes had dug a little hole in my heart.

Knocking on the door, I waited for Wyatt to let me inside his home. The sky was open and clear tonight. It was beautiful. I would make him leave the gloomy trailer and come outside for some air. I knocked on the door again. Twisting the knob, I stuck my head inside. "Wyatt? You in here?"

Gus and Gatsby came from his bedroom. I scratched them both on the head. Gatsby seemed better. Actually, he seemed ten times better. The brown dog had been a heap on the floor since he'd arrived. This didn't even seem like the same Gatsby. I heard a noise coming from the bedroom. "Wyatt?"

I wasn't sure if it was appropriate to just barge into his bedroom. I hesitated as my mind slipped through a few scenarios that might be waiting around the corner.

Wyatt would be angry if I invaded his personal space while he was wearing a towel. I wasn't sure why I went to the idea that he was in a towel, but that's where my thoughts stopped. I really couldn't just go into his bedroom once I'd decided he was naked, wearing just a towel. I waited a moment longer for Wyatt to come into the living room.

"Wyatt?" I tried to stand still on the brown shaggy carpet, but my impatience slipped into fidgeting. I finally gave up and poked my head around the corner, only to find Wyatt sprawled across his bed, wearing clothes. The sheets were tangled up in every direction around his body. I walked slowly over to the side of the bed, but he didn't move.

"Hey," I whispered. "Are you okay?"

At the sound of my voice, Wyatt rolled over. He blinked a few times, trying to adjust his vision. "Emma?"

Wyatt seemed confused. His hollow, sunken eyes stared at me, trying to determine if I were real or a figment of his imagination. His T-shirt was soaked in sweat. I sat down on the edge of the bed. "Are you sick?"

"I-I don't know." He swallowed hard, closing his eyes. Wyatt seemed vulnerable and weak.

"How long have you been like this?" I put my hand against his forehead. The heat burned into my skin. "You've got a fever. I think you should go to urgent care. Let me help you to my car."

"*No!*" Wyatt's eyes flipped open fast. He grabbed my wrist, removing my hand from his forehead. "No doctor."

I was ready to fight him on it, but Wyatt seemed to be on the verge of some sort of panic attack just by suggesting a doctor. "Okay. I won't take you to urgent care."

Wyatt's fingers burned into my arm. It wasn't the kind of burn that I wanted to feel from him. I loosened his grip on my wrist. "Have you taken any medicine?"

"Yes. No. Or yes. I-I don't know."

"That doesn't make sense, Wyatt. Have you taken any medicine?"

"I don't think so." His eyes closed. "I thought about it, but I don't think I did."

"Do you have a thermometer?"

"No," he muttered. I put my palm on his forehead again, feeling the scorching heat. His fever was really high. My fingers trailed over his cheeks. They had a couple of days' worth of stubble. Wyatt had been sick longer than he was letting on. His eyes stayed closed as I touched him. He *really* must be sick.

"Do you have any Tylenol?"

"Bathroom." The word crackled from his pale lips.

"I'll be right back," I whispered. "Oh, have you eaten?"

"I-I . . . maybe. I'm not hungry."

"Okay. I'll just get the medicine."

Going to his bathroom, I opened the first drawer, finding shaving cream and razors. I opened the second. It was easy to spot the red bottle in his perfectly organized medicine stash.

I moved to the linen closet next to the tub, which had a few towels, washcloths, and a clean set of sheets. They were folded like Wyatt worked at the bed store. He was painstakingly detailed in every level of his life. Taking out a washcloth from the closet, I ran cold tap water on the brown fabric and squeezed it out.

In the kitchen, I flipped open the pantry doors. His shelves were virtually bare, containing only a few items, including three boxes of Cap'n Crunch, a jar of peanut butter, and a loaf of bread.

Opening the refrigerator, I found milk for the cereal, three kinds of jam, a package of bologna, and another of cheese. I opened the freezer, discovering ten packages of hot dogs.

This was disgusting. I wouldn't be surprised if his digestive system was revolting against him, making him deathly sick.

Opening the next cabinet, I found a few plastic Eskimo Joe's cups and one that said Texas Westmiller University. I studied the odd, out-of-place item mixed with the others before grabbing the maroon and gray cup from the shelf. After filling it with tap water, I made my way back to his bedroom. I found Wyatt resting amidst the tangled sheets just as I'd left him.

"Hey, I need you to sit up."

His eyes flipped open slightly like I'd surprised him. He scooted up against the pillows. It was slow and painful and required all of his energy. Sitting next to him on the bed, I held the pills up. "It's okay. Just try to get these down."

His green eyes gazed back at me as I pushed the pills against his mouth. My fingers brushed across his soft lips before I pulled my hand away. I put the cup against his mouth and Wyatt took a few swallows. His eyes flickered to the maroon and gray letters in my hand. I didn't ask, and he didn't tell. Yet I knew from his reaction that cup meant something.

Pushing the brown hair off his forehead, I situated the washcloth across his skin. My fingers trailed over the stubble on his cheeks.

"It's cold," he mumbled.

"It needs to be. You really should try to take a cold shower too. It will help with the fever."

He contemplated my words before muttering in his raspy voice, "The questions weren't enough? You're trying to see me naked now?"

"No." I smiled at him. "Tonight, I'm your nurse. That's all."

"I think you'd be a good nurse," he muttered. "You should finish school."

"So you actually listened when I was talking?"

"Yeah." He smiled faintly. "You told me that first day when you came back. You kept talking about stuff. Asking me questions. You wouldn't be quiet. Talking and talking, over and over again, driving me crazy."

I laughed under my breath. "That Tylenol must already be working. You're back to being a jerk."

"I wasn't being a jerk. You drive me crazy, Emma. I want to hate it, but I like it." His eyes drifted closed, but the smile lingered on his lips. Reaching for my hand, he wrapped his fingers around mine, pulling it against his chest in a loose grasp. "Your hand is so small. I feel like I'm gonna crush it."

"You won't crush it," I whispered.

His eyes remained closed as a wry smile brushed his lips. "I think the same thing about you sometimes too. You're so tiny. I'd crush you."

The shock came in small waves as his words registered. I think Wyatt was talking about sex in his feverish semi-coma, which meant I probably should've insisted on taking him to the doctor.

"Maybe you should try to eat something. I didn't see much in there, but Cap'n Crunch. But I could go get you something in town?"

His fingers ran over my palm and circled around my wrist, each touch radiating up my arm. My pulse beat strong under his hand. With his eyes still closed, I heard him whisper, "I like Cap'n Crunch."

"I know," I muttered, feeling the burn of his feverish hand as he brushed my skin. His face stayed relaxed, his eyes closed.

Even in his sickness, I was attracted to Wyatt Caulfield. I didn't care if I were in bed for days because of this visit. His guard was down. It was down, and I was getting closer to him.

"I need you to do something." His eyes opened for a minute and bore into my face like he could read all of those thoughts floating around in my head. All the thoughts of how I would kiss him, even if it meant getting the flu. "I haven't fed the dogs. I need you to do it."

"Gus and Gatsby?"

"No. All of them. Put twice the amount in there. It will hold them over. And there's a list of medicine on my desk. It's in a locked case." Wyatt let go of my hand and pointed next to his dresser. "The key is in my drawer."

I scooted to that side of his bed. Reaching for the handle, it was strange to think I was about to rifle through his nightstand. Not that I was trespassing, since he was right there. But Wyatt was allowing me into another layer of his life.

I glanced over at him before pulling it open. Stress lines formed around his eyes, and then he closed them again. He was letting go. Wyatt was giving me permission to look inside his personal stuff.

My fingers tugged the metal handle. The inside of the drawer contained two packages of cough drops, a worn-out Bible with Wyatt inscribed in faded letters on the bottom right corner, and a key ring. Lifting the set from the bottom, I shut the nightstand.

"It's the smaller one that doesn't look like a door key. The case with the meds is in the bottom right drawer of my desk in the office. I keep it locked up because there's pain meds in there. There's a list with it. Tells you who gets what."

"Okay," I muttered, getting up from the side of his bed.

I let Gus and Gatsby out in front of the trailer to use the bathroom before going to the kennel. It took close to an hour to feed, water, and dish out medicine to all the residents. I played with Charlie for a few minutes. He covered my cheeks with wet slobber. I loved that little dog with everything in me. Putting Charlie back in his kennel, I pulled out my phone to send Blaire a text.

"Wyatt is sick. I'm going to be here late."

I braced for a slew of protests, but all I got was a simple, *"Okay."*

I made one last stop by Cye's pen before I returned to the trailer. Crawling on my hands and knees, I placed a bone a few feet from him. The tortured face of the poor dog broke my heart. He tolerated me at this point, poking into his life. Cye didn't embrace my actions, but at least he didn't run.

I walked the trail in the moonlight. Opening the door, I found Gus and Gatsby waiting together at the entrance. "Don't worry. I brought you some too."

I put the food in their bowls. After washing my hands, I peeked around the corner in Wyatt's room. He was lying against the pillows. His hair was a little damp and the covers were pulled up to his waist. Kicking off my flip-flops, I stepped softly across the old, shag carpet. Wyatt opened his eyes. "Are they okay?"

"Don't worry. Everyone is fine." I sat next to him on the bed. He stared at me, his eyes blinking at half the rate. Placing my palm against his forehead, I felt the temperature of his skin, which seemed to have decreased to a shade less than scalding hot. Maybe the Tylenol was working. "You take a cold shower?"

"Yeah."

"You feel any better?"

"A little." His voice grated on the words. "Diana was sick.

She must have given it to me."

"I'm sure she didn't mean to."

His face tensed up. "I wasn't blaming her."

"It's okay. I didn't say you were." I moved my hand away, seeing his eyes flash something I couldn't read. The stubble on his cheeks reflected slightly in the lamp light. I wanted to run my fingers over it again. I swallowed hard. "So . . . um . . . how often does Diana come out here?"

"Once a week. Usually on Sunday, but she came Friday after you'd left. She had plans."

"So I could meet her sometime? If I came on Sunday?" I wanted to talk to someone else who knew Wyatt. Maybe it would give me some clue into his *why*. Because a big *why* existed with this broken man. Why was he hiding out here? Why was he in so much pain? Why was he afraid of me?

"You have met her. Diana sent you out here."

"The lady with the rescue in Stillwater was Diana?"

"Yes. Diana is more of an extravagant dog foster with a kennel license. She volunteers with Red Dirt Claws. She keeps some of the dogs here and tries to place them through the rescue."

"So she could've just taken Charlie from me that day," I muttered. "Instead, she sent me out here to see you on purpose?"

"Yes." His eyes were tired and plagued with fever. There wasn't much fight in him tonight, and it wasn't right that I was using it to my advantage. But this new piece of information was very intriguing.

"Why did she send me out here?"

"Do you really have to ask that question?"

"She wanted us to meet?"

"Yes." He let out a deep breath, coughing a little. "She thinks I should be more open with you. Tell you things."

"What things?" That statement caught me off guard.

"Please . . . don't ask me anymore questions tonight." The

sadness came over his eyes first and then dipped across his cheeks down to those lips. It extended into his shoulders as he sunk into the pillows. I felt incredibly guilty, seeing how visibly he was crushed.

"I'm sorry," I whispered. And then I did something I figured would make him angry. I scooted up beside Wyatt on the bed, pushing myself next to his body. My shoulder touched his shoulder. My side touched his side. I nestled myself against him, bracing for his reaction. His body moved as he took a ragged breath, and then Wyatt rested his head against my shoulder. I felt his hair against my bare arm.

And then I froze as he took it a step further. He leaned over, placing his head across my lap, resting his cheek against my thigh. Hesitating, I fought the urge to touch him until I gave into the feeling. I ran my fingers through his soft brown hair. I smelled the faint scent of shampoo.

His hard body relaxed against my tiny one as I touched him. It felt good being this close to Wyatt. I smiled to myself, savoring every second of this moment because tomorrow might be a different story. But I didn't care. Tonight, he was going to let me comfort him.

Looking over on his nightstand, I saw a book sitting open. "You're reading *Call of the Wild*?"

"Yeah. Have you ever read it?"

"Actually, I did. About six years ago for a book report."

"You should experience it for fun. It means something entirely different when you do."

I smiled at the passion coming from his voice. My fingers drifted from his hair to his neck and to his shoulder. I wanted to keep touching him, but I rested my hand against his side. "Have you always read books?"

"No," he muttered. "It's more of a recent thing. Have you ever read one out loud?"

"No. Not since I was a kid, I guess."

"You should try it sometime. The story sounds different. I think it means a little more when you speak the words, when you hear them."

"Maybe you could read one to me sometime?" The comfortable words slipped out of my lips, and I braced myself for his reaction.

"Okay."

"You would?" I couldn't hide my surprise.

"Yeah," he whispered. "When I feel better, I'll read you *Emma*."

I smiled. "That wouldn't be weird at all."

"Have you read it?"

"No." I laughed. "But I saw the Gwyneth Paltrow movie."

"That doesn't count. And I haven't read it, so it would be a first for me too."

Reaching over to his nightstand, I pulled *Call of the Wild* over to us. "How about I read to you tonight?"

He didn't answer for a moment. I glanced down to where Wyatt was resting in my lap. His eyes were heavy, but open and full of sadness as he muttered, "Okay."

I opened the book. "Don't make fun of me."

"I won't." His answer was serious without a hint of laughter.

My voice came out soft at first, picking up where he'd left off at the turned-up page on chapter eight. I was nervous reading to Wyatt. It was strange speaking the words into the open air of the room. "How am I doing?"

"Your voice is nice. I like it."

The warmth spread through my heart, hearing the rare compliment. As I turned through the pages, I forgot how my voice sounded as I got caught up in the story.

Wyatt drifted in and out of sleep as I reached the end of the next chapter. I closed the book and put it back on the nightstand.

My fingers found their way back into his hair. I brushed a few strands off his forehead.

"Thank you for taking care of me," he whispered as his warm breath drifted across my legs. "I don't deserve it."

"Don't say that. Everyone deserves to be taken care of when they are sick."

"I don't think that's true."

"You just have a hard time letting someone else handle things."

"Maybe so." Wyatt said the words, but I didn't believe he meant them.

Turning off the lamp on his dresser, the room was flooded with the moonlight and shadows. I lifted his head from my lap, placing it on his pillow. I scooted down so I was even with him. Lying on my side, I stared into his green eyes. My lips were just a few inches from his soft ones. "What's your favorite Stephen King book? You haven't mentioned any, but you said he was your favorite."

"*The Stand.* But sometimes I think it's *Shawshank Redemption*," he whispered. "Because most people don't know it's his."

"I was afraid you were going to say *Pet Cemetery*. And that would be weird if you read that one to the dogs."

"I'm not that twisted." He lips turned up a little on the edges. "I didn't read *Cujo* to them either."

"Yeah, that would be pretty twisted."

Wyatt rested in silence as his eyes blinked heavy with sleep, the shadows flickering across his pale face.

"You're beautiful," he mumbled. "I wanted to hear it out loud and not just in my head."

His words hit me right in the middle of my chest and spread like wildfire under my skin. Hearing something like that from Wyatt burned deep.

"Did you decide that tonight in your flu delirium?"

"No." A faint laugh came from his throat. His eyes peered into mine before drifting lower. "I think you have sexy lips too, like the fake kind girls have on TV."

"They're not fake."

"I know. There's nothing about you that's fake. Not even on the inside." His eyes finally closed for good, leaving just a wry smile on his lips. "That's why you're so beautiful."

I was mesmerized by the thoughts he'd released into the safety of the darkness. Touching his face, I traced over the dimples. His breathing got deeper, sending the warm air over my face. I wanted to lean forward and press my mouth to his lips, but I would wait for him. Kissing Wyatt while he slept wasn't a good idea.

He shifted his body, putting an arm around my back. Wyatt clutched me against his chest. My muscles froze for a moment, feeling the sudden full-body contact with him.

The fever burned through his shirt and radiated against my skin. It burned with the electricity that existed between us even as he slept.

I let myself rest against Wyatt, and it felt good. With each breath, his face became more relaxed. He seemed younger, sweeter, and full of innocence. A version of Wyatt that was free of the constant pain that always remained on the edges.

I woke up, seeing the early-morning light coming through the curtains. My eyes darted around for a moment as my thoughts registered. I was in Wyatt's bedroom and his arms were circled around my body. His green eyes blinked back at me. He was awake. He was watching me. My stomach tightened, knowing Wyatt would be angry about me staying the night.

"Hi," I whispered.

He didn't respond, which caused a hundred bad thoughts to

circle through my head. His face was blank and unreadable when his gruff voice finally answered. "Hey."

"Do you feel better?"

"A little."

My breasts pressed tight into his chest each time I took a breath. I wasn't sure what I should say or do in this situation. After all, it was Wyatt and one wrong word could make him agitated.

Hesitating, I touched my fingers to his forehead. "I think your fever is gone."

"That's good. I hope I haven't made you sick. I breathed germs all over you last night."

"I'll be okay." Except I knew I wasn't ever going to be fine again. He was like an infection that spread through my body, replicating in my mind and heart. Every breakthrough with Wyatt just made the infection invade new parts of my soul.

"I think I changed my mind about you being a nurse, though."

"Why?"

"I don't think you are supposed to sleep with your patients." His lips were soft as he said the teasing words. He was flirting. I tried to calm the rush of feelings that flooded my heart. The more I felt his solid body touching me, the more I sucked in air, which pressed me tighter against his chest.

I was nervous. But a good kind of nervous. The kind that spoke of anticipation and excitement. I embraced the nervous jitters. They filled the space between our bodies, tightening the hold. It was a rush, a blissful surge under my skin that settled right behind my belly button and trickled down between my legs, lighting me on fire.

"Are you okay, Emma?" His gravelly voice hung on my name.

"Yes." I felt embarrassed as I whispered the truth. "I like waking up with you."

The words slipped out, and I regretted what I'd shared as I witnessed this new layer of Wyatt disappear right in front of me.

His face tightened and sadness pulled at his lips, twisting his jaw against his teeth. Wyatt let go of my body and rolled over to his back.

"Well, it's not like you're the first girl that I've seen in the morning." His words came out rough. "Most of them just had less clothes on."

I sat up in the bed. Leaning over, I stared down into his troubled face. "People have pasts. I have a small one, but every guy I meet will have some kind of past."

"Not like mine."

"But all of that existed before."

His eyes sharpened as fear settled in over his cheeks, making his skin even paler. "What do you mean *before*?"

"The before Wyatt. The person who existed before you decided to barricade yourself up out here."

The muscles in his arms tightened. His fingers balled into fists. "You don't know anything about who I was before here."

"Then tell me. Let me decide."

The battle raged inside his mind as I waited for Wyatt to come to some conclusion. His past had deep hooks right in the middle of his soul. A glaze slipped over his eyes. His fingers relaxed a bit and a wry smile brushed his tight face. "I was unapologetically sad."

"That almost sounds poetic," I whispered. Our eyes met, twisting into one of our stares. It pulled me closer to him as I looked down at his face. He was so captivating at times with his cryptic words.

"I read it in a book once. And I knew exactly what it meant. But I'm not sure you really do."

"You underestimate me, Wyatt Caulfield."

"And you're too good for me, Emma Sawyer." His gruff voice whispered my name as his fingers touched my cheek. They ran over my bottom lip. I closed my eyes, feeling the warmth spread through my body.

An aching pain simmered just under my skin. I kissed the end of his finger. I opened my eyes, seeing the guilty desire written all over his face as he touched my lips.

"You shouldn't do that," he whispered, leaving his fingers in place. I kissed his index finger again as he tugged at my bottom lip. "Emma . . . I wish this was possible."

"I don't understand why you think this is impossible."

"There's lots of reasons why." His hand slipped away, leaving me wanting more. The muscles in my stomach tensed as he continued to gaze up at me. I wanted him to touch me again, dragging his lips over my skin until every place on my body knew how it felt to be kissed by Wyatt.

I heard a vibrating sound. Reaching over to the nightstand, I grabbed my phone from his dresser, seeing the text from my sister.

"You have to take me to campus. Come home."

"I have to go. My sister needs me to take her somewhere. She doesn't drive." I climbed off his bed.

"Do you tell her the truth about me?"

"What's there to tell?" I said, putting on my shoes.

"So you lie to her?"

"She knows you exist. And you live here." I looked back at Wyatt, getting in one last stab. "You do realize not telling me things about yourself is the same thing as lying."

Wyatt sat up in his bed as his eyes glazed over with a dizzy spell. "I'm trying to protect you, Emma."

"From what?"

"*Me*." The desperation ached in his voice.

"Maybe I want to make my own decision about you. Have you thought about that?"

"You don't know any better. You are sweet, Emma. I see that about you. It's like second nature for you to take care of everyone.

You've got a whole weekly agenda designed around the people you help. You are a good person. Your heart is pure. I hurt people like you. I break them. Falling for me would not make sense."

"It's a little too late for that," I muttered.

His face seemed to crush right before my eyes. "I told you not to."

"You can't control who cares about you, Wyatt. You can't control my feelings for you."

"I-I didn't want you to feel this way."

"How could I not? You're so . . . so . . . *you*," I whispered.

He seemed more scared than angry as my words hit their mark. "I'm sorry, Emma. I tried to stop it."

I walked over to the side of his bed. My breath came in nervous bursts as I touched the stubble on his cheek. I ran my finger over his soft bottom lip, like he'd done to mine earlier.

"My heart aches for you, Wyatt. Every time I come here. You're so sad and sweet and caring even though you're convinced that you're some awful person." My fingers trailed down, coming to rest on his chest where his heart beat under my hand. "I think you're beautiful in here too."

Wyatt swallowed hard, making the skin around his throat move. "I'm sorry."

"You haven't done anything to be sorry for," I said, turning his own words back on him.

The sadness resumed in lines around his lips. It pulled me to Wyatt just like it had done all the other times. I was still worried about him being alone and sick, but I needed to do my *good deed* and get my sister. "I have to go. Are you going to be okay by yourself?"

"Yes," he muttered.

"Take some more Tylenol."

"Okay."

He settled back against the pillows. As I turned to leave the room, my flip-flop twisted beneath my foot. It happened fast. My knee buckled as I gasped in pain. I fell down on the brown shag carpet. I sucked in air, rolling around on my back. The pain spiked through my knee and down into my calf.

"Emma?" Wyatt was next to me on the floor. "Are you okay?"

"I-I'm." I tried to scoot to a sitting position. A cry of pain escaped my lips as I stretched it out. Wyatt put his hands under my arms, pulling me the rest of the way up.

"Maybe I could—" His words dropped off as Wyatt realized how close his lips were to my face. He was touching me in a hundred different places as the pulsing vibe between us got stronger than the pain. His eyes flickered to my lips and back up. His breath brushed in slow waves over my cheeks.

Wyatt leaned forward, pressing those soft lips against mine. The pain disappeared. I forgot my leg even existed. The world stopped spinning and nothing mattered except the fact that this broken man had finally given into the desire that plagued his conscience.

He kissed me slowly, letting our mouths gradually burn together before he even dared to move. Wyatt made this a waiting game of sweet erotic torture as he sucked on my bottom lip. He teased and pulled it gently, letting his tongue trace the outside before slipping inside my mouth.

Slow, sweet, delicate movements until we merged, until I melted on the shag carpet. I melted as every thought disappeared into oblivion.

His fingers twisted up in my blonde curls. Every stroke of his tongue sent a spark shooting through my body. The strange electric pull between us got stronger, making our movements grow more intense. I needed to touch him. I needed to feel him. Digging my fingers into his shoulders, I pulled myself closer to Wyatt.

A noise came from low in his throat. He kissed me deeper, rougher. The slow torture moved to a desire that seemed just out of reach. Wyatt slipped a hand under my butt, pulling me into his lap. My knee draped over his thigh. I moaned a little from the pain as it gripped my leg.

He lifted his mouth from mine. "I'm hurting you."

"You're not hurting me."

His arms circled around my whole body, crushing me against his chest. He held me tight as he tried to slow down his breathing. His green eyes gazed into mine, showing a mix of fear and desire. "Emma, I . . ."

"Don't make this harder than it has to be," I whispered.

"I tried, Emma," he muttered, resting his forehead against mine. "But I couldn't see you in so much pain and not kiss you. I had to. I'm sorry. I tried to stay away from you. But you just kept coming back here. And I didn't want to stop you. Every time I saw you. I wanted to just . . . grab you. Kiss you until . . . it didn't matter. But it's wrong. No matter what I do."

"I'm okay with this. With all of it. It's not wrong to want me."

"I don't want you." His words came with a vulnerable catch in his throat as he whispered, "It's like I . . . I crave you. And it scares me. Because I think you make all of this better."

A sweet flood of tingles swept under my chest and heart and down into my fingers, which clung to his shoulders. I held on to his flesh as those words rocked my very soul.

"That's okay too."

My pulse beat fast in my veins. His fear stayed just on the edge as Wyatt absorbed my words. Our eyes morphed into a stare before mine closed.

And then I felt him. His mouth, pressing against mine. His tongue, slipping through my lips. He kissed me, over and over again, as we held on to each other with our pace set by the electric force, pushing us together.

I crave you.

His words vibrated through my body. They tossed around

inside my head as his fingers clenched my waist just below my breast. I knew this was a battle inside of him. He held onto my side like an anchor, afraid to touch the rest of me.

Trailing my fingers down his back, I explored the hard muscles I felt through his shirt. I wanted to touch his skin and dig my fingers into his flesh. I craved him too.

My hands moved under his shirt, making contact with his bare stomach. He was soft and hard and so very Wyatt. I traced the faint trail of hair that disappeared into his pants.

"Emma . . ." He pulled back. "Don't. I . . . um. Just don't."

"I'm sorry. I didn't . . ." The words disappeared on my tongue.

His eyes shut for a moment, then opened. They seemed hazy and tortured. "You need to go get your sister."

"Yeah. Okay." I agreed, but I didn't move. I wanted to spend the rest of the day with Wyatt. I wanted to taste his lips. I wanted to feel his hands on my skin, but he wasn't ready for it. A very odd thought about someone who was way more experienced than me.

Wyatt shifted me out of his lap and back to the shag carpet. His fingers trailed over my thigh to the swelling around my knee. He worked the muscles. He worked the pain. The burning tingles of desire floated through my body, leaving an achy feeling trailing up my thighs, settling between my legs. He was just as sexy and meticulous with his fingers as he was with his tongue.

"Why don't you want the surgery?"

"I don't know. Past issues." The words came out breathless. I forced my nose to take in tiny gulps as his fingers remained on my skin.

"Issues?"

"I had the first surgery when I broke my leg. And it ruined my life in some ways." I closed my eyes for a second, steadying my thoughts. "I didn't go to school, but I lived in a college town. I missed out on all those next-step pieces. I didn't make new friends or go to exciting date parties. I floated around, living on the fringe of what was supposed to be my life."

"You missed out on all that crazy college shit. That's your sad story?"

"I didn't say that. I know my story is not exactly tragic. People have way worse stuff than some busted-up knee derailing them. I guess mine is more of a detour. And I just haven't found my way back on the road."

"I get it, but that doesn't really explain why you won't have the surgery."

"I don't know. Maybe it's the idea of having this stupid injury control my life again. Or maybe . . ." I grinned at him. "I don't have a good reason, and I'm just stubborn."

"I never would've guessed that one about you." His lips curled up at the corners, letting the dimples settle on his cheeks. Wyatt stopped moving his fingers, but the flutters in my stomach remained just as intense. I focused on breathing as our eyes held in the rare humorous moment that was laced with the achy desire, pulling me to him. I glanced at his lips, wanting him to kiss me again.

Wyatt swallowed hard, reading my thoughts. "Let's see if you can stand."

He shuffled up from the floor, holding out a hand. Clasping his fingers, I used his strength to maneuver up from the carpet without putting weight on my leg. Testing the water, I put my right foot on the floor. The pain remained pretty strong, but I didn't crumple to a pile on the ground. "I think it's better. I should be able to drive."

"I'll walk you to the car." And then before I knew what happened, Wyatt scooped me up in his arms.

"What are you doing?"

"Walking you to the car." He carried me out the front door. The flutters in my stomach got stronger as he clutched me tight against his hard chest. Circling my arms around his neck, I held onto Wyatt as his bare feet went down the steps and across the path to my car. He set me down next to the driver's side door.

He shuffled around, digging his bare toes into the dirt before saying anything. "All joking aside, you really need to go back to the doctor. That knee is a damn mess."

"I know." I nodded in agreement. The summer air pressed against my body, making sweat trickle down my back as I struggled to keep the weight off my knee.

"Well, bye, Emma. And um . . . thank you." The words came with a surge of emotions he tried to push down. "You know, for last night."

"You're an easy patient." I joked as the nervous energy bounced between us. Our parting moment, for now or forever, depending on how he reacted to kissing me. I might return only to find him back behind the curtains. "Promise me something, Wyatt. Promise me you won't sit here all day regretting that you kissed me."

"I can't promise that." His raspy voice hung on the words. It took everything in me not to sling my arms back around his neck and do the very thing that caused him so much agony. I wish he would just let me in, let me help.

"You want to know why I was so good at running cross country before my leg got busted up?" I gave him an even stare. "My coach always said that I was small, but I had the determination of ten people. Running trails is not for the splash-in-the-pan runner. It's for someone who is willing to stick with it for miles. Someone who has to pace herself and keep going despite the blisters and the bugs flying in her teeth. That's who I am. I trained for years to be that person, and it doesn't just disappear. Yes, I'm stubborn, Wyatt. And I have determination. There's nothing you can throw at me that will shake that. So I want us to talk more when I come back. I promise. I can handle it."

His hands balled into twitchy fists as fear settled in around his eyes. I had pushed him. I wanted him to know despite my appearance, I was solid on the inside.

"Fine," he grunted.

I let a deep breath trickle out my nose, trying to calm the excitement of a possible breakthrough. "I'm not sure when I can get back out here. I have to cover at work again this week. A girl quit, and I need the extra hours before classes start back."

"Well, I'll be here. So whenever you get back." His jaw gritted up in a death grip like he swallowed acid. "We can talk."

It was hard to leave him. My phone dinged again. Without taking it out of my pocket, I knew my sister was having another fit about me coming to get her. I got in my car, driving away as he stood in the yard looking guilty and tortured. My heart felt a thousand different emotions as his face disappeared in my rearview mirror.

CHAPTER 13

Emma

WITH EACH MILE I TRAVELED DOWN THE ROAD, HER TEMPER hit me with little stabs in the chest. My sister was angry. The sensation grew stronger the closer I got to my apartment.

My car rolled into the parking lot. I slammed on the brakes, coming to a stop right beside the stairs where Blair sat on the bottom step, waiting with her arms crossed. I tossed the door open with an apology on my lips.

"Don't even." Her fingers flicked up, dismissing me.

Hitting the trunk button, the flap popped up, allowing her to put the tuba case inside the back of the car. "Come on, Blaire. I really am sorry. I didn't mean to . . . to spend the night."

"I don't give a shit that you spent the night."

"Then what's wrong?"

"I texted you almost two hours ago. I know it doesn't take that long to get here from his weird compound. Then I felt all those butterflies and shit. You've been cramming your tongue down his throat while I missed rehearsal."

"I really am sorry. I made progress with him and I just couldn't leave."

"Just where have you been, Emma Sawyer?" The deep voice came out with a nasty twist. I spun around, seeing Kurt next to Blaire. He was too close to her. Glancing at my sister, she grew flustered at his sudden presence.

He spit tobacco straight on the cement, which splattered a little on Blaire's foot. His beady eyes drifted slowly back and forth between us. The little brain in his head still couldn't get over the fact there were two of us. His *other* little brain got it very clear, which made the sick feeling creep inside the pit of my stomach.

"What do you need, Kurt?"

"I'm just asking the same questions as your little sis here. We were both so worried that you didn't come home last night. I'm getting a little concerned. You're always coming and going . . . *somewhere*." He shut the trunk on my car. Kurt looked at the red dirt on his hands that came from the white paint. Watching my reaction, he smeared it across the thighs of his jeans.

"Bye, Kurt. We are in a hurry." I ran to the driver's side as Blaire climbed in the passenger's seat.

"You just had to provoke him over some dog."

"Stop it." I put the car in drive, speeding out of the parking lot. "I didn't know he would get all crazy about it."

"I told you stuff doesn't seem right about him."

"I know. I know." I blew a blonde curl out of my eye as I came to a red light.

"By the way, I did a search on Wyatt."

"You did?" I glanced over, bracing for whatever incriminating information she'd found on him. "I didn't even think about looking him up."

"I figured. And no. I didn't find anything. Are you sure that's his name?"

"Yes. I saw it on a Bible in his dresser. People don't make that kind of stuff up and stamp it in gold on a Bible."

"Well, I guess whatever is wrong with him is personal and not criminal."

"This has never felt like something criminal. He's hurting. I just don't know why." I parked in front of the building, clicking the trunk button. I thought my sister would jump immediately from the car, but she stayed in her seat, staring blankly out the window.

"That's your heart talking, Emma. Not your common sense. But I get it. I felt it from you today." She hesitated, letting the words form in her mind before speaking. "Do you think I will ever feel something like that? Am I capable of it?"

My heart broke a little for Blaire as her voice betrayed her true emotions. My sister wanted something she couldn't even understand. I hoped one day it would be true. I hoped Blaire Sawyer could experience everything in life.

Reaching over, I grabbed her hand in mine. "I think you are. I *believe* you are. Those feelings only exist when you meet someone who makes them happen. I believe it's possible. You just need to meet the right person."

"I don't know. We both know I'm not like other people."

"There's love inside of you, Blaire. But love is not the same for every person. It will be different for you than me. But it will make you happy."

"You *love* him?" Her identical eyes caught mine.

"I-I don't know." It wasn't exactly love, but I sure felt something for him, especially since I was so close to a breakthrough. I think Wyatt was finally going to let me help him.

CHAPTER 14

Emma

THREE DAYS LATER, I DROVE DOWN THE TRAIL TO THE KENNEL. Three agonizing days of wishing I could see him and worrying that everything would blow up in my face when I finally had the opportunity to return. What if I went two steps forward only to fall five steps backward when he tried to shut me out again?

I got out of my car, seeing Wyatt in the distance. His gaze followed me as I walked the path to the fenced-in play area. Gus and Gatsby were inside, waiting for him to throw the tennis ball again.

His soft lips turned up on the corners, just briefly, just enough, which caused his dimples to slowly roll into place. Pausing with my hand on the gate, a rush of anticipation shot through my chest as his green eyes bore into mine.

"Hey." I moved the latch, letting myself inside the fence. I fought the urge to run across the grass and throw my arms around him.

"Hey."

This was far better than I'd expected today. In my absence, I'd assumed Wyatt tortured himself into some level of a fit. Instead, he seemed *okay*. Yet I planned to proceed with caution. His promise of talking would come at his own pace.

I wish he would just trust me. There was nothing Wyatt could say that would make me leave at this point. I knew the inside of his heart. I saw the deep compassion that encircled the broken pieces, holding it together. I saw it very clearly as he clutched a worn tennis ball, grinning at two very impatient animals.

"Gatsby is like a whole new dog." I went for the safe topic, the one I knew would be easy for him without ruining his current mood.

"You should watch this."

Wyatt tossed the ball across the grass. Gus ran beside Gatsby as the yellow fabric rolled in front of them. Moving into the lead, Gus stopped right beside the ball. The little Jack Russell waited for the old Labrador to grab it between his teeth, never darting for it himself. Once Gatsby captured the tennis ball, the pair returned to Wyatt.

"Did you teach Gus to do that?"

"No." Wyatt tossed the ball again. It was sweet, seeing the little dog guide the older one to where it landed in the grass. "I think Gatsby has bad eyes. That's why he's gotten better with Gus. He stays glued to him now."

Walking over to the dogs, I rubbed the older one on top of his head. His brown eyes were glazed over like he was in a far-off place, but his tongue hung out the corner with the impression of a smile. Sweet, old Gatsby. Sometimes this place was just too much.

"You kinda work a little magic out here with the dogs."

"Maybe."

"I mean, you are really good at this. I hope you know that. You're making a difference with them."

Wyatt didn't respond. He went over to the water faucet, refilling their bowl. The dogs made their way to the large plastic container. Gus let Gatsby get a drink first.

I walked across the pen in my tennis shoes. His eyes drifted down to my swollen knee. "You talk to the doctor?"

"Yes. I'm having the surgery in September. I'll have to be off my feet for several weeks, which is good for homework. But not for summer and working. This way, I'll have more study time while I'm banished to my apartment."

"You got a date for it?"

"You don't believe me?" I flashed a mischievous grin at him.

"Not when it comes to you and whatever stubborn shit is keeping you from getting it fixed."

"Not stubborn. Just . . . unwilling to be controlled by it. My surgery. My terms. Besides it's more practical in September. I'm taking more classes this fall." I stepped a little closer to Wyatt. "You feeling better?"

"Yeah." The gruff word rolled off his lips. I slipped a look at them and then back to his eyes. I wanted to kiss Wyatt again. I wanted to taste his lips.

I touched his freshly shaven cheek with my fingertip before cupping his face with my hands. Leaning up on my tiptoes, I pressed my mouth over those soft lips. I kissed Wyatt. My pulse moved in anxious beats with my brazen action.

Releasing my hold, I backed away a few inches, waiting for his reaction. The battle raged right behind his green eyes. He swallowed hard before slipping his hands around my waist, pulling me tight against his chest.

He needed to feel me. I knew from the desperate way his hands clutched my body. And a strange realization settled just inside my heart. Wyatt may have a past, but I don't know the last time he'd felt the touch of another person. Not even in a sexual way, but just in the casual emotional embrace.

Wyatt held onto my body, digging his fingers into my lower back. He pulled me tighter and kissed the side of my head. And then his lips drifted to my cheek before coming to rest against my mouth.

Wyatt kissed me slowly and deliberately. I had never met a guy who focused so much on using his lips. The soft movements caused a ripple of burning agony under my skin. I was alive and tortured by the desire he ignited. If Wyatt was this good at just kissing, the feel of his hands on my bare skin might just push me over the edge into oblivion.

"You're a good kisser," I whispered as he lifted his lips from my mouth.

"I've never taken the time to enjoy it before. I always rushed through that part. Or I guess I never cared enough about another person to enjoy it."

"So you're enjoying it with me?"

"Yes. More than I should." His eyes glazed over for a moment before he pushed back whatever tormented thought that plagued his conscience. Wyatt rested his forehead against mine. "I feel it too, you know. This thing . . . pulling us together. But what I'm doing to you isn't fair. I know you want me to talk, but I just don't know what to say or think."

"Then don't think right now."

I kissed him again, holding onto the taste of his lips. I ran my fingers through his soft hair. Pressing myself against him, I wanted to reassure the broken man that his feelings were safe with me. Not talking was just as good as talking. He uttered not a single word, but shared so much of himself in the way he took over the kiss.

His tongue touched mine like a match to a firework. The sparks ignited as his right hand moved over my butt, pushing me tighter against his hard body, tighter against his hips.

I couldn't get close enough to Wyatt, and he needed to hold

on to me too. As he pressed us together, I melted against him, letting his lips take control of my thoughts. I drifted away. Kissing Wyatt was erotic and intoxicating and pure agony—and then he was gone.

He pulled back, staring out in the distance. I closed my eyes for a moment. My heart beat so fast in my chest that I was getting a head rush.

"What's wrong?" An ashen color slipped over his cheeks as his jaw clenched tighter. "Wyatt?"

Looking in the direction of his piercing eyes, I saw a trail of dirt before I saw the car. Someone was coming down the trail. Someone was coming *here*.

"Go inside the trailer." The bite to his words caught me off guard.

"No." I wasn't going to miss this piece of the puzzle. I should wait for him to tell me on his own terms, but I couldn't wait for that to happen. I needed to know this information. I needed to crash down the wall that held him captive. Whoever was inside the car was a key to the secrets he kept locked inside his heart.

As the car got closer, Wyatt shifted a few feet away from me. "Get inside the trailer. *Now!*"

A small trickle of fear trailed like sweat down my back. I wasn't budging, and he knew it. This person in the car was causing Wyatt to slip into a borderline panic attack. He looked at me with wild eyes and then back to the Tahoe. The SUV with blacked-out windows parked in front of the trailer.

Wyatt ran a hand through his brown hair, gripping the short pieces in a tight wad. His shoulders went ridged as he braced for the driver's side door to open. I waited to see the face of the man who had scared Wyatt into practically shaking in his boots, but a lone girl stepped out in front of us.

Her tall, slender figure paused, glancing at the trailer before surveying the rest of the property. She noticed us standing in the fenced-in play area. Even from a distance, I knew their eyes locked tight on each other. I knew because the contact made his body shudder.

She stepped across the dirt with the grace of a dancer. The mysterious stranger came closer and closer as the silence from Wyatt filled the space with his visible anger. The girl paused at the gate, taking in the scene in front of her.

Looking from Wyatt to me, she eyed my presence with open curiosity. The girl brushed a few pieces of brown hair from her shoulder, making it fall in long strands down her back. She was beautiful in that natural sort of way, the kind that graced face wash commercials.

A white and brown blur went past me in the grass. Her face lit up bright, flashing a stunning smile as she came inside the fence. Bending down on his level, her delicate hands touched the little dog who was just short of passing out from excitement.

"Gussy." Her soft voice laughed as he licked her cheeks. "I've missed you too."

I stood paralyzed, taking in her presence. The sun cast a spotlight on the girl like the halo of an angel. She glanced back up at Wyatt. "I see you've been taking good care of him."

My gut twisted, and I backed up until I touched the fence. My fingers gripped the metal wire. This scene had an eerie familiar hint that made me think of Charlie, made me think of me. Gus was not Wyatt's dog. The little Jack Russell belonged to the mystery girl.

Out of reflex, I slipped a look over to Wyatt. His hands were clamped into tight fists, making his knuckles glow white. His green eyes darted from the girl and then back to me.

She let a hesitant smile flow in my direction. "I'm Willa, since he's obviously not going to introduce you."

"Emma," I muttered, staring at her. I wanted to ask questions, but too much was happening at once.

"You're not supposed to be here." Wyatt came alive, growling the words in her direction.

"I brought you some stuff."

"Leave, Willa." His teeth gritted tight against his jaw.

"You can't just keep doing this. I won't let you. It has to stop."

"I can't do anything else, but I can stop you from coming out here. I can do that much at least. Besides, you're not supposed to be driving, anyway."

"I've made a little progress. Sometimes I can go a week or two without an episode."

"Really?" Wyatt's face changed briefly as his emotions flooded his cheeks.

"Yes." Her eyes pleaded back.

I didn't know the identity of this girl. But she meant something to him. Something deep and slightly crazy. Something so strong, it brought tears to the corners of his eyes as he processed her words.

"That doesn't mean you should come here. You know my conditions on this fucked-up arrangement."

Hearing his words, a sudden chill shot up my spine even though the temperature was in the nineties.

"Why? Tell me why it's so horrible that I come out here to see you."

"You know why." He glanced slightly in my direction, acknowledging my presence in the middle of their fight. Fear gripped in tight lines around his flat lips—fear mixed with the panic of a trapped animal. Wyatt was afraid she would say something in front of me.

Maybe she was his ex-girlfriend. *Or girlfriend.*

"This isn't fair to me." Her voice quivered a little as she faced him. "I know you are angry. And you feel guilty. But to me? It's not fair."

"If life were fair, I wouldn't be *here!*"

"Don't say that."

"Then get back in your fucking car, and you won't have to hear it."

Her face went white as they stared at each other. Somewhere during the exchange of heated words, they had drifted closer together. Her hands clenched into fists as she processed the vile words slung in her face.

"I still love you. And I'm going to keep telling you every time I come out here. You can say every awful thing you want, but nothing is going to change how I feel about you. Nothing you do will either."

A hard, granite mask slipped across his face, blocking out his emotions so her words had no place to land. Tears fell down Willa's cheeks as she gazed at him. Her pain was strong.

And in that moment, I didn't care about her identity.

I felt the pull to her broken heart. Her shoulders sagged, and I wanted to hug the poor girl who *loved* Wyatt because part of me understood her agony. I wasn't the first person who had tried to fix Wyatt Caulfield.

As he failed to react to her powerful words, Willa wiped away a few tears and turned to leave. She opened the gate, and Wyatt grabbed Gus before he darted out the fence. The little dog whined as his apparent *owner* left him. My gaze followed her long, graceful legs back to the Tahoe. Willa climbed inside, but she didn't start the motor.

The shock of the confrontation had left me as a petrified statue. I didn't notice Wyatt take Gus and Gatsby toward the kennel until the door slammed, getting my attention. I looked back toward the SUV. The dark windows blocked her from my view. I had more questions than answers for the mysterious girl, but I went toward the kennel instead of risking his anger by going after Willa.

I stopped inside the door, seeing Wyatt put the two dogs in

the holding pen by the office. He never put Gus in the kennel room, and Gatsby lived in his trailer now too.

"Wyatt, are you okay?"

"You shouldn't be here either." The bite to his words came as strong as those he'd thrown at Willa. I cringed at the sudden change in his personality toward me. His lips remained flat and white. Just a few moments ago, those same lips had clung to my mouth in desperation.

"I'm not going anywhere."

He laughed with a strange, cryptic edge. "You almost had me. For a brief moment, you almost had me convinced that I was someone else."

"Look, I don't know what just happened out there."

"This is over. That's what happened. I don't want you here anymore, Emma. Stay off my damn property. Take Charlie with you or leave him. I don't give a shit. I just want you gone."

"Wyatt, I—"

He disappeared out the door before I could finish the sentence. I walked slowly out the entrance just as he slammed the trailer door shut. The whole building shook on the cinder blocks.

My confused thoughts cluttered all the rational ones right out of my head. The parking area only held my car. Glancing out across the pasture, the black Tahoe disappeared into a cloud of dust.

I could push him. I could march right inside his cave and push him into talking, but I wasn't sure if that was the right course of action. This Willa had set him on fire. Maybe I should wait until it burned down into something not so angry. Leaving was a risk because I might return to only find the ashes with all my progress, blowing away in the summer air.

The questions and options were endless and not promising. Maybe he loved this girl and that's why I was an impossible fantasy. Maybe there was truth to all those warnings and her *episodes.*

Willa's cryptic comments raised a different set of questions that haunted my thoughts as I walked to my car. Pulling open the door, I saw a note lying in the front seat on the back of a Walmart receipt.

Emma,

I don't know who you are. But the fact that you are here means Wyatt trusts you. I don't know what he's told you. I'm sure you have questions. If you want some answers, at least the ones I know, give me a call. 405-555-5309. If you want to wait for him to tell you, I understand too.

I'm not some psycho ex. I'm his sister. I doubt he's ever mentioned his family. He's got one of them too.

Willa

His sister? The shock hit me hard in the chest. All those times I'd worried that no one thought about him, Wyatt had kept a secret sister and a family. He had people but chose to live out here in complete misery. As the anger flickered in tiny bursts through my thoughts, I knew his isolation came from something much bigger than I'd realized.

Gripping the receipt in my hand, I slammed my car door and marched over to his trailer. The pain went through my knee in sharp stabs, but I ignored the irritating reminder. My fingers grasped the knob on the aluminum door, expecting it to be locked, but it turned loose in my hand.

Wyatt sat in the old chair that held the shape of his body. His eyes glowed back from the darkness of the trailer. Every light remained off and the thick curtains cut off all traces of the sun. I left the door open so I could monitor his reaction.

"Start talking." I threw the slip of paper in his lap. Wyatt grasped the Walmart receipt tight as he skimmed the words and then crumpled it in his fist.

"Fine. Destroy it. But that doesn't make any of this go away." Except I'd forgotten to write down her phone number, but that little detail wasn't relevant. "You need to talk to me, or I'm going to call Willa. I'll let her tell me everything you are so desperately trying to avoid. Just tell me, Wyatt. Talk to me."

That strange laugh came from deep in his throat as he shook his head. "You're so naïve. It's been right in front of you. I thought you would figure it out, but you never did."

"Figure what out?"

"Dammit, Emma." His hands gripped tight, making his knuckles turn white. "Fine."

He kicked off his boot and yanked up his jeans leg. A three-inch scar ran down his skin right under his knee.

Just above his white sock, a black strap circled his entire leg with a little box attached to the side. I was confused, and then it all slammed into place.

Wyatt couldn't go to the doctor. Wyatt couldn't go to dinner. Wyatt couldn't ride his motorcycle. *Wyatt couldn't leave.*

My eyes stayed locked on the ankle monitor as the puzzle pieces swirled around in my head. "How long have you been here like this?"

"Over two years."

"You haven't left here. *This place.* In over two years?"

"Yes," he muttered. "And it's only the beginning."

"What happened?"

He watched me as the raw pain twisted through his face. Wyatt pulled his jeans leg down. "When a guy out in the middle of nowhere tells you that he has been in his own personal prison for the last two years—*that* should be your cue to leave."

"Not until you tell me why. I'm tired of fighting you on this." I sat down on the couch, feeling the scratchy fabric on my thighs. I crossed my arms in defiance. "Stop trying to push me away by being a jerk. Just spit it out. Rip the Band-Aid off."

"How do you know I won't lie and just sugarcoat it with a bunch of fake shit?" He was trying his best to scare me, but I was in too deep to run. I saw through his façade. He was afraid. He was terrified for me to see the broken pieces of his life.

"I know you don't lie to me. You're not that kind of person."

"You don't know what kind of person I am. Not really."

"Then tell me." Staring into those mocking green eyes, I dared him to give me his worst. "Who are you *really*, Wyatt Caulfield?"

He hesitated, letting out a deep breath. "Well, for starters, my last name is Carter. I stole Caulfield right out of *Catcher in the Rye*. If you tried to look me up, I'm sure you didn't find a damn thing."

The words came out with a cruel twist, causing my heart to falter and question everything I thought I'd known about this person. I was so sure, and then like a flash—I wasn't. Wyatt *Carter* got up from the chair and kicked the door closed, sending us into darkness.

Part II

Wyatt

CHAPTER 15

Wyatt

NO ONE STARTS OUT THE MORNING THINKING, *I'M GOING TO screw up everyone's lives today.* Instead, they go about their day believing, *I'm so damn invincible, not even God himself can touch me.* But that's the thing about believing you're more powerful than God. At the end of the day, everyone is really just a product of their piss-poor choices and ultimately the consequences.

I don't know when I'd become the guy who contemplated a bunch of theoretical shit. Maybe it was my freshman year when my advisor stuck my ass in that philosophy class—or maybe it was the night I learned the truth the hard way.

CHAPTER 16

Wyatt

2 years, 6 months, 17 days ago

MY EYES LOCKED IN A DEAD HOLD WITH MY FATHER. ONE whole hour. That's all it took. "Are you coming down for dinner, Wyatt?"

Simple, harmless words, but laced with years of issues. Sometimes I wished he would just hit me. Break my nose. Knock out a few teeth. People had a way of understanding violence. It's easy to explain: *my dad beats the shit out of me.*

But our disagreements were different. Oil and water and gasoline and fire. Words and resentment and control. That's what it always came down to with him. He wanted me to say and do everything just like those he commanded at work.

I crossed my arms over my chest without saying a word. We held our spots, each of us frozen in our attempt to take a stand. My father expected me to follow him down the stairs like a puppy. But I wasn't coming until I damn well felt like it.

My phone buzzed as Trevor Higgins sent another obnoxious

text. Looking at the screen, I cringed at the words, describing my high school ex-girlfriend.

"Melissa Cox is here. I think her tits got bigger."

My fingers gripped around the phone before tossing it on the bed. Taking another look up at my father, his jaw clenched in a tight hold. He knew who had sent the message without even reading it.

"I'll be down in a minute," I muttered.

I wanted him to leave me the hell alone tonight. I was exhausted from finals. Over the last three days, I'd slept a total of five hours and I couldn't shake the uneasy feeling that still gripped my gut. I hoped my psychology professor took my end-of-semester term paper since I'd slipped it under his door late. My scholarship required me to keep a certain GPA, or I would find myself right back here in this shit-hole on a permanent basis.

"I'm warning you. Don't pull one of your stunts and ruin dinner."

"Yes, sir." I struggled to tone down the sarcasm. He gave one last commanding glare before stepping around my suitcase and leaving my bedroom. Hearing his shoes on the stairs, I got up and slammed my door before falling down on the bed. My phone lit up again with another message from Trevor.

"Get your pussy ass over here. This is your fucking party."

I didn't want any damn homecoming party, but we both knew this had nothing to do with me. Not really. Back in the fifth grade, his mom had left with some guy who grew hemp on a commune in California. Mr. Higgins had never really gotten over that one. He slowly spiraled into a worthless father who spent all his time and money at the Indian casinos. I'm sure Trevor was all alone and my trip back for winter break was an excuse for some bender blowout at his house.

I felt that usual pang of guilt when it came to my old friend. After all, tomorrow was Christmas and I bet he was spending it by himself again. He was like some ripped-up teddy bear, tossed in the dumpster and forgotten. Letting out a deep breath, I picked up my phone, shooting off a quick reply.

"Be there soon, asshole."

Heading downstairs, I heard their voices before I even reached the landing. I grabbed my black hoodie from off the back of the couch. Glancing in the direction of the laughter, I saw my family gathered around the table in the kitchen—waiting for me.

Hopefully, I could slip out the door without my parents knowing I was headed to Trevor's house. Just the mention of his name would make my dad get all preachy and shit again. *You need to stay clear of that Higgins boy.* I'd heard it most of high school.

"Where are you going, Wyatt?" Her soft voice made me stop in my tracks. I looked over my shoulder, seeing the sad smile on my mom's face as she stood under the curved archway that led into the kitchen. "Are you leaving? You just got here."

"I'm just going for a little ride. I won't be gone long."

The visible hurt flashed in her eyes. "Well, it's already after eight and I just got finished with dinner."

I got a whiff of something that resembled pie. Only a complete asshole cut out on Christmas Eve, but I needed to get to his house, make an appearance for Trevor's sake. I would spend some time with the guys, and then take it easy the rest of winter break.

Ever since I'd gotten the scholarship to play for Texas Westmiller University, my life was an endless looping circle of football practice, class, and homework. Coach was a hard ass, but he was damn good. It's the reason our football season ended in the Division-II semifinals.

But now I was here. I was back in Gibbs and the same old claws of the monster pulled me right back down into the depths of his debauchery. But I'd be lying if I said I wasn't just a little excited. I'd missed Marcus and Trevor while I was away.

"I'm sorry, Mom. But there's something I gotta do."

"You going to Trevor's house?" Her eyes probed with the questions I knew she would never ask of me. The whole town of Gibbs heard the rumors of the crazy shit that went on just over the city limit line—my father more than any of them.

"Yeah. Just for a little bit."

"You should invite him over tomorrow." Even though my dad hated the guy, my mom on the other hand had a soft spot for the delinquents.

"You sure that's okay?" I asked, glancing toward the kitchen at my father. His large frame seemed three sizes too big for our old dining chair. I stared for a moment as he talked to my little sister Willa. She laughed, flipping her brown hair over her shoulder. It seemed so normal and easy with them.

"Yes, invite Trevor. I'm the one making the food. I can give it to anyone I want to."

My father picked up a six-inch knife, taking a stab at the roasted turkey. I moved out of eyesight before he noticed my presence. "Thanks, Mom. That's um . . . that would be nice."

"Don't stay out too late. Grandma and Grandpa will be here early. They want to see you and Willa open presents."

"Okay, Mom." I laughed under my breath. "Early, as in?"

"Seven."

"Fu . . . I um . . . mean. That's nice." The Christmas show still went on like I was five. My pocket vibrated again. *Shit.* Trevor needed to calm the hell down.

"Bye, Mom." I gave her a quick kiss on the cheek.

Flipping the hood over my head, I left through the old front door, leaving my mom standing alone in the living room. I went around to the storage building where they kept my bike. I didn't take it to college. I didn't want any of those stupid assholes touching it as a prank.

Lifting the tarp, the moonlight reflected off the shiny chrome and black. The motorcycle had been a gift from my grandpa when

I turned sixteen. He'd restored the old Harley himself. My father had wanted to send it immediately back over to his garage. He said it played right into the path of me becoming a felon. Personally, I think it saved me from it.

I pulled a pack of Marlboros out of my pocket. Lighting up a cigarette, I took a couple of drags and studied the clouds. The air was chilly and smelled of winter rain. I'd probably get soaked on the way back, but it was a better option than my truck.

I straddled the seat, feeling a deep rush of freedom under my thighs. It had been too damn long. I took a few more puffs before tossing the butt on the ground. I'd get shit from my father over that one tomorrow once he figured out my smoking habits were still alive and well. He'd be pissed that college didn't fix *everything* about me.

Putting the key in the ignition, I fired up the engine, letting it get warmed up. The sound sent chills down my back. My grandpa did a hell of a job on it. I drove down the driveway, glancing back at the house. My father's broad shoulders cast a dark shape against the window as he watched me leave. I felt the anger from his face without actually seeing it.

I dared him to come out and yank me off the seat, pull me by the arm right back in the kitchen and throw my ass down in the chair. Force me to stay for one of our typical discussions that was more yelling than talking. Giving him one last look, I gunned the engine a few times and peeled out in the street.

The football scholarship changed more than one thing about my life. It got me away from my friends—*and* my father. I only came back for holidays and I didn't give a shit if he showed up at my games. Another perk of going to college in south Texas.

That's the thing about being a PK. Not the preacher's kid, but a more destructive one. My father was the police chief for the town of Gibbs. He'd always expected the same authority at both work and at home, which only caused me to push back against an unmovable force. I was the round object he'd tried to cram into a square hole. And sometimes I still provoked him on purpose—just for the hell of it.

Sucking in a deep breath, the air settled in my lungs as I watched the streetlights glow under the cold mist. My nerves seemed to relax the farther I got from my house. Cruising through the comfortable darkness, I looked around my old hometown. The whole place was lit on fire with the familiar Christmas lights—the same ones they'd pulled out of storage each year that had faded to a pink color instead of shiny red.

Once I cleared Main Street, I kicked it up to seventy. The bike went over the rough metal of the railroad tracks to the literal other side of town. The chilly wind slapped my bare face, making me feel better than I had in months. As much as I loved college, it was brutal at times—and so very different than here.

As I pulled in the driveway full of three-foot tall weeds, I thought about Trevor. His life was an overgrown mess of shit. Unlike me, he wasn't going to do anything about it. He was a follower right down the path of his father and it all happened because his mom was a selfish bitch who had left him.

The yard was full of cars and an assortment of trash. The low bass from the music was louder than the motor on my bike. Pulling up in front of the garage, I looked at the mangled door. The damn thing must have broken months ago, and no one had bothered to fix it. I cleared the lopsided hanging metal and parked inside to keep the rain off the old Harley. An arm grabbed me as I slung my right leg over the seat.

"I was beginning to think your ass was too good for me."

"Shut up, Trevor. You don't need me. Looks like you got a full house." I hugged the guy who had been my friend since kindergarten. Trevor was so damn needy sometimes. He never could stand on his own. He'd always had Marcus and me at his side. "By the way, my mom wants you to come over for dinner tomorrow."

"Really?" His face lit up. "She making that stuffing shit?"

In that moment, I felt bad for the guy. That was the thing about Trevor. He made sure I never forgot him. It was the eyes. The sad, pathetic eyes that spurned pity from his friends and made the girls fuck him.

"Yeah, I'm sure there's stuffing." I followed Trevor around the busted bags of trash and hundreds of old containers and bottles, scattered across the cement. The smell caught my stomach. Some kind of animal must have died in here too.

"Everybody is here. And wait until you see Melissa. *Damn.*"

We entered through the garage and for a split second, I froze. The world stopped spinning and it was senior year all over again. I swear he'd invited our entire class.

"Carter!" Marcus reached me first. "You got here just in time. We're lining up another Crash."

"Shit, man. I can't be doing that stuff tonight."

"Sure you can."

I hadn't done that kind of drinking since I'd left this place. Crash was a game Marcus had invented our sophomore year. The fastest to down four shots of vodka plus a can of beer, without hands, was the winner.

Trevor had me on one side and Marcus on the other as they pulled me through the kitchen. The three amigos. Growing up, they had been my best friends. Inseparable in T-ball and football and all that shit that boys did in small towns. Even when we got older, everything stayed the same between us—even when our *activities* got a little wilder.

The guys pushed me over to where Becca Fenton was lying on the dining room table. A night-and-day difference from what I'd just left in my parents' kitchen.

"I can't." I protested as Marcus poured the clear liquid into the glasses. Glancing across to the other side of the stained-up table, I saw Jimmy Meisner, sticking shots on some girl I didn't recognize. I felt the old hatred brewing under my skin like a lit match. I despised the guy. He was an obnoxious asshole who had tried to break my nose in PE class in elementary school.

All the internal conflict dissolved into the excitement of crushing his ass. One round wouldn't hurt. Looking back down at Becca, her nipples poked through the tight, white shirt. I pulled the bottom of the fabric up just enough to show her tan stomach and belly button ring. She giggled, pushing it up higher, exposing her see-through white bra.

"Shit, man. Here." Marcus handed me two oversized shot glasses. As I tucked one against her neck, she leaned up for a kiss. Her mouth grabbed mine with a quick bite to the lip. I pushed her back to the table, catching the shot before it slipped to the floor.

"Be still," I warned.

"Sorry, Wyatt. I haven't seen you in a while." She grinned, showing off the wide smile I remembered very well. I laughed, shaking my head at her attempt to flirt with me. Becca and I had history going back to ninth grade. She was the first girl I'd ever fucked.

"Let's just win this, and we can catch up later."

"Sure."

As I balanced the second glass between her tits, I caught myself looking into her eyes. She smiled again. Becca was better than this shit, but I guess things never really changed—not even me in this moment.

Marcus handed over another two glasses. Flipping up her skirt, I shoved the third shot against her purple-lace crotch. She giggled again as my fingers grazed her inner thigh. I put the fourth shot inside her knees and the can of beer between her red painted toes.

"You assholes ready?" Marcus shouted across the noise of the house. Jimmy and I stared at him, waiting for the signal.

"Go!"

I clasped each glass between my teeth. They went down fast. The beer trick was always the hardest, but once I got the can balanced between my elbows, it was over for Jimmy.

"Wyatt Carter!" Marcus yelled across the room. He slapped me on the back. "Damn, you still got it. That college shit hasn't whipped your ass."

"I told you. Same lame-ass parties, just hotter girls and better liquor." Except that wasn't exactly true. Coach would cut me faster than I could blink if he caught me drinking. Texas Westmiller didn't approve of that sort of thing.

"Well, Mr. Preppy. Don't say that shit to Trevor. He went all out for you tonight." Marcus poured two shots of vodka, pushing one in my hand. He tapped the glasses together for a toast. "Here's to the cheap stuff. I hope it lights your ass on fire and gives you the shits."

I tipped it back, rolling my eyes at the guy who I considered my best friend. Tonight was like a damn time warp. In a brief moment, I remembered the first time we had downed shots. I was thirteen. Trevor had stolen a bottle of tequila from his dad's stash. Marcus and I had taken turns until I saw him pass out on the floor—even though he swears I crashed first. Trevor wouldn't ever tell us the truth. Said he was taking it to his grave.

We'd had some fun times growing up. Marcus, Trevor, and I had been so different, but it had worked for us.

Marcus Tucker was the actual preppy of my friends. The good one. His dad was a former city councilman who got himself elected mayor last year. Marcus even went to a state university in Arkansas but flunked out his freshman year. When we talked a few weeks ago, he thought the school might let him back in for the spring semester.

"So? What's the verdict?" I asked.

"Hopefully hooking up with Zoey tonight."

"Jackass." I rolled my eyes. "You going back to Arkansas?"

"Yeah. Probation is over. They let me back in. Trevor's pissed of course since I won't be around." Marcus laughed, glancing over to where our friend was smoking a joint. "But I'm going to do it right this time. No more of this shit. You know what I mean?"

I let out a deep breath. "More than you realize."

"Zoey said she would marry me if I could keep it together this year."

"Really?"

"Crazy, huh? I bought a ring and everything. I haven't given it to her yet though. I'm trying to figure out a way to surprise her. Who knows. I might just do it tomorrow. That would be a hell of a Christmas present." He laughed, the happiness glowing in his eyes. Marcus put an arm around my shoulders. "You'll be my best man, right?"

"Shit, man. I'm the closest thing you got to a brother. I *better* be."

He grabbed the vodka bottle, topping off the glasses again. "To getting married."

"To not flunking out of school." Tipping the shot back, the alcohol burned all the way down my throat.

"And there she is. My girl is looking hot tonight. *Zoey!*" Marcus yelled over the music at the tiny brunette who came in the front door. He poured one final shot in my oversized glass, slapping me on the back. "I'll see you later. And try to have a little fun tonight. You can go back to being a Texas nun after break."

"Asshole." I shook my head, swallowing the contents of his parting gift.

Marcus ran off across the living room and grabbed Zoey Lemming, lifting her right off the nasty carpet. She squealed as he spun her around before sticking his tongue down her throat. She was the only girl Marcus had ever hooked up with and the only girl he'd sworn to ever love.

As he whispered in her ear, Zoey turned in my direction. She waved, and I nodded in return. They were the perfect couple: the quarterback and homecoming queen kind of shit.

My eyes drifted around the room at the bare walls. Half of the paper was ripped off next to the couch. An area of the kitchen still had fire damage from the time we had gotten smashed junior year—the kind of drunk that made us think spiders were edible if we set them on fire.

Then I saw her. My ex-girlfriend Melissa, wearing a tight, red sweater. Damn, Trevor was right. My hands and eyes were very familiar with that body—and that shit was no longer real. She looked up in my direction, sending over an icy stare. Melissa was still pissed at me for ending it before I'd left for college.

"What are you doing over here alone, Wyatt?" Becca handed me a can of beer.

"Just taking a breather." I tipped the can back, swallowing half of the cold liquid. "What are you doing these days?"

"Not much. Still doing hair at the Glamour Shack."

"Sounds nice." I didn't know what else to say. Swallowing the rest of the can, I leaned against the wall. The noise in the room got vague and hazy in my head as her hand rubbed along my thigh. I knew what she wanted. Things had always seemed to continue between us, off and on through the years, after our first time together.

Removing her fingers off my crotch, I pulled Becca into the bathroom. Her kisses were familiar. Her body moved in all the same ways as I pressed her against the white ceramic sink. Becca slipped her fingers down between us and tugged the zipper on my jeans.

I let go long enough to pull the broken drawer open on the cabinet. Grabbing a condom from Trevor's stash, I lifted Becca onto the sink. We fit together just like a hundred other times.

The bathroom door opened, and Ronny Burkett walked right past us. He took a long piss in the toilet before stumbling back out the door, slamming it behind him.

"Oh my gosh." Becca burst out laughing, her forehead leaning into my chest as she struggled to stay sitting on the sink.

"I don't think he even saw us."

"But I saw more than I ever wanted of Ronny. That's some nasty stuff he keeps down there." Her nose squinted up. "And he didn't even wash his hands after touching it."

"So I guess those rumors of you and The Burkman weren't true." I grinned back at her.

"Asshole. You know I got better taste than that."

Becca jumped down, fixing her skirt. She kissed me briefly, leaving the taste of beer and strawberry lip gloss on my mouth.

Someone beat on the door. "Stop fucking in there. I need to take a piss."

Becca whispered against my lips. "This was fun, you know. Catching up."

I smiled back at her. "I should come home more often."

"You should."

The flimsy door rattled as someone took a fist to it again.

"I guess we better get out of here."

"Bye, Wyatt." I let Becca kiss me one last time before opening the door. She gave the middle finger to Jimmy Meisner who was waiting to come inside the bathroom. Damn, that guy was everywhere tonight.

I walked back into the crowded living room, picking up a couple of cans of beer. I took a seat alone on the couch. I never made actual plans to have sex with Becca when I came back into town. But we always had a tendency to find each other. There were no delusions. We both knew it would never be more. I never loved her or Melissa for that matter—even with her new tits.

I wasn't like Marcus. I'd never felt something even close to what he shared with Zoey. I cared about Becca in a friendship kind of way, but Melissa could go to hell. She had a scary-evil temper. After one of my games, she'd burned all my jerseys when she decided I'd lied about what I did at one of Trevor's parties. My high school coach almost kicked me off the team.

A glazed-over Marcus half-fell down on top of me. "Come on, buddy, you ready to go again? I've got money riding on you."

"I think I've had enough."

"Come on. One more round of Crash. I've got a hundred bucks on this one. You'll crush it. Win one more for me. Remember. You're on *vacation*." The words slurred from his grinning mouth.

"Marcus, I've got grandparents coming at seven in the morning. I'm out, man." And I needed out of this house too. I needed some fresh air or rather a little nicotine. "I'll catch you later."

Grabbing my hoodie, I made my way outside into the trash dump known as Trevor's yard. I took a piss next to an old washing machine.

Leaning back against the house, my fingers touched the rotted siding. I remembered a time when it used to be yellow. Digging inside my pocket, I pulled out my cigarettes and lighter. I sucked in a drag, letting the smoke settle in my lungs before releasing a puff into the air. A slight gust of wind hit my neck. I flipped the hood up over my head, blocking out the freezing drizzle. It was going to be a nasty Christmas tomorrow.

Noises from the party drifted up into the quiet night. None of this ever changed. Life here was strange and yet so familiar. Taking another drag from my cigarette, I heard laughter coming from the back porch. I listened for a moment, catching the low voice of Trevor.

With a house full of girls, it wasn't a surprise that he'd lured one outside to his usual spot on the covered back porch. Dropping the butt, I watched the faint embers disappear in the drizzle. The voices laughed again. I stepped around the old washing machine and through the overgrown weeds into the backyard . . . and then I froze in place.

My sister. My little sister Willa was on Trevor's lap in a lawn chair. Sitting on the wooden deck, her friend Layla leaned against his legs, holding a cup in her hand. The girls laughed at something he said too low for me to hear.

A slight gust of wind hit my face as I remembered the night Trevor had gotten drunk and tied a girl to the railroad tracks in some freaky-shit dare. I knew better than anyone what he liked to do with women. He bragged about it until I wanted to punch him sometimes. But like a moth to a flame, those girls always fell for him anyway.

"Hey, man." His face took on that charming grin and my fists clenched into a death grip as I watched my *friend* touch Willa's knee. "Look who showed up tonight. I've been trying to get your little sis out here for months since she got her license."

"How did you get here?" I said, looking directly at her and ignoring him.

"I drove." She scooted out of the chair, holding onto the plastic cup. Her arm moved in an exaggerated circle, sloshing the red contents all over her Ugg boots. The smell of alcohol drifted up around us.

"You need to go home." I tried to keep my voice steady when everything about this situation made me sick to my stomach.

"I can't," she giggled. "Dad . . . um. He will . . . be mad if he sees me . . . like this."

Shit. She was drunk. The idea of Willa being hammered at one of Trevor's parties sent a deep chill down my spine.

"Come on, Carter. Let her stay just a little bit longer." He flashed that pathetic grin, but it wasn't going to work on me tonight. He knew better than to mess with my sister.

"Get your stuff. I'll deal with Dad when we get home."

"You're leaving?" Trevor got out of the chair and came down the steps into the yard. "I had to beg your ass to come over here.

Now you're leaving. That's fine. Get the hell out. But maybe *she* doesn't want to leave. You were having fun, right, Willa?"

"Shut the hell up, Trevor. You may act like you're still in high school, but she's the one who's actually sixteen."

"When did you become such a fucking tool?"

I punched him. He fell over backward before my fist even registered the pain. I shook my hand out a bit. Trevor spit blood on the ground. "Last damn party I ever throw you. College did nothing but make you into an ungrateful prick."

My sister's stupid friend Layla came over to his side, dabbing at his busted lip. Her sweater slid up a little around her waist, showing off a silver belly button ring. That lazy grin reappeared on his lips. I stared down at Trevor, shaking my head.

"She's also sixteen. So keep your dick in your pants."

"Go to hell, Carter."

Grabbing Willa under the arm, her cup spilled down the front of my sweatshirt. I took it from her hand, throwing the blue Solo cup down on the ground with the rest of the trash.

"Come on." I dragged my sister through the backyard. We stumbled down the grass path and into the front around a pile of beer cans. I walked too fast for Willa to keep up, but I didn't want to risk Trevor following us.

"I didn't mean for you to get in a fight," she mumbled as she clung to my arm.

"It's fine." I hated the fact that I'd punched him. But he'd eventually get over it. We didn't store up all that resentment shit like girls.

"I thought it would be okay to come to the party since you were here."

"No. It's not okay to be at Trevor's. *Ever.*" I growled the words. "What the hell were you thinking?"

"But he's your friend."

"Yes, but Trevor and Marcus are not *your* friends. And *never* will be."

She tripped, but I caught Willa before she fell completely in the grass. "Sorry. My foot got caught in some wire."

"It's fine. Just keep walking so we don't get that wet."

I stopped at her Tahoe, which was parked between a yellow Cavalier and a beat-up white truck. The smell of that red punch had followed us all the way back to her car. I didn't know what the hell Trevor had poured down my sister, but it stunk like toxic sludge.

"The um . . . the keys are in here somewhere." Her lips puckered up as she dug around in the large brown purse.

"No. Give them to me."

"What about your motorcycle?" Willa handed over the ring with a little cross dangling next to the ignition key.

"I'll come back for my bike tomorrow."

I opened the passenger's door, helping my sister into the seat. Going around to the driver's side, I climbed behind the wheel of my old SUV that my parents had given to Willa. The fifteen-year-old motor fired up a little clunky. I took a deep breath, gripping the steering wheel.

"Promise me something. You will never come here again."

"Okay." Her eyes stayed fixated on the darkness outside. "I only came because of you. I know I shouldn't be over at Trevor's. But when you got home, I thought you would be excited to see us. I wanted to watch *Christmas Vacation* like we used to. I thought it would be fun. But you didn't even stay."

Hearing the pain in her soft voice, I felt like a complete asshole. My jaw gritted tight as I watched a tear fall down her cheek.

"Maybe," I muttered. "Maybe we can watch *Christmas Vacation* when we get back to the house."

"Nah. It doesn't matter now." She wiped another tear from her face. I swallowed hard, seeing Willa lean against the window glass. I had crushed her tonight, just like I'd done a hundred other times through the years. I'd never done much when it came to her. She'd always asked me to come to her dance recitals and piano concerts and all that shit, but I'd never given her the time of day.

Someone beat on the driver's side glass. I rolled down the window, seeing Marcus outside. "Can you um . . . shit. I'm drunk. Like *really* drunk. Can you give me a ride home?"

"Sure."

Marcus climbed in the back door. He scooted to the middle, draping an arm over each seat. "Hey, Willow Tree. I didn't know you came with Wyatt?"

"She didn't," I snapped.

"What's wrong?" His words slurred into one.

"Nothing," I muttered.

I went forward, tapping the yellow car slightly on the bumper. Throwing the Tahoe into reverse, I floored the gas pedal. I needed to get the hell out of here.

I was the black sheep of the family, the one who wreaked havoc and butted heads with my dad. My sister was the good one. She had no business being anywhere near this place. I picked up speed, trying to get Willa away as fast as possible before this house of hell seeped into her innocent skin.

As we cleared the railroad tracks, the vehicle lifted slightly off the ground. I flicked the windshield wipers on to clear the drizzle. My phone buzzed from inside my pocket. Pulling it out, I saw Trevor on the screen.

"Sorry, man. I would never touch your sister. Can I still come for stuffing tomorrow?"

Oh, hell. If Trevor didn't come over, he would be alone on Christmas Day. Tossing the phone down in the cup holder, I would wait and text him back when I got home. I let out a deep breath, feeling the irony of the whole situation. The guy still made you feel sorry for him, even after he'd caused you to punch him in the face.

"How long you staying in town this time?" Marcus said next to my ear as he leaned on the back of the driver's seat.

"New Year's Day. Coach wants us back early."

"Shit. You're always running off. But you always loved football more than me. I only played because of you. Remember? You made me play varsity. I was going to quit."

"I couldn't play without my QB. I hate it now. Wish you would've come with me."

"Too damn far away, Carter. Zoey would leave my ass. I'd never come back like you."

"Asshole." Glancing over in the passenger's seat, I saw a tear fall down my sister's cheek. I knew the comment about me leaving had crushed her all over again. I should come back more. I should be here for Willa.

"I'm sorry," I muttered, but the apology came a second too late. I said the words as her face shattered into a million pieces.

I drifted away, feeling the world spin in circles, around and around as my body slammed hard against the door and the seat belt cut into my neck. Grinding metal echoed with screams as the SUV rolled sideways, flipping upside down before landing right side up and smashing into the electric pole. She screamed and screamed until she didn't scream anymore.

I struggled to catch my breath. I struggled to see as blood ran down into my eyes. Wiping my face with my right hand, my left arm no longer felt connected to my body. The pain in my chest hurt like knives, stabbing over and over with each breath.

Glass covered everything in the front seat. The windshield was completely gone. Looking over in the passenger's seat, Willa's head rested against the shattered door. Blood soaked her pink sweater as it ran from her head.

"Willa. Wake up." It took everything in me to reach over to where her head hung lifeless from the shoulder strap. I shook her arm, but my sister didn't budge.

"Come on, Willa." The desperation in my voice came out like a tiny screech. Blood poured out of her nose, soaking everything in her lap. Panic overtook my thoughts. Everything got blurry as I shook her arm in a frantic attempt to get her to answer me. "*Willa!*"

I tried to open my door, but my left hand refused to clasp the handle. I think my shoulder was pulled out of socket. Reaching over with my right hand, I pushed and pushed against the warped metal.

"Hold on, buddy."

I heard a voice somewhere outside the car. Looking through the mangled door, I saw a man talking, but I didn't recognize him.

"It's okay. I'm gonna get you out."

He pulled and pulled until the door moved on the hinges. I tried to climb out, but nothing seemed to work correctly. Taking a step, I fell to the street. Blood soaked the front of my jeans. I tried again, feeling a ripping pain through the bone. My leg was broken and bleeding through the skin. I kept on trying to walk despite the agony.

"Let me help you." The older man with brown hair had a busted-up lip. Dark, bloody spots covered his green sweater. I held onto the stranger as he dragged me around to the back side of the SUV. Sparks shot out of the electric pole as it rested on top of the old post office. Everything around us smelled like burning rubber.

We reached the passenger's side door. Willa seemed worse than when I'd seen her inside the car.

"Have to um. Have to get my um sister out." I think I spoke the words, but I wasn't sure if they actually left my lips. My vision got cloudy again, and I leaned against the busted-up metal.

"Okay. Let me see what I can do."

I struggled to stay conscious as my body slid down the side of the car and onto the ground. Sparks shot out of the pole again as the roof caved in on the post office. Lights flashed each time I blinked. I swallowed, tasting blood in my mouth. And then I saw flames.

"How did this happen?" I muttered. None of it made sense. I couldn't remember what had happened or how the SUV had become a crumbled pile of metal.

The stranger stopped fiddling with the door and looked down at me. "You were swerving all over the road."

"Wh-what?" I mumbled to myself, trying to remember the last few moments in the car.

"I tried to miss you, but I couldn't. We hit, and your SUV rolled over into that light pole."

"I wasn't. That's not—" My mind went blank. Fear burned right through my gut. Why couldn't I remember what happened? Running a hand across my forehead, tiny shards of glass cut into my skin.

The man worked to get the door open, but he didn't seem to be making any progress. Something gnawed at the back of my mind like a scratch I couldn't touch. Maybe it was the glass in the side of my head. Maybe it was cutting away into my brain cells.

Then it flashed. *Marcus.* The faint memory burned in my mind. Marcus was in the backseat. I pulled myself off the ground and to the crunched-up backseat window glass. Peering inside, I tried to focus on the middle row.

"My friend," I mumbled.

"Your friend?" The man asked as he stared at me. His face spread into two and then back to one. A frown appeared on his lips.

"He's in there too."

The man froze for a moment. "There's no one else in there."

My heart stopped, and I second-guessed myself. I went to Trevor's. Marcus got in the car. He asked for a ride. He was in there, talking about football and shit. I *know* he was in there. That was real.

Stumbling away into the street, I saw a black dually truck with the hood crunched like a beer can. It was completely totaled.

Smoke billowed out in front of me, filling my lungs and I doubled over coughing. My chest hurt as I gasped for air. Looking up into the sky, I saw the old post office on fire. The building went up like kindling and lighter fluid, spreading to the new bank next door. And the furniture store. *Shit!* The flames were everywhere.

Staggering out into the middle of Main Street, I tripped over a broken side mirror. Pieces of bumper and metal covered the wet ground. A pinkish-colored Santa was lying in the middle of the street. Dragging my leg along the pavement beside me, I searched until I found his crumpled-up body in the debris.

Marcus. The pain grew to a hot fire under my skin, seeing his body twisted at an odd angle.

"Marcus?" I whispered. He was just lying there in a pool of his own blood. I wanted to help him, but I didn't know what to do. *Shit.* He looked dead. So very dead. What have I done? My gut clenched like someone punched me.

My heart gripped in my chest as my thoughts raced widely and I gasped for air. The night spiraled around as I remembered going to Trevor's house. I saw my sister. I made her leave. Marcus got in the car. We crashed. I crashed. I killed my oldest friend. I killed my sister. They were dead. I killed them.

My mom. Her face came to me under the misty rain. What would I tell my mom? Willa was dead. I was supposed to take care of her, but I'd forced her in the car. She trusted me. Willa had gotten in the car because she'd trusted me.

Everything spun in circles. I fell down beside Marcus in the middle of the street. I couldn't feel my leg anymore. Sirens echoed in the distance. Maybe I was dead. Maybe I should be. Maybe the fire truck would come through the street and plow me down, kill me like I'd destroyed them.

The sirens howled in the night, getting louder and louder. I remembered the time we dressed up like Ghostbusters for Halloween. Me, Trevor, and Marcus. My mom had made the costumes. She'd even created a little white ghost one for Willa. We'd taken her through the neighborhood as she carried a tiny flashing red light in case she had gotten lost from us. It had made a little sound like a siren if you pushed the top.

Tears rolled down my cheeks. Sucking in a deep breath, I smelled the stench of alcohol on my clothes. I knew why I couldn't remember. The whole evening was a haze for a reason. It was my fault. I should rot in hell. I killed them.

Looking out into the darkness, the bank clock glowed above my head with the time. 12:12 a.m. My eyes slipped out of focus and the numbers faded away as I lost consciousness. It was officially Christmas.

CHAPTER 17

Wyatt

AS I TOLD MY STORY, THE CURTAINS BLOCKED THE SUN FROM the room and the vivid images of that night haunted the shadows. Emma remained on her side of the couch, and I stayed on mine. I was afraid. I was afraid she would reach out and grab my hand. I didn't want her comfort. I didn't want her damn sympathy.

But Emma did none of those things. She stayed in a ridged lump just two feet away. This was the moment I'd dreaded since the day she'd appeared outside my door. My hands got shaky. I clenched the right one over the left. My heart beat fast in my chest. It pounded away with the strength of a jackhammer. I wished for a cigarette. I wished for the bitter taste of nicotine to calm down the rush of feelings.

"So um." Her voice cracked a little. "What happened after . . . um . . . after—"

"After I *destroyed* everyone's lives? After I *forced* my little sister to get in the car with me?" I closed my eyes for a moment, trying to figure out a way to explain all of this shit. Things would be easier if Emma were some coldhearted bitch. Someone without feelings. Someone who wouldn't be crushed by the truth. "I woke up in the hospital with my leg in a cast. My dad was staying with me. Officially and unofficially, I guess. My mom needed to be with Willa."

I swallowed hard on the bitter words, wishing for some intervention to keep this conversation from happening. But I continued, feeling every word cut on my tongue. "She had um . . . something wrong with her brain. Something I caused in the accident. And it never went away."

Hearing the truth out loud made the ugly parts seem even darker. I had inflicted a very cruel and horrible curse on my sister.

"The doctors here sent Willa to some hospital in Baltimore, but they couldn't help. She has some permanent traumatic brain injury that causes seizures. They sent her home with a box of medicine. And things just got worse. Willa couldn't drive, and then the school couldn't deal with the episodes. They wouldn't take her back. So she finished out the last two years at home. Without any friends. Or a normal life."

I lost my train of thought as I pictured Willa at her dance recital. At least, the only one I could remember. The only one I'd ever bothered attending. In my distant memory, I saw my sister moving across the stage in some gray shiny dress and her feet bound in those pink shoes. She couldn't dance anymore either.

"I-I'm sorry," Emma muttered.

"I don't want your damn pity. I'm the one walking around here just fine."

"That's not what I meant." Her voice spoke as barely a whisper. "What, um. What about your friend?"

I swallowed hard. "The guy driving the pickup was named Cam Reynolds. He was on his way back from the twenty-four-hour pharmacy. His kid had gotten sick on Christmas Eve. He'd been in Afghanistan. I didn't know that at first. Cam had only been back a few months. He knew all this triage shit."

I clenched my fists, feeling the tremors shoot up my arms. Every time I thought about Cam, my mind flashed to the images burned inside my head, watching him do CPR on Marcus as I lay next to him on the cold street. My thoughts drifted off in the darkness, feeling the familiar chill down my spine. I smelled the burning rubber. It coated my nose as I sucked in a deep breath.

"Wyatt," she whispered, pulling me back to the present. "Did Marcus live?"

I swallowed the bile back down, trying to keep my voice steady. "Yes."

I heard the breath release from her lungs.

Reaching over, I flipped on the lamp. I couldn't hide in the darkness anymore. I needed to see myself in her eyes. "But he's paralyzed from the middle of his back down. He's in a wheelchair. He can't do anything. Can't drive. Can't run. Can't really use his arms. He was in the ICU for six months. And I did it to him. I destroyed a guy who was the closest thing I had to a brother. I fucked him up so bad that . . ."

I couldn't breathe. They said Cam had saved him. If I had crashed with someone else, my best friend would've died right there in the middle of the street. The images of Marcus strangled my throat. His life was total shit. Every time I pictured him trapped in that chair, it triggered a panic attack. I took a slow breath through my nose, struggling to calm down the pressure in my tight chest.

"But he's alive," she whispered. "You didn't kill anyone."

"There's different ways to kill a person, Emma. Psychotic killers don't just walk up and shoot someone. They make it the worst possible scenario. They drag it out so the person feels every damn thing until the end."

I let the words sink in as her beautiful tan skin turned white. I let those vile words hit that innocent heart before I finished her off.

"You don't think Marcus wishes he just died that night? I put him in a front-row seat, watching his body slowly disappear while he's trapped inside. And what about my sister? I screwed up her head. And right now, she's like a bomb driving down the road. She could be killing an entire family as we speak. No, Emma. What I did was worse than death. I've made them both live every day in their own personal hell."

My whole body started to shake. The words. The thoughts. It was getting to me. I had never talked to anyone about that night. Not really. Not in a way that I was telling Emma.

I held her gaze, seeing the deep emotions flash across her sweet face. A faint wetness glowed on the edges of her lashes. I wanted to reach out and touch it. Our eyes stayed locked in one of our probing stares. I saw a flash. She felt sorry for me. Somewhere inside that soft heart, she believed I was still fixable.

"They hated me." I faltered, seeing a tear roll down her cheek. "My father didn't sit at the hospital because he was worried about his son. He had to stay there to keep people away from me. I'm hated by just about everyone in Gibbs. I'm the guy who brought the whole town *literally* to their knees. They prayed for Marcus to live. And they prayed for me to rot away in jail."

Her hands trembled. She balled those perfect fingers into a tight fist, working hard to keep her composure. Why couldn't Emma just break and run out the damn door? I wanted this over. I wanted her gone. She needed to leave me here and go back to her life.

"But you said it was freezing rain. I mean, you were a kid . . . it was an accident."

"It wasn't any damn *accident*." I slapped the arm of the chair, making her jump. "And I wasn't any damn kid. It was just another *incident* by a guy who couldn't keep his shit together. They tested me, you know. My blood alcohol was off the charts. Like a walking coma, but I was completely awake, driving a car down the damn road."

I was yelling at this point, but I didn't care. It was the truth. "It plays over and over again in my head. Every day like a horror movie, and I want to scream at myself to wake up. To not get in the car. But it's not a dream. It's all very real. I forced Willa to get in there. I let Marcus think I was better off than him that night. I did it. There's no excuse or way for you to rationalize it. I'm responsible."

"Then why aren't you in prison?"

"My father. The judge. I don't know. They waited for a couple of months to have the trial. The court didn't know how to prosecute me because Marcus was in ICU. When they decided he would live, my father pushed for probation. They laughed in his face. Marcus's dad is the mayor and half a city block burned down that night. The insurance office, the new bank, some clothing store, and the post office. Millions in damages."

I let out a cryptic laugh. "People get really crazy when you burn down a post office. Between his dad and business owners, they fought hard for me to go to jail. And I wanted it. I had wanted it so damn bad. My father and I argued, over and over again. He said he was looking out for my future. But he didn't understand."

I would've done anything to trade places with my sister. With my best friend. But that wasn't possible. So I wanted prison. I wanted to be there until someone figured out a way to fix them.

"Fighting for me was the last thing my father did before they fired him. The whole town had loved my dad until he went to bat for me, and then everyone turned on him. They wanted him gone. From his job. From town. But he didn't budge. He fought for me anyway."

Letting out a slow breath, I thought about the meeting that had sealed my fate. "The judge knew all of us and offered a choice.

Three years in prison with possibility of parole. Or five years here on house arrest if I pled guilty to a couple of felonies. My father made the decision for me. And *here* I am."

"He was right," she whispered. "This is better than prison."

"No. He wanted to control the courts and my punishment—the way he *always* wanted to control everything in my life. But this wasn't about him. I should be locked away with the other selfish bastards who destroy people."

"I don't think. I mean. Wyatt, I . . ." Her eyes watered up again as she struggled to continue her faith in me. "But you aren't that person. Not anymore. Not now. This place has done you good."

"You *still* want to believe in the good even when you see the bad. But that's not me, Emma." I swallowed the lump in my throat. "I purposely got drunk. I got in a car. I drove down the road. I hurt people. I hurt their families. I hurt their friends. I hurt *my* family. That's who I really am. That's the person you want to kiss. The person you want to touch. The person you are trying so damn hard to save."

Her brown eyes betrayed every painful emotion in her heart. Maybe I should've spat out the awful truth on her second visit when she insisted on hearing my story. I could've stopped the feelings. I could've shut them off with the slice of a knife. Instead, I let Emma get close. I let her think I was safe. And now, I burned this innocent girl with the heat of the same fire that had destroyed everything else.

"You should go," I whispered, hearing the catch in my voice. The pain of telling her goodbye wasn't something I deserved to feel. I didn't deserve to care or mourn for her. I wanted to shut it down. Her sweet face stared back at me. Crushing me. Killing me.

"Get out!" My voice grated on the words with a slight growl. "I said get the fuck out! I don't want to see you here again."

Another tear fell off her long lashes. It rolled down her

cheek, leaving a wet streak that trailed down her neck.

"I said leave. This isn't a game anymore. I want you out of my damn house. And never come back."

She stood up from the couch. Her leg twisted a little as she put weight on her right foot. I wanted to pull her against my chest. I wanted to carry her so it didn't hurt. Those thoughts floated through my heart as Emma limped with her messed-up knee. She stopped just in front of me. Staring at me. She cried in open sobs. Her pain punched me in the damn gut.

"Get the fuck out!"

"Or what?" Her lips quivered just a bit. My fists clenched tight. The war ragged inside my heart. I wanted to kiss her so damn bad. Wipe away the tears. Taste the salt on my tongue. Run my hands over her soft skin. I needed to hold her. I needed to feel her body wrapped around me. I needed Emma and I hated the very thought.

"Or I will physically throw you out the damn door."

The sadness twisted up on her face as she listened to my empty threat. "I know you would never hurt me, Wyatt. But I'll go. Let you calm down."

Emma turned to leave, her limp making those hips sway back and forth. She didn't shut the aluminum door. Maybe she did it on purpose. Maybe she left it wide open, hoping I would call for her to come back. Instead, I got up from the couch and just stood in the doorway, making sure she got to the car without falling in the yard. Just like I always did when she left.

The motor came to life, and she slowly left the kennel. I let out a deep breath, feeling the weight on my shoulders grow heavier as she disappeared. I couldn't even go after Emma if I wanted to.

Slamming the door shut, the whole trailer shook with the impact. I threw the lamp against the wall, sending the room into darkness. I fell into my old chair. My body found the familiar groove.

The silent air filled each breath of my lungs. I embraced the empty solitude. The pain in my chest grew stronger. She was gone. Emma wasn't coming back. I deserved nothing. I deserved no one. I sure as hell didn't deserve a girl like her.

They had banished me to the middle of nowhere, yet I still managed to hurt someone. As I stared into space, another layer of guilt pierced into my heart. I thought about the part I didn't share with Emma. The part that still felt like a fresh stab wound in my chest.

Trevor had always struggled to keep his shit together. In those months following the accident—somewhere in the course of the hearings, and the hospital, and Marcus being in ICU, and me being in jail—Trevor must have decided it was all too much for him.

His friends were gone. The whole damn town was pointing fingers, blaming his parties and blaming the sheriff's office for not condemning his rundown house years ago.

Right before they sent me out here, Trevor overdosed on a cocktail of drugs and alcohol. I don't know if it was an accident or on purpose. As usual, his dad didn't come home for days. Trevor had just laid there—his body mixed in with the trash on the dirty floor—forgotten even in death.

My fingers gripped the arms of the chair. They dug deep into the leather as I closed my eyes. I would be lying if I said I hadn't thought about it myself—but death would just be the easy way out of my guilt.

CHAPTER 18

Wyatt

MY EYES OPENED AT EXACTLY SIX IN THE MORNING. I KNEW this fact without ever looking at a clock. It had taken me almost three months of discipline to accomplish. Now, it happened like second nature—even after a day as fucked up as yesterday.

Pulling off the covers, I went straight to the bathroom. Everything progressed along like the cogs of a damn wheel in a grandfather clock. I put on a T-shirt and old athletic shorts before slipping into my running shoes.

Leaving the trailer, I felt the heat of the early sun as it rose in the sky. Sweat soaked my shirt even at this hour in the morning. I followed the familiar dirt path in the worn pasture grass—one I could've run even on the blackest of nights from memory.

My actions were not for the physical exercise. Instead, they served as more of a reminder of my confinement. I wanted to feel the exact extent of my prison.

Each morning, I ran a path based on my ankle monitor—every step exactly four inches from where the box would signal the authorities. It took me over a week to get it marked out with precision based on the yellow warning light.

As I went farther out in the pasture, I reached the area where Emma had fell down in the grass during her run. I cursed under my breath as she invaded my thoughts.

Ever since the day she'd appeared at the kennel, I'd woken with the same question: *Would Emma come back today?* The simple thought was always followed by the torrid ones, like how I imagined her lips would feel if I touched them with my tongue.

But today was different. I *knew* she tasted like cinnamon from the tube of ChapStick she kept in her pocket, always smearing it across her soft lips out of habit.

But that wasn't the biggest change. I knew deep in my gut she wasn't coming back. This fact caused my chest to catch. Emma wasn't coming back because I'd told her the truth and then threw her ass out the door.

"Shit," I cursed out loud, trying to snuff the thoughts. I wanted to punch something.

Instead, I pushed myself harder, pounding my feet into the ground until I was sprinting through the pasture. By the time I reached my trailer, my lungs begged for air. I sat down on the cement steps of my home. I hated the place. Diana had insisted on bringing the trailer out to the kennel even though I told her a cot in the office would've been just fine.

After I stretched my leg for a few minutes, I walked inside and took a shower. In my brief time in county jail, I'd never experienced the luxury of warm water. So I never used the hot water tank in the trailer. I always ran it cold, even last January when Oklahoma had the record-setting snowstorm.

I figured regular prison would be similar to those days I'd spent in lockup after Marcus's dad had me arrested. The experience should've scared the shit out of me. But it didn't.

I knew real fear, deeper than any damn prison. The kind that shocked the words from my throat and made my blood turn cold. I'd felt it every single time I'd witnessed Willa have a seizure. I'd felt the guilt like nails in my heart as I watched her eyes roll back in her head and her body beat against the floor while I waited to see if this attack would be the one to finally kill her.

The images gripped my whole body, and I couldn't think. Willa in the ER. Willa lying on the floor of the living room. Willa flopping around in the front yard. My mom crying because there was absolutely nothing she could do to help my sister. Me looking into my mom's eyes as she struggled to look back.

As those images paralyzed my muscles, I found myself frozen in place, holding the razor next to my cheek. My hand jerked, causing a small cut right above my jaw.

"Shit." The word whispered from my lips.

I saw the red trickle down my skin. I watched it for a moment, remembering the bad seizure that happened when I'd taken Willa to the grocery store. The one where she'd fallen down in the aisle by the apples and blood rolled out of her mouth because she'd bitten her tongue so hard it had needed stitches. The one where everyone had just stared at us—*at me*—while judging and blaming instead of helping.

I let out a deep breath, blocking out the memory. I needed to get to work. Wiping the blood off with my thumb, I applied another layer of shaving gel and continued to remove every single hair from my face.

I dressed in jeans and work boots. After a bowl of Cap'n Crunch, I headed to the kennel. Gus and Gatsby were both still in the holding pen. I felt bad for sticking them in the kennel all night, but I hadn't left my old chair until after midnight. The Labrador lifted his head as I approached. My sister's Jack Russell was curled up next to him.

Willa had gotten Gus from this very place on her fourteenth birthday. Most girls her age begged for makeup and shit, but my sister wanted a pet. My dad had arranged for her to pick one from the assortment Diana had kept at her kennel. Back then, she only had a few dogs in residence even though she'd built the facility to hold fifty rescue animals. The place didn't grow to its full capacity until I came to live out here to take care of them.

My sister had wanted Gus from the moment she'd seen the little guy. She brought him home, and he immediately ruled our house as king. She loved him. My whole family loved him.

My thoughts disappeared into the memory of the night Gus and I had come out here. They twisted away, paralyzing me, sending me back to that moment.

I leaned against the wall next to my closet. I just wanted to get this over with and not speak to them. I just wanted out of this damn house. I couldn't bear to look at them. I couldn't bear to see myself in their eyes. I'd caused so much pain and destruction.

I looked around the room. I was supposed to be packing, but I wasn't planning to take a damn thing. Gus came into my room, resting his head on my knee. He knew something was up. I scratched behind his ears.

Glancing up, I saw Willa tiptoeing into my room. She took a seat on my bed. The sad look on her face just about destroyed me. My throat got tight as I struggled to look her in the eyes. I'd fucked up her head and now I was breaking her heart by being sent away.

I stared at the floor as she fidgeted around, twisting her fingers. If she broke down in a teary goodbye, I just might lose my damn mind. It was all too much. I couldn't handle seeing her like this. My chest constricted into the beginning of another panic attack.

"I think you should take Gus," she whispered.

My eyes flashed to hers. "No."

"I know you blame yourself. You want to fix this. Fix me. You know that's not really possible. I hate that you're going away. We won't see you. I'm so sorry. I never wanted this to happen. I'm going to worry about you every day."

"Please don't," I whispered. "You need to just focus on getting better."

"I will always worry about you, Wyatt. Don't you know that? But it won't feel so bad if I know that Gus is out there with you. I don't think I can handle you being all alone. It will stress me out, and I don't do so good when I get stressed out."

I'd refused, but my sister had pulled out the king of daggers. I couldn't say no to those words and that sadness in her eyes. So I packed a suitcase full of boxers, jeans, T-shirts—and Gus.

Snapping out of my twisted thoughts, I sucked in a deep breath, trying to calm the tightness in my chest. I let the two dogs out of the kennel. They followed me over to the door and down the path to the trailer. Gatsby walked a little sluggishly and the Jack Russell slowed his steps for the older dog. I think Gus knew who needed him the most these days. Opening the aluminum door, they went inside and headed for the bedroom. I knew those two would spend the day stretched out on the pillowtop mattress.

Returning to the kennel, I went to work on pit row. I did a few pens each day, instead of one massive cleanout. I'd learned my lesson the first couple of months. Fifty kennels at one time was insane. Ten a day. Very reasonable.

There wasn't much shit on the inside since each pen had a dog door to the outside. But the cement did get its share of dirt and other crap. I took a bucket of soapy water over to Lola's pen. I scratched the pit behind the ears as she leaned against my leg. Her square head tilted up, grabbing my hand between her gummy lips.

Maybe I didn't tell Emma the truth when she asked about my favorites. I thought back to the day Diana brought Lola out to the kennel. She had just picked her up from the vet. All the wounds had been still fresh as blood, and puss drained from the ripped-up sores. My boss handed me tubes of cream and a list of instructions for Lola.

It was the first time I'd asked Diana about the kennel. It was the first time I'd cared about my new world. As we talked, my questions had gone from Lola to the kind of people who did this sort of thing.

I'd never thought much about animal abuse before that night—or dog fight rings. But her words lit a fire in my chest. I'd wanted to beat the shit out of the man who had sliced up Lola. I'd fantasized about ripping his arms off and shoving them up his asshole. I might have done it too if that ankle monitor hadn't been attached to my damn leg.

Regardless, that night had changed things for me. I couldn't fix Willa or Marcus, but I damn sure could fix Lola and all of the other dogs. I had one job and one job only: make sure the animals lived, make sure their lives were better than where they had come from out there in the cruel world. From that day forward, I had taken my duties seriously.

Pulling my hand from Lola's mouth, I led her out the kennel door to the fenced-in play area. I got Ponyboy and Indy, taking them out to join her. Returning back inside, I used a scrub mop on the cement. I cleaned each of their areas and then moved to the outside runs to scoop the shit from the ground.

Once I was finished, I washed up and then went out to join the dogs outside, carrying a tennis ball. I laughed as I got to the fence. As usual, Lola thought she was a badass. She had Indy on the run, chasing him around in a circle. He should've figured it out by now—the girl had no teeth. But I couldn't blame him. Indy had been burned with a firework. Or rather, someone had tied a firework to his collar, trying to blow his brains out.

"Come on, boy. You can take her." I threw the ball out across the grass. He scooped it up in his wide mouth before Lola got close, which just made her run faster. Glancing over in the corner, Pony was stretched out like a frog in the sun. Even though I always brought him out with the other dogs, he never gave a shit. Diana had rescued Pony from some hoarder who had kept him crammed in a tiny cage with a bunch of other mutts. The dog still went crazy anytime he was placed in small spaces.

Each of the dogs at the kennel had some story. Some were worse than others, but they were all outsiders in some way, fighting to stay alive or just become a pawn in someone else's game.

I played with the pits for a while before taking them back inside. The dogs stretched out on the cool cement for a nap. Over the next four hours, I did the same thing, over and over again until I was finished. I went back to the trailer to make a bologna sandwich for lunch.

Afterward, I went to the work shed for the Weed eater. I glanced over at the tarp covering my bike. Every so often, I got it out and washed the dirt off. I figured I owed my grandpa at least that much, and I hated the fact that it just sat neglected in the corner.

My dad had insisted I have at least some form of transportation in case something happened at the kennel. Being alone in the middle of nowhere, I might have an emergency. The court agreed to that one little request of his—considering if I ever left the property, I would violate the agreement. If I ever caused that monitor to light up red, I would go back to court and probably to prison.

I'd be lying if I'd said I never thought about it. I wanted to go to prison, and I could make that happen by stepping over the line. But I would have to see my mom and sister sitting in the courtroom. I would have to see their torn-up faces as they took me away, which would cause another layer of guilt to choke my conscience.

Putting some gas in the Weed eater, I used it around the kennel grounds. It scared most of the dogs so they stayed inside the building. I finished up and did the daily feeding in the kennel. Once everyone had food, I headed to the trailer for another cold shower.

After eating a hot dog for dinner, I went to my bedroom and

grabbed *The Hobbit* from my dresser. I'd never finished *Call of the Wild.* Emma had ruined that book with the sound of her sweet voice, the way she got lost reading me the story as my face rested against her soft, sexy thighs.

I shook off the feeling and headed for the door. The sound of cicadas filled the blackness. I hated the evenings the most. Being in the country was always just a little bit darker than in town, enhancing the demons that haunted my thoughts. Maybe that's why I read to the dogs. The spoken words kept the monsters at bay.

I stopped by Cye's pen. His dark eyes watched me from the back corner. I took the bag of treats Emma had left for him. Crawling on my hands and knees, I put a little peanut butter-flavored bone on the cement. I stared at the dog for a moment. He knew something wasn't right with this scenario.

"It's just you and me now," I muttered. I doubt he would eat the damn thing since it had come from me. Not that I blamed him. Cye liked Emma, even though he made her think he didn't.

Most people would've never noticed a change in him. But I did. When she was here, Cye didn't lie on the cement. He sat up on his hind legs and watched her move around the kennel. It was a small change, but more than I'd ever accomplished with him. As I closed the gate, I whispered softly to the black dog with dents in his skull. "I'm sorry, but she's not coming back."

CHAPTER 19

Wyatt

OVER THE NEXT FEW DAYS, I DID MY USUAL ACTIVITIES UNTIL one morning I returned from my run and the box unit in the trailer was blowing hot air. The whole single-wide was already a damn sauna. Falling in my old chair, I considered my options. I could just stay in here and let it go, sleeping with the windows up, embracing the late summer heat. But shit. They had no screens. The damn grasshoppers would be on me like a swarm of locusts.

I pulled in a deep breath, which felt like sucking the end of a hair dryer. Gus and Gatsby couldn't stay in this heat. Either I tried to fix the unit or move the dogs over to the kennel. Maybe all of us should go to the other building. But I knew Diana would flip out if she came back and saw me living with the dogs.

Climbing out of the chair, my legs stuck to the leather. I left my running clothes on and headed out to the work shed. After digging around for a few minutes, I found a toolkit. Time to learn about air conditioners.

Three hours later, I had the unit reassembled after removing every movable part and washing them in the bathtub. What didn't come out, I wiped down with a rag or cleaned with the end of the vacuum hose. I think the old unit was blowing more dirt than air inside the trailer.

Sweat rolled down my face, burning my eyeballs. I swore under my breath as I plugged the newly cleaned box back into the wall. This better work, or I was taking it outside and killing it with a shovel.

Cool air hit me in the face. Letting out a sigh of relief, I headed out the door to the kennel. Time to get to work. I was already behind schedule. Today was bath day for half of the dogs, and it was already noon. I wouldn't get today's chores done unless I worked after dark.

I grabbed Ricky Bobby, carrying him out to the wash area. The rat terrier morphed into one of his feisty streaks as I scrubbed him in the porcelain tub. As I held him down, the little dog covered me with soap. That three-legged guy had more energy than ten other dogs combined. After I was finished, I put his wild ass in the play area to run around and dry.

Going back inside, I took the next dog on the aisle. *Charlie*. My chest gripped for a moment. Since Emma left, it had been a struggle to be around him, which wasn't fair to the dog. His ears shot up as soon as I unlatched the gate. That dog looked so damn weird. His body didn't fit those strange rabbit ears. Scooping him in my arms, I carried Charlie outside as he licked my chin.

After a good scrubbing, the dog pranced around in the tub as I tried to wash the soap off. I grinned, thinking about Emma. She sure knew how to pick them. I leaned over and turned off the water. I froze, remembering when she'd come out here for bath day. It was stupid. My life was total shit, but I'd wanted her to come back anyway.

I thought about the way she laughed as Ricky Bobby shook the muddy suds in her face. The way it felt as our hands accidentally bumped under the water. I thought about her smile and the way the white T-shirt had clung to her breasts, showing off the yellow bikini hidden underneath.

I'd tried not to look at her. I'd tried not to take a peek. But I couldn't stop myself. I'd let my eyes drift down to what I knew existed right in front of me. I'd let myself watch her, fussing with the water hose, trying to get the mud off her legs. Her arms. Her stomach. I'd watched her even though the image caused my jeans to get tight.

I hated the fact she'd possessed the power to cause that reaction. I'd tried to rationalize it. After years of being in this place, of course I would get turned on by a girl in a wet bikini. But I knew it wasn't just some random sexual pull to her. This was different.

Emma was so beautiful. So full of life as she laughed. So kind. So sexy. So sweet. She cared about the dogs. She cared about me. She made me crave her body. The feel of her skin. The way those brown eyes said *kiss me slowly while tearing off my clothes.*

Whether she realized it or not, Emma had always shared her thoughts in those innocent looks she sent in my direction. I knew her attraction to me had existed from the moment I'd made her stammer in the front yard.

I thought about that first day. Other than my weekly visits from Diana, I'd seen virtually no one in over two years. But Emma had landed on my doorstep like some sexy angel with bloody pawprints all over her shirt, so beautiful and sweet, holding the weirdest-looking dog in her arms, asking if I could help her.

At first, I thought the girl was a hallucination—like one of my trances had taken hold and I'd imagined her out of thin air. But she had kept talking and asking questions, probing into my life, making me realize the girl with blonde curls was very real.

And then she tried to leave. I panicked. I had to stop her. But I'd regretted the decision the moment I'd asked her to come back to see Charlie. I'd regretted it because Emma sent a look that reached straight inside my chest.

She'd touched me with her eyes and not her hands. She'd held on to my body from ten feet away, boring into my soul, ripping me apart. And I craved it. I craved something from Emma that had nothing to do with sex. And I still craved it.

Emma saw things I didn't want her to see. Or *anyone* to see. But in some twisted way, I needed her to see those shit-filled pieces. And I hated the very idea that I needed someone like her. I hated every damn second of it.

So I was an asshole. I tried to drive her away. But she didn't care. Emma had hope for me even though I had none of my own. And it scared me. It was a tug-of-war raging inside me. She made me *want* something, and I didn't allow myself the privilege of *want* in my life.

Charlie whined, and I jumped.

"Damn it," I muttered. I'd let it happen again. I wasn't sure how long I'd stood there beside the tub, but I snapped out of my psychotic break and wrapped the little guy in a towel. At least I wasn't holding a razor or knife this time.

It was the time alone. That had to be it. When a person spent every day with only animals as companions, I'm sure they were allowed a certain amount of unexplained episodes.

Or maybe it was the glass. The doctor never did get all of the pieces out of my head. They surfaced sometimes when I washed my hair—little shards, climbing out of my skin as reminders.

CHAPTER 20

Wyatt

I WAITED FOR DIANA TO ARRIVE ON SUNDAY. SOMETIMES I FORGOT the days of the week. They blended together into the daily chores of the kennel. It didn't matter if it was Tuesday or Friday—the dogs had to eat and the place had to be cleaned. However, I usually got my bearings when Diana came out to the kennel on Sundays to drop off food and supplies.

Sometimes she picked up a dog for adoption or brought in a new one. Sometimes they were injured and they arrived with a bag of medicine and a list of instructions from the vet. I didn't know what to expect today. It's not like she'd phoned and told me in advance of her plans.

Diana pulled up in front of the kennel after lunch. I waited for the tiny woman to climb out of the one-ton beast of a truck. From a glance, some might dare to accuse her of trying to overcompensate for something in her life—like flat tits or a husband's small dick.

But that was far from the truth. Diana Sweetwater overcompensated for nothing and bowed down to no one. She was a classy lady with real grit who could cut down any man with a few quick words. She didn't give a shit what people thought about her—*or* the decisions she made to help clean up the crap in the world, which included me.

In her stubborn resilience, Diana had believed this place would right the wrongs in my life. She had been the reason the kennel was even an option on the table. As the police chief and the mayor fought over their sons, she had come up with an alternative solution. Marcus's dad thought Diana had lost her mind. But she'd fought Fred Tucker, toe to toe and eye to eye, swearing on the Bible and God and the President of the United States that this would work for everyone.

I'd known both of them as long as I could remember, but my actions that night had turned friends into enemies. His dad had blamed me for everything that had gone wrong in his son's life. I was the reason Marcus ever had a drink of alcohol. I was the reason he was friends with Trevor. I was the reason he went to *my* homecoming party instead spending Christmas Eve with his family. I was the reason he was a crippled-up piece of shit in a chair. I was the reason he would never walk Zoey down the aisle or teach his kids to play football—if he could even have any.

It had been strange seeing Fred Tucker turn on me—after all the nights I'd spent at his house and all the times I'd ridden home in his Suburban from football games. Not to mention all the Sundays I'd eaten dinner at his house after church. Our families had even gone on three vacations together.

But *Mayor* Fred Tucker had turned on me in a blind rage, full of pain and helplessness as Marcus sat in the hospital. He'd wanted me to pay for every business that had gone up in flames on *his* main street and every bone I'd broken in *his* son's body.

"Snap out of it, kid," Diana spat as she slammed the large metal door on the truck. Her jet-black hair was pulled high on the back of her head, making the gray piece in front resemble a white stripe. "Hurry up and get your stuff out of the backseat. I don't want your Popsicles melting all over my leather."

"I didn't ask for Popsicles."

"It's too damn hot. You need Popsicles." She walked around to the bed of the truck, leaving a trail of soft perfume. Her white button-down shirt was tucked into formfitting jeans that ended with a pair of custom-made ostrich boots.

Diana had married some rich guy who was twice her age, but he'd died about ten years ago, leaving her a pile of money to piss away in the wind—or so says the stories floating around Gibbs.

I opened the back door, taking out the sacks. I never asked for much. She knew what I liked to eat at this point in our arrangement. I also never gave her a reading list, but Diana always dropped in a few books with my supplies.

She had asked me once about my classes in college—which ones I'd liked and shit. I'd mumbled something about a literature class and reading as we traveled to the away games. After that conversation, Diana dropped off a large black shelf and some books. I think she was just happy that something seemed to interest me.

I unpacked my sacks, glancing at the grape Popsicles before adding them to the freezer. I found three new books and placed them on the counter. Seeing the title of the first one, I flipped it over to read the back cover. I guess Stephen King had a new one out.

I thought about the outside world sometimes. Things were changing while I was here. I knew nothing of the world news. Technology would keep advancing. I had no idea what had already been invented or what would come in the next couple of years. But I was okay with it. I didn't want to know anything about life outside of the fence.

As I walked back out the door of the trailer, I frowned, thinking of the one exception that had landed on my doorstep. I caught myself wondering what she was doing right now, and it pissed me off.

I found Diana with an old bulldog sitting on the bed of her truck. Walking over to the edge, I looked into the dazed eyes of the poor dog.

"So who's leaving?" I asked, knowing if I were getting a new one, she must have found a home for one of the others.

"The one you call Ponyboy." Diana snickered a little as she said it.

"So the antisocial one found a home before the others."

"I'm surprised I didn't find him one before now. He's actually not a bad sell. Mild-mannered dog. Potty trained. Doesn't give a shit if you just leave him alone. He's going to live with a workaholic who has a dog door. The dog gets free reign of the house and a half-acre backyard. Perfect fit."

"Until you put him in a bathtub. He freaks out because it's too small for him." I shrugged. "But maybe he'll do better there."

"And it makes room for Betty here. Sorry, kid. You don't get to name her. She's lived too long with that one to change it now."

"Owner die?"

"No. Family surrendered her to the pound. They got tired of her or some stupid shit story. Like someone would adopt an old, cranky bulldog. She was scheduled to be put down on Friday so I scooped her up. She's been staring at the wall of my house the last two days. I don't know if she's in shock or depressed or senile. Maybe you can work with her some. I would like to think she's not a lost cause."

"Okay." I lifted her up from the bed of the truck and headed to the kennel. The old dog hung from my arms like a lifeless bag of rocks. I felt sorry for Betty as I placed her in the holding pen. I ran my fingers over the wrinkles around her face as she stared blankly back at me. The poor girl had some serious issues.

Diana spoke from behind me. "So I guess from the looks of you, Emma finally knows why you are here."

"What's that supposed to mean?" I turned around, staring down into her blue eyes. I towered over the woman, but not a bone in her body was scared of me.

"Kid, you look like shit."

"I don't know what the hell you're talking about. I took a shower. I shaved."

"Your eyes, Wyatt. You got dead fish eyes today."

"Shit, Diana. What did you expect? We both knew how this was going to end."

"No, we didn't. So the question is—did she decide to drop your mopey ass or did *you* decide for her? Considering your pissy attitude, I assume the latter."

Hearing her accusation, my fingers gripped into tight fists. "This is your fault, you know."

"How, exactly, is it *my* fault?"

"You told Emma to come out here. Practically drew her a damn map." I shook my head. "I still don't understand *why* you thought that was a good idea?"

"Because I saw a girl with spunk *and* compassion as she begged me to take that dog. One who might be able to tolerate your self-absorbed pity-party. And she was cute too. Figured that would get your attention."

"I'm not here to be dating," I growled under my breath.

"I sent her your way. Whatever kind of relationship you had with Emma was your business. I just thought it was time for you to have friends in your life again."

"We know what happens to the *friends* who are around me," I muttered.

"Here we go again. You've got all those books in your trailer. Maybe you should start paying attention to that big important one I know you read. There's whole sections inside of it on forgiveness and grace."

"Yeah, well, there's whole sections on retribution too. Eye

for an eye, and all that shit. I'm pretty sure there's a list of commandments devoted to it too. I think I saw it plastered on the wall in your office."

She let out a deep breath. "You are a pain in my ass sometimes, Wyatt."

"If you feel that way, then send me back." My lips hardened into a thin line as I challenged her. I wasn't joking, and Diana knew my request was very real.

She sized me up for a moment, all four-feet-eleven of her. "I've known you for a long time. And when I saw your punk ass sitting in that courtroom, you were still a boy to me—hell-bent on going off like a man to something you didn't really comprehend. Prison makes some people better, and others, well, it just finishes rotting out their insides. You were at a crossroads that day. And you're still at one, even out here. Don't fuck this up. *I bet on you.* Don't prove Fred Tucker right."

Our eyes held for a moment, my heart beating in my chest until my lips curled up slightly on the edges. "Does anyone else know you curse like a trucker?"

"I only do it when I need to hit a home run. So, if she comes back—"

"Stop. It's time to let this idea go, Diana." I shook my head. "She's not coming back. Not after what I said to make her leave."

"*You* stop this self-loathing nonsense. If she comes back, do it right this time. Let her make the decision. And if she chooses to like your sorry ass? Let her."

"I can't," I whispered.

"Let me ask you something. Are you planning to be alone forever?"

"I don't really have a plan. I don't feel like the future is something I should be thinking about, I guess." But deep down, I knew that wasn't true. No matter how much I wished for permanent retribution, one day I would be released from my prison.

"You need to. You're almost half done. The rest will fly by. And then what? You need to figure out what will make you feel like you deserve to exist out there in the world again."

My eyes cast down on the floor. The whole idea of having a future made the pain start in my chest. It made me think about Willa and Marcus—and Trevor. People without futures. How was it fair that I got one? My breath stopped in my lungs as I fought a panic attack.

"Snap out of it, kid. There's no reason to take it all in at this very moment. Just start thinking about it."

I nodded, seeing the concern in Diana's eyes. She cared about me and didn't want this arrangement to fail. And it would—if I lost my damn mind out here. We both knew it.

"Good," she muttered, patting me on the arm. "Now, let's get Ponyboy ready to go."

"We will have to drug him to go in the crate. Or his PTSD will flare up."

"I'll get it." Diana walked toward the office to the medicine cabinet. She returned with a vile and syringe.

"If you want, I could have someone come out here to talk to you," she said as I held Pony down, watching her insert the needle into his skin. "A preacher, counselor, or maybe a priest?"

"I'm fine." I knew what she was getting at with me. Confession was good for the soul. But confessing of one's sins meant letting go of one's guilt. And I wasn't ready for that in my life. Maybe I never would be.

"How's everything else going out here?"

I looked up, catching the concern still hovering on her face. I ignored her probing glare. "Next week I will need a tank of gas for the Weed eater. It's running low."

"Okay. What else? Any special requests?"

Diana always asked that same question, and I always gave the same answer. "No."

Pony relaxed against the cement as the drugs took hold. I rubbed the side of his head as his brown eyes closed. I hated the idea of knocking him out for the ride into town, but it was better this way.

"Well, I've got it from here if you want to unload the rest of the stuff."

Without a word, I went outside to the bags of dog food, weighing down the bed of her truck. She always bought the expensive stuff. I bet those dogs ate better food than me, which is funny. I knew Diana would bring me grocery sacks of steaks if I asked her.

I carried the fifty-pound bags inside the kennel, stacking them in the storage area next to the office, over and over again until the truck was empty. Afterward, I opened the cab to retrieve the cases of canned food for the dogs like Lola who couldn't eat the crunchy stuff.

I wiped my sweaty face off on my shirt before going over to where Diana sat with Pony in the pen.

"You ready?" I asked, trying to catch my breath.

"Yeah. Let's get him loaded."

The hundred-pound dog was complete dead weight in my arms. I carried him out to the crate she kept in the back of the truck. Sliding him inside, I latched the door tight. I wiped the sweat from my forehead onto my sleeve. Diana came over to stand in front of me.

"Told you it was too damn hot out here. You should take it easy the rest of the day. It's Sunday, you know."

When I didn't answer, she just shook her head, giving me one of her looks. "Well, I guess I'm gonna head out."

"Hey, I . . . um . . . I think it's time we took the hold off of Charlie. You should start looking for someone."

Her eyes narrowed as she stared up at me. "You sure about that?"

I nodded, feeling like I was betraying Emma. But there was no need for him to stay anymore.

"Just remember, that one's on you. I'll see you next week. Take care, kid." She climbed inside the cab, slamming the door. I stood in the yard until her truck disappeared down the road.

Going back inside, I went to the holding pen with Betty. She had her back turned to the gate, staring at the wall. "Okay, girl. This is not going to work."

I opened the door, but she never seemed to notice. Picking up her potato-shaped body, I carried Betty down the aisle. I went past Cye's pen and stopped. He was slunk in the back corner, staring at *his* wall.

Either this would be a stroke of genius or end in bloodshed. I opened the metal latch and carried the old bulldog inside, placing her on the cement about four feet from Cye. I swear his single, dark eye narrowed, saying, *What the hell?*

I looked from one dog to another. "You two can stare at each other."

Leaving the kennel, I went inside the trailer and opened the freezer. I held the door open a good two minutes before taking the grape Popsicles out of the package. I went back out to the porch steps. Purple drops hit the cement as I sat down.

After I finished the Popsicle, I chewed on the stick as I gazed out in the sky. It would be dark soon, making it one step closer to Monday. The day after Diana's visits always seemed to be long. Maybe that's why I'd never bothered to pay attention to the days of the week. They were all the same, except for those weeks when Emma had decided I was worth seeing.

CHAPTER 21

Wyatt

THE CLOUDS GREW DARK. A DEAFENING ROAR HURT MY HEARS. I spun in circles, hearing the screams, but I couldn't find a face to go with the voice. Stumbling around in the freezing rain, a storm of ice pellets scratched my skin.

I tripped over a mound on the wet pavement. Catching my balance, I looked down and saw Willa with a dark-red line across her throat. She was dying. She needed help. I wanted to scream, but my voice didn't work.

Stumbling along, I saw a man lying facedown with his back split open like someone had planted a grenade inside. Marcus. I couldn't breathe as I stared at the ripped-up remains of my friend.

Red streaks shot across the clouds. Looking up, I froze in place as Fred Tucker appeared in the middle of the street. He towered over me—the way clowns looked at the circus when they walked on stilts. He screamed and yelled, making the skin around his eyes glow red as flames spewed from his mouth.

I tried to back away, but the muscles in my legs remained paralyzed and I couldn't move.

The air went from ice cold to scalding hot as drops of fire rained from the swirling clouds. My shoes stuck to the melted pavement. Right beneath my feet, the asphalt turned into a pool of black quicksand. I fell through, landing with a hard thump on the floor.

It was quiet. Not a sound anywhere, except my heart pounding in my chest. The air was still. Not a color glowed in the gray and white shadows.

"Don't leave me here alone, Wyatt."

I spun around at the sound of his voice. My stomach clenched like someone had punched me in the gut. I saw Trevor's lifeless body on the floor with his head propped up on an old pizza box.

"You know I hate being alone."

I heard the words, but his lips were rotted out and unmoving.

My eyes flew open and I pulled in a deep breath, sucking spit down my windpipe. Rolling over on my side, I succumbed to a fit of coughing. My lungs finally relaxed, and I fell onto my back, staring up at the stained white ceiling of the trailer.

Some mornings started out worse than others. Some started in the pit of hell. Gripping my hands into fists, I braced for the shakes—the damn involuntary muscles spasms that always followed those kinds of dreams.

My arms twitched against the mattress. I took in a deep breath, holding it in my lungs before releasing the air slowly through my nose. My legs jerked wildly under the covers. I repeated the breathing exercise, over and over again until my heart rate got a little less sporadic and the panic released itself from my body.

Uncurling my fingers, I let my neck relax against the pillow. And then I remembered the last flash of my dream. *Trevor.*

The cold chill went over my skin as I pictured his face. In this new nightmare, Trevor had been about eleven. I swallowed the knot in my throat, knowing why my subconscious had pulled that particular memory. It was the way Trevor had looked the summer his mom had left him.

Here one minute, and gone the next. Selfish bitch. Our school had just let out for summer break. About a week later, Trevor had knocked a can of Pepsi off of the counter. As the brown liquid poured out on the clean tile, she'd stared at Trevor and said, *I can't do this anymore.*

Not to his dad. Not to her husband. But to Trevor. Her child. As he tried to clean up the pop, his mom had packed a suitcase—and then she left him. We later discovered her decision to leave wasn't really out of the blue. She'd met that hippy asshole a few weeks before that afternoon, but none of those facts had mattered to Trevor. Her words had already done their damage.

Marcus and I had spent that summer camped in a tent we put up in their yard—back when it was full of grass and flowers instead of rotting bags of trash. We'd stayed with Trevor because he hated being alone while his dad worked nights at the Walmart distribution center.

As I thought about Trevor, his familiar face haunted my thoughts. I wondered who had attended his funeral. With Marcus and I out of the picture, did anyone else care enough to even go? Most of those assholes in Gibbs had only liked Trevor for his parties. Or rather, the freedom his piece-of-shit house had offered them.

But that wasn't the case for me. He was my friend and had been since the day our teacher had sat us next to each other in kindergarten. And I missed him. I even missed all of his wisecracking one-liners, and all of his annoying texts he'd sent while I was in Texas.

I had a vague memory of our last encounter. My eyes closed as the pain in my chest got deeper. Flashes of that night spun through my head. I remembered yelling a bunch of shit before punching Trevor in the jaw. It wasn't the first time. I just never thought it would be the last thing I ever said to the guy.

But that's the thing about lasts. No one ever plans those last moments. Last words. Last actions. I bet Marcus never dreamed his last normal steps would be into my damn car.

I jumped, feeling a wet nose pressing into my cheek. Gus reached his tongue out for a lick. I stared into his black eyes. The little guy was concerned for me this morning.

"I'm okay, Gus," I mumbled. Blinking a few times, I tried to brush off the ghosts that still lingered in my thoughts. Climbing out of bed, I went to the trailer door and let the two dogs outside. The internal darkness followed me to the bathroom as I got dressed to go running.

I slowly lost my grip on reality as I trotted along the trail of the perimeter. The sun rose in the sky, but I only saw the gray shadows from my dream. I couldn't shake the feeling it had left inside my chest.

I wasn't the person who had crammed a handful of pills down his throat. And there were no charges against me for Trevor. No *mayor* fighting for him. But I knew the hand I'd played in his death. And it ate away at me, little by little, dream by dream as my subconscious made sure I never forgot him.

I found myself lying on my back in the grass. Somewhere in my thoughts, my body had shut down, causing me to fall to the ground. As the clouds passed over my head, I struggled to remember the day of the week. Was it bath day or lawn day or Tuesday?

Sweat beaded up on my forehead as I stared at the sky. I tried to swallow, but my throat was too dry to cooperate. The sun got hotter and brighter. Maybe the sun would burn so hot, I would catch on fire and disintegrate into a puff of smoke. If I just stayed in this very spot, I wondered how long it would take for someone to find my burned-up body.

Diana had already come and gone again—this time taking Ricky Bobby. She had found the energetic, three-legged dog a family with three boys. Even those thoughts hurt today. I shouldn't be sad to see him leave. But something about it made me think of

Emma. She wouldn't like the fact that I'd sent him away without letting her say goodbye.

I allowed myself to think about Emma. I allowed myself to want her. To hear her voice. Kiss her skin. I wanted to see her sweet face and those lips. I wanted to bury my nose in her hair, and bury myself inside her body as she whispered my name.

That beautiful girl consumed my last thoughts as I waited for the black birds to come pick me clean. But that was the thing about the darkness. Once you allowed the light inside, the shadows exploded into a million pieces.

"*Ahhhhh!*" I screamed up into the sky.

I had to snap out of it before I lost my damn mind. Even in my insanity, I still had a job to do at the kennel. Dogs to be fed. Pens to be cleaned. I had responsibilities.

I crawled up from the ground, walking slowly back to the trailer. My shoes moved at the speed of a sleepwalker. Getting in the shower, I let the cold water shock my skin. I shaved. I ate my cereal, doing my best to hold it all together.

Some days were tougher than others. Some were darker as I clung to the fringes of sanity. But I always snapped out of it. Sometimes it took hours and sometimes those feelings lingered for days. And sometimes I prolonged it by reading Poe.

I left the trailer, shutting the metal door softly behind me. As I reached the side entrance of the kennel, I paused, hearing the sound of a motor. I turned around just as the cloud of dirt spit out of a little white car.

Emma.

The tires got closer, and I struggled to think straight. Was she real or had I imagined Emma on this dark morning? The car skidded to a stop just a few feet from where I stood in the dirt. As the car door opened, my lungs stopped working. I held my breath, seeing my angel of mercy come into view.

My thoughts were still jumbled. It was hard to transition

from the gray nightmares to seeing actual people. To seeing her. I'm sure everything about me screamed crazy as I stared at her.

But I couldn't help it. Emma held me captive as she leaned against the hood of the car in her cutoff shorts and pink shirt. I couldn't take my eyes off of her. The way she smiled. The way her hair touched her neck.

As she stared back at me, the darkness seemed to fade away and the ghosts disappeared into the shadows. I saw the light of the sun shining down from the sky.

And then I moved. My legs moved faster than they had all morning. They took me over to Emma. My heart pulsed in frantic beats in my chest as my nerves took over, strangling the words in my throat.

Her eyes flashed uncertainty and fear and happiness and worry. "Wyatt, before you say anything—"

But I didn't let her speak. I wrapped my arms around her body, holding Emma in a death grip against my chest. I needed to feel her. I needed to know she was real. The thoughts I heard banging around inside my head scared the shit out of me.

Placing my hands on her cheeks, I stared into her eyes. Emma looked back at me with her usual open heart full of compassion and desire and tenderness. It flowed with every breath as she let me hold on to her body. And then I felt a glimmer of peace. She was the one person who seemed to make this shit inside of my head better.

"Wyatt, I was so afraid you would think that I wasn't coming back. I wanted—"

I kissed her. I needed to feel her again. My mouth pressed hard against her lips. Emma needed to know how much I wanted her. It was rough and hard and slightly possessive as my tongue pressed into her mouth. But I couldn't stop. I needed to taste her. Crush her. Hold her. My hands moved over her arms and waist, digging into her skin to the point she would have finger-shaped bruises.

I loosened my grip, not wanting to hurt Emma. I couldn't bear the thought of causing any type of pain to anyone again. Letting go of her lips, I buried my nose in her hair. She smelled like honeysuckles.

"I don't know what scared me more when you left," I finally whispered. "That you wouldn't come back. Or that you would."

I felt a stab of panic as I admitted my fear, but I couldn't stop the words. She brought it out of me. Her sweet face and those lips that tasted like cinnamon.

"I wanted to come back. Like, the moment I left. I wanted to turn back around."

Staring down at Emma, something sparked inside my chest. *Hope*. It came out of nowhere. My mind struggled to comprehend the thought.

"You did?" I asked, assuming she'd spent the last couple of weeks processing some internal and moral conflict of coming back to see me.

"Remember?" she whispered. "You can't get rid of me that easy."

I slowly grinned as I remembered the day she'd stood on the trailer steps, yelling all that shit through the door. I'd watched Emma through the curtain, seeing her face get all red and angry. I'd pissed her off good that time, but she had the resilience of an MMA fighter. She had never given up on me.

"You're right. He's got some serious dimples." Hearing the voice, I froze as I looked over Emma's head to the parked car. My eyes darted back and forth between them. *What the hell?*

"Wyatt, um, this is Blaire. My sister."

Emma's twin shut the driver's side door and came over to us. Her piercing glare seemed friendly and menacing all at the same time. They were just alike, yet very different. I felt it radiating from their personalities as well as their looks. She had the same little turned-up nose and sexy lips. But Emma's shiny blonde hair fell in curls around her shoulders while her sister's was held up in some stringy blob on top of her head.

"I didn't think you drove," I asked in confusion.

"I don't. But she's been driving me crazy. Wyatt. Wyatt. Wyatt. Blah. Blah. I finally just said fuck it. I'll waste my morning in that death trap."

"Blaire!" A nasty look passed between the girls. "Sorry, she can be an *acquired* taste."

I laughed a little, seeing Emma with Blaire. They were both so animated and full of life. So different than me. But it felt good to be around them. They made this dark day come alive and seem real. I hated that feeling and craved it all at the same time.

"What?" Emma stared up at me and I got nervous, knowing I'd slipped away into one of my trances.

"Nothing. It's just funny seeing both of you together."

"Not him too." Blaire rolled her eyes. "Please tell me you won't fixate on it like Kurt."

"Who's Kurt?" I asked, feeling surprised at the sudden pang of jealousy in my chest. I shouldn't be upset by another guy in Emma's life. What did I really know about her or who she spent time with outside of here?

"She's never told you about Kurt? Typical Emma." She shook her head, making the messy blob of hair fall to the side. "Kurt is the reason her knee got messed up, *again*. And the reason I had to drive out here today because his little *obsession* put Emma in the hospital."

Part III

Emma

CHAPTER 22

Emma

13 days ago

I CRIED. I DIDN'T WANT TO CRY, BUT I COULDN'T STOP THE TEARS. They poured down my cheeks, blocking the sun and my view of the road. I came to a complete stop in the middle of nowhere and put my car in park. Snot dripped out of my nose. Opening the center console, I found an old Sonic Drive-In napkin with traces of dried ketchup on the edges. I wiped my face with it anyway, smelling the stench of tater tots.

I'd known he was messed up. I'd known something terrible was haunting Wyatt. But I think in the back of my mind, I'd created a romantic fantasy story—one where he was the wounded hero who had lost the girl. He had loved her so deeply that it had wrecked him. And I was going to put him back together. I was going to show Wyatt that it was okay to have feelings for someone again.

But this was a different kind of tragedy. His pain was so much deeper and complex than I'd ever imagined. And he wasn't any hero. By most people's standards, Wyatt *was* a bad guy—just like he'd warned on all my visits.

I wrestled with my thoughts. What if I'd done something like that to Blaire? What if I'd gotten high and cracked her skull open? Just the idea caused a flash of deep guilt in my chest, which I knew she would feel all the way back into town. And I seriously doubted my twin would be as forgiving as Willa if I'd messed up *her* head.

All the twisted bits of truth caused every emotion inside my body to come alive. I thought about the rest of his story and all the people who had suffered because of his reckless stupidity. Some guy was currently sitting in a wheelchair because of Wyatt. Some guy who had been his best friend.

Letting out a deep breath, I leaned my head back against the seat, feeling the cold air conditioner as it blew in my face. My red puffy eyes burned from all the tears.

This was so confusing, but even in my search for clarity, I still hurt *for* Wyatt. The way he couldn't even look me in the face as he told me his story. And the way he struggled to breathe at times from the shear agony of saying the words out loud. He cared about these people. *His* people. The people he hurt.

Wyatt might be the bad guy, but I'd seen the shame in his eyes as he told me the truth. I'd felt the guilt tormenting every thought inside his head. And those feelings made me want to turn my car around and go back. Maybe it was crazy, but I knew the truth and I still wanted to save him. I still believed Wyatt *Carter* wasn't a lost cause.

I remembered the way his voice had sounded as he spoke. I knew Wyatt had never shared any of this with anyone. The accident. His grief. His remorse.

I'd pushed him until he confessed. I'd pushed and pushed until he'd broken, turning him into a wild animal backed into a corner, yelling all those terrible things—lashing out, trying to hurt anyone who came near him. He had done his best to push back. And his words still hurt.

I swallowed the knot in my swollen throat. Maybe I should just give him some space. I wiped my face again on the dirty napkin, blowing out a hunk of snot. My heart beat in ragged pieces from being ripped to shreds. Maybe we both needed some space if I planned to continue on with this insanity of trying to help someone who felt he should be left to rot like garbage.

When I pulled into the apartment complex, my mind was numb. The strain of trying to drive with swollen eyes had caused a pounding headache. I just wanted to get in my apartment and bury myself under the covers in my bed.

Crawling out of the seat, I slammed the door and limped toward the stairs, keeping my face cast down. I prayed my sister was away on campus. Blaire would know something had happened, but right now, I couldn't deal with her stealth-level doom-and-gloom questions.

I'd already made up my mind. Not that I really had much to consider. My cosmic fate had been sealed after our first meeting. Wyatt and I were intertwined now—even when the truth got messy. Helping people wasn't for the faint of heart and saving them might border on self-inflicted torture.

"Why so sad, Emma?"

My good knee froze in mid-step, leaving all my weight on the bad one. My fingers gripped the handle on the staircase as Kurt came out of my apartment.

"What were you doing in there?"

My mind played a film reel of torrid thoughts, involving Kurt sitting on my couch, running his hands over my bedspread, digging through my drawers, touching my clothes, smelling my panties.

Get a grip! He didn't smell my underwear. As the apartment manager, there had to be a reasonable explanation as to why the guy was in my home—except he didn't answer my question. I swallowed hard, trying not to be nervous.

"Why were you in my apartment?" I asked again, hearing my shaky voice.

Kurt came over to the staircase as I stayed perched just a few steps down from the top. His lips curled up on the corners under his wiry beard. "Your neighbor smelled gas. So I took a look around. Thought you might have left the stove on or something. You girls are always running in and *out*."

"Was . . . um . . . everything okay?"

"Didn't smell any damn gas. But that bedroom shit you got in there is gonna cost you. I'll have to take that out of your deposit when you move out."

"What bedroom stuff?"

Kurt took a step down to the spot just above my foot. His grin got even bigger, showing bits of chewing tobacco stuck in his teeth. "You painted it some girly purple color. You know that ain't in your lease."

"It was that way when I moved in. You even knocked off an extra ten dollars a month if I didn't make you haul a bucket of paint up there to fix it."

He pondered my words for a moment as he stood in my personal space. "I suppose I did."

"Okay, well, thanks for checking on the gas leak."

He grinned, leaning a few inches closer. "Your eyes are all covered in black shit. You been crying?"

I frowned, leaning backward until I stood at a crooked arch with his face hovering. I put my good leg back one step.

"You have a fight or something with that guy you go see?" His eyes traveled over the smeared mascara to my neck and down to the low V-neck of my shirt. "A pretty thing like you deserves someone better than a piece of shit like him."

My eyes glanced to my door and then back to where his body blocked most of the staircase, preventing me from running past him. And I wanted nothing more than to get away from this uncomfortable situation.

"I need to get to my apartment, Kurt." I tried to be firm. He couldn't keep this up for very long. Someone would pull into the lot soon or open their door.

"I'm just trying to be helpful, *Emma*." His drawl pulled on my name. "Girls like you shouldn't be running off to see guys who live out there in the sticks. All kinds of bad shit can happen."

I stepped backward with my bad leg, feeling it wobble on the wooden steps, and then it crumbled. My fingers grabbed for anything—the railing, his shirt, his arm, his stupid face—but everything slipped through my hands as I tumbled down into the parking lot.

I landed in a heap at the bottom of the staircase. My head throbbed from hitting it eight times against the wooden steps. The pain caused me to black out for a second. And then I screamed, feeling the stabs in my knee bringing me back to life. It hurt like someone had emptied an entire revolver of bullets straight into the bone.

"Hmm. You really should be more careful." Kurt took his time walking down the stairs before hovering over me. "Well, I guess I better get you off the ground before you scare the other tenants."

He scooped me up in his arms. I struggled to get free, seeing stars as I blinked. "Let me go."

"Now, how in the hell are you going to get yourself to the hospital?"

"You're taking me to the hospital?"

"You act like I was going to tie you up or something." He laughed, giving me a strange side smile.

Reaching his truck, I noticed a bunch of chains and ropes in the back. Up next to the cab were several metal cages. I'd never paid much attention to it before since he'd kept it parked out of view on the other side of the manager's office.

I screamed in pain as Kurt dumped me in the passenger's seat. He slammed the door, and I slid down in the floorboard as my head throbbed. I struggled to get back up in the seat. My hand slipped under the edge, feeling something cold and metal. *A shotgun.* I panicked. Kurt had a shotgun crammed under the seat.

Not unusual in Oklahoma, but in this precarious moment of relying on Kurt, I panicked. I kicked with my good foot, trying to get back in the seat. I grabbed at the door handle just as he climbed in the driver's side.

"Just settle down over there. You ain't walking to the hospital."

The motor fired up, and he put the truck into drive. I concentrated on breathing amidst the burning pain. He was taking me to the hospital. He was taking me to the hospital. He was taking me to the hospital.

CHAPTER 23

Emma

This morning…

The car slammed to a stop in the middle of Duck Street, throwing me against the seatbelt. The impact knocked the wind slightly out of my lungs.

“It’s an automatic, Blaire. That’s not a clutch. It’s a break.” I tried to use a calming tone and not glare in horror at my sister. “You only use it at, like, lights and stop signs.”

“Emma, I swear. One more word, and I’m getting out and walking back to the apartment.”

I steadied my thoughts, knowing this wasn’t an idle threat. She would leave me and the car right there in front of Garth Brooks’s old yellow house. And I couldn’t drive. Not for another two weeks.

“I’m sorry. I know this is a big deal for you. Just go slow and everything will be fine. We are not in a hurry.” I turned to face the front, praying a big farm truck didn’t ram us from behind. “Thank you for doing this.”

"Yeah, yeah." Her foot lifted from the brake. She smashed the gas and we shot forward, slinging my neck back against the seat.

I knew driving scared Blaire and I was starting to understand why. She was going to wreck our car. After all these years of joking, I wasn't exactly thrilled with the idea of actually sharing *my* car. Not when she drove like Jeff Gordon with Fred Flintstone's feet.

I didn't relax until we had left the city limits and drove down the vacant dirt road. Staring out the window, I tried to calm the apprehension that spun through my nerves.

I'd left his trailer thirteen days ago. Thirteen very long and very eventful days ago. And I'm sure he thought I wasn't coming back. After yelling all those terrible words, I bet Wyatt assumed he'd finally driven me away for good. And that had me worried.

The guy was in bad shape. I'd never seen a person ripped apart like Wyatt. His insides were raw with guilt and pain that manifested as serious depression. I didn't need to be a psychologist to put that one together.

"Turn in here." I pointed toward the silver metal gate.

"Seriously? The place with the cow skulls? Are there human ones too?"

I knew she was trying to get a reaction out of me. Instead of responding to her condescending remark, I focused on the positive instead of the negative. She had taken a huge step by driving the car. She had brought me to see Wyatt. "Blaire, you will have to open the gate. Just pull the chain out of the hook. Don't worry about shutting it."

"*Okay*." She said the word like I asked her to push me to the top of Mount Everest in a wheelchair.

My hands got fidgety as I watched her struggle with the gate. She managed to get the silver metal pushed to the side and got back in the driver's seat. "Where's the road?"

"Just follow the tracks in the grass."

"That's not a road. I'm not messing up my car over this."

"Just." I took a calming breath. "It's fine. Just follow the tracks. You will see the buildings better once we get in there."

She stared at me like I was crazy. I imagined a hundred different *Criminal Minds* episodes running through her head. Even though she knew Wyatt wasn't technically dangerous, it didn't mean she necessarily approved of him or where he lived. And when did it become *her* car?

Blaire touched the gas, making sure she hit every rut and bump. My knee was still in a brace from ankle to midthigh. And thanks to Dr. Westbrook and his tray of nuts and bolts, my bones were tied all back together and my ACL was good as new. I did therapy every day, but I couldn't put weight on the leg for another week—and no driving for at least two, which only happened because it was my left leg.

Thirteen days ago, Kurt had dropped me off at the hospital. I'd had surgery and then I'd moved in with my parents, at least for the time being, until I could maneuver around on my own again. Thirteen long and torturous days where I thought about nothing but Wyatt.

I strained to see his trailer and the kennel, trying to find him somewhere in the distance.

"What are you going to do if he flips out again?" Blaire asked.

"I don't know," I whispered, searching for his familiar shape in the distance. And then I saw him.

Wyatt.

He walked slowly out in front of the kennel, watching us get closer. Blaire hit the break, slamming me against the seatbelt and leaving a small cloud of dust from the tires.

Opening the door, I struggled to get out of the seat. And then I saw his face, so twisted and almost gray instead of the usual tan from the sun. I didn't bother to grab my crutches from the backseat. I bounced on one foot, stopping next to the hood. Leaning against the metal for support, I gauged his reaction.

Wyatt seemed spooked—his eyes were wild and crazy and even a bit scary. His hands were shaking to the point of distraction with his palms flexing into fists and releasing. The guy was on the cusp of a physical explosion. And then he came toward me.

I was right to be worried. "Wyatt, before you say anything—"

But the words disappeared the moment I felt his arms circle around my body. He clung to me the way a drowning man would hold onto a tree limb. So tight. So desperate.

My heart broke into a million pieces. And I couldn't breathe as he pulled every bit of strength from me. But I gave it freely. I gave everything I could to Wyatt as he held on to me under the hot sun.

After what seemed like an eternity, he loosened his grip enough to look at me. Our eyes morphed into one of those deep, probing stares. So lost. So alone. I almost cried right there in front of him. "I'm so sorry. I was afraid you would think that I wasn't coming back. I wanted—"

And then he kissed me. Hard. It was different from the soft lips he had used in the past. The desperation fueled a spark that transcended into some frantic desire. Wyatt kissed the same way he'd clung to me earlier—like his life depended on it.

He trailed over my cheek and neck, letting his lips rest against my ear. His gruff voice spoke low, and I struggled to hear the words.

"I don't know what scared me more when you left," he whispered. "That you wouldn't come back. Or that you would."

I knew this was the turning point. I had finally broken through his defenses. I had torn down the walls, and he was letting me inside for real this time.

"I wanted to come back. The moment I left. I wanted to turn back around."

"You did?" He seemed surprised or maybe relieved.

"Remember?" I whispered. "You can't get rid of me that easy."

His grin came slowly, painfully, like he needed to process his thoughts, pushing the worried ones aside. But Wyatt finally smiled and his whole face moved. I wanted to kiss him again. I wanted to go inside his trailer and let him run his hands over my skin. I wanted to feel that same desperate spark as he moved inside of me.

"You're right. He's got some serious dimples."

I mentally gasped, hearing my sister's voice. I had forgotten she was in the car witnessing my entire makeout session.

"Wyatt, um, this is Blaire. My sister." I didn't know why I added that last part. It wasn't like he couldn't tell from just looking.

"I didn't think you drove," he asked, seeming confused.

"I don't. But she's been driving me crazy. Wyatt. Wyatt. Wyatt. Blah. Blah. I finally just said fuck it. I'll waste my morning in that death trap."

"Blaire!" I shot her a death glare. "Sorry, she can be an *acquired* taste."

Wyatt didn't say anything. His eyes traveled back and forth between us, taking in the similarities. And then his smile grew a little hazy as he looked off in the distance.

"What?" I asked.

He laughed faintly. "Nothing. It's just funny seeing both of you together."

"Not him too." Blaire rolled her eyes. "Please tell me you won't fixate on it like Kurt."

"Who's Kurt?"

I cringed at his question, not wanting to explain Kurt the pervert to Wyatt. Blaire eyed me, sensing my dilemma, but she went for it anyway.

"She's never told you about Kurt? Typical Emma." She smirked. "Kurt is the reason her knee got messed up, *again.* And the reason I had to drive out here today because his little *obsession* put Emma in the hospital."

"You were in the hospital?" His fingers dug into my shoulders.

I nodded, looking down at my black-encased leg, the one I held slightly off the ground. "Surprise. I got that surgery after all. That's what I was trying to tell you. It's why I didn't come back sooner."

"Emma. I-I'm sorry. I didn't realize." His face twisted up as he slipped back into a guilt-stricken panic. "Shit. You shouldn't be standing here. Did I hurt you? I am so stupid. I was mauling you out here. You can't even stand. Shit."

I grabbed his cheeks on each side of his face, getting his attention. "I'm okay. I promise. And Kurt is my apartment manager. We were talking. And I slipped on the stairs. He drove me to the hospital."

Standing behind him out of view, Blaire visibly choked as she heard my explanation. I would deal with her later. Telling Wyatt about Kurt would just make things worse. He would get more worked up over something that was beyond his control. It's not like Wyatt could even leave this place to confront my slightly obsessive apartment manager. And maybe I'd made too much of it—after all, the guy did drive me to the hospital.

"Let me help you inside." The wild look in his eyes got stronger. "We can talk or something."

"I would like you to take me to the kennel. I want to see everyone. I want to see Charlie."

He nodded before bending down and picking me up. I settled into the crook of his arms with my leg sticking straight out in that stupid contraption. We made eye contact, and my heart beat faster.

"Is this okay?" Wyatt asked. His desperate need for reassurance was transparent.

"Yeah." I traced a finger down his jaw, right over the spot that kept his hidden dimple. His familiar scent of clean soap filled my nose. I smiled at Wyatt, wanting to kiss him again. I leaned up, brushing my mouth against his.

"I'll be in the trailer," Blaire said as she pulled her giant backpack out of the backseat.

"Okay," I mumbled. She went up the steps and disappeared behind the old door. I looked back at Wyatt. "I don't know about her being in there alone. She might have some weird forensic kit stuffed down in that backpack."

"It's okay. I've got nothing to hide." Even though his words came out like a joke, I saw the way his jaw tightened up.

Wyatt carried me to the kennel. Once inside, the familiar sounds of the dogs filled the whole room, echoing off the metal walls. He took me down the main aisle toward Charlie.

"Wait." I grabbed his arm. "I want to see Cye. I don't think I can get down in there, but I want to see him. Did you give him the bones while I was gone? Did it work?"

"Well, I'll let you see for yourself." He sat me down next to the gate, and I held onto his arm for support.

"I don't understand." My eyes traced the perimeter of the pen. An old bulldog was perched in the back where Cye had always sat. "Where is he?"

"Right under your nose."

"What the—" About two feet away, the battered dog sat in the corner by the gate. He was angled just right so I couldn't reach through and touch him. But he was close enough for me to see the gold flecks in his one dark eye. "I don't understand."

"Well, Betty arrived and she stared at the wall. So I put them in the kennel together. I wasn't sure what would happen. Not all of their problems are solved. But I guess Betty gave Cye the stare-down until he moved. I can't touch him yet. And he seems a little angry at me. But he moved."

"Wow. Well, that is not what I expected. A lot happened while I was gone."

"Yeah. I guess so."

I turned to face him. "I need to say something to you."

Wyatt didn't answer immediately. He let out a deep breath. "Okay."

"I researched you while I was at home. I had plenty of time to do it. I read about the accident and all the stuff printed afterward. And I . . . um . . . I read about Trevor," I added cautiously, unsure of his reaction since I knew Wyatt had left that part out of his story on purpose.

His eyes got a little dark as he stared off in the distance past my head, but I continued anyway. "I read all of it. But I also found the articles from high school. You were a football player. A pretty good one too. I even tracked down the stuff from Texas. You were the reason they made the Division-II national finals."

"Well, all of that is gone now."

"I know. But that's not the point I am trying to make. You did a bad thing, Wyatt. I'm not going to act like you didn't. But I don't think it makes you a bad person. And before you say anything, I realize that I will never know the guy who existed before the accident. But that doesn't really matter. I know the person I see now. And I know right here." I rested my hand over his heart. "That person is not bad. He's just a little lost and really broken."

Wyatt put his hand over mine, holding it tight to his chest. The torment twisted around on his face like a visible tug-of-war over my words.

"Emma." His voice grated on my name. "I try to sort it out in my head, but it's all a damn mess. I haven't really talked about it with anyone. And I don't even know if I told you the whole truth. I honestly don't remember everything from that night. And that messes with me too."

"I can't imagine what it's like, being out here all alone, living with those feelings every day."

His green eyes bore down into mine, letting me see the deep pain rotting his insides. I slipped my arms around his neck, pressing myself into his body. He tucked his nose against my cheek.

"This is hard for me to say." He muttered so quiet the words almost disappeared. "But I need you in my life, Emma."

"I know," I whispered. "It's why I kept coming back."

He let out a deep breath. "But I don't know what I'm doing. You. Me. Us. Here. I don't know how this works."

"Honestly, me either." I laughed faintly. "Look. I can't drive for another couple of weeks. And I won't force Blaire to bring me out here again either. But I'll come back once the doctor clears me. I want to help you. I want to be there for you. I want to be with you. I know it will be hard, but I can handle it, if you just let me. Because I want this with you."

He swallowed, making his throat move with emotion. "I wish I could give you more than this. But it's all I can do for now."

"What? Like dates to stupid places that just cost money? I think we both know that other stuff is overrated. I'd rather just spend time with you here."

"You say that now."

"It's the truth. I want you, Wyatt. Just the way you are."

I gazed into his troubled eyes until Wyatt leaned down and kissed me, letting his tongue slip through my lips. His mouth moved slowly and sweetly as his hands trailed over my body until they cupped my butt cheeks before scooping me up in his arms. I held on tight as he carried me down the aisle to see Charlie.

CHAPTER 24

Emma

A WEEK LATER, I SAT IN THE APARTMENT NEXT DOOR TO MINE, playing checkers with Mr. Hughes. After I got clearance to put a little weight on my leg, I made my mom bring me home. I was tired of staring at their walls while everyone was away at work. I thought it was better to at least have some company. It didn't take much to maneuver the few steps next door. I could hang out with my neighbor while Blaire wasn't home.

"Well, I've finally caved."

"Uh?" I looked up from the black and red board. The old man had me cornered. For the last ten minutes, I'd run ever scenario through my head and it was official—he was going to beat me again.

"You folding?" I teased.

"You young'uns know nothing about real games. There's no folding in checkers."

"Then why are you caving?"

"My daughter. I talked to her last night. She's made Nebraska sound tolerable."

"Tolerable?" My heart hurt, seeing the pained expression on his face.

"Well, she put it to me this way. When she comes at Thanksgiving, I'm either getting shuttled off to some old nursing home or I'm going to live with her. Like I said. Nebraska sounds tolerable."

I nodded, feeling the undeniable sadness for him and for me. I would miss the old guy. "Well, I guess Nebraska sounds pretty nice then."

"Yep. And you might as well fold and we'll start a new game. You're not getting out of that corner."

"Okay." I gathered up the plastic pieces, stuffing them back down in the box. "What else you got?"

"Since you keep talking about folding, you ever play poker?"

"It's been a while." I shrugged, giving him a smile. "I played some when I traveled for track meets. I'm about as good at poker as I am at checkers."

"Well, it looks like I'll be winning my bet against you."

I cocked an eyebrow up at Mr. Hughes. "What bet?"

"When I beat you, no more salads. I really hate green things."

"I accept your challenge since we are playing for salad. Where are the cards?"

He coughed faintly. "Hall closet."

I took the checkers box with me as I hobbled to the door in the entryway. I dug around the shelves filled with pieces from his life. All of those items would soon be packed up and in a truck going to Nebraska.

"I guess you got one more week before you can go see that boy." I heard his voice come from behind me and the waves of feelings overwhelmed my thoughts. For a brief moment, I'd stopped thinking about Wyatt. I missed him and craved him. I worried about him.

I couldn't imagine what it must be like for Wyatt. What it

must feel like, going days and days without seeing another person. Not talking. Keeping all your words bottled up inside. It was enough to make a normal person go crazy. I couldn't imagine what it must be like for a person carrying enough baggage to sink a ship to the bottom of the ocean.

My hand clasped around a beat-up deck of cards. Closing the closet door, I made my way back to the couch and the TV tray we kept between us for the games. "He's not a boy, Mr. Hughes. He's twenty-two."

"If you say so. So what's his name again?"

"Wyatt."

"Wyatt what? This boy not have a last name?"

"Caulf—um. I mean, Carter." It was still a little hard for me to keep that one straight.

"Wyatt Carter. Well, that explains a lot. You never told me he was that Carter boy."

My eyes snapped up to his old, wrinkled blue ones. The confused thoughts tumbled around. "You know Wyatt?"

"Can't burn down half a town without a few people noticing."

I cringed, hearing the reference come from Mr. Hughes. I knew when people found out about my involvement with Wyatt, they would start judging me. I knew it was bound to happen. We lived in Stillwater, but Gibbs wasn't that far away. And small-town news had a tendency to travel, especially when it got picked up by the big-city affiliates: *Drunk Driver Burns Down Main Street, Paralyzes Mayor's Son.*

And like Wyatt had said—taking out a federal post office really did make people crazy. It was the biggest leverage Fred Tucker had used against Wyatt. I'd read it all in the papers. And I guess Mr. Hughes had read it too.

"Don't get all worried, Emma. That's not how I know your boy. He's Orville Carter's grandson. Wyatt's grandpa owns a motorcycle repair garage in town. Or, well, he used to own one. I think he's retired now."

"Oh, I um—I remember Wyatt saying something about that. He's got a bike out there at the kennel. Keeps it under a tarp."

"You don't say." A whimsical grin took over his face.

"How would you know about his shop?"

"How do you think? I couldn't have just anyone work on Priscilla." He gave me an ornery smirk. "I used to ride her every weekend."

"Priscilla . . . is a *motorcycle*?" My thoughts tumbled around, remembering all of his references to that name and their trips across the country. "I thought she was your wife?"

"My wife?" He let out a wild laugh. "My wife was named Margie. And she didn't care much for Priscilla. Said I was going to end up with half a brain left in my head."

"But when you talked about . . . I'm confused. Never mind. So where's Priscilla now?"

That whimsical grin returned. "Well, I reckon she's sitting out there at the kennel with your boy. Orville had spent so much time putting her back together through the years. He was just as fond of her as me. When I couldn't ride her anymore, he wanted Priscilla as a birthday present for his grandson. And I thought, that's where she belongs, with some young'un who could give her the road time she deserves."

I was stunned. As the reality of his words settled into my heart, I leaned back against the couch holding the deck of cards to my chest.

"Maybe one day he can take her back out," I mumbled.

"Make sure he takes you with him. Oh, the memories. Nothing but wind and speed on the road. You'll love her."

"Yeah, I'm sure I will."

CHAPTER 25

Emma

BY THE TIME I GOT OUT OF MY CAR, HE WAS ALREADY COMING down the steps of the trailer. I'd missed Wyatt, every broody, rotten, sweet piece of him. If I could run, I would've run in a dead sprint. But I didn't have to. Wyatt walked quickly to me, wearing a grin as big as any I'd ever seen from him. His arms came around me. My body lifted up from the ground as he crushed me to his chest, leaving my feet dangling against his knees. I felt every inch of him pressing into my skin under the sticky summer sun.

"I missed you," he whispered next to my ear.

I wanted to wrap my legs around his waist, but the new brace still restricted my knee from bending in that direction. And my physical therapist might just kill me.

Wyatt backed me up against the hood of the car. The hot metal burned a little as I sat on the edge. As our lips found each other, I no longer cared about the slight scorches on my dangling legs. My mouth opened, letting his tongue slip inside and drag slowly out to my lips. His fingers gripped my butt cheeks, pulling me closer until my thighs split and I straddled his hips.

"How's your knee?" he asked as he moved his lips down my neck. "Does it hurt like this?"

"No," I managed to say. Every time he kissed me, I swear all rationale left my brain. I wanted him and he needed me. Wyatt transferred all his pain and loneliness into a mind-blowing physical explosion—and I didn't really think that was such a terrible thing.

His hand moved up my waist and slipped in between us and over my breasts. He cupped me through the T-shirt, rubbing lightly with his thumb, over and over again as his mouth sucked on my bottom lip. Wyatt tugged the low V-neckline of my pink shirt until my left breast was free and he pressed his lips against the lacy fabric. Only a few delicate flowers composed of tiny threads separated his tongue from my skin.

Wyatt pushed his hips tighter against me. My fingers dug into his shoulders, and I held onto his body as he made my insides experience things I didn't know were possible.

Five minutes ago, I was missing Wyatt and now he was holding me, kissing me, touching me, setting my body on fire—and then he stilled. Wyatt lifted his head up, letting his forehead rest against mine. He let out a deep breath. "I told myself I wasn't going to do this when you got here."

His voice had a painful catch to it. I stared into his eyes, trying to let him know it was okay. He could kiss me, hold me, take my clothes off—preferably not on the hood of my car, but inside his trailer would be just fine.

"It's okay, you know." I ran a finger over his cheek, feeling the smooth skin covered with faint stubble. "To want me that way."

"I know. Just not yet. Not like this." His warm breath drifted slowly over my skin. "We are just getting started. I want us to be different than all that shit I did in the past. Because you are different. I've never had this part with someone. And I want this part with you. The beginning stuff. The stuff that is supposed to happen before sex."

Wyatt pulled my shirt back up before releasing me. He backed away, and I sat on the hood alone. Hearing his words made me fall for Wyatt just a little bit more. I understood completely as his eyes held onto mine, showing his tormented thoughts full of pain and desire.

"I want that too," I reassured him.

He smiled, letting his dimples take over his cheeks. And then he leaned forward, touching me with nothing but his lips. Wyatt kissed me softly, and I melted all over again. His sweet, simple kiss burned me just as hot as the one before, because I knew that simple kiss came filled with his actual emotions—deep ones that I'd tried to pull out of him all summer.

He released my lips slowly and backed away. "That's the way it was supposed to go instead of mauling you in the driveway."

Even though he put a stop to our makeout session, his earlier thoughts were still very obvious as his eyes traveled over my whole body. Wyatt had decided not to touch me—just torture me with those looks. He lifted my foot up, looking at my knee. "So that's the new brace? It doesn't look that much better. When do they set you free for good?"

"I don't know. Depends on the physical therapist. He's holding me hostage." Yesterday, the therapist had removed the giant black contraption and replaced it with something about half its size.

"But you are doing what he says?"

"Yes," I answered, but Wyatt's eyes narrowed. "You don't believe me."

"You seem to do whatever you want despite what other people tell you to do. So I'm not sure."

I got off the hood of the car and walked slowly over to him. "I promise. I'm doing everything by the book. If I wasn't, then I would've driven out here, like, five days ago." I gazed up into his eyes and whispered, "I missed you too. And I was worried."

His eyes filled with a mix of sadness and longing. I figured in my absence, demons had filled his lonely days. Wyatt cleared his throat. "So school started back?"

"Yeah. A couple of days ago. Blaire had to help me get to my chemistry class, but I should be able to go on my own with the new brace. I go back to the bookstore tomorrow. They are going to let me sit on a stool and just work the register."

He nodded. Our conversation seemed to lull, making me want to kiss him again. I glanced at his lips, so soft and puckered. They traveled up to his eyes, which held mine. His haunting gaze was truly the window to his soul.

"Oh, I brought you something." I grinned.

"You shouldn't bring me stuff."

"Why?"

I waited for his reply, but he didn't answer. Wyatt got a little fidgety, twisting his eyebrows up. Something was eating away at him. Wyatt seemed at a loss for words, struggling with the casual conversion. Kissing was easy. Talking—well, that was a whole other beast.

I went over to the car and pulled out my surprises. Tucking the book under my armpit, I held a small paper bag against my chest with my wrist and a Styrofoam cup in each hand. "I brought dinner."

Wyatt seemed conflicted as I carried everything over to him. I grinned, trying to loosen up the sudden seriousness that coated the air around us. I gestured to the Sonic Drive-In cup. "It's Cherry Coke. I thought everyone likes cherry."

"Yeah, I like cherry," he muttered, playing along with my joke about the last time I'd tried this with him. Wyatt took both drinks from me. "What's in the sack?"

"I thought you should eat something besides hot dogs. That's disgusting, by the way. So I brought hamburgers. Not that it's super nutritious. But it's better than hot dogs. Oh, and some tator tots. You like those, right?"

He let out a deep breath and nodded. "Yeah, I like tator tots."

"So do you actually like the food I saw in the refrigerator or is that the only thing they will buy you?" I asked as I followed him up the steps and inside the trailer.

"It's just easier." He sat the cups down on the coffee table and took the bag from my hands. "Diana brings my supplies. I just wanted to make it as simple as possible."

"I see." We both sat down on the couch, leaving about a foot between us. I pulled out the book. "Here's your surprise."

I passed the paperback over to him. He took it cautiously from my hand like it was rat poison. "It's just a book, Wyatt. I thought you might like a new one."

"Emma, I can't get you anything. So I don't want you bringing me stuff. Not even books."

"It's okay."

"No, it's not." He let out a deep breath, closing his eyes for a moment. I felt sorry for him, watching the struggle go on right in front of me. I reached over and slipped my fingers between his. After a moment, Wyatt looked at me again. "What's the book about?"

I paused, seeing he was trying to put aside his reservations. "Well . . . it's about these aliens, I think. And they take over people's minds, but not everyone's. And I think there's a love story between this girl who gets possessed and this guy who wants to hate her because she's possessed. But he, like, falls in love with her anyway. And eventually doesn't care that she's possessed. I think they may save the world."

"Sounds interesting." He laughed faintly.

"Are you making fun of my book?"

"No." He grinned before breaking out in a deep, throaty

chuckle.

His laugher filled my chest with happiness. I rolled my eyes and teased him. "It's supposed to be good. I promise. And you like Stephen King. I thought it sounded Stephen King-ish."

"Okay, I'm sure it is Stephen *King-ish.*"

And then my heart melted a little, seeing him struggle to contain his laughter again. But he couldn't. His chest moved up and down as he laughed at my present. I wanted to see Wyatt this way—all the time, every day—full of these kinds of emotions instead of the ones that ripped him apart.

I leaned over, placing a chaste kiss against his mouth. He caught my bottom lip between his, making it last a little longer.

"Thank you," he whispered. And I didn't know if his gratitude was about the ridiculous book, the food, or the fact that I gave a crap about him.

"I don't know about you, but I like my cheese melted and it's getting cold." I pulled away and picked up the silver-wrapped hamburger. I opened the corner and looked inside. "That one is yours."

He seemed puzzled when I handed it over to him. "So what do you think I like on my burgers?"

"You seemed like a pickle-only guy. With mustard. I know—a gamble, right?"

He held my gaze for a moment. "Good call. How did you figure out the mustard?"

"All those nasty hot dogs. You had to be a mustard guy."

He laughed again. "That's funny. So what's on yours?"

"Guess," I teased.

"Lettuce and tomato since you are concerned about my nutrition."

"Keep going."

"Pickles. With mayo?"

"So close. Ketchup. Keep going?" I held up the stacked burger so he could get a better look at it.

"What? How could there be something else?"

"Well, I kind of cheated this time." I gave him a flirty smile. "I got a jalapeno, mushroom, and cheese burger. The Sizzling Summer Special."

"That's gross."

"Says the guy who lives on processed pig organs."

He rolled his eyes. I took a bite of my burger, chewing on the gooey, stacked mess. Out of the corner of my eye, I watched Wyatt take his first bite. His face drifted off into a slow trance of pleasure. I smiled to myself. I would have to do this more often. Just force it on Wyatt, knowing I would be met with resistance followed by this kind of payoff: forgotten happiness.

We finished off the burger and fought over the last tator tot. I gave it to him, while he wanted me to have it. I won, of course. And I got to see him enjoy the serendipitous moment of eating the last crunchy fried potato covered in ketchup.

After dinner, I followed him outside to the kennel. It was getting close to dark. Wyatt hadn't fed the dogs yet since I'd interrupted his late-afternoon schedule. I helped fill the bowls with food and water, pausing occasionally to scratch the irresistible faces.

When Wyatt had told me about Ricky Bobby, I expected to feel a rush of sadness, but I didn't. He was such a crazy character, and I knew a family of three boys could wear down all that energy. After all, adoption was the goal of the rescue. Find a place better than where they had come from. Find a place better than being stuck in here.

"Hey, do you need to leave?" I heard his voice behind me. Wyatt slipped his hands around my waist, pulling my back tight against his chest. I'm not sure if I would ever leave him if given a choice.

"I can stay a few more hours."

He let out a deep breath that I knew was a sigh of relief. Wyatt continued to hold on like he was afraid to let go. Our difficult reality would always be just on the edge, surrounding each visit. I knew this was our future—at least for a couple more years. I just hoped Wyatt continued to get better and not worse.

"Okay, I'll be right back." He released the gripping hold on my body and walked out the side door. He quickly returned, carrying a familiar book, but not the one about the aliens.

"I figured you would've finished *Call of the Wild* several weeks ago."

His grin faltered. "I couldn't bring myself to finish it without you."

"Oh." We stared at each other for a moment, lost in the thoughts of those weeks after he'd thrown me out of his trailer. I knew that time had played a toll on Wyatt, pushing him down even further into the darkness. "Well, I'm pretty sure you promised to read to me that night too—when you felt better. So you better get your game face on. I expect earth-shattering spectacular."

"Okay." He seemed to relax again, hearing the teasing side come back between us.

"How does this work in here? Where do you normally sit?"

"Different places. Lately I've been next to Cye's pen."

"Okay. Well, I'm getting Charlie out. I think he needs a good cuddling."

Making my way down the aisle, I heard Wyatt getting situated on the other end. I watched him for a moment as he spread a blanket across the cement. He messed with the edges, trying to make it perfect. He moved over to the wall panel by the door. The lights dimmed as he flicked off most of them in the room, sending us into a shadowy darkness with the exception of the spot where he planned to read.

I lifted Charlie up from the ground, cradling him in my arms. I made my way slowly down to Cye's pen. Wyatt helped me get settled down between his legs. Leaning back, I rested my head against his chest. I felt his lips brush the back of my neck as he planted a kiss. And then another, letting his lips linger. I smelled of dogs and sweat, but I'm sure he didn't care.

Wyatt put the book in front of us, turning to the page where I'd left off the night he'd gotten sick. His sexy, raspy voice carried throughout the building. He sounded better than I'd imagined—so articulate and full of passion. Wyatt held on to each word as his breath came in waves next to my cheek.

The rustling noises in the kennels settled down. Across the aisle, Lola crawled into her bed. Indy stretched out against the cement in his pen. I scratched Charlie behind those giant ears as he slept stretched across both of our thighs. The whole room seemed to breathe together in peace.

Wyatt paused and whispered faintly next to my ear, "Wait for it."

From behind us, I heard a stirring. I wanted to turn around and see what was going on, but I knew it would disrupt the natural progression of whatever Wyatt had put in motion. He continued to speak, letting his voice become consumed with the story. I listened until I fell deep into my own trance and my eyes drifted closed. He was a gifted storyteller, speaking the words of Jack London, making them come alive in the darkness.

Wyatt took my hand and moved it slowly behind us. My fingers brushed the side of his T-shirt, and then I felt the soft hair of a dog. *Cye.*

As the powerful story of a dog named Buck mesmerized a room full of animals, one in particular had found the strength to let go of his fears. Cye pressed himself against Wyatt's back with the safety of the fence separating them.

My small hand fit through the metal wire. Cye remained still as I scratched his head. My fingers brushed over the dents in his skull. My breath held for a moment, embracing the magnitude of the moment. The poor dog, who had suffered at the hands of a vile and evil man with a hammer, had finally allowed me to touch him.

Tears beaded up in the corners of my eyes. The rehabilitation had moved at a snail's pace. Not very many people possessed the patience to keep helping an animal like him. But in my book, it showed Wyatt's inner heart.

While I'd never given up on Wyatt, he'd never given up on Cye.

I pulled my hand out, leaving the dog alone to his peaceful slumber. I settled back against Wyatt's chest, feeling it move up and down as he spoke the words.

And I knew in that moment, I was in love with Wyatt Carter, in every way a girl could be in love with someone else: mind, body, heart, and soul.

CHAPTER 26

Emma

OVER THE NEXT SEVERAL WEEKS, MY LIFE SHIFTED INTO A pattern of school, work, and Wyatt. The therapist released me from his clutches, leaving me with just an elastic brace. I started my shifts again at the nursing home and my tea sessions with the girls.

Vera forced me to sit for an additional three hours on my first visit. I got updated on all the gossip about the evil grandson with the debutant wife and how Mr. Robson sneaked into Hazel's room last week when he was supposed to attend movie night with JoAnna. It was like I'd missed a whole month of *Real Housewives of Shady Pines*.

Blaire and I were forced to come up with a car schedule since she'd decided driving was tolerable and she wasn't going to die in the few blocks we lived from campus. Sometimes she dropped me off at work and sometimes we fought over me taking the car to Wyatt's trailer "*again*" as she liked to add.

After all these years, I had to admit—I didn't like sharing the car. Not one bit. But deep down, I was happy for Blaire because

I loved her. And I wanted my sister to succeed in life, which required driving on her own. However, it was just another thing I had to schedule around my visits to Wyatt.

Despite the car situation, I saw him as much as possible. Each time, we discovered a little more about each other. Sometimes joking and laughing, and then sometimes, I still couldn't get him to talk at all.

I don't know what triggered those moments. Occasionally, I would find Wyatt in his trailer, zoned out with a wild spark in his eyes. And I would wrap my arms around his body as he clung to me in his gray silence. Those were the days that made it hard to leave him.

I pulled into the apartment complex, hauling a trunk full of our groceries, the items on the list from Mr. Hughes, and the food I bought to take out to Wyatt. It wasn't the first time I'd purchased stuff for his trailer. He hated it. But I told him it was my food and his stubborn choice. He could choose to have some or just watch me eat it.

I popped the trunk but stayed sitting in my seat, thinking about him and the haunting eyes that had watched me leave this afternoon. Just when I thought Wyatt was getting better, he'd experienced a day like today. I wish he would tell me what set off those depressing moments that made me worry about his sanity. Instead, he swore everything was fine, making my heart ache for his tormented one.

Pushing open the driver's side door, I went to the trunk and slipped a few bags over my wrists. It would take multiple trips with this much food.

"Let me help you."

I froze out of instinct, hearing Kurt's voice come up behind me. After he drove me to the hospital, I hadn't seen much of him.

He made an appearance when necessary. Even when I hand-delivered the rent check last week, he'd been polite. Maybe my stumble down the staircase had given him a good scare—enough to forget his curiosity in me.

"Thank you," I muttered.

He grabbed several bags and followed behind me to the stairs. "Sure is a lot food for a little thing like you."

And here we go. "I grocery shop for other people."

"You buying stuff for someone besides that old man up there? Got someone stuffed in that apartment with you? That's against your lease, you know."

He stayed close on my heels as I went slowly up the stairs. "Yes, Kurt. Blaire and I have an entire motorcycle gang living with us in our apartment. Do you charge by the person or by the night or by the hour?"

He snorted. "I might have to check that shit out, you know. I'd like to see that weird sister of yours wrapped up with some biker."

I didn't mean to laugh, but the idea sounded pretty funny to me too. I was still chuckling as Blaire opened the door and quickly moved out of the way as we came inside the apartment together. She eyed Kurt, shooting daggers as he set the bags on the counter.

"I . . . um . . . thanks for the help." I gave a quick dismissal to our apartment manager, feeling suddenly aware of him inside our home.

"All right. I'll get out of your way."

Neither of us spoke as he walked toward the door. As soon as it shut, Blaire ran over and clicked the deadbolt. Not that it mattered. The guy had a key.

"What was that about? You were laughing with him." She plopped down on the couch, watching me unpack the groceries. Her blue crocheted hat covered the top part of her fuzzy hair while the rest hung in clumps around her shoulders.

"I don't know. Kurt's been decent lately, and he offered to help me."

"Hmm." She smirked. "He's just happy that you didn't turn him into the police."

I stopped mid-sack with a can of green beans in my hand. "For the last time. Kurt didn't push me down the stairs."

"Riiight." She pulled her computer off the couch cushion and placed it in her lap. I stood there for a moment, watching her type while my fingers tightened around the can.

I walked over in front of her. "I'm tired of you implying that I'm some idiot who let a guy push her down the stairs."

"I didn't say you were an idiot. I just think you are oblivious sometimes. And I have to be aware of things for the both of us."

"I don't think that's true."

"Really? Let's see. You have Kurt thinking his behavior is okay and he's going to start getting close to you again, little by little, until something else happens. Or maybe you get knocked up by Wyatt. Maybe that will happen first. You don't think twice about that kind of stuff. You'd do anything to help him. But how will he help *you* with a baby? The guy is stuck out there in some shit-hole with a court-mandated ankle monitor while you flitter around him."

"That's enough, Blaire." I felt a flash of true anger at my sister. "Wyatt is not going to get me pregnant and then abandon me."

"It only takes once, Emma. And we all know how you get too comfortable with things. It's how you *fell* down the stairs."

I struggled to keep my patience by picturing a deserted island with a single palm tree. My feet walked through the sand as the tide washed up around me. But then Blaire appeared out of nowhere—our internal twin connection, bringing her along to my peaceful retreat. So I imagined the palm tree falling on her.

The thought startled me back to reality. I just mentally crushed my sister with a tree. Letting out a deep breath, I clenched the can tighter in my palm. "I'm safe, Blaire. Nothing is going to happen to me. You don't have to get so worried."

"Whatever. Your ability to be oblivious to the world is going to catch up to you one day." She mumbled something under her breath that sounded like, "And I'm not taking care of some baby."

She fiddled with her laptop while I continued to stand in front of her. I guess that was her way of dismissing me back to unloading *our* groceries. Blaire typed something quickly, cutting her eyes up at me. "*What?*"

I leaned over the top of the screen to see why my continued presence seemed to agitate her. "What are you doing?"

The lid slammed closed, almost hitting me in the nose on the way down. Her eyes were level with mine as we stared at each other. "None of your damn business."

"But my life is yours?"

"Forget I even said anything." Blaire jumped up from the couch, grabbing her laptop. "You always do whatever the hell you want anyway—regardless of what I say. So just continue to live in your bubble with the birds chirping around you while you skip through the forest. Oh, wait. That would be some nasty dirt road in the woods to see a convict."

My jaw hung open a little as Blaire and her irrational thoughts stormed off to her bedroom—and mine went to Wyatt. I wasn't wrong about my relationship with him. I was good for him. He needed me, and helping people was the right thing to do. I knew without a shadow of a doubt I was supposed to save him. Because he needed saving more than any person I had ever met.

And besides, that part of our relationship had not changed. Wyatt always kept himself in check while in the trailer, even though it turned into something else when he walked me to my car. Sometimes it took five minutes to leave and sometimes it took thirty as he pressed me against the car door.

I guess it made him feel safer if he touched me in the driveway rather than on his couch. Either way, I think the impending loneliness triggered the desperate moments from him. The more he thought about me leaving, the more he clung to my skin and my lips.

Going back into the kitchen, I separated the groceries out, making a sack to take to his house. After his terrible day, I knew Wyatt needed me tonight for nothing more than my physical presence as I slept next to him.

I had yet to tell Wyatt that I loved him. Sometimes I wanted to share the depth of my feelings as a way to comfort him. And sometimes the words almost slipped out as his lips rubbed over my skin. But I knew those feelings needed to be reserved for the right time—when he was ready, when I knew Wyatt wouldn't lash out.

Our conversations were never angry or hurtful, but I'd never said those significant words. Saying "I love you" might make Wyatt kiss me, scream, and yell, or just break down crying.

I'd seen him cry twice on those random nights when I'd slept beside him. Once he'd shaken the bed as his shoulders clinched up in some muscle convulsion. And the other time, it had been in silence as hot tears ran down his cheeks, leaving giant wet spots on the pillow. Honestly, I'm not sure if Wyatt was even aware of the episodes. And that bothered me more than if he'd just broken down in front of me.

I gathered up the two sacks for Mr. Hughes and the one for Wyatt. I slammed the front door hard behind me, making sure Blaire knew I was headed to Wyatt's trailer *again.*

CHAPTER 27

Emma

I SHIFTED AROUND ON HIS COUCH, TRYING TO GET COMFORTABLE. I had chemistry homework strung out across the cushions and the coffee table. Sometimes it was either a choice of visiting Wyatt or doing equations. So I started combining them into one and the same. He usually disappeared outside when I brought my backpack, poking his head back inside the door ever so often to check on me.

And right on cue, the aluminum door cracked open and I saw his brown head look around the corner. He smiled at my obvious frustration.

"Still not going good?" he asked, coming into the living room and sitting down in his old chair.

"Uh, no. Are you sure you know nothing about chemistry?"

"Positive."

I fussed with the question a little longer, applying my eraser more than the lead. Glancing up, his gaze was still on me. He grinned, letting his dimples burn into his cheeks.

I play-frowned at his flirting. "I can't concentrate with you staring at me. I have to get this done before my study group tonight."

"Why do you have to take chemistry anyway?"

"Because I'm applying to a program that requires it." Sometimes he asked me questions about my classes, and I wondered if he missed school. Or maybe he associated all of his time there as the *unapologetically sad* guy.

I leaned back against the cushion. "Do you ever think about going back to school?"

"I don't know." His voice grated slightly on the words as his smile faded.

"You finished three semesters, right?"

"Yeah." He looked down at the floor.

"Did you have a major?"

He shrugged. "Not really."

"Oh." I figured it was best to let this one go. I turned my attention back to the equation. One more eraser mark, and I would have a hole in the paper.

Out of the corner of my eye, I saw Wyatt get up from the chair. He went into the kitchen, opening the cabinet to retrieve two mugs. Pushing the Folgers container over to the side, he grabbed my bag of fancy hazelnut coffee. I smiled to myself, seeing what he was doing.

I went back to making a hole in my paper as the room filled with the smell of the dark brew. Hearing a slight clinking noise, I sneaked another glace over to the kitchen. Wyatt was carefully stirring my container of liquid creamer into *both* cups. I had to bite the side of my cheek to keep from laughing. I knew he liked that stuff.

As he turned around, I looked quickly back down at my paper. I didn't want Wyatt to know I'd been watching him.

"Come on. Break time." He gestured toward the door. Gus and Gatsby beat me to it. I crawled off the couch, feeling the ache in my leg. I had sat there, twisted up like a pretzel, for over two hours.

Wyatt sat down on the small steps, and I squished in beside him, feeling my right hip smash against his. Summer had ended several weeks ago, and the chill of the fall breeze blew through the air. I snuggled closer to the side of his body since I didn't wear a jacket outside.

Handing me one of the cups, Wyatt put his left arm around my shoulders, pulling me tighter against his warm sweatshirt. I sipped on the sweet coffee. A wet nose pushed at my leg. I reached down, taking the tennis ball from Gus, tossing it out in the dirt driveway. He ran like a flash of lightning, and returned with it clamped between his teeth before I could even take another sip.

Wyatt chuckled beside me. "Remember, you started it."

"How can I say no to him?"

"Well, he's an addict, and tennis balls are his crack."

"That's because you spend all your time out in the kennel with the others."

"That's not true. Besides, he sleeps with me. What more does he need?" Wyatt pushed his nose into the side of my hair, letting his lips hover before pressing a warm kiss against my neck. His mouth moved an inch lower as the electric energy seemed to pick up between us.

So I nudged him a bit. "You should take Gus running with you instead of going by yourself in the mornings."

He let out a deep breath, and my body soaked up the warmth as it drifted over my skin. "You know why I go alone."

"Just think about it." I tossed the ball again, putting my full arm into the throw so it bounced across the dirt and into the grass. I gave Gatsby a scratch on top of the head. His old body was stretched out on the ground next to the stairs, completely oblivious to Gus and his addiction.

"Okay," Wyatt finally muttered. Sometimes he just needed a

small push to see things a little differently.

Taking another sip, the hot liquid rolled down my throat. I leaned over, letting my head rest against his shoulder. "Thank you for the coffee. I needed this."

Wyatt's hand moved down my back and held onto the side of my waist. He pulled me even tighter to his body, placing another kiss just below my ear. Reaching down, I set my cup on the step below us. I circled my arms around his stomach, burying my face into his chest. My nose filled with the scent of laundry detergent and the soap he'd used in the shower.

Gus nudged at our legs with the yellow ball. Wyatt's chest moved a little as he laughed. "Told you."

He threw it this time, jostling me a little in the process. I loved these moments with Wyatt. So simple and peaceful. Maybe I really didn't need all of that other stuff that went along with dating. Maybe I told the truth when I said it was overrated. Wyatt and I didn't need the rest of the world. Except that wasn't the truth. I still saw the outside world every day, and he didn't see anything but here.

"Do you miss things?" I whispered into the soft folds of his sweatshirt.

"Things?"

"I don't know. Like doing stuff and going places. Things."

Wyatt rested his chin on top of my head. "I try not to think about that kind of stuff. I guess it defeats the point. Don't you think?"

Given the opportunity, I gave him another small nudge. "No. I think it's okay to miss things. Or wish you could do things."

"I miss you when you're not here."

Wyatt knew just how to get me right in the heart. I was tempted to give in to his sweet answer, but I tried to push one last time. I lifted up my head and looked Wyatt in the eye. "I miss you too. But that's not what I mean. Wanting to do something and actually doing it are two different things. You focus so much on trying to deprive yourself of things on purpose. It's okay to talk about what you want or what you miss. It doesn't mean you are going to run over the fence line and break the rules. But I think talking about this stuff helps calm some of those thoughts that twist around in your head."

My tiny, delicate nudge had transcended into a full-on shove. When he didn't answer, I chose not to push him any further. I didn't want it to come across as an attack.

Wyatt got that look again, where he seemed to drift away into another dimension. I didn't interrupt like I'd done in the past. Instead, I studied his eyes as they hung open wide, staring off into the distance.

Maybe this was too much for him to discuss with me today, but I knew my hypothetical question had sparked somewhere in his twisty thoughts. Wyatt needed to come to terms with his *actual* punishment and the difference in levels of restrictions he'd chosen to impose on himself. But I knew none of those issues would be resolved in an afternoon or even a week.

I leaned over, taking the ball from Gus, tossing it out into the grass. I cuddled up against Wyatt's warm sweatshirt again. His chest moved in ragged breaths under my cheek. I held on to his body as the conflicts wrestled to some form of a conclusion inside his head.

"I miss riding my bike." His voice came out soft.

The revelation startled my thoughts and warmed my heart as I imagined him on Priscilla. I'd told Wyatt about Mr. Hughes a few weeks ago. He didn't say much at the time. I think it had bothered him to be gifted with something so significant from another person. The bike had meant a lot when it had come from his grandfather. Now it had an ironic sentimental tie from someone in my own life. Maybe he didn't feel worthy. Or maybe he just hated talking about the outside world.

"I miss going to the movies," he continued. "The giant screen. And the noise. I have always liked the way loud movies make your seat shake like you are literally standing in the middle of whatever you are seeing on the screen. I liked that part the best. Even more than the popcorn. But I miss that too. I swear I can smell it right now."

I held onto his body, listening to his words and smelling the scent of butter. His voice always had the ability to bring the imaginary to life. When he read his stories—and even now when he told me his secrets.

"And playing football," he spoke again with a soft, nostalgic ache. "I always loved the simple act of playing the game. Way before the whole crowd thing. But I liked all that shit too. I loved playing in the stadium. The way it sounded, hearing everyone stomping in the bleachers, chanting all that "go team" shit—chanting my name. You get this high unlike anything you can imagine. Thousands of people who love you. And they know nothing about you. But they love you anyway."

He paused, resting his chin on my head again. "And they can just as easily hate you. Thousands of people who know nothing about you. I deserved the love or at least I thought I did when I was scoring points. And I deserved the hate too when I screwed it all up."

I had come to realize the pain in Wyatt had many layers. He blamed himself for the accident, yet it also hurt to have others blame him too. And I think he felt some twisted guilt about those thoughts. He felt guilty for being hurt by their hate.

"And I miss seeing the texts from Trevor." My heart immediately clenched, hearing the raspy catch in his throat. "He always sent the craziest shit after he heard my score on the college games. He was always rooting for me. All the way back here even though Trevor never saw one of my games."

His voice faded out, haunting the quiet air. And I couldn't

bear to look at him. I didn't know what to say to the answers he'd given to my question. Wyatt had made progress, at least to me it was progress. Gus pushed the ball to me again, and I took it from the little Jack Russell without throwing it.

"I want to go sky-diving," he muttered.

I sat straight up and stared at him. "Sky-diving?"

"Yeah, Trevor, Marcus, and I tried to go once. But we got drunk in the parking lot, and they wouldn't let us go up. Trevor had always talked about going back, but we never did."

"So you've never jumped?"

"No," he muttered. "You said *want.* That's what I want to do. I want to feel that kind of freedom, falling through the clouds, seeing the world float below me. I bet it's an unbelievable high. Maybe even better than a whole stadium of people shouting your name."

He paused, letting the thoughts cloud his green eyes. "What do you think about that, Emma?"

I clutched the yellow ball in my fingers, feeling Gus paw at my hand. "What do I think about you sky-diving?"

"No, um, what do you think about going?"

"Like, with you?" I stared at him, feeling my heart beat faster in my chest.

"Yeah."

"Are you asking me?" And my breath caught. Because it was the first time Wyatt had acknowledged anything about our future. He seemed to accept me in the *now*, but we had never talked about what happens *after*.

"Yes." For a moment, the ghosts of the past seemed to disappear. His lips rolled into a faint grin, letting me see his dimples. "Emma Sawyer. Would you jump out of a plane with me?"

I weighted the sincerity of his question and decided to push him just a step further. "On one condition. You put your request in writing."

"Seriously? You'd jump with me? You're not scared?"

"Seriously? You're going to put it in writing? A commitment to me for something on the other side of this?" Our eyes locked for a moment, and I knew the struggle was still very much alive in his head even with the dimples shining from his cheeks.

"Yes," he finally answered.

"Okay then. I'll be right back." I jumped up before he could change his mind. Going inside the trailer, I came back with my notebook. I wrote the following and handed it over for Wyatt to sign.

I, Wyatt Carter, commit to jumping out of an airplane with Emma Sawyer.

Wyatt scribbled his name below the words. I saw his handwriting for the first time, and it wasn't surprising. The letters were all squished together like he gripped the pen with the intensity of a grizzly bear.

I signed below his name and looked up, catching his gaze. "Well, I guess I will see you on the other side then, Wyatt."

"Yeah, I guess it's a date."

He seemed a little torn at the realization. Pulling me into a tight bear hug, his fingers pressed into my skin. I struggled to breathe as his emotions transferred into the tight embrace. Wyatt and I stayed like that until my coffee got cold and Gus gave up on the ball.

"I need to go to my study group," I whispered.

"Okay." He reluctantly released me. "Go get your stuff together. I'm going to stay here."

Going back into the trailer, I shoved all my papers into my backpack and paused before leaving. I hated this part. When I walked out the door, I would see his face. He always tried to hide his thoughts, but it was impossible for me not to see them written so clearly on his cheeks. Wyatt did this every time I got in my car, every time I drove away back into the world, leaving him standing alone in his dirt driveway.

Taking a deep breath, I gathered a big smile and turned the knob. "So you gonna walk me to my door or what?"

Getting up from the steps, he gave me that heartbreaking grin, taking my backpack from my hand. "What do you got in here? Rocks?"

"No. I shoved several of those cow skulls inside from the gate entrance. I'm taking them back to scare Blaire. You know, like the horse head in *The Godfather* movie."

Wyatt carried my backpack as I followed him out to the car. His eyes studied me like he wasn't sure if I was kidding. "I um . . . okay?"

"Go ahead. You know you want to look."

"I'm just going to pretend you didn't put one in here." He chuckled, putting the bag in the passenger's seat. "You know. I have never seen *The Godfather.*"

"Really? I thought that would be one of your favorites. You seem like a Mario Puzo fan."

"So you've watched it?"

"Well, not exactly."

"I didn't think so, you little liar." He smirked. "Well, I may not have seen the movie either. But I read the book."

"Ha. I knew you were a fan." I leaned up on my tiptoes, laughing right into his face. He leaned forward, capturing my lips with his mouth. And then his hands pulled my body to him.

Everything between us did a one-eighty from sweet and joking to a needy burn. His lips moved slowly, drawing out each pass so they took twice as long. Every tiny movement amplified as Wyatt took his time, touching my mouth, stroking back and forth with his tongue.

I leaned into him, wrapping my arms around his neck, digging my fingers into his shoulders as I tried not to fall over from the cloudy thoughts in my head. I turned my cheek to the side, gasping for air. I knew he did it on purpose. The more I was wrapped up and consumed with the taste of his mouth, the slower it took for me to get in my car—to the point I almost forgot about even leaving.

Wyatt rubbed his hands over my waist, pulling me tighter against his chest. I took a step back and gave him a sly grin. "Hold on."

His fingers clenched into my skin before releasing my body. Reaching behind me, I opened the door to the backseat of the car. I sat on the edge of the soft cushion with my feet dangling outside. I tugged his hand.

His eyes held my gaze as a thousand thoughts circled around inside his head. "Come on. Don't overthink it. Just get in here with me. I don't bite."

Letting go of his hand, I scooted inside the car, lying down on my back. Wyatt hesitated in the doorframe before climbing inside. Our bodies shifted around in the tight space of the backseat. My elbow hit the seatbelt buckle, causing me to squeal. And I couldn't help myself from giggling as Wyatt's head whacked the side of the other door before we got situated, but that didn't stop our lips from finding each other again.

They moved softly over my cheek, nibbling on my ear as he whispered, "You may not bite, but I do."

His teeth teased at my earlobe, making me smile. My fingers traced over the side of his jaw as Wyatt kissed me full on the mouth, sucking on my lower lip. It was easy to get lost in these feelings. These moments of abandonment, the overwhelming physical pull that came alive as our bodies squirmed to get closer.

Wyatt slid his hand up the side of my black yoga pants, pulling my leg over his thigh. "I like these."

"Because it lets you grab my butt easier."

"I don't do that," he whispered with a hazy grin.

"You do too. And when I first started coming out here, you

used to watch me walk to the car, staring right at it. Even when you acted like a jerk, you still liked to look at my butt."

"I'm not an ass man. I was afraid you would fall down on the driveway."

"And I look at your lips because I'm afraid they are going to fall off your face. And I kiss them like this." I pressed my mouth to his. "To make sure they stay on tight."

His lips latched onto mine as his fingers moved over the soft fabric of the pants until he grabbed my round butt cheek, squeezing lightly. Wyatt pulled me tighter against his hips as my leg curved around his thigh, keeping me in place.

In the nights I'd slept beside Wyatt, he'd held me, but he didn't touch me. Not like this. Those moments were different because he needed someone to chase the ghosts away. But in the backseat of my car, I closed my eyes and let him touch me, feel me, want me with the burning desire of a person craving another person.

And I liked it. I liked it so very much that I forgot about the kennel and my study group. I forgot everything except the touch of his lips and his hands as they rubbed against my body.

Wyatt traced his nose down the side of my cheek, leaving faint kisses on my neck. His hands ran under my shirt. They trailed over my breasts and stomach. Every brush of his fingers caused warm sparks to shoot under my skin. I wrapped my legs around his hips as he rocked slowly, back and forth against my body. Each time he made contact, I let out a faint little gasp. I had on every stitch of clothing, yet I was about to lose my entire sense of time and place.

His breath floated over my skin as his mouth found mine again. Wyatt slipped his tongue inside my lips. And he was touching me. Each place registering separately until my senses exploded and I felt him everywhere. A faint gasp escaped my lips. And I couldn't get enough. I wiggled as close as I could to his body as he rubbed against me.

Wyatt pulled back a little, staring me in the eye. I didn't want him to stop touching me. I needed him to keep touching me. He held my gaze, and then his hand slipped slowly over my stomach and down between us. My eyes closed as his fingers moved against the yoga pants, touching me, over and over again, and then I lost it altogether. As my body drifted away, a smile formed on my lips. I relaxed, savoring the moment. And then I got embarrassed. And then I was falling.

My eyes shot open, and I grabbed at his body, but my hip whacked the back of the front console and I landed on my back in the floorboard. Wyatt looked down at me and started laughing. I tried to rise up, but I was stuck. The more I tried to move, the louder he laughed until I was giggling with him.

"Stop laughing. You have to get me out of here. I'm stuck."

He climbed out of the car and extended a hand down to where I was lying on the floor. After a couple of pulls, he had me dislodged from the disgraceful pile of twisted limbs.

He wrapped his arms around me, staring in my eyes as his tried to hold back the laughter. "You okay?"

"Yeah." I nodded.

He grinned, rubbing his nose down mine until the ends touched.

"I like this before stuff," he whispered.

"Me too."

The longer we stared at each other, the more his lips turned serious. "You're going to be late to your study group."

"I know," I whispered.

But we didn't let go. We held on for another five minutes until I was the first to break contact. I didn't whisper goodbye. And neither did Wyatt. Sometimes saying goodbye was harder than saying nothing at all.

CHAPTER 28

Emma

MY EYES GLAZED OVER AS I STARED AT THE EMPTY bookstore. The last customer had left thirty-seven minutes ago. I knew because I'd watched every tick of the clock on the slow Tuesday afternoon. My thoughts slipped away to Wyatt and my visit yesterday. So many emotions rushed through all at once like a tidal wave from the memories of his confessions and his kisses. I think he was my addiction in more ways than one.

And I loved him. Every day, I loved him a little more than the last—a little more completely and wildly and deeply. And I wanted to do something for him, something for Wyatt, but I wasn't sure exactly what I could offer that he wouldn't reject.

My mind toiled over my thoughts. I shifted on the stool by the register, looking around the room. On the shelf in the back, projectors were lined up for student groups to check out for presentations. I smiled as the idea formed in my head.

I crawled off my perch and went in search of my manager. He was a nice guy who wouldn't mind me borrowing a few things.

I pulled into my apartment complex with my backseat full of everything I needed for my surprise. I just had to run upstairs and change clothes before going out to the kennel. Tonight wasn't going to be a T-shirt or sweatshirt visit.

After taking a shower, I curled my hair into precise ringlets and coated them with a layer of hairspray. I ran my fingers over the soft waves to make sure they were not sticky. After applying an intricate layer of eye makeup, I covered my lips with a faint coating of clear cinnamon gloss. Looking out the window, I noticed the afternoon sun was going down slowly.

I wanted to get out of here before Blaire came home. We had barely spoken to each other over the last couple of weeks. I hated that our relationship was in such turmoil. We used to have such a deep-rooted connection to each other—one that lacked human explanation. But now even that rarely sparked. The closer I got to Wyatt, the less I felt my twin.

I needed to come up with some sort of plan to fix this with Blaire. I just didn't know how to communicate with her anymore. We had ridden in silence to our weekly dinners with our parents. Lucky for us, my mom and dad liked to talk. And lucky for me, Blaire had decided not to reveal my relationship with Wyatt.

I wasn't sure how to explain our situation to them. He wasn't dangerous. I wasn't doing something unsafe by being with him. He just was . . . tied up for the moment and lacked the ability to do most of the things my parents would expect from a guy—like, come to their house for dinner and shake my dad's hand.

I had no idea what kept Blaire silent. Maybe she didn't hate me as much as I imagined. Or maybe she was waiting for the right moment to drop the brick on my head.

I didn't even know where she went every day since my sister no longer required me to drive her places. Over the last few weeks, she had skipped her scheduled days to use the car. I had no idea how she got around town.

I let out a deep breath—another problem for another day.

I slipped on a pair of spandex leggings and a deep-purple dress, which fell mid-thigh. I added my short black boots and smiled in the mirror. Sexy yet warm. Digging through my top dresser drawer, I looked at scarves until I found the one with gold embedded sparkles that matched my gloves. Draping it around my neck, I left the ends hanging down next to the scooped neckline of my dress.

Grabbing my keys, I went bouncing down the stairs as I thought about my surprise for Wyatt. I hoped it all came together once I got out there. The excitement sent chills down my back.

"Weeell, look at you, Emma. You're like some pocket-sized Barbie."

My feet stilled on the cement by my car, hearing his voice get a little lower with a chuckle. "I sure as hell wouldn't mind having you down there in my pocket."

He didn't really just say that to me. Did he? The words seemed to hang in the air around us. I continued the last few steps to my car. I had my hand on the door handle before I looked up.

"Hey, Kurt, gotta run."

"Of course you do." His eyes traveled over my clothes, touching each piece. I couldn't move. I knew I should get in the car. But the leering glint was so unnerving that I froze as he mentally peeled the dress from my skin. "Guess that guy of yours is waiting for you."

I nodded quickly and ducked inside the cab. My fingers hit the lock button before I ever put the key in the ignition. I threw the car in reverse. Out of the corner of my eye, I saw Kurt walking back to the manager's office. He picked up a dog crate and carried it inside.

Oh no. He got another one.

My hands shook on the steering wheel as I drove out of the parking lot. I couldn't tell Wyatt anything about Kurt. It might just push him over the edge into some meltdown. He would want to drive over there and do something about it. But yet, he couldn't go any farther than a precise radius from the trailer.

And I couldn't tell Blaire. Even if we were still talking, my sister would freak out. I couldn't tell anyone. And what was there really to tell?

So this Kurt guy said he wanted to stick you down in his pocket. Did he touch you? No. Did he actually try to stick any part of your body down in his pocket? No. So he really didn't do anything to you? No.

I let out a heavy breath, trying to shake the rattled thoughts. Kurt didn't really do anything to me. Not really. It was just Kurt being Kurt—airing his colorful thoughts. But I knew something he would actually touch, and it was in that crate. I had no idea what I was going to do about his new dog.

My excitement had dimmed some after my run-in with Kurt, but the long drive helped settle my nerves. Wyatt came out of the trailer as my headlights touched the windows. And I forgot about everything in the outside world as his smile melted my heart.

"I didn't think you were coming tonight."

I got out of the front seat and walked slowly to him. "Well, the bookstore was boring so my boss let me off early for date night."

"Date night?"

"Yep."

"Hmm. I like date night if that means you look like that." Wyatt gave me a sweet kiss, lifting me up from the ground. I wrapped my legs around his waist. Letting go of my lips, he whispered, "You are so beautiful."

My arms held on tight around his neck as I got sucked into the heated gaze from Wyatt's eyes. He kissed me again and then smiled. "So what is date night exactly?"

"I brought you something. And before you say anything, it's not a present that stays. And you have to help me set it up."

"A riddle." He chuckled, setting me back down on the ground.

"Come on. It's all in the backseat." Lacing his fingers between mine, I pulled Wyatt over to the car.

"The backseat?" He grinned. "You do like that backseat. Or maybe it was the floorboard."

"Stop it." I swatted his arm. I opened the door and pulled out the projector. "Carry this and don't drop it. I don't want to know how much that costs to replace."

"What is this?" He held the bulky box in his arms.

I grabbed my laptop bag, slinging it over my shoulder. Picking up the extension cord, I stacked the orange wad on top of the projector and lifted the giant speaker to carry myself. "Let's go. I'll come back for the extra-special part. I know it wasn't your *favorite* part, but it's mine. And I couldn't stop thinking about it after yesterday."

Wyatt's face glazed over for a minute. I guess my surprise had finally made sense. I waited for him to process the thoughts.

"You okay?"

He nodded, holding my gaze. "So . . . um . . . I guess you brought the movies to me."

"Yeah. And this is a subwoofer. Not sure it will make you shake, but it should be loud. We need to get this set up before it gets pitch black out here." I started walking toward the back side of the kennel and he followed slowly behind me.

We ran the large cord from inside the building. Wyatt took the coffee table from the trailer for the projector, and I hooked up my laptop with the speaker. He pulled out some old blankets and pillows to put on the ground while I got the popcorn out of my car. Not just any popcorn, but actual buckets from the movie theater in town. They had even given me a few containers of butter to warm in the microwave.

I went inside the kennel and pulled Charlie out of his pen. He got in a few good licks to my face as I carried him outside to the blanket.

Wyatt was sitting there, staring at the bucket of popcorn that was dripping in butter. "Are you not going to eat any of it?"

"Oh," he muttered, looking up at me. "I was just um . . . waiting for you, Emma."

"Okay, well, you don't have to wait on me." I put Charlie down on the blanket and he cuddled up next to Wyatt's leg. He absently ran his fingers over the little dog's fur. "You get to pick. I've got several movies loaded on the laptop."

"What are my choices?"

"*The Godfather*." I let out a faint laugh, seeing his eyes roll. "And I saw that you had some Michael Crichton books on your shelf. So I have the classic *Jurassic Park* movie. Have you seen it?"

"No."

"And I have a couple of Stephen King *thrill-ers*." I let my voice get a little crazed on the end, which made him smile. "Let's see. I have *The Mist*, *Carrie*, and *The Shining*."

"Holy shit. You want to watch *The Shining*?"

"Have you seen it?" I crawled down on the blanket next to him, making sure my dress was smoothed down.

"Yes. It's awesome. And um, intense, but it's different than the book. And I don't think you will like it. Let's do a different one."

"You pick." Reaching into my bucket of popcorn, I took a handful and munched on the puffy kernels. The butter melted on my tongue. Wyatt's eyes trailed up my legs and over my dress and stopped on my lips as I pushed in another bite of popcorn. I poked his leg with the toe of my boot to get his attention back to the movies.

"Okay. Okay." He let out a deep breath. "Well, I have also seen *Carrie*. But not *The Mist*. And I don't know about watching *The Godfather* out here."

"So it's a toss-up. *Jurassic Park* versus *The Mist*. I have an idea." I gave a flirty grin. Leaning over, I took a giant piece of popcorn from *his* bucket—the one he seemed conflicted to eat. "I'm going to throw this in your mouth. If I miss, then it's *The Mist*. If I can make it inside your mouth, then it's *Jurassic Park*."

I scooted back a couple of feet, but Wyatt rolled his eyes like I was crazy. "Either you participate, or we watch *Twilight* because I have that movie on there too."

Wyatt's jaw immediately dropped open. Our eyes held on to each other as I took aim. The soft piece of popcorn traveled between us and my eyes became huge as it landed on his tongue. I fell over laughing. "I really can't believe I made it."

Rolling over on my side, I saw his face relax into some euphoric haze as he chewed on the buttery popcorn. Wyatt looked so incredibly sexy in his black sweatshirt and the black wool hat, which covered most of his head. It made his dark eyebrows and soft lips stand out. As I watched him lick the salt off of those sexy lips with his tongue, the warmth in my chest expanded through my whole body. I loved him. I wanted him. I craved him.

His gaze drifted down to where I was lying on the blanket. And I smiled, not bothering to hide a single thought in my head. "How does it taste?"

"Incredible." He dipped a hand inside the bucket, shoveling a whole fistful into his mouth.

"Good." I grinned at him, feeling my own euphoric rush. I wanted nothing more than to just stay in this very spot, watching the happiness as it radiated across his cheeks. But I knew we should get the movie started or it would end late.

I crawled off the blanket and went to the laptop. After a

few clicks, the projector broadcasted on the back of the white metal building—the only wall without pens or doors attached to the sides. I adjusted the picture as the sound boomed out of the speaker. It remained slightly crooked. Fiddling with the lens, I just seemed to make it worse until I finally gave up.

I glanced down to where Wyatt sat with Charlie. His face was no longer alive with excitement but veiled in sadness and wrapped in guilt. His self-punishment had surfaced, keeping a strong hold on his thoughts, tainting my surprise with his demons.

I just wanted Wyatt to have a good night. And I didn't think there was anything wrong with a good night. He was confined to living at the kennel. Wasn't that enough? None of his self-inflicted restrictions would change the past. I wish he could just see it that way.

I made my way back to the blanket, stopping next to his feet. Wyatt reached a hand up to pull me down to the blanket. I clasped my fingers around his, giving him a teasing grin to lighten his mood. Settling between his thighs, I pulled the extra blanket up over our legs before leaning back into his chest. His arms circled around my body, holding me tightly, squeezing me with the intensity of his thoughts.

"Thank you for all of this," he whispered. "I don't deserve—"

"Shh." I turned my neck enough to press my lips over his. "Just enjoy tonight for me, okay?"

"Okay," he whispered, and I heard the surrender in his gruff voice.

Wyatt seemed to relax, letting his hands wander over my skin until his fingers intertwined with mine. We leaned back into the mound of pillows he had propped up against the coffee table. His chin rested next to my cheek. I felt his warm breath on my skin as the opening credits spilled across the side of the building, just slightly crooked and just a little blurry, but very peaceful and sweet and wonderful—and just as I'd imagined as I'd sat daydreaming at the bookstore today.

We finished off one of the buckets of popcorn as the sounds of the movie filled the quiet air of the open country. It wasn't loud enough to shake our seats, but the speaker worked pretty well when the dinosaurs crashed across the screen. I learned that Wyatt liked Spielberg even though he thought the movie wasn't very close to the book. But neither of us cared. We loved it anyway. I stayed curled up in his arms even after the end credits disappeared and the screen went black.

"You want to watch another one?" I looked up at him. He pushed a curl off my face, letting his hand cup the side of my cheek. I kissed the tip of his thumb as he touched my lips.

"Don't you have to work early at the nursing home?"

I let out a sigh. "I do. I have a five-a.m. shift tomorrow."

"We should get this packed up then so you can go home."

"I don't want to leave," I muttered.

Wyatt clutched me to his chest. "I don't want you to leave either."

So we didn't move. My eyes closed, listening to the quiet sounds around us—the bugs and the chilly breeze moving the grass. And I drifted away into the feel of his body. The way his chest moved as he breathed. The way his fingers stayed curled around my breast. The way his left hand rested on my thigh. The way his nose stayed buried down in the scarf around my neck.

It wasn't wild and breathtaking. Instead it was the stillness that made this moment weave around my heart as Wyatt held me in a comfortable and sleepy embrace.

"I liked movie night," I mumbled. "But I know it wasn't as good as a real theater."

"It was better," he whispered. "Because you did this for me. I don't think a real theater will ever compare. Even when I take you to a real one, I will still think about this night with you."

I couldn't find the words to say back to Wyatt. He was making plans and promises again. He made me feel like I was falling right through the sky as he held me tight, while on a simple blanket spread out across the ground.

So I didn't say anything and snuggled as close as I could to his body. I wanted to stay like this forever. I wanted the future he was gradually promising. My thoughts got sleepy, and then I drifted slowly away.

"Emma." He shook me a little. "Wake up. It's really late."

"Okay." But I didn't move.

"Come on." He shifted me off his lap, disturbing Charlie in the process. "Why don't you take him back to the kennel? I'll put all of this back in your car."

"Okay." I didn't have the energy to argue.

Lifting up Charlie, he gave me a half lick before closing his eyes again. We stumbled back around to the side door. I carried him down the aisle. A few dogs woke up enough to come to the gates. Placing Charlie inside, he walked slowly over to his bed and fell against the soft padding.

I shut the pen and I dragged my sleepy body through the building. If I didn't have to be at work so early, I would just stay the night. But I didn't bring my scrubs and I would have to leave at 4:15, which was in about three hours.

Something caught my attention and I stopped walking, realizing my feet were next to Cye's pen—or rather, the home of Betty and Cye. Bending down, I saw his single brown eye, watching from the other side of the fence. I swear, every time I looked at him, he broke my heart just a little bit more until there was nothing but dust in my chest.

I stuck my fingers inside the pen and waited. He slowly came over, lying down against the wire. And he let me touch him, very softy, very lightly, behind the ears. And then he rolled over, giving me his fuzzy belly.

Tears threatened to pour down my cheeks. This was a new one, something he had never done for me or Wyatt.

"That's a good boy," I whispered. I loved this dog. Plain and simple. I loved him and his courage to trust again. If Cye could make this kind of progress, he might just get himself adopted.

I heard the door open at the front of the building. Giving Cye one last rub on the stomach, I got up from the cement and made my way over to where Wyatt stood by the office.

"Cye rolled over for me," I whispered. "He let me pet his belly."

"His belly?"

"Yeah. His big ol' fuzzy belly."

"Huh," he muttered, giving me a grin. "Well, he always liked you better."

"He likes us the same."

Wyatt put an arm around my waist as we walked out to my car. "Everything's packed up in the backseat."

"Thank you."

He rested his hands on my shoulders, fiddling with my scarf. I knew he was sad that I was leaving and he was worried about me driving in the middle of the night. I wished that I could say, *I'll text you when I get home*. But that's not how things worked between us.

"I'll be okay," I whispered.

"I know. I just . . . I know." He let out a deep breath, pulling me to his chest. His mouth found my lips, tugging possessively until they were slightly sore from his kiss. And then he abruptly released me. Backing away a few steps, Wyatt let his eyes wander over me as he slipped away into some hazy stare in the moonlit shadows.

"What?"

"I'm just trying to remember you like this." His low voice hung on each word. "With your hair falling down around your shoulders and that sleepy look in your eyes. And your lips all red from me kissing you. That's what I want to remember. When I'm out here alone and I feel like I'm losing my mind. I want to picture you like this."

I stared back at him, feeling my heart beat wildly in my chest. After a few moments, I climbed inside my car and drove away as my insides turned into complete mush. That might be the sweetest and most heart-wrenching thing Wyatt had ever said to me.

CHAPTER 29

Emma

THE LAST SEVERAL DAYS HAD BEEN A WHIRLWIND OF CLASS and work. Sitting at a stoplight, I rubbed the back of my neck. A knot was forming right under the base of my skull. My eyes drifted closed as the fatigue sat into my body. I had studied almost all night for my chemistry test. I didn't know how the full-time students handled the pressure. I only had two classes.

I knew it took me longer than some people to understand things. School had never been easy for me. And Blaire had more time to invest in being some award-winning student. She gave a few music lessons on the side, but her scholarship pretty much paid for everything else while I worked two jobs. Not that I saw it as an excuse. Lots of people worked while in school, and I didn't need a first-in-class medal. I just needed to make a B. That would get me into the nursing program.

A horn blared from behind, making me sit straight up in the driver's seat. I put my foot on the pedal and shot forward from the light. I just prayed I did well on my test even though my head wasn't quite together today.

The blood was still pumping fast through my body as I pulled into my apartment complex. My neck spasm had grown into a full-fledged migraine. I wanted to rest my head against the steering wheel instead of taking the effort of going upstairs, but I peeled myself out of the seat anyway.

My dark-blue scrubs smelled from spilling applesauce down the front this morning at the nursing home. I still wore the stained clothes at four in the afternoon because I didn't have a chance to change into something else before going to take my test.

Ugh. I needed a shower. And I needed to check on Mr. Hughes. It had been a couple of days since I'd seen my neighbor or Blaire for that matter. She had run through the living room yesterday, clutching her laptop with her big tuba bag over her shoulder. It was hard not to see a giant elephant smashing through the apartment even though she pretended I wasn't there.

Shuffling over to the bottom of the stairs, I paused, seeing something out of the corner of my eye. Those same two dog crates had reappeared outside the manager's office. I told myself to let it go. My whole life would be much simpler if I could just walk away, but I just wasn't that kind of person.

Besides, that's what started this whole new chapter of my life anyway. I couldn't walk away from Charlie. I couldn't walk away from Wyatt. If I had to do it all over again, I wouldn't change a thing. Wyatt and those dogs consumed a huge chunk of my existence. And it was the thought of another one bleeding in Kurt's crate that stopped me from going up the stairs.

Letting out a deep breath, I checked around for signs of anyone else in the parking lot. I moved swiftly over toward his door. I just needed to take a quick peek inside the crates to see if they were empty or if they contained another Charlie. The thought made my stomach ache.

I looked quickly in the first, seeing nothing but an empty cage. My nose filled with the rancid odor of urine. The other was just the same. I straightened up, wanting to take a peek around the corner into his office. Kurt must have put them somewhere. I just didn't know if it was here or off the property.

"You need something or just poking your nose into other people's shit?"

The blood drained from my face as I heard his voice come up behind me. Turning around, I gave him a half smile. "Just you, Kurt. I . . . um . . . Mr. Hughes's kitchen faucet has been dripping. Thought you might have some tools to fix it."

The lie came off clunky, but I hoped it was at least believable. Kurt licked his bottom lip, giving me a half smirk as his eyes slide over to the crates and back up to me. He shifted his weight to his other leg, sticking his hand down in his front pocket of his ragged jeans.

"You tell that old man I ain't doing shit. He's leaving soon and can just deal with it. I don't give a damn if the water don't work at all." The glint in his eyes was just a little off, just a little creepy as he stared at the applesauce stain on the front of my scrubs. The chilly wind hit me in the back, and I shuddered.

"Well, thanks, Kurt. I'll give him the message." Not wanting to argue with his stupid statement, I walked quickly over to the stairs without looking back at his strange glare.

I shoved my key into the lock and darted inside my apartment. With the door shut behind me, I turned the deadbolt and walked slowly to the kitchen to grab a few Tylenol. I noticed Blair's door shut. For once, I guess my sister was home.

I rinsed off in the shower and put on a pair of sweats with my fuzzy boots. Slipping on a T-shirt, I went back out in the hallway, looking at her closed door again.

All joking aside, I missed Blaire. I missed talking to my sister. Not that our conversations were exactly normal, but our discussions had always been that way. So to me, they *were* normal. For the last several years, she'd been the only friend in my life. My weird, eccentric, paranoid friend—and I missed her.

Giving Blaire's door one last glance, I headed over to check on Mr. Hughes. I walked across the upstairs landing between the apartments. Looking down in the parking lot toward the manager's office, I noticed the crates were missing. Whatever game Kurt was playing, he had decided to hide the evidence again.

I gave my neighbor's apartment door a few hard knocks before turning the knob. It was open as usual. Mr. Hughes was more trusting than me.

"Hello," I yelled inside. I closed the door behind me, seeing the whole living room surrounded in a wall of brown boxes. The realization of his move hit me again. I had chosen to ignore the reality until I couldn't anymore.

"In here, Emma."

I followed the sound of his voice until I found Mr. Hughes sitting on the side of his bed with more boxes.

"Where did you get all of the stuff?"

"Well, your sister was a sweetheart and dropped them off."

"Blaire?" I couldn't contain the gasp. Oh no. Mr. Hughes was getting worse and hallucinating.

"Yeah, thought I should get started packing since I'm leaving in a couple of weeks. Blair has been helping me some. That girl's not like you. She's got a mouth on her. Always back-talking and swearing."

Nope. No hallucination. "What do you mean my sister has been helping you?"

"You know, running some errands and helping me clear up some stuff before I leave. I let her drive my car since I'm not using it."

And that answered my question on her means of transportation the last couple of weeks. My sister had been using poor Mr. Hughes for his car to avoid talking to me.

"I'm sorry. I hate to run, but I need to take care of something. I promise to come back later with *Blaire*—and we will help you start packing stuff."

"Okay. Whatever you need to do."

I heard part of the words, but I was already halfway out of the apartment. I stormed through his door and back into mine, slamming the heavy metal behind me. I stopped outside of Blair's bedroom and decided knocking would accomplish nothing. I barged inside, seeing her eyes widen and her skin turn a little pale. I plopped down beside her on the bed as my sister scrambled to get her laptop as far away as possible from me.

"Get the hell out of my room!" Her gaze burned deep with anger.

I replied with a simple and smirky, "No."

"I mean it, Emma."

I crossed my arms over my chest and my legs like a pretzel on her bedspread. "I'm not moving until you get over whatever has you mad at me."

"Damn it. Get out!" she growled.

"I mean it, Blaire. I'm sitting on your bed until this is fixed. And you know I will."

She shook her head, rolling her eyes. "I will just leave you in here."

"Then I will follow you like a shadow. I'll stare two inches from your face as you sleep. And while you eat. I'll even sit on the toilet while you are in the shower. Or maybe I'll get in there too. I'll haunt you, Blaire. Every step. I'll follow you to class. And band practice. I'll be right there, Blaire. Every single step until you think I'm some ghost you can't shake."

"And people think I'm the crazy twin." She scooted away, but I caught a glimpse of her laptop screen before she could get off the bed.

"What are you doing with that?" I gasped.

I lunged for the computer as she tried to twist away. We

fought for a moment—me tugging and climbing on top of Blair while my sister tried yanking the laptop out of my fingers. I hadn't physically fought with my twin in years. Neither of us was really stronger than the other. I got in a few elbow jabs and she rammed her knee into my stomach. But it was the small push with my hip that sent Blaire down in the floor, ending the scuffle over the computer. She shoved her glasses back on her nose.

"Emma, *don't!*" she squealed. My eyes took in the image and I shot a confused look at my sister as she got up from the floor.

"Why do you have a picture of me up on your screen?"

"That's not you. It's me."

"No. I'm pretty sure I know what I look like. That's me. Not you. So what are you doing with a picture of me—that you *think* is you?"

"Fuck." She fell on the bed next to me, covering her face with a pillow.

"Whoa." I flipped through the screens open on the laptop. "You are trying to send someone called M-Attack815 a picture of yourself? But it's really of me?"

"Same thing." Her voice came out muffled.

"No, that's not the same thing. And who is M-Attack815?" I yanked the pillow from her face. "Do you have a *boyfriend*?"

"No, he's just someone I . . . um . . . talk to online."

"Are you serious? How did you meet M-Attack815? Does he know where we live? Did you give him our address? You seriously did not give him our address."

"Calm down. I'm not you."

"Oh, that was low, Blaire. For all you know, he could be some sixty-year-old man who likes feet—or Kurt. He could be Kurt pretending to be normal. You could have found Kurt on the Internet and you're sending him a picture of *me*."

"Oh, hell, he's not Kurt. Besides, he could get his own picture of *you* without me. You'd just waltz right into his office and pose for him, Emma."

We stared at each other until I started laughing at the absolute ridiculousness of our fight. I stretched out on the bed next to my sister.

"Tell me about him," I whispered.

Blaire didn't answer me for a while. "We met playing a game online. It's that stupid one with the avatars. The one you make fun of."

"So you met him in your game. How long has it been going on?"

"About a month. His name is Matt. He's goes to school in Norman. Engineering major. I checked him out. Everything seems legit. He sent me a picture last week, and I don't know. I've been stalling."

"Why?"

"It's easy talking to him online. I don't have to be something I'm not. The part that is hard for me is gone. I can think about everything I say before I type it. But if I give him a picture, then he will want to talk on the phone and eventually meet in person. I don't know if that's something I can do."

I felt sorry for Blaire. She was odd. Maybe even strange at times, which could easily be hidden while typing behind a computer screen. But even the socially incompetent wanted to find someone in life who was just as much of a recluse as them. That had to be a very difficult situation. "Why did you try to send him a picture of me?"

"Because I thought it would be the same thing. Just with all that frilly shit you do. I don't know. It's all so damn stupid. I should just tell him goodbye and stop talking to him."

"No. Don't do that. Go take a shower."

"Why?" She turned her head to face me, giving a skeptical glare.

I smiled. "Because I'm going to help you."

She sat up straight in the bed. "Like, how?"

"We are going to send him a picture of the real you. You don't have to be something you're not. But this"—I waved my hand around in front of her—"needs a little scrubbing. So go take a shower. I think you forgot to wash your hair, like, two days ago."

Blaire grumbled something under her breath that was strong and explicit. Her eyes locked with mine, and I felt that slight familiar buzz in my chest. My sister gave me a quick hug, just long enough for me to feel the pressure of her arms before she leaped off the bed. I would swear it didn't happen, but I was in the same room so I knew it had taken place. I knew Blaire had hugged me on purpose.

I smiled as the guilt stabbed me a little in the heart. She had missed our friendship too. And my absence had caused the only feeling my twin was capable of expressing to me: anger. Blaire had shut me out and stormed around instead of just saying, *Stop spending all your time with Wyatt.*

As I waited for my sister to finish in the shower, I flipped through her emails until I found the one in question. M-Attack815 was adorable. His face had a little scruff on the cheeks. And he wore a stocking hat over his blonde hair. But it was the shy smile that got me. This guy was a sweetheart. I could feel it all the way through the computer screen, which made me understand why Blaire was nervous about eventually seeing him in person.

She came out of the bathroom, wearing a frown. "I don't know about this, Emma."

"Will you just trust me?" I forced her to sit down in a chair while I dried her wet hair. Then I disappeared into my bathroom, returning with a large curling iron. I styled her hair in simple, flowing waves around her shoulders.

"Now, go put on that red shirt you like so much."

"It has a hole at the bottom."

"He won't see it in the picture. Just put it on because that's what I see when I picture you in my head. You in that red shirt."

"Because I don't like change," she said under her breath.

"I know you don't."

Blaire grumbled again, digging through her closet until she found it and a pair of jeans. She sat back down in the chair. "Does this work?"

"Yes, but you are not done," I teased. "Where's that little blue hat you like?"

"You want me to wear a hat?"

"Stop asking questions."

She glared at me before pointing at the back of her door. I took the crocheted hat and placed it on Blaire's head, fluffing her hair out around her shoulders. "I think you're done."

"No makeup?"

"That's not you. This . . ." I smiled. "This is you. At least the cleaned-up version. Go look."

Blaire went into the bathroom, staring at herself for about five minutes before she returned. "Okay. Let's get this shit over with."

Using her cell phone, I snapped several pictures of Blaire until she grew fidgety. "I think you got several to pick from. Want me to help?"

"No." She sighed.

"He's cute, Blaire. Seems sweet."

Her eyes narrowed at me. "*Emma?*"

"So I may have looked at him on your computer. Just don't worry, okay? You will be fine." I gave her a hug and I swear she whispered *thank you* against my shoulder.

CHAPTER 30

Emma

I PULLED THROUGH THE SILVER FENCE ONLY TO HAVE MY CAR consumed in a field of ominous white fog. If this had been my first visit, I would've turned right back around and drove with my foot pressed to the floorboard. Except, it wasn't my first visit and I liked the way the hazy mist wrapped the whole place in its own secret blanket.

Parking next to the trailer, I felt a spark of anticipation. I still got a little thrill in the pit of my stomach every time I came to his place. I craved that moment when his face lit up with a smile because he was simply happy to see me. Sometimes it was strange to remember the way it was in the beginning—before I knew the *why* behind his pain. Those days seemed like a lifetime ago.

Pulling my laptop bag from the passenger's seat, I squealed when I turned around, seeing Wyatt standing just a couple of inches from me.

"Don't do that." Even though the beginning seemed so long ago, he still had the ability to sneak up on me the way a leopard tracked its food.

Taking the bulky bag from my hands, he leaned down, giving me a peck on the lips. "But it's so easy. You're always like ten miles away in your head."

"That's not true."

"I just figure you're thinking about me." His arm slipped around my shoulders as we walked toward the door.

"That's *really* not true," I protested, sitting down on the couch. Reaching for my bag, Wyatt refused to give it to me. "Come on. I have an English paper to write. And I haven't even started."

Placing my computer out of reach, he sat down next to me on the same cushion. His eyes were no longer laughing. Wyatt cupped the side of my cheek with his hand.

"You may not have been thinking about me, but I've been thinking about you the last three days," he whispered. "Every minute. Every second you were gone. I thought about you."

And then he kissed me. Not that flimsy brush-of-his-lips-by-the-car. This was a mouth- and mind-consuming madness. And then I fell slowly against the couch cushions. His lips never left mine as we settled into a comfortable spot with his full weight on top of me.

My hands ran over his shoulders until my fingers trailed through his hair. The short pieces felt soft against my fingertips. Moving my palms over his back, I slipped my fingers under the bottom part of his shirt. I loved the feel of his skin. I loved touching him—the way he responded, the way he seemed almost surprised at his own reaction.

And without even whispering a single word, I knew in those moments, Wyatt felt something deep and different with me. No one had ever touched him the way I touched him. The kind of touch that started on the skin, but was felt inside the heart.

"You smell so good," he whispered. "Sometimes I think about the way you smell. And the way you taste. And the way you make those little sounds when I kiss your neck. Sometimes it makes me feel crazy. And I think you aren't real. That I imagined you because I couldn't handle this anymore."

As those words slipped out, the vulnerability of his confession gripped his face. He didn't mean to say it. He didn't mean for me to hear those dark thoughts that twisted away inside his head.

"It's okay," I whispered. "I'm not going anywhere."

Our eyes held for a moment as our bodies begged us to keep going. I wasn't sure where he would stop this time. But he always stopped, denying himself of what he needed from me—what he craved.

I closed my eyes as Wyatt continued, feeling his tongue trace over my lips, before moving slowly inside my mouth, stroking my tongue. The intensity grew between us. His confession seemed to open the floodgates. I shifted beneath him as Wyatt moved his hands over my body, gripping and holding possessively, almost like he was afraid I would disintegrate into the foggy mist outside the window.

My shirt inched up, and then he leaned back enough to pull it over my head. The scratchy couch rubbed against my bare skin as he kissed down my neck. Every single brush of his lips sent a lightning bolt of tingles through my stomach until there was no space between them.

Wrapping my legs around his waist, I arched against him, trying to get closer even though several layers of clothes separated us—separated our skin and the way I wished we could fit together.

I tugged at the hem of his shirt until I had it pulled over his head. His bare chest felt solid and warm against my skin. I let out a gasp, feeling his tongue trace the edge of my bra. His eyes caught mine as his fingers pushed the strap off my shoulder. He removed my bra, leaving me exposed as his mouth dipped lower, gently tasting my skin. My eyes closed. I couldn't process another thought in my head.

That mouth of his was the devil. When he smiled, it melted my heart. When he used those lips on my body, I crumbled into a million pieces.

"Well, I guess you two are getting along fine."

Her words boomed out of the clouds like the voice of God. My eyes flipped open as Wyatt stilled and looked over his shoulder. Very slowly, I met the gaze of the woman responsible for his confinement and for bringing us together. Diana Sweetwater.

"For the record, I knocked, but I see why you didn't hear me." She turned to leave, yelling over her shoulder. "Get your shit together, kid. I got a new one for you."

Neither us moved an inch until the trailer door was shut. His stricken expression was worse than I'd expected. Wyatt rested his forehead against mine. He let out a deep breath. "I can't believe that just happened. I'm sorry, Emma."

"It's okay. Neither of us thought someone would just show up. I mean. What are the odds?"

"It's not that. I, um . . ." He lifted himself off of me, leaving my half-naked body cold and alone on the couch. "You can stay in here if you want. I'll go. She's brought a new dog. It must be a bad situation if she didn't wait until Sunday."

The stress lines showed deeply around his eyes as his once-soft lips flattened into a white line. Without another word, Wyatt disappeared out the door. I sat up, trying to decide if the change in him was because of Diana, the dog, me, or something else I wasn't factoring into the equation.

I pulled my long-sleeved, blue shirt back over my head. Somewhere in the middle of our makeout session, my shoes had ended up on the floor. I pulled the fuzzy boots back over my clingy yoga pants.

Opening the door slowly, I peered outside, seeing Wyatt and Diana next to the bed of the truck. Their voices caused me to pause with my hand on the knob and the old aluminum door half open.

"There's nothing wrong with you having a relationship with Emma."

"Well, Fred Tucker would shit rocks and throw them at me if he found out," Wyatt grumbled.

"Maybe so, but what he doesn't know won't kill him."

"No, but he would like to kill me. What if he did something to Emma?"

"Like what?" Diana spat. "He's not in the damn mafia."

"Not like that. What if he messed up stuff for her or something? I don't know. I just don't want my shit to screw stuff up in her life."

The door slipped in my hand, making the creaky hinges shriek, causing both of them to look over at me.

"Hey." I hesitated before coming down the stairs toward the truck, feeling the embarrassment of getting caught shirtless by this woman.

Wyatt's fists were clenched at his sides, which meant his agitation was continuing to grow. He watched me with wild eyes. The passion and tenderness from just a few moments ago had disappeared into a puff of heated smoke.

"Well, you are just as cute as the last time I saw you, dragging that little bloody dog to the rescue. Good to see you again, Emma."

"Thanks. Um . . ." I paused, trying to figure out how to address her.

"Just call me Diana out here."

"Good to see you again too, Diana."

I fidgeted, looking back over to Wyatt. His eyes were still on me. The anger seemed to be replaced with sadness—that deep, overwhelming sadness.

"Okay, kids. We need to get moving before the tranquilizers wear off. I got you a wild one this time. He's sedated, but you will have to watch your fingers when he comes to. He's like a gator with those teeth."

I peered inside the crate, sitting in the bed of the enormous truck. A brown muzzle was wrapped around the mouth of a medium-sized Australian shepherd.

"What's his story?" I muttered.

"Let's talk and walk. Wyatt, unlatch the crate and carry it inside. I don't want you handling him in case he wakes up."

And in a flash, his demons went back inside their cave. Wyatt snapped alive, pulling the bulky crate from the truck. As he walked to the kennel, I followed behind him, seeing his arm flex with the weight of the heavy animal.

"Are you taking one of them?" he asked Diana.

"About that. I have someone who wants the one you call Gatsby."

"Gatsby?" I gasped. I wasn't expecting that one.

"Yeah, Gatsby. Nice old lady. She sits in her chair all day, watching *Wheel of Fortune* and talk shows. She would like a dog that just lies around to keep her feet warm. What do you think?"

Tears burned the corner of my eyes, but I refused to let this tough and eccentric woman see me cry. This was the business. The dogs would come and the lucky ones would go. And even more rare to find a home—the old ones who were destined to end their life without a true family. "Sounds like a good fit. Don't you think, Wyatt?"

"Yeah."

His eyes caught mine as the thoughts traveled between us. For once, his sadness and my sadness mingled together. These dogs did have a family. A family name Wyatt, and he cared about each and every one of them.

They made him laugh as he bathed the wild ones in the porcelain tub. They chased away the ghosts in his head as he played ball in the grass. They kept him company on the lonely nights as he read books to them in the kennel. And in return, he made sure their days were filled with clean pens and food and hugs and scratches behind the ears. Wyatt made sure they saw love—even if he didn't always realize it happened that way.

We reached the holding pen. I opened the gate so Wyatt could carry the crate inside. Setting the large box on the ground, he looked at Diana. She knelt down beside the door, opening it slowly.

"They found him down in a water drain that went into a small lake. Not sure how he got in there. When that hard rain came the other day, one of the city workers was checking on it and found him. He snapped like a crazed gator. Scared the shit out of the worker. You know, it took four men over the course of two hours to get him out and about two seconds to put him on the kill list. But that's what happens when they get labeled a biter. That little girl who works in the intake room called me. She thought he was cute."

Diana ran a hand over his sleeping head. "I guess I did too. And maybe he's just scared. I'd go for the jugular too if I got trapped down in a damn cement drain."

I stood there mesmerized, watching her fingers run over the dog's head as she told his story. So this is what it's like in the beginning—when the forgotten and the neglected, the beaten and the abused, and those dubbed a killer arrive at the kennel.

"Well, let's get him out." She moved out of the way, letting Wyatt take over. He got a hold of the dog under his armpits, dragging him out onto the floor. The sleeping eyes opened briefly, revealing one blue and one brown eye before closing again.

"He seems pretty harmless with that Hannibal mask," he muttered.

"Don't fool yourself, kid. Be careful with him until he's got his bearings." She unbuckled the brown leather, setting him free. Diana handed the muzzle over to Wyatt. "You keep it just in case."

We backed out of the pen, leaving him to sleep. Wyatt filled the water bucket up and placed food in the bowl. I headed over to Cye's pen, grabbing some peanut butter bones from the sack. I stepped carefully back inside with Gator.

"Emma . . ." I heard his voice warn, but I ignored Wyatt. Placing the bones next to the sleeping dog, I studied him for a moment, itching to run a hand over his gray-speckled head. He might be like Cye. This might be my only chance for the next year. I ran my fingers through his fur, feeling the silky softness. And then I left Gator alone.

"Diana and I have some stuff to do in the office. Could you . . . um . . . could you get Gatsby ready?"

"Sure."

Leaving them to their business, I went outside of the kennel and over to the trailer. I was already inside when I realized I'd forgotten a leash. It was better to have him on a leash inside the truck. I didn't think she would put poor old Gatsby in the crate.

I returned inside the building and felt a stab of guilt, hearing their voices. But I couldn't stop myself from eavesdropping. Wyatt was sitting in the office desk chair while Diana was standing in front of him.

"I don't need any of that shit. I've told you over and over again. I'm doing better."

"Don't be blowing all that smoke at me, kid. We both know she can't fix everything. But I'm glad she's helping you. Just don't bite my head off for asking. I just wanted to check your mental state before I told you."

"Told me what?"

Diana walked in the direction of the office door, and I smashed myself to the wall. She stopped, picking up something from the shelf, and then went back over to Wyatt. "Well, the Tuckers finally had that wedding last weekend."

"Did you do what I asked?" he muttered.

"You've asked me to do exactly one thing since you got here. So what do you think?"

"Stop dragging this out. Just tell me." His deep voice cracked with anguish. "Did you see him?"

My breath caught as I waited for her to speak again. "Yes, I went to see Marcus, which was difficult because it's not like he gets around much on his own. He's got a whole hen's nest around him."

My stomach caught, hearing the name Marcus and the implication of the words.

"But you got him alone and you told him?"

"I did. And he gave me something."

I heard Diana's shoes on the cement as she walked closer to Wyatt, but I couldn't see the exchange. The sound of crinkled paper drifted out to my hiding spot, and I realized it was a note. I could only imagine the way his heart must be breaking right now—the torment wrestling around in his chest. I had no idea if the words were scribbled in compassion or anger toward Wyatt. I had no idea how his friend really felt toward him—the same friend who had just gotten *married* while trapped in a wheelchair.

I let out the breath I was holding. Maybe it was better if I got Gatsby loaded up with Diana and she left. Maybe it would be better for me to handle his potential wave of debilitating depression without her at the kennel.

CHAPTER 31

Emma

WE STOOD SIDE BY SIDE, WATCHING DIANA DRIVE AWAY with Gatsby. The old guy was riding shotgun in the front seat of the truck on his way to a new home. Wyatt never said much as we loaded the dog. Right before we shut the door, I'd slipped away and talked to Diana, giving him a moment with Gatsby.

As the truck disappeared into the white fog, I felt Wyatt's presence next to me as he slowly morphed into a statue. I stepped in front of him, and he gazed down at me. I knew his looks at this point—the happy and the sad, and the tormented, and the one that said, "I just want to disappear into a hole and slowly die." Yeah, Wyatt had that one too. I didn't see it very often, but it terrified every piece of me when it surfaced.

Today conveyed a mix of every feeling as his firm jaw hung in defeat. The news from the outside world had brought the gray clouds with it, which made me question how I should approach the information I'd learned by eavesdropping. I wasn't sure if I should bring up Marcus or just let him eventually tell me on his own. It didn't take long for Wyatt to come to a conclusion. His eyes stayed glued to mine as he fished inside his front jeans pocket, pulling out a crumpled piece of paper. He shoved it roughly into my hand as I stood there.

"You might as well read it," he mumbled. "I know you were outside the door when Diana gave it to me."

I swallowed hard, glancing down at a program from a Sunday church service. "I'm sorry. I didn't mean to. I'm sorry, Wyatt."

"It's okay. I would have eventually told you anyway."

Defeat rang so loud in the air that my heart clenched in my chest. I reached up, touching the side of his face. Wyatt closed his eyes for a moment, resting his cheek against my hand. Turning his head ever so slightly, he kissed the inside of my palm.

"What did you ask Diana to do for you?" I whispered.

His eyes flipped open, letting his gaze settle on me. He took my hand, pulling me over to the steps. We sat down on the small landing at the top, leaning back against the door with his arm around me. I rested my head against his chest as the fog thickened around us.

"A couple of weeks ago, Diana told me that Marcus and Zoey were getting married." His raspy voice was low, and I turned my head up slightly to hear him better.

"So she stayed with him after the accident?"

"Yeah," he muttered. "She's his nurse and all that shit. Zoey doesn't really like me very much. Hates my guts, actually. She yelled it at me in the hospital lobby."

"Oh."

"And after I told you about my last attempt to talk to Marcus, I got to thinking. I just wanted him to know. I *needed* him to hear the words even if I couldn't say them myself."

"Know what?" I whispered.

"That I'm sorry." He swallowed hard. "The guy got married in a damn wheelchair. And she has to take care of him. Forever. I just wanted Marcus to know I was sorry."

My mind drew a vivid and sad picture of the couple I'd never met, at the altar—there without the best man. Because even though Wyatt didn't say the words, that part must have hurt too.

Looking down at my hands, I slowly unfolded the Sunday school program. I saw the black pen marks in the margins.

"Wish you were here, Carter. I'm okay. Don't blame yourself. Not your fault. —M"

"Diana only got a couple of minutes with him before the wedding," he muttered. "He must have grabbed that off the table or something at the church."

"He doesn't blame you," I whispered, feeling the burning knot in my throat.

"I know. But how is that supposed to make me feel? Should I feel angry that *he's* not angry? Or should I feel relieved? And if I feel relieved, what kind of person does that make me?"

I nodded, understanding the cobwebs that circled around every thought in Wyatt's head. One thing always meant another and so on until he drove himself crazy.

"If you wanted Marcus to know that you are sorry, then you have to accept the fact that he forgives you. Or maybe he never did blame you. Either of you could've been the driver that night. Have you ever thought about that? Maybe he feels guilty too. For the accident. For his father's determination to destroy you. Maybe he feels just as bad as you."

The silence carried for what felt like an eternity as the ghosts of the past floated around in the foggy mist. I folded the program back up, holding it tightly in my hand as I rested my head against his chest again.

"You're right," his voice cracked. Wyatt's arms crushed me against his body. A tear fell down my cheek as the emotions ran strong between us. I was his strength, his hope, and sometimes his voice of reason that talked him off a cliff.

"We should go for a run," I muttered against his shirt. "It will make you feel better."

"I think it's drizzling rain."

"Nah." I looked up at him, seeing the redness around his eyes and nose. "It's been like this all day. Gus is alone in there now without Gatsby. Let's take him and Charlie out for a quick run. I'll get my running shoes out of the car."

"Okay." He let out a deep breath. "Let me go change. I'll meet you in the kennel."

It didn't take long for Wyatt to change from his boots and jeans into running shoes and old sweatpants. He checked on Gator, but the new arrival was still passed out on the floor from the tranquilizers.

We started out slowly, letting me get used to the pace. I was completely fine, but it made Wyatt feel better. This wasn't our first run with the dogs. After I'd suggested it a few weeks ago, he ditched his carefully executed running plan every morning. Instead, he went several times a day, taking different dogs for short runs through the tall grass until he started wearing down a new path in the dirt.

"You okay?" he called over to me as Gus pulled tight on the leash. His excitement for running might have overtaken his tennis ball addiction.

The cold northern wind picked up, hitting me in the face. "I'm good. You?"

"Better." He didn't have a smile, but it was close. I caught him watching me from the corner of his eye. He didn't have to tell me how he felt in a bunch of flowery words or take me on some fancy date. A simple look from Wyatt carried the weight of a hundred gifts. Just like I knew in the very beginning of my visits here—he didn't just hand those looks out to everyone. I knew

Wyatt reserved them for me and only me.

The first drop hit me on the nose. And then five more on the forehead.

"It's raining," I gasped.

"Time for a sprint." He scooped up Gus under his armpit. I grabbed Charlie as he tried to lick the drops from my cheek. I ran fast, pushing my body to the limit. But it didn't matter. The sky opened with the buckets of water it had threatened to spill all day—and not the sexy and warm stuff from the summer. This was a brisling fall rain that sent chills all the way to the core.

By the time we reached the kennel, I was out of breath and shivering. And Wyatt was laughing as we stumbled inside the door, carrying the dogs.

"This is not funny." I smiled at him.

"Would you rather I laugh or say I told you so?"

"Laugh." I was kidding, but for some reason the words came out almost serious as the reality of the moment hit me hard in the chest. He was better. At least for the moment as our wet clothes froze our skin.

He paused, holding my gaze. The storm picked up outside. He spoke, but the sound of the rain hitting the building drowned out his voice.

"What?" I yelled.

He leaned in close to my ear as drops of water dripped from his hair and onto my cheek. "Thank you."

"For what?"

"For being you."

I gave him a quick kiss, feeling the coldness of his lips before I pulled away. We took the shivering dogs into the office and grabbed a couple of towels. They both had short hair so it didn't take long to clean them up.

I put Charlie in the kennel. As I shut the gate, I watched the little dog make five circles in his bed before burrowing down in the warmth. When I returned to the front of the building, Wyatt was standing with the door open, watching the downpour. He had Gus wrapped in a raincoat so he didn't get wet again.

"You ready to make a run for it?"

"I don't see how I could get any more soaked."

"You go first." He moved to the side so I could run through the door. The cold drops shocked my skin as I made a beeline to the trailer. I ran inside, hearing Wyatt come up behind me. He shut the door and unwrapped Gus from inside the bundle. The dog trotted off to the bedroom to get in his warm bed just like Charlie.

"I don't think one single piece of you is dry." His eyes drifted over my body. "I'll get you something to wear."

"Okay. I probably should get started on my paper," I said, following him into his bedroom.

"That's right. You were going to write a paper when you got here. Sorry for all the distractions."

"It's okay."

Opening his dresser drawer, Wyatt pulled a long-sleeved shirt and sweatpants from the carefully folded piles of clothes. I laughed as he held up the gray pants. "I'm going to need a belt to keep them up."

"I've got some duct tape in the kitchen. I could just tape them to you."

"Haha." I rolled my eyes, taking the clothes from him. I disappeared into the bathroom, shutting the door behind me. Turning on the shower, I waited for the steam to fill the room. I just wanted to feel the warm water for a moment to get rid of the chill from the rain.

I rinsed off, wishing I could sit under the spray for hours instead of working on my paper. Climbing out, I grabbed the towel next to the tub since I'd forgotten to get one from the meticulously folded pile in the closet.

I did my best to get the water out of my hair until it was only damp. Burying my face down into the soft fabric, the overwhelming smell of Wyatt filled my nose and my thoughts. Glancing at the door, I felt a nervous idea forming in my head.

I loved him. I wanted him, and he wanted me. Plain and simple. But he wasn't going to let himself have what he wanted. Not without a push, just like I had to push him with every other issue in his life.

Wrapping the towel tight around my body, I tucked a little piece down between my breasts to keep the brown fabric in place. I took a few steps back from the mirror to get a good look at myself. It wasn't glamorous, but it should at least get his attention.

As I slowly opened the bathroom door, my heart hammered away at a thousand beats per minute. My silent feet made their way across the carpet until I found Wyatt in the kitchen, drying his chest off with a dish towel since I'd hogged the bathroom. Pausing next to the refrigerator, I watched as he rubbed the rag over his head. He made one more pass down his chest, stopping on the edge of his gray boxer shorts.

Wyatt glanced up, seeing me standing there in just a towel. His hand froze in place as his eyes touched my skin, my breasts, my arms, my legs.

"What are you doing, Emma?" His voice struggled to say the words.

"Well, I figured if I got this far, you would take care of the rest," I whispered.

Wyatt didn't move as I closed the last few feet between us. And then slowly, he cupped the side of my face, tracing his thumb against my skin. He stared into my eyes as the past and the present battled around inside his head.

"Emma," he murmured. "I don't think we should do this."

"But I want to. And I know you want to."

His hands moved down around my waist, holding me gently

as his fingers rubbed against the soft fabric of the towel. Wyatt gripped me tighter, pulling me closer to him.

My arms went around his shoulders as his lips brushed across my neck. He held me like that for a moment before whispering, "I don't even have condoms out here. It's not like I could tell Diana to add some to the grocery list."

I steadied my thoughts, knowing this conversation would need to take place at some point. "I take birth control pills."

"For how long?" His paranoid eyes bore into mine. "Because I can't get you pregnant. Not now. Not like this."

I didn't think it was possible for Wyatt to look any more haunted, but that particular thought had pushed him right over the edge into a different kind of stricken. The rain picked up outside, filling the quiet air of the trailer.

"Since I had the leg surgery. And I knew that I was coming back. So for several months now."

He didn't say anything. So I kissed him, gently and slowly until his resolve gradually caved and his tongue slipped between my lips. He held me tight against his chest. The only thing separating us was a small brown towel and a thin pair of gray boxers.

Wyatt let his hands relax as they drifted past the frayed edge of the fabric until he touched my thighs. His fingers slipped under the towel, cupping my bare butt cheeks, making my legs quiver. I dug my toes into the carpet, feeling the warmth spread through my body. He whispered against my lips, "I know you haven't done this before."

"No." I had assumed Wyatt had already figured it out, but I wasn't embarrassed to admit it out loud to him. Maybe if I hadn't gone on my detour in life, I would've met someone who I'd wanted to share this with. But the truth is—I had never met someone who made me feel the way Wyatt could with a simple glance. Maybe he was my obsession. Maybe I was addicted to helping him and saving him and doing whatever it took to fix him. But I also felt something deep in my heart.

I looked Wyatt in the eyes, trying to calm the storm I saw inside of him. "I love you. I love the part you think is bad and the part I know is good. So just let me love you. Okay?"

He nodded slowly as a hundred different emotions flickered through his eyes as he processed my words. "I would do anything for you, Emma. But that's not really possible while I'm out here. I can't give you much of anything. So if you want me to love you, then I'll love you. At least I can do that."

Everything inside of me melted and ached with his words. The pull between us got thicker and heavier, and then his lips were on my mouth. His hands were on my skin. Wyatt picked me up from the floor. My legs wrapped around his waist as he carried me the short distance to his bedroom.

Wyatt set me down next to the bed. My toes dug into the carpet as I gazed into his eyes. His lips lingered against mine. Reaching between us, he pulled the little piece of towel that I'd tucked down between my breasts. The brown fabric fell to the floor as the cool air hit my back.

But I didn't feel it for long. His eyes trailed over my exposed body, followed by his hands as they warmed my skin. The back of my legs touched the side of the bed as we fell against the comforter.

"You feel so good." I barely heard him over the sound of the storm outside. Our bodies intertwined as we found our way under the covers. I had been in this bed many different times, but never completely naked. It was a little awkward as we got used to each other, and at the same time, incredibly beautiful.

He kissed me as his hands explored my skin. They moved softly, making me squirm against his fingers. I needed more. I craved more as his lips followed the slow path down my body, pressing little kisses against my stomach and thighs. His warm breath brushed my skin as he licked me softly with his tongue. It felt incredible. He felt incredible. I was breathing hard, fighting to keep it together. Closing my eyes, I let him kiss me. I let him kiss me everywhere as I twisted around against the sheets. His mouth moved slowly and sweetly until my body finally gave away, letting me fall into the hazy afterglow.

My eyes caught his, and I knew my cheeks were pink. I was a little embarrassed, but I loved this with him. I loved every moment. Every touch. Lying on my back, I watched as Wyatt tugged the gray boxer shorts off. He flashed a smile, letting me see his dimples. I felt a warm spark of anticipation inside my chest. I had wanted this with him for such a long time. And he was finally letting himself be with me.

A faint clap of thunder echoed outside the window. Wyatt hovered between my legs, putting his weight on his arms and knees. In the shadows, our eyes held onto each other as he slipped gradually inside my body, letting the pain come slowly. And then he stopped as the conflicted thoughts filled his head.

"I'm okay," I whispered.

"I don't want to hurt you. I *can't* hurt you."

"You're not." I bit back the gasp as he moved again. "I'll be okay."

I know Wyatt tried to go slow, but the pull between our bodies was greater than us, rolling into a momentum he couldn't really control. Every push of his hips made me gasp as I drifted somewhere between pleasure and pain. I felt him everywhere, kissing my neck, touching my skin, pressing deeper inside me as he whispered things I couldn't hear.

I held on to Wyatt, feeling the pain slowly disappear—for both of us. With every breath, I loved him a little bit more as he let go and loved me back.

A few hours later, the trailer was almost completely dark. Night-time came earlier in November even without the rain. I crawled out of bed, leaving Wyatt asleep under the covers. In the bathroom, I cleaned myself up before putting on the clothes he'd given me earlier.

I smiled at myself in the mirror. I wanted to go back into the bedroom and wrap myself around him, never letting go. But I had a paper to write. One that was due first thing in the morning.

Tiptoeing through the trailer, I made my way into the kitchen. I poured water into the coffee pot and added my favorite hazelnut-flavored dark brew into the filter. Leaning against the counter, I stared into space as the warm steam trickled out of the machine.

A smile slipped on my lips from the residual effects of my runner's high. I loved running. When my feet hit the ground, I was one with the trees and the grass as the cool air slapped me in the face and I disappeared into the free fall.

But tonight was beyond anything I'd ever experienced. Being with Wyatt was a complete free fall with another person. I had let go and he had let go, and nothing else mattered except the moment in which we had fallen together.

I jumped, feeling his hands around my waist. "You have to stop doing that," I whispered.

Pulling me back against his chest, Wyatt kissed the side of my forehead. "Haven't you figured it out by now? I like scaring you."

"I *know* you do." I laughed softly.

Wyatt held me in his arms as the coffee dripped down into the silver pot. I sucked in a deep breath, inhaling the scent of hazelnut and the smell of him.

"Are you okay?" he whispered.

"It hurts a little, but I'm okay." I turned around in his arms, seeing the concern etched in the creases of his eyes. "Don't worry. You can't have love without a little pain. Right?"

His lips gently touched mine. "It will be better next time."

"It was good this time. I promise."

"I love you," he whispered. He clutched me in his arms with a tight grip, giving those words the depth of saying them a thousand times. In the shadows, I was his tree limb. I was his rock. I was pulling him slowly to shore as he allowed himself to feel something deep and passionate for another person.

He held me for a little bit longer before letting go. He flashed me a sweet smile complete with his rugged dimples. "I'll let you get to work. I've got a Gator to check on. Maybe if I'm there when he wakes up, it will make it better for him."

Wyatt grabbed a book off of the shelf and a small umbrella. My heart grew five sizes bigger as I watched him disappear out the door, knowing he was planning to read to the poor, scared dog in the kennel.

CHAPTER 32

Emma

I LEFT WYATT'S AS THE SUN DRIFTED SLOWLY INTO THE SKY. MY paper had to be submitted before eight in the morning, and I still needed to stop by the computer lab and use their printer. This professor preferred the good old-fashioned printout to mark it full of red lines.

I was exhausted when I pulled into the apartment complex. Last night, it had taken five hours to finish my paper and then at three in the morning, we had sex again. I was sore, but it was already better than the first time. And honestly, I didn't even care if being with Wyatt still hurt a little. I simply loved the way it felt as we got tangled up together in the darkness.

I got out of the car, seeing Kurt perched on the wooden stairs leading to the second floor. He had a hammer in one hand and a box of nails sitting on the steps. I wonder what lit a fire under our apartment manager to cause him to do work this early considering Lanie, the girl who lived on the other side of Mr. Hughes, had reported the broken banister about three months ago.

I made my way over to the stairs, wishing I didn't have to pass by Kurt to get to my apartment. He stopped beating the hammer against the wood once he noticed my presence.

"Well, well. Emma's doing the damn walk of shame. What do they call that? Rode hard and left . . ." His words faded into a grin that held the pictures I knew must be dancing around in his head. I had on my damp yoga pants from last night and Wyatt's sweatshirt since mine was still wet.

I gave him a tired glare at his disgusting statement. "Move your stuff, Kurt. I seriously doubt you want me falling down the stairs *again* while you are out here."

Under the wiry beard, his face stiffened at the subtle hint. One time was enough to make people talk. But twice, well, that kind of stuff made people start investigating, even if Kurt didn't *push* me down the stairs.

The burly man dusted the step clean of all the loose nails and scooted over next to the railing. I moved quickly past him without giving a second glance. As I reached the top, his voice came out almost as a low growl.

"Why doesn't he ever come here to see you? Instead, he just leaves his girlfriend here *all alone*."

My skin crawled at his implication. This little banter with Kurt was getting ridiculous. Putting the key into the lock, I went inside the apartment only to find Blaire pacing around the living room, cursing under her breath. Glancing back outside, Kurt still had his eyes on me as I shut the door. I turned the deadbolt even though it failed to give me any kind of comfort.

Blaire made another pass in front of me as she wore down our carpet with her feet. I figured my sister was worked up again over our creepy apartment manager. "What's wrong, Blaire?"

"He wants to meet. I knew it. And I *told* you it would happen. But you just had to make me look all nice and send that damn picture. Now he wants to meet. I can't do it. I'm not ready. I just *can't*, Emma."

"It's going to be okay. You can do this."

She paused, gaping at me like I'd grown horns. "You had sex with him. I thought something was off last night, but now it makes sense."

"I did," I muttered. My skin bristled as I waited for some tirade. I'd expected one of her explosions since M-Attack815 already had my sister wound up tight.

"Did you *like* having sex with him?" Her expression seemed more curious than crazy as she asked the blunt question.

"I did."

"Hmm. Well, that's good. So you are happy with Wyatt? The way things are with him?" Her words came out cautious as she probed the controversial subject between us.

"Yes, but it's not like it's going to be like this forever. You do understand that he will eventually get to leave. It's not that long of a wait. And then everything will be normal."

"That's true." She started pacing again. I glanced out the kitchen window, seeing Kurt walk back to the office. He picked up the dog crate next to the door and disappeared inside. I didn't know what kind of game he was playing, but I swear the creepy man was taunting me after he'd caught me snooping.

"You're not helping," she spat from behind me.

I turned around, seeing her face a little wild as her feet moved quickly to the back wall of the living room and spun in a complete circle as she headed back toward the kitchen.

"You should just go meet Matt. Get it over with."

"I can't," she gasped.

"Then why did you ask me to help you? Just go meet him. If it's terrible, then leave."

"Like, just get up and walk out of Starbucks?"

"He wants to meet at Starbucks? That sounds good. It's usually loud. And you are not required to eat dinner or play twelve holes of mini golf. Starbucks. It's simple. You should go."

"Shit!" Her face exploded into a panic attack. "I'm just so . . . just . . . shit. I'm not good at this. I'll freak out. I won't even get in the door."

My heart hurt, seeing Blaire's sudden meltdown. In this moment, I was reminded of our differences. I had barged into Wyatt's life, forcing him to take notice as I slowly pulled his kind soul from the dark clutches of his mental anguish. My sister couldn't even have coffee with a guy who *wanted* to see her.

"I'll go with you." I tried to reassure Blaire. "I'll stay in the corner. I'll even wear a disguise. Like, a wig or something and my big sunglasses. He will be looking for you in that little blue hat anyway."

"You'd go with me?" she asked weakly.

"Yes. And if things get crazy, then we will walk out the door *together*. Now go figure out a day to meet him."

And I needed to figure out what Kurt was doing with that dog crate. I peered out the window again, seeing him carry the white box around the corner to where he parked his pickup truck. Something was up with Kurt again. And I wasn't sure how easy it would be to rescue another Charlie from his clutches.

CHAPTER 33

Emma

OVER THE NEXT COUPLE OF WEEKS, I SECRETLY WATCHED Kurt through the curtains. Something just didn't make sense. When I was home, I studied his comings and goings from the apartment complex, but I never actually saw Kurt in possession of another crate. I wasn't sure what I could do if I did catch him with a dog. Yank it out of his hands and make a run for it. Call the police and report a man with *crates*. All of my irrational logic had me thinking crazy thoughts until I questioned my sanity and gave up on my surveillance of Kurt.

Besides, I had a full work schedule keeping me busy. I helped decorate the nursing home for Thanksgiving. Vera said her grandson was picking her up for the holiday. She was going to their fancy house in Nichols Hills for the whole day. After a cup of Earl Grey tea, Vera showed me the pink dress she was planning to wear, the one she saved for special occasions.

As for Wyatt, our relationship grew deeper, sweeter, and more intense. He loved making love to me, which sounded cheesy for a guy like him. But I couldn't call it anything else with Wyatt.

Those moments were not just sex or the hundred other torrid terms used to describe it. In his mind, there was nothing he could give me but love—so he *loved* me over and over again.

Sometimes when I arrived at the trailer, he pulled me through door, touching me, kissing me, until I was swept away into the feel of our bodies melding together in a fiery collision. And sometimes it was a slow burn like the embers had all of eternity to smolder into oblivion.

I wasn't sure what side of Wyatt I would get when I showed up unexpected on Tuesday. My chemistry lab had ended early so I sought out the only person I wanted to see in my free time. As I climbed out of the driver's seat, he came out of the kennel door covered in sweat, looking a little bewildered. I ran over to him, jumping into his arms, wrapping my legs around his waist. He kissed me briefly before pulling back.

"What's wrong?" I looked into his green eyes, seeing the creases around the corners.

"I've been wrestling a *Gator* most of the morning." I felt the warmth of his breath against my cold face.

"That bad?" I said, letting go of his body. He pulled me back close, keeping his hands in a possessive hold around my waist.

"He got loose when I tried to fill his food bowl. I honestly thought he was going take my damn arm off. I'm not sure if he wouldn't just eat me if he had the chance. It took forever to put him back in his pen. Shit was flying everywhere in the kennel room as he knocked stuff around. And he got some of the others all worked up as he tried to attack them through the gates."

"What are you going to do with him?"

He shook his head as his face twisted up a bit. "Honestly? I don't know. I guess give him some time and keep trying."

"Maybe that's all you can do. Keep at it until he has no choice but to let you help him."

His eyes caught mine. "I guess so."

"Do you need me to help you in there?"

"Nah, I've got it all put back together. What are you doing here? I thought you wouldn't be back until tomorrow."

"Well, my schedule cleared up a little bit today. So I thought I would stop by."

"Hmm." He grinned. "I like that you decided to stop by."

"You do?"

His lips touched my mouth as my eyes drifted closed. His fingers rubbed softly against my back as he teased me with his tongue. I relaxed against him, feeling the sweetness of the slow burn.

"I can't reach you under all of this," he whispered against my lips.

Wyatt tugged my scarf, twirling it slowly around and around until he pulled the red wool free from around my neck. The brisk chill hit my skin, but his lips quickly made a slow descent toward the neckline of my purple sweater. We moved around in the cold breeze—almost like it pushed us into a slow dance, swaying back and forth as his hands stayed on my waist and his warm mouth on my skin.

"I want us to go dancing sometime," I whispered.

His eyes caught mine. "Like, country dancing or something different?"

"Can you two-step?"

"Yes," he whispered as a flash of sadness mixed in with his gaze. I knew it bothered Wyatt to be reminded of how our relationship was anything but normal. "You want me to take you sometime?"

"Yes."

"Okay." He let out a deep breath. "We will go dancing."

"With a live band?"

Wyatt kissed my forehead before running the tip of his nose down the length of mine. "Yes. I'll bring you flowers and take you to dinner. You'll wear some short, sexy dress, which will make me not want to leave your apartment. But I'll take you dancing anyway. And there will be a live band. I'll hold you against me on the dance floor as I fight the urge to touch your ass. And I'll probably step on your toes with my boots."

"I wouldn't care if you did," I whispered.

"I know." Wyatt's lips found mine and my eyes closed. I got lost in the dream he'd painted of dancing as our bodies swayed to the imaginary music that played in the cold air. I wanted those dreams. I wanted those moments to come true. I wanted our future. The one we built brick by brick as we gradually made promises of a life together in the outside world.

The sound of a car brought me back to our current reality as the beautiful moment crumbled right into a ball of dust. We both turned in the direction of the dirty cloud coming up the grass path to the trailer. I recognized the vehicle immediately as the black Tahoe parked in front of us. *Willa.*

Wyatt tensed up before stepping away from my embrace. I dreaded every second as the door opened. I didn't want another episode like last time. But things were different. We were different.

Willa got out of the passenger's side, her long brown hair hanging in silky waves to her elbows. She wore a flowy white shirt with a frayed jean jacket and black skinny jeans. She was just as angelic as the last time I saw her.

Another woman got out of the driver's side. She hesitated as her eyes latched on to Wyatt. I knew immediately she was his mother. Glancing to my right, the chill of the air was nothing compared to what I felt coming from Wyatt. He remained perfectly still, watching her get a giant picnic basket out of the back of the vehicle. His mother lugged the heavy load over to us, setting it down on the ground.

"Hi." I smiled, trying to break the tension.

"Hey." Willa's eyes flickered from me to her brother.

His mother focused on me. "You must be Emma. Nice to finally meet you."

She was younger than I'd expected. But I assume the last couple of years had played their toll on this woman. Dark circles haunted her blue eyes from the many nights she must have stayed awake, worrying about her children.

"Nice to meet you too, Mrs. Carter."

"Call me Karen." She looked over at her son, but he focused on the ground instead of acknowledging her presence.

"I got my diploma today." Willa grinned. Her excitement overshadowed the awkward situation.

Wyatt had yet to say a word so I spoke up. "For high school?"

"GED. I finished the program and did the testing."

"Wow. That is really awesome. Isn't it, Wyatt?"

He said nothing, and I saw tears on the corner of Karen's eyes. "She's been watching the mail for a week. And it finally came this morning. I asked Willa what she wanted to do to celebrate. And she said have dinner with her family."

Her voice broke a little on the last part, but she kept talking, addressing Wyatt directly. "Your father was going to come, but he wasn't sure how you would feel about it. So it's just us. I . . . um . . . I have everything in there. Pulled pork. Baked beans. Some mashed potatoes. It's still hot."

The familiar look of panic gripped his face. Not the explosive angry kind, but the one where he fell down in a deep hole. The one that made me worry about his mental state.

"It sounds really good. Give us just a second." Grabbing his hand, I pulled Wyatt inside the trailer. I shut the door behind us. His stricken expression hurt my heart. Cupping a hand on each side of his face, I forced him to look at me.

"Before you freak out and start cramming your family back in the car, have you ever thought about this from their perspective?

They have lost you. They don't see you. They worry about you."

"I know, but—"

"No buts. Just stop whatever nonsense you are about to tell me. Your sister just accomplished something really big. And you sit out here, acting like you killed her. She's not dead. Stop pretending like she is. Willa is alive, standing outside your door. And she wants to celebrate with you. And it's a big deal. I'm sure it was hard for her to study and do this on her own. But she did it."

Wyatt chewed around on my words. I had pushed a mountain of reality on him all at once. I prayed my approach didn't backfire. And then his eyes turned sad. "It hurts to see her like this. That's why I make them stay away."

"I know. But it hurts your mom *not* to see you. It hurts Willa." I pleaded with him. "This dinner will not be easy. It's going to be awkward. But let them stay."

It took a moment, but his shoulders relaxed. He put his hands over mine. "Okay." His voice cracked thick with emotion. "Let's have dinner."

A tear fell down my cheek as I stared into his eyes. He kissed my forehead. Wyatt took my hand, leading me back outside. He picked up the picnic basket.

"Thanks, Mom," he mumbled. She followed him back inside the trailer, and I felt a heart rush, seeing it happen. I lagged behind with Willa. She threw her arms around me for a brief hug.

"Thank you," she whispered.

"Don't thank me yet." I rolled my eyes.

As we joined them inside, I heard Wyatt muttering something about not having a kitchen table.

"That's okay." I smiled, trying to keep everyone moving. "We can eat on the coffee table."

His mom paused, taking in the contents of the trailer. Her eyes drifted across the living room and into the bare kitchen. I realized it was the first time she'd seen the inside of where her son lived.

"Is water okay?" I asked her.

"Yeah, it's fine." She finally sat down on the couch, unpacking the basket. Her eyes glanced up to the bookshelf several times until she finally asked the question that had plagued her thoughts. "Have you read all of those books?"

"I have," he muttered, getting the plates out of the cabinet.

"Huh, well, that shouldn't surprise me, I guess."

"No?" I asked. His love of books honestly surprised me.

A whimsical smile slipped on her lips. "As a little boy, Wyatt always liked me to read to him. He would say, 'Again, again.' I had to read some of them twice or three times before he would go to sleep. But he eventually got older and grew out of it. I guess he didn't like hearing his old mom reading out loud to him. I don't remember the last time I saw Wyatt pick up a book that wasn't for school."

I set the cups of water on the coffee table. "Well, he actually reads them out loud to the dogs in the kennel."

Wyatt froze in mid-step with the plates in his hands. Maybe that wasn't something I should've shared, but I knew it was the right decision the moment I saw his mom's face. Karen looked at him with a sense of awe and relief. So I kept on talking. "He will have to take you out to see the dogs after we eat. Show you around the place. See what he does out here. He's like magic with them."

"That sounds nice." Karen looked at Wyatt. The obvious yearning was there in her gaze. He gave her a quick nod in agreement. I took a drink of water, trying to calm down the nervous flutters. This was going better than I'd ever expected.

Willa picked up Gus, holding him like a baby in her lap. He licked every inch of her fingers, and I smiled at their reunion. She obviously loved her dog, yet she had given him to her brother because she loved him too. Gus was the piece that still held them together.

As we ate, the conversation grew easier. I gushed over his mom's wonderful food. Willa told us about the GED program and studying for the test. They both asked me a hundred questions about my classes and working at the nursing home. I can't say Wyatt contributed that much, but he made an effort to speak when asked a question.

And then out of the blue, he looked at his sister. "You should take Gus back with you."

"I can't do that," she protested, but her smile couldn't remain hidden.

"I think it's time. I've been thinking about moving Charlie in here anyway. I'm going to keep him." His eyes sought mine. As far as I knew, my little dog was still on the adoption list. But now Wyatt wanted to keep him, which meant he was *keeping* him for me. Another little brick for our future. Neither of us said anything, but I think Willa caught the exchange. Her grin got a little bigger as she looked at me.

"Well, I guess Gussy is coming back with me then," she said, clutching the Jack Russell in her arms.

Taking their plates, I headed toward the kitchen. "Why don't you take them out to the kennel and I'll clean up in here."

"I'll help you. Wyatt can take Mom to see it."

I stilled, waiting to see his reaction, but he simply got up from his brown chair and looked at his mom. "It's this way."

I held my breath until I saw them disappear out the door. Swallowing the knot back down in my throat, I washed the food off the mismatched dishes, placing them in the cabinet. Willa packed the refrigerator with the leftovers. "Gross. Does he eat this stuff?"

"Yes. Unless I bring food. Did he always eat that many hot dogs?"

She shook her head. "No. Actually our mom cooks all the

time. She doesn't even buy hot dogs and bologna."

"If you think that's gross, the cabinets are only full of Cap'n Crunch. He *lives* on that stuff."

She burst out laughing. "Well, that would be my fault. I got him hooked on that one."

"You seriously eat that nasty cereal like him?"

"Yep. Every morning. And sometimes for dinner on Sundays. I get cranky if I don't get it. It's my sugar crack."

I made a gagging motion, and she laughed. "Oh, Emma. You are *so* missing out."

We finished and returned to the living room, sitting side by side on the couch. I looked over at Willa, and then my mouth got the best of me. "How are you doing?"

"You mean with my head stuff?"

"I'm sorry. I shouldn't pry. I only know what he told me."

"No, it's fine. I'm sure Wyatt gave you the Frankenstein version. I'm okay. I still have several episodes a week. I kind of *lied* about that one the last time I was here." She laughed faintly.

"Yeah, I think he figured that out."

"True. But the episodes are not as scary as they were in the beginning, like when he was around. Actually, since you asked . . ." She smiled with a grin that was very familiar. I had seen that one on Wyatt a few times when he was teasing me. "I haven't told anyone this yet because I'm afraid they will freak out."

"So I guess the rest of your family is like Wyatt?"

"Haha. Not usually as intense, but they don't process news very well. Especially my father. They're kind of alike, you know. Wyatt and my dad. It's why they struggled so much."

I nodded, hearing something I'd already figured out. "So what is your news?"

"Well, I found a doctor who thinks he might be able to help me. It's *brain surgery* of course, but there's a real possibility he can stop the episodes."

"But?"

"Ah yes, there's a catch. There's risks. Like the big one involved with any type of brain surgery. I could be a vegetable. And the lesser side effect but still a biggy. I could go blind. The area with the problem is close to the place that controls my vision."

"But you want to do it?"

"I don't know. I'm thinking about it. I mean. I *should* consider it. I think I should consider all my options. The doctor is in Boston. We have been emailing. And technically, I'm not ruled incompetent or anything. I'm eighteen, so they can't stop me from jumping on a plane and letting some guy rip my head open. Although my parents will probably try."

I laughed at her blatant candor. She didn't let her condition wear her down. "That's incredible. It really is. I'm glad that you have options."

"And who knows. Maybe I will let this guy cut my brain into mush or maybe I'll end up doing nothing." She rested her head back against the couch. "I like you, Emma. You're easy to talk to. Easy to spill my secrets. I see why he's drawn to you."

"I don't know if he was exactly drawn to me." I chuckled under my breath, picturing that very first day I'd arrived at the kennel.

"Either way, I'm glad you found Wyatt. Because I worry about him."

"Me too," I muttered.

Her face fell as her thoughts got darker. "Is he okay? I worry sometimes that he might, you know. Do something crazy. And sometimes I get terrified that we will get the call because someone found him like Trevor."

Her voice faded out as her eyes watered up over the same guy who haunted Wyatt. I didn't know what to say to make his sister feel better. I had often felt the same concerns and fears when it came to her brother.

"He's better, I think," I whispered. "He talks to me about some of the stuff. I don't know what will help with the guilt. That's something he will have to figure out on his own, I guess."

"I know he feels guilty. And Marcus's dad didn't make any of this easy. He even tried to get me to testify in court against him. I was a minor so the DA couldn't force much." Her eyes drifted off across the room. "It's my fault, really. If I hadn't been on the porch with Trevor, none of it would've happened. Wyatt got so angry. He was drunk. I was drunk. Trevor was drunk. It was like a match dropped in gasoline. So I let him take me to the car instead of trying to sort it all out."

She stopped talking and a tear rolled down her cheek. I reached over, gripping her hand in mine. Willa looked up at me. She smiled a broken grin. "Like I said, you make a person want to spill all their secrets."

My heart ached for the other person who lived with the aftermath of the accident. We talked for a little bit longer until Wyatt and Karen returned. They loaded Gus and the empty picnic basket into the car. Willa grabbed her brother in a quick embrace, and then Wyatt allowed his mom to properly hug him goodbye. She gripped tight to his tall frame while his eyes briefly closed.

"Maybe we could do this again?" Karen reluctantly released her son, her expression hopeful with the question.

Wyatt hesitated, and I was afraid he was going to decline the offer. "Okay. What about Thanksgiving?"

"I think we could do that."

He shuffled around, not making eye contact. "And I guess bring Dad and . . . um . . . maybe Grandma and Grandpa."

His mom didn't have any words. The emotions were too much. She just nodded in agreement, jumping in the car before he could change his mind. As we watched his family drive away, Wyatt clutched my hand in his large palm. His nerves were shaking hard, making my whole arm move with him.

"Thanksgiving?" I whispered.

"It sort of just slipped out. And I want to take it back."

"You can't really take back an invite, Wyatt."

"I know," he muttered.

"It's going to be okay."

The brisk wind hit me in the back, making me shiver. Yet we didn't move. Neither of us budged from the spot even after their car disappeared from view.

Today was a huge step for Wyatt. His emotions were raw and torn from just seeing his family, and then he accidentally invited them back for Thanksgiving. Except, I didn't think it was an *accident.* Just like inviting *me* back here wasn't an accident. His subconscious had gotten the best of him, spitting out the words he needed to say even when he preferred to keep them silent.

I let go of his hand and went to my car. His stoic expression stayed in place as I unzipped my backpack. Reaching inside, my hand clasped around the hardback book. I pulled it free and zipped the pack closed, slamming the door behind me.

"I brought you something." His troubled eyes held mine for a moment, and I wasn't sure if he was even going to speak. "I have a new one for you."

He shoulders moved as he took a deep breath. "So you are going to make me suffer through another alien love story?"

"No. This one is vampires."

The corner of his lip twitched into an almost smile. "Shitty vampire love stories now."

I laughed, knowing he would read any story I brought, even if he acted like it was the worst book in the world. I handed the old hardback over to him. He studied the title and then smirked a sad grin. "I admit. You got me on this one."

"Bram Stoker's *Dracula.* The *original* vampire story. You told me once that you wanted to read it. And I didn't see it on your shelf."

"No. I haven't read it. Thank you." His gaze held mine.

"You're welcome," I whispered.

"Maybe I should read it to Gator so he will know there are things with teeth bigger than his."

I laughed faintly. "Maybe."

He held the book in one hand, keeping his eyes on me. His gaze turned into something deep and needy. I felt the growing heat between us even in the cold November air. The events of the day had taken their toll on Wyatt. He needed something. He needed me.

Slipping his right hand in mine, Wyatt pulled me slowly to the trailer. As we reached the top of the stairs, he pushed me up against the old aluminum door as he fumbled with the knob until he gave up altogether. His lips found mine. His emotions were wild and on fire, making his kiss rough and almost possessive. My back pressed tightly against the door, and I feared it would crash through into the living room, taking the flimsy wall of the trailer down with it.

"We should go inside," I pleaded.

But Wyatt didn't answer. He silenced my words by slipping his tongue between my lips. He kissed me like I was the very air keeping him alive, making the achy warmth spread through my legs. Wyatt pushed his hips tighter against my stomach. I was trapped between the hardness of his body and the fragile old door. A loud creak echoed behind me, causing Wyatt to freeze in place.

"Hold on," he muttered. He turned the knob. We finally made it through the door without breaking it off the hinges. *Dracula* got tossed on the coffee table, and I fell on the couch. I pulled my sweater over my head at the same time he struggled to peel the skinny jeans off my legs. My fingers unzipped his pants and he stepped out, dragging his boxers down to the floor with them.

Wyatt never paused as he climbed on the couch. I sucked in a sharp breath, feeling him press inside of me. And then we were together, bound in a haze of gasps and moans. Wyatt clutched my body, moving faster with every push of his hips.

"I just don't feel like I can get close enough to you." His words came in short breaths against my neck.

Yet I felt every bit of his closeness. He was inside of me and outside of me. I gasped as he pushed himself deeper and deeper until he pushed me right to the edge. My thoughts blurred as I sought what only Wyatt could give me: a melding of our hearts and bodies and souls. And then I crashed. My eyes closed, letting the world disappear into suspended time. I felt utterly and completely happy. I loved him. And I knew he loved me too.

Wyatt continued to rock into me, over and over again, and then he stilled, wrapping his fingers into my hair as a low groan escaped his lips. We held onto each other until the silence of the trailer came back into focus. Yet he still didn't let go, gripping my bare skin tightly beneath him. If it were possible, I think Wyatt would've buried himself inside my body and soul forever.

He eventually pulled the blanket from the back of the couch, draping it over our sweaty bodies as we shifted ourselves around into spooning on the scratchy cushions. Wyatt circled his arms around me, snuggling his face up against my hair. His lips briefly kissed my neck.

We didn't speak, not even after the darkness enveloped the trailer. I knew Wyatt was awake, processing the emotions of seeing his family today. I let him work through the thoughts in silence. Sometimes he needed a push and sometimes he just needed to hold on to me. I closed my eyes, listening to his soft breaths until he finally rested his lips against my ear.

"I want to tell you something," he murmured.

"Okay."

It took a moment before he found the words. "I have nightmares sometimes. The really graphic stuff. It's all crazy shit that isn't real. But when I'm asleep, it feels so real."

"I know," I whispered. "I've heard you before in your sleep."

"I figured, but I don't have them as often anymore. Not since you. And sometimes I have different dreams. And they mess me up in a different way."

"Why?"

He let out a deep breath that warmed my skin. His fingers trailed over my stomach, making little circles around my belly button. "Because they are about you and me. I see us on the other side of this. I see us in a real house, walking down the street, going to stores and dinner and movies. I see us together, laughing like there's nothing holding us back. I see us hanging out with your sister. Meeting your parents. Having this normal life. Having a future. And I want it, just as much as I *hate* it."

His words made my heart ache. "You shouldn't hate it. I want those things too."

"I know, but I just can't stop feeling like I don't deserve you."

"Wyatt." I tilted my neck around so I could see his face in the shadows. "You can't think something like that. No one really deserves anyone. People choose to be with other people. I chose you. I chose to have these moments with you. And I chose to make future plans with you."

"I know. But how is that fair? Diana keeps telling me to think about the future. And you make me imagine that future. But then I look at Willa and I think—how is that fair? Her life is a struggle because of me. And I'm making plans with a girl I don't deserve."

I didn't know how to answer his question without sounding cliché so I just told the truth. "It's not fair, Wyatt. None of this is fair. But you can't stay still in life, thinking that will make it fair. You have to keep moving forward."

"I don't know how." His frustration seeped into the words.

"You keep trying until you do."

He didn't say anything, but I felt his silent thoughts as his chest moved quickly up and down against my back. I had pushed, and as usual, he just needed time to absorb the words.

And then his gravelly voice spoke in the quiet darkness of the trailer. "Maybe I've looked at this all wrong. Maybe there is a way to live with the guilt." His voice broke with emotion. "Maybe I can stop people from being me."

"How?" I whispered.

"I don't know. But if I can stop just *one* person from being me or even Trevor. Then maybe I will be able to live with myself. Maybe I will be able to move forward and live in the world again. And I can have a life with you. The one I want to give you."

A tear fell down my cheek, followed by another. They ran down my face until they dripped onto his hands. "I think that sounds like a good plan."

Wyatt brushed the wetness from my cheeks. "Emmy, don't cry."

"It's okay. They're good tears."

Wyatt kissed my neck, leaving his lips in place as he whispered against my skin. "I love you. Whether I deserve you or not. I love you. Don't ever forget that."

CHAPTER 34

Emma

On Thursday night, one week before Thanksgiving, I finally told my parents about Wyatt. I figured if he could let his family back into his life, then mine deserved to know what I'd kept hidden from them all these months.

After Blaire said she needed her own car, I slipped the news into the conversation. They were stunned. My dad stopped eating his lasagna in mid-bite. My mom gave a teary smile like she understood my need to help Wyatt while silently questioning my sanity. She saw my boyfriend as another of my *Emma* projects. My dad's eyebrows narrowed, similar to Blaire's, as he said, "I remember seeing the story on the news about the kid who burned down that town."

Apparently I was the only person who didn't remember Wyatt's story being splashed in the headlines. I politely explained it wasn't an *entire* town, but my accurate description didn't relieve any of the concern expressed by my father.

I'm sure he would love to have a discussion with Wyatt, but that would require a drive out to his confinement, which currently wasn't a good idea. Showing up unannounced with my *parents* would be a disaster.

And then I flipped the tables around in my mind, looking at it from their perspective. Daughter finds guy with ankle monitor on house arrest because he got drunk and burned down a town, almost killing his friend and sister.

Those thoughts smothered the argument right out of me. The rest of dinner was relatively quiet. Blaire never said anything while my dad randomly brought the conversation back to my *boyfriend.* I had buzz-killed the whole meal.

As we left the house, they hugged us each goodbye. I decided to let my parents mull it over for a while. And maybe in a few weeks or *months*, I would take them to meet Wyatt. Maybe that would make it better.

"Have you ever been to Gibbs?" Blaire asked out of the blue as she leaned against the window in the passenger's seat.

"No. Why?"

"Maybe you should see the place. You know, see where it happened."

I thought about her suggestion. The dark sky had a decent moon. We should be able to see the buildings tonight.

"Okay," I muttered. "Let's go see the infamous Gibbs."

I turned around in the middle of the road and headed south, crossing the county line as we traveled the thirty-something miles to Wyatt's hometown.

Blaire didn't say much as we rode in the darkness. I glanced over a few times, seeing her deep in thought. "So when are we going to meet Matt?"

"Geez," she spat. "I'm working on it."

"Okay, okay." I decided the rest of the trip might be better in silence. As we reached the city limits, I realized the town was smaller than I'd imagined. I continued driving past houses until the street opened up to the main corridor. The moonlight illuminated the broken shadows, sending a chill up my back.

"Shit . . ." The word slipped out of Blaire's mouth.

The fire had happened almost three years ago, but like many small places, it had taken time to rebuild. I'm sure there was plenty of red tape with insurance and bills. Parking on the side of the street, I got out of the car, walking slowly over to the brand-new electric pole. My fingers touched the rough wood. This is where it had happened. My eyes closed briefly as I remembered the words of his story. I heard the sound of his deep voice, filling my mind as the ghosts of Wyatt's past floated around me.

The breeze picked up and the moment was over. My eyes opened back to the present. I walked over in front of the post office, looking at the centrifuge of the destruction. The large lot had been cleared down to the dirt. In the front part by the sidewalk, a single-wide trailer was parked on cement blocks with a tiny sign: US Post Office. I had a sickening feeling *this* was the permanent new office. Given the terrible economy, I'm sure the postal service questioned the necessity of reconstructing a grand building.

As for the three buildings to the right, they were still charred and black, haunting the residents every day as they drove down the street. Half of the burned furniture store sign still hung in front of the largest building, and caution tape flapped in the breeze, blocking out trespassers, even though the black words had faded from the weather. There were just three buildings, but those *three* buildings consumed an entire city block of the old main street.

On the left side of the post office, a construction billboard sign read: Future Home of the First Bank of Gibbs. I assumed this was the only business that could afford to rebuild. The walls were slowly going up behind the sign. At this rate, it would be spring before the new bank was finished—over three years after the accident.

My heart beat faster in my chest. Maybe in my naïve thoughts,

I had wanted to believe the events of that night were slightly exaggerated. But Wyatt Carter, in his drunken carelessness, had destroyed a large chunk of this town. Gibbs wasn't a big place, which made any type of destruction hit right in the emotional gut of the residents. And it hit mine.

I felt their pain. I felt his guilt. Wiping a tear from my eye, I quickly got back in the car. They continued to run down my cheeks as we pulled out on Main Street. And then I saw the multicolored light boxes and decorations stacked on the street corner by the chamber of commerce. They must be getting ready to decorate the light poles for Christmas.

And my heart broke for all the people in this town whose lives had changed in a matter of seconds on that cold Christmas Eve. Blaire reached inside her backpack, grabbing some tissues. The tears continued to fall as we left the city limits of Gibbs so I pulled over to the side of the road. My sister voluntarily gave me a brief hug before switching places behind the wheel.

But even in my sadness, I knew something these people couldn't fathom about Wyatt. A reckless kid had almost burned down this town, but a kind and responsible guy had emerged from the ashes.

CHAPTER 35

Emma

THE NEXT DAY, BLAIRE AND I STARTED PACKING BOXES AT about eight in the morning. Neither of us talked about the road trip as we helped Mr. Hughes empty his apartment. His daughter wanted to leave a few days early so they could get settled before the Thanksgiving holiday.

I had never met Nancy, but the tall woman hugged us both immediately when she came in the apartment, thanking us repeatedly for helping her father. Once everything was sealed up tight, we took a breather. Nancy had hired movers to put his furniture and boxes into the moving truck. All we needed to do was sit back as they carried everything away.

Once they finished, it took all three of us to get Mr. Hughes down the stairs. My nerves were frayed by the time we put his frail body in the front seat of the truck. He took a deep breath of the cool air and smiled. "I don't know the last time I've been out here. Smells good."

All I smelled was the strange food cooking in the other apartment building, but I nodded along like it was the best thing in the world. Blaire hugged him first, and I secretly smiled. Two voluntary hugs in twenty-four hours and she didn't self-destruct. That was definite progress.

"You get these." He pushed a set of keys in her hand.

"Your car?" She gasped.

"No sense in you two sharing anymore. And what am I going to do with it?" And then Blaire wrapped her arms around him again. I think the bristly ice queen might be going soft.

My eyes watered up before I ever hugged Mr. Hughes. I swore I wouldn't cry, but swearing never really helped me keep it together. Like Wyatt said, my emotions were as transparent as hell.

I slipped my arms around his old bony neck, holding Mr. Hughes tight as he whispered in my ear. "You keep an eye on Priscilla for me."

"I will," I promised, smiling through the tears.

"And when you finally get to take her out, hold on tight to that boy. I don't want you falling off on the pavement."

I laughed, picturing him riding his motorcycle down the highway. I still had a hard time believing he was a biker. But there was always more to a story than what people saw on the surface. "Bye, Mr. Hughes."

"Bye, Emma." I shut the door to the moving truck. My sister and I waved until they made the wide turn into the street.

"So the old bastard is finally gone," Kurt spoke up, leaning against the brick wall of the lower-level apartments.

"Don't be an ass," Blaire spat at him.

Kurt chuckled, enjoying the reaction he'd caused in my sister. He reached up, stroking the long, wiry ends of his beard. His old work shirt was half open down the front, flashing a nasty amount of chest hair.

I wasn't against chest hair. Wyatt had a soft patch right in the middle of his chest. But seeing Kurt's exposed skin just plain gave me the creeps. He came over closer to us, spitting a wad of tobacco out on the ground. He stopped next to me as I got a whiff of sweat and that strange body spray he thought covered it up.

"You don't have to get all mouthy. I truly feel bad for him. That damn daughter really messed up his life. I think the old bastard had it pretty good here." Kurt let his eyes drift between us. "But I still can't figure out why he always needed *two* of you in his apartment. Maybe that walker was just for show."

"You really are an ass." Blaire tossed the insult in his direction, mumbling more curse words under her breath as she headed for the stairs. I didn't say anything and followed behind her to our apartment.

As I closed the door behind us, the explosion erupted from my sister. "*Shit!* I hate that man. And I'm counting down the days until I never have to see his nasty face again or hear his fucking voice or smell whatever dead rat he rubs on his skin."

"I know."

"I mean, seriously. What shitty apartment owner lets that crazy pervert run this place?" Blaire was pacing back and forth in the living room. At this rate, we would owe Kurt new carpet when we moved out.

"Probably his father."

"You think? Maybe it's his mother. Because I think he has a face that only Norman Bate's mama would love." She stopped mid-step, gripping her fists. "It's so damn frustrating because I don't remember Kurt being that bad when we signed the lease."

"All you remember is the discount. Admit it."

"Fine. Whatever. I'm taking a nap." Blaire's pacing feet carried her out of the room.

I knew that was code for chatting online with M-Attack815. She hated naps. Even as kids, my mom would force us to lie in bed and I would be asleep in minutes. And Blaire would get up, moving all around the room, which was the beginning of her pacing issues.

I went in the kitchen, peering out the curtain to the parking lot. My eyes stayed glued for his whereabouts. I wanted to make sure Kurt was minding his own business, and then I saw him, carrying a dog crate as he walked toward the office. A few seconds later, he came out empty-handed and went around the corner. My nerves tightened as his old truck pulled out of the complex.

I turned around, looking at Blaire's door. She wouldn't approve. So I wouldn't tell her. Grabbing my keys, I shoved them down in my jeans pocket. I sneaked outside, shutting the apartment door softly behind me.

I ran quickly across the open parking lot, trying the knob on the manager's door. It was locked. Checking around the corner, I saw the small window that overlooked the area where Kurt normally parked his truck. My heart beat fast in my chest, making the adrenaline course through my body. I looked down the driveway several times, seeing no sign of the man coming back. Taking a deep breath, I ran over to the window.

Peering through the dirty glass, I saw the crate sitting next to the wall. I tried the edge of the window and it pushed up without any effort. I climbed inside, knocking a spit cup of tobacco off his desk and all over the floor. I stepped around the brown sludge and knelt next to the metal door of the crate.

A face peered back at me, followed by another pair of brown eyes in the black shadows. The smell of rancid urine burned my nose and trickled down the back of my throat, making me gag. I didn't know how long the puppies had been inside the box, but the stench indicated it could have been several weeks.

Going back to the window, I listened for the sound of his truck pipes. My hands were shaking as the thoughts battled around in my head. I wanted to take the puppies. I wanted to drive straight out to the kennel and give them to Wyatt, just like I'd done with Charlie.

The terrible feeling churned stronger in my stomach. Kurt might be a mouthy pervert, but he wasn't stupid. I wasn't sure if I could fool him a second time around. Not that I really did the first time. He had just chosen to harass me with leering comments instead of calling the police.

Glancing back over my shoulder, the two faces were no longer visible. They had slunk back out of view. I went to the front of the office, unlocking the door and propping it open so we could make a run for it. I noticed a sweatshirt in the corner of the junky office. Picking it up, I made my way back over to the crate.

Opening the little door, I pulled the first one out. It was some sort of bird dog. He didn't put up a fight. Neglect did that sort of thing to a dog. His entire stomach was caked in a layer of dried poop from sleeping in the filthy bottom of the crate.

I paused for a moment, waiting to see if I heard the sound of his truck. Kurt might be gone for hours or he could've run to the gas station for more tobacco and be back any second. Hearing nothing but silence, I reached in the back, grabbing the second one. The little puppy let out a yelp when I pulled it across the bottom of the crate. Once I got it out in the light, the tiny animal shrank back in fear, letting out another cry. The poor thing was terrified of me. Tucking the second one in the sweatshirt, I held the dogs close to my chest, feeling their trembling bodies.

My heart pounded hard as the beats echoed in my ears. It was now or never. I needed to take the puppies and face the wrath of Kurt later. Standing up, my legs went wobbly as I left the office. My head whipped around in every direction as I made my way to the car. I put the little puppies in the passenger's seat and then climbed in the driver's side.

I pulled out of the apartment complex, trying not to draw attention. Once on the main road, I passed every car and even ran one stoplight. I just needed to get out of town. I just needed to get to Wyatt.

My thoughts tumbled around, overlapping and twisting up. Kurt would flip out when he returned to find them missing. I didn't know what that crazy man had planned to do with these puppies. Those thoughts were vivid and wild as my foot pressed harder on the gas, making the tires fishtail on the dirt road. Matter of fact, I never had figured out why he had Charlie.

I reached the entrance, skidding to a stop in the dirt. Jumping out, I pushed open the silver gate, not bothering to even latch it back shut. I drove fast across the beat-down grass trail until I reached the kennel. Hearing my erratic arrival, Wyatt came running out of the kennel door. I jumped out of the driver's side. He caught me before I could get the passenger's door open.

"Hey, what are you doing here?" His hands grabbed my waist, pulling me close to his chest. And then he backed away. "Shit, you stink. Like shit."

"I know. I've got these two puppies in the car." My words came in frantic pants. "Help me get them out."

"Whoa. What's going on?"

"I had to save them. I didn't know what he was going to do with them."

"Save them from who?"

"Kurt. Mr. Hughes left, and Kurt was saying weird stuff." I struggled to catch my breath. "And then I saw him carry another crate in. And so I waited for him to leave. And I took them."

"And he doesn't know you took them?"

"No," I whispered, wincing at the look on his face.

"You stole your apartment manager's dogs . . . and brought them *here*?"

"Technically, yes."

His hand went up, running his fingers through the short pieces of hair. "Shit, Emma. You have to take them back."

"*What!* Why? I thought that's what this place was for. I thought you would be glad that I helped them."

"You can't just steal dogs from people. Maybe if we talked to Diana, she could get some sort of order to take them away. But until then, you have to take them back."

My heart froze, hearing his words. "You need to see them. They are so little and covered in their own poop. He's not even *feeding* them."

"I'm sorry. I don't like this either. But I'm in a very awkward situation here with this place. I would do anything for you, Emma. You know that." His hands pulled me closer even though I smelled something awful. "I wish I could take them in. But if I let you leave stolen dogs here, this could backfire on all of us. Including Diana."

Panic filled every pore of my skin. In that moment, I realized Wyatt had no clue about Charlie. Our first meeting had been sporadic and strange. By the time things had leveled out, I'd forgotten to tell him the circumstances involving Charlie. I didn't really see a reason, I guess—until now.

"Hey, don't get all upset. No harm done yet."

He kissed me, but it didn't make anything in my body feel good. A cloud of fear penetrated every thought. I would have to face Kurt if I didn't get to moving. "I better go. Maybe I can get them back before he notices the puppies are gone."

Wyatt kissed my forehead, letting his lips rest gently against my skin. "I wish I could take them back for you."

"I know." And that was the truth. He would walk through fire for me and swim through lava and sneak dogs back into the office of my dog-abusing landlord. And maybe one day, he would have the chance.

"Will it be hard?" The concern etched around his eyes.

My thoughts went back to how I'd left Kurt's office. Returning the dogs back to the original spot, *undetected*, seemed virtually impossible.

"It will be okay." I lied to Wyatt. If Kurt got back before

me, then I would just have to think of something. Maybe I could turn the puppies loose outside his door and hope for the best. Maybe he would be pacified enough with just getting them back. Or maybe he would meet me in the parking lot before I ever got out of my car. The image of his leering face made me shiver in the cold air.

"Here, let me see them before you go." His warm hands released my body. I followed Wyatt to the passenger's side as he slowly opened the door. The two puppies were curled up around each other asleep in the old sweatshirt. "Damn. That smell is terrible."

"I know."

Wyatt ran a hand over the skinnier one. His terrified eyes opened, peering back as his body visibly trembled. "These are some pretty expensive bird dogs. Does your landlord hunt?"

"Maybe. I don't know."

"Well, they seem okay. No broken bones. They just need food and a bath to get rid of all that shit."

"But he keeps them locked in a filthy crate."

"Not ideal, but it's probably not enough to get them taken away. You better get the pups back." Wyatt stood up, shutting the door. The sound of a car filled the quiet air. We both turned in the direction of the dirty cloud coming up the grass path. The dim light of early evening prevented us from seeing much of the vehicle until the pickup was almost to the trailer. My stomach clenched into a spastic knot as the blood drained from my head.

"It's . . . it's . . . h-him," I stuttered.

"Who?"

"Kurt. I-I don't. I don't understand." My thoughts spun wildly. I couldn't figure out how he'd found me out here. Kurt must have followed me. Nothing made sense. But the fear was real. *So very real.* I tasted it on my tongue. I felt it burning under my skin. This wasn't some strange comment tossed out in the parking lot.

Kurt had *followed* me to Wyatt's.

"The dog owner?" Wyatt's low voice was hard to hear.

"*Yes*," I hissed.

"Just go get in the trailer. Let me handle it."

I thought about his suggestion for about half a second before running through the old door. Peering through the thick curtains, I waited for Kurt to arrive. I couldn't breathe. The anxiety had me twisted in knots. It engulfed every piece of my senses.

I wasn't sure how this would go with Wyatt. I didn't want some showdown or fight. Maybe if he handed over the puppies, Kurt would just leave. But nothing about this felt remotely easy. This man had followed me all the way out here.

The driver's side door opened. Kurt stepped out, wearing the same clothes as earlier today. And then the passenger's side opened. My throat let out a strangled gasp as the world stopped spinning, the air stopped blowing, and my lungs stopped breathing.

I went running out the door before I realized my feet had moved across the carpet. Blaire's terrified eyes caught mine. In that split moment, I realized the anxiety I'd felt thrashing around in my chest was twofold. I ran across the dirt, making a beeline in the direction of my sister while she took a step toward me.

"Not so fast," Kurt spat. "As much as I would like to see this little reunion, we still got shit to settle."

I froze in place, seeing the black handgun clasped in his fingers. Kurt had a gun? *Kurt had a gun!* He must have forced Blaire to show him the way out here.

The muscles in my legs wobbled. I stared at my sister, seeing the deep panic etched in her skin. Her fear burned me cold from the inside out. But there was absolutely nothing I could do for Blaire. I retreated quickly over to Wyatt. His lips were pressed down tightly, making them deathly white.

"Now that's better." Kurt's dark eyes studied Wyatt before

drifting over to the kennel building. Some of the dogs were outside in the kennel runs. His lips curled up under his beard. "You know. I wasn't sure you even existed. I thought your girl here only fucked old men."

Wyatt's hands gripped into tight fists. "You're trespassing. So get the hell off my property before I call the sheriff. Or maybe I'll just shoot you."

His grin turned into a laugh. "I doubt that. I've heard about you. That pussy-whipped judge put your ass out here instead of jail. You won't be doing much of anything."

"What do you want, Kurt?" My voice failed to hide the tremble. My eyes were locked on my sister as we stayed invisibly connected in fear. I had never seen Blaire so subdued as the *Criminal Mind*'s junkie had her own worst nightmare come true.

"Well, Emma. I just want what's mine. Then I'll get out of your hair. No harm done."

"The pups are in the car. Take them," Wyatt growled.

"That's all good. But I also need the other one too."

"What other one?"

"You know. The first one that little bitch stole. I want them all, then I'll be gone."

Wyatt's eyes drifted to me before putting the piercing glare back on Kurt. The crazy man started laughing. "I guess she's not all that honest with you. Your girlfriend here stole a dog from me a few months ago. The little bastard had these big fucking ears. Had a client really interested in that one too. Then the bitch stole him."

Wyatt glanced at me again with a flash of irritation before it was snuffed back down. "Go get Charlie."

"No," I whispered. I couldn't even believe Wyatt would suggest it. I knew our situation wasn't good. Wyatt had threatened to shoot Kurt, but I knew he wasn't allowed to have any sort of firearm out here. The three of us were currently at the mercy of my insane landlord. But I couldn't believe he wanted me to hand over Charlie.

"Just do it," he pleaded.

"What are you doing with the dogs?" I glared at Kurt.

"You really are one nosy bitch. You really shouldn't ask so many damn questions." He fondled the end of his beard while holding the gun in the other hand. "I pick up stray dogs. Then I sell them to people who don't like *me* asking *them* questions. I don't give a shit if my clients drag the mutts behind a car or chop 'em up for fish bait. I'm just in it for the cash. People tend to pay a lot of money when no one's asking questions. And *none* of this is any of your damn business. So just get your ass in there and bring me the other one."

Kurt pointed the gun a few inches from Blaire's head. "You get the pups out and put them in the truck."

My sister moved stiffly over to the passenger's side of the car. All the spitfire and venom from earlier must have disappeared on the ride out to the kennel. She lifted the two puppies out of the seat, holding them in the bundled-up sweatshirt.

"Looks like you steal more than just dogs. Now get that sweet ass of yours moving, Emma."

The safety of my sister rattled every thought in my body, causing my muscles to become paralyzed. I didn't budge as I watched Blaire carry the two puppies over to the back of his truck. She placed them in the nasty crate stored in the bed.

A gunshot fired, and I screamed, seeing the dirt billowing up from where the bullet had hit the ground. "I'm not fucking around anymore, Emma. You're wasting my time."

Feeling the sudden rush of fear, my hands started shaking and I almost peed my pants. The dogs were barking like mad in the outdoor pens. Kurt shot another bullet about four inches from my shoe.

And then everything happened at once. Wyatt lunged toward

Kurt, tackling the burly man to the ground. They wrestled around in the dirt and the gun fell to the side. Everything in me said run. But I couldn't move. I couldn't breathe.

Kurt tried to ram Wyatt's head against a rock. But Wyatt was faster. He rolled over, grabbing the gun. Kurt's body slammed him into the ground, making the barrel tip wave around as he tried to pry the gun from Wyatt's hand. The trigger fired sporadically in the air. It fired again, and I heard Kurt grunt in pain as the bullet hit his leg.

Blaire took off in a dead sprint for the trailer. Seeing my sister free of that crazy man, I finally moved, running in the same direction. But the gun fired again before I reached the door.

The impact shook my very core. And then I heard the screaming. I heard my *sister* screaming as she fell to the ground in front of me. A bloody spot formed on her upper back.

There's no preparation for the worst. No mental planning to make it easier. There's nothing I could've done, leading up to that moment. The pain came from my chest as I gasped for words and air. The screams came from my mouth and my heart. I felt the burn. It engulfed my very soul. It melted my insides.

Reaching my sister, I pulled her into my arms. I held her to my chest, whispering incoherent words of comfort. My thoughts flashed a hundred miles a second. I couldn't imagine a world that didn't include Blaire. Our bond was irreplaceable. It would be strange to even begin to explain that bond to someone else.

I loved Wyatt. I hopelessly and utterly *loved* Wyatt. But Blaire? I don't think the correct word even existed to describe my connection to my twin. We were born of the same blood and flesh. We came from the same cells and brain matter and skin.

And as her body cried, mine cried too. The tears were everywhere, pouring down my cheeks, dripping onto her pale face as my identical eyes stared back at me in fear. She trembled in pain. I trembled in pain. She struggled to breathe. I struggled to breathe.

And in that very moment, everything else disappeared. We were different sides of the same coin. But it's impossible to destroy just one side of a coin. The whole piece had to go down in flames or nothing at all. And that's what happened on the cold ground as everything else faded away and we struggled to stay afloat.

I gripped Blaire tight in my arms, praying for *us* to be okay—because this was my fault. My stupid, childish actions had provoked this mess. I had caused Kurt to drag my sister out here.

The guilt slapped me in the face. It gutted my very soul, making it black and charred. For the first time, I truly understood Wyatt's struggle. I'd never felt something so gripping and hopeless inside my heart. "I'm so sorry, Blaire," I whispered, rocking her blood-soaked body back and forth in my arms.

Wyatt touched my shoulder, and I jumped. "Is she okay?"

He knelt down beside me on the ground. I tried to answer, but my tongue got stuck to the roof of my mouth. So I didn't speak. I focused on the closed eyes of my sister. She wasn't okay. I wasn't okay.

"Emmy baby, look at me." He traced along the side of my jaw, pulling my chin up. "It's going to be okay. We are going to get an ambulance out here. But I have to take care of him first. That asshole is half-conscious over there. I need to get some rope to tie him up. Hold this in your hand." Wyatt transferred the gun to me. The black object felt strange in my fingers. "If he comes near you, shoot."

I stared blankly back at him.

"Come on, Emma," his gentle voice pleaded. "Answer me. What do you do?"

"Shoot," I mumbled.

Wyatt seemed hesitant to leave me. His face had streaks of blood on one side from being shoved into the dirt. My dazed eyes drifted over to where Kurt was on the ground. Wyatt ran toward the kennel as I watched for any sudden movements from that evil man. I didn't have a clue how to shoot a gun, but my shaking hand kept it pointed in his direction.

"I told you that Kurt was obsessed with you. And that he was *crazy*."

Her voice pulled me out of the foggy coma. "You're okay," I gasped.

"No. Having a bullet in me is *not* okay," her weak voice replied. "You people are crazy. Shooting and fighting over damn dogs."

Blaire still had her prickly personality despite her paleness. The exasperation made the giddiness surge through my skin, making me almost drop the gun.

"Does it hurt?" I whispered.

"What the hell do you think?" She coughed for a moment before closing her eyes. She mumbled something about resting as she drifted back to unconsciousness.

Wyatt returned with the rope. He tied it around Kurt's hands and legs. The man woke up in the middle of it. My nerves clenched, preparing for another fight to break out, but he allowed the rope to bind him tight without a complaint.

Wyatt came over to us. He pried the gun from my stiff fingers. "Where's your phone? I need to call 911."

"In my pocket." My sad eyes met his. I swallowed the thick lump down in my throat.

"It's going to be okay. Take a deep breath."

I sucked in the cold air as he instructed.

"Now let it out."

My lungs released, but the tension remained. Wyatt kissed my forehead and pulled the phone from my jeans pocket. I listened as he talked to dispatch. He made a second call to Diana. My eyes darted back over to Kurt, seeing his nasty glare fixated on me and Blaire.

After Wyatt hung up, he sat down beside me on the dirt. He grazed my cheek with his lips. "You okay?"

"I-I don't know. What's going to happen to you? I'm sorry." The tears fell down my cheeks as I choked on the words. "I've messed this all up for you."

"You didn't mess up anything. This wasn't your fault."

"No, but it's yours." Kurt spoke up from a few feet away. His beard twitched as he gave us a sly grin. "Everyone out here knows who shot the mouthy bitch. Your hand was on the trigger, firing shots everywhere."

"Yeah, well, who do you think they will believe?"

"I don't know. I'm not the felon." His voice cackled with a laugh. "I just came out here to get my dogs. The ones your stupid girlfriend stole. And then you threatened me. Took a swing at me right here in the face. I had to protect myself. I've got myself one of those concealed carry permits. It's all legal. And of course, there's that bullet in my leg where you shot me too. I was lying on the ground, unarmed, of course, since you took my gun. And then you just walked up and fucking plugged me."

My heart sunk right into my stomach. Kurt seriously couldn't turn this around into his favor. But my thoughts filled with terrifying doubts. The pained expression on Wyatt's face didn't relieve any of the turmoil. Maybe Kurt was just messing with our heads.

"You better stay over there with your damn mouth shut," Wyatt growled.

Kurt laughed and laughed, falling over sideways on the ground. That man tried every piece of patience in my body and terrified every thought in my head. He really was insane.

"Just ignore him. He can't do a damn thing."

But I didn't feel any relief. I guess somewhere in our busy lives and absent thoughts, that's where the Kurts of the world sneaked in. I'd never really considered him an actual threat. I'd never *dreamed* he would show up with a gun when I took the puppies. I thought Kurt would get mad and maybe curse me out while giving me the once-over with his leering eyes. But I never thought it would end like this. Blaire once said my stupid trust in other people would get me killed one day. She was almost right.

Holding my sister in my arms, I felt the sticky blood on my fingers. I leaned my head against Wyatt's shoulder. I wondered if he was scared. Glancing over at his stoic expression, I knew Kurt couldn't read his thoughts. Wyatt had them sealed up tight behind his firm, pressed lips.

But I knew that face. He was retreating, deep inside a hole full of darkness. The guilt hit me again. Wyatt caught my gaze. Nothing about his features changed, but his solid arm slipped around my back, holding me close as we waited together, for absolution or condemnation.

The ambulance reached the kennel first. Blaire woke up again as they strapped her to the stretcher. The medic said the gunshot went into the upper part of her shoulder, missing any major arteries or organs. I guess Wyatt was a pretty good shot. The relief flowed through both of us.

Several sheriffs' cars arrived with Diana right on their heels. I sat in the back of the ambulance with my sister, watching the officer handcuff Kurt as the medic looked at the gunshot wound on his leg. And then another set of metal cuffs were placed on Wyatt.

My heart cracked into pieces. It was a mistake. The police must have listened to Kurt. I had to stop them. Jumping out of the ambulance, I scrambled to get over to his side, but Diana stopped me. "You need to let them take Wyatt into the station."

"But he didn't do anything. He was protecting us."

I pulled against her, trying to make my way to him. The lights flashed in colorful strobes across the growing darkness, but I found none of it pretty. Wyatt saw my struggle and his deep agony was highlighted by the red lights. Our eyes locked across the space of the driveway. A painful and heart-wrenching moment burned between Wyatt and I as the police placed him in the back-seat of the cop car.

"They have to take him in so we can sort it out." She put an arm around my sagging shoulders. "Emma, I'm afraid this is going to be complicated. We had rules about Wyatt staying at this place. I'll do what I can to help him. But you need to understand this is serious."

Tears rolled out of my swollen eyes as they shut the door. The officer climbed in the front seat, putting the car in drive. After all this time, Wyatt Carter was finally leaving his confinement.

I had imagined this moment in my mind. I had imagined the day he would cross the line back out into the world. I had imagined him riding that motorcycle he kept stored under the tarp. I had imagined him leaving with me. But instead of our joyous moment of flying off into the sunset together, I watched Wyatt leave the kennel alone in handcuffs.

CHAPTER 36

Emma

BLAIRE WAS IN THE HOSPITAL. WYATT WAS IN JAIL. AND I WAS just short of a mental breakdown. After my sister had surgery to remove the bullet, I sat in a chair next to my twin, leaving only for a brief moment when I tried to go see Wyatt at the sheriff's office, but I was denied access.

Instead, I answered a plethora of detailed questions from the police *and* from my parents. They all grilled me about Kurt and Wyatt, making my head and heart hurt with the accusations as I fought to clarify the truth. When Blaire felt better, they did the same exact line of interrogation to my sister.

After she was released from the hospital, we returned to our apartment against the protests of my parents. We both insisted the threat was over. Kurt was currently being held until the police could sort through the convoluted mess.

And that is exactly how I described my own life. It was a complete and utter mess. My sister was angry at me *and* sad for me, which manifested into a depressing silence between us since I couldn't bring myself to talk anymore about the situation. Wyatt was still in jail, and I honestly didn't know how this would end for him.

So I cried raw, burning tears, which seemed to be the only words I could say to anyone. I cried for Blaire, and then I cried for Wyatt until I felt the rotting sickness in my chest, which I'd come to identify as guilt.

My thoughts stayed on a looping "What if?" film reel. What if I'd told someone about Kurt? What if I'd left the puppies alone? What if I'd never taken Charlie out to the kennel? What if I'd never met Wyatt? And then everyone's lives would be much better.

But I loved him. I couldn't imagine not meeting Wyatt. Not caring about him. Not falling in love with him.

And the film reel started all over again, reminding me of the way his dimples hooked in the corners of his cheeks. And the agony of his pain as he held me tight. And the sound of his voice as he read out loud. And the sweet way his lips kissed mine. And the way it felt as he *loved* me. And the whispers of the promises we had made for our future.

On Tuesday, I got a phone call from Diana Sweetwater. There was a hearing for Wyatt the following day if I wanted to be there. I showed up alone at the courthouse. Wandering the halls, I found the small courtroom jam-packed without an open seat. I didn't understand why so many people wanted to witness this hearing. Willa turned around in the second row, giving me a small wave like she'd been waiting for me. His mom was next to her. A man with wide shoulders sat on the other side. I assumed he was Wyatt's father.

Reaching their row, all three sets of eyes landed on my swollen face. No amount of caked-on makeup could hide the days and hours of incessant tears.

"Hi." My throat scratched on the words.

"You must be Emma." His dad cased me with his stern glare before sticking out a hand. "Willa has told me a lot of good things about you."

I took his large fingers in a firm grasp. I wanted to babble a string of incoherent words of apology, but I kept my mouth shut, nodding only my head. His family stood up, making room for me. Once seated on the cold, wooden bench, his mom gave me a hug. I felt the desperation in her lengthy embrace, and it reminded me of all the times Wyatt had grabbed me in a similar way.

And then I froze. My breath stilled in my lungs. A man brought Wyatt into the room. I stared at his familiar body dressed in the orange jumpsuit. A purple bruise had formed behind the scrapes on the side of his face from where Kurt had slammed his head into the dirt.

His eyes drifted across the courtroom, seeing all the people in their seats. They locked briefly on a man in a wheelchair, sitting on the other side of the room. A small gasp came from my lips when I realized it must be Marcus. They each did a quick nod to each other. So brief that everyone else probably missed it. A tear fell down my cheek, and I reached up to smear it away, but it was followed by several more.

Wyatt reached the table that sat in front of us on the defense side. I noticed the dark circles around his eyes. They ran deep and haunting. He nodded at his father. As his gaze reached his mom and sister, a weak smile formed on his lips. And then he looked directly at me.

Our eyes morphed into a deep stare as the pain twisted up on his face. My fingers gripped the wooden seat as he let me see inside his troubled heart. The vulnerability almost crushed me. I wanted to run to him, slinging my arms around his neck, wrapping my legs around his waist. I wanted to touch him. Hold him. Kiss him. I wanted to let him know it would be okay.

Wyatt mouthed *I love you* before looking away. Tears fell down my cheeks as he turned around, taking his seat. Seeing him like this hurt more than I'd ever imagined. I just wanted things to go back to the way they were a week ago. I wanted to turn back time. I wanted to roll back the clock, making this all disappear.

A man in a gray suit joined Wyatt at his table. He whispered something in his ear. I hoped this man could work magic. I prayed this man would make this okay.

The bailiff stepped forward, making his announcement. We all stood up as the judge entered the room. It was strange seeing her dressed in the black robe. I assumed it was even stranger for Wyatt. Judge Sweetwater reached the bench, looking over the crowd with an annoyed look that bordered on disgust.

Diana had just been *Diana* to me in Wyatt's story about his confinement. That was until I did my Internet research to learn more about the accident. Seeing *Judge* Diana Sweetwater listed in the news stories, I couldn't believe Wyatt had omitted that one very important detail. The woman who had cared for Wyatt in his imprisonment was the very same person who had sentenced him to the kennel.

"Well, ladies and gentlemen. If I can actually call you people that. It saddens me that we are all here *again* to discuss the fate of Mr. Carter."

"Your Honor, may I approach the bench?" The man with the dark hair, peppered with gray, stood up from his seat. I assumed he was the prosecutor. Another man with dark-blond hair sat next to him.

"No, you may not. You made it perfectly clear that you wished to do this *publicly* and not in my chambers." The strained glare from Judge Sweetwater made the man sit right back down in his seat. "As I was saying. We are here to discuss the fate of Mr. Carter. I am very aware of the agreement signed by all parties, including myself, that allowed Mr. Carter to reside in my protective custody. And if any of the stipulations were broken, the agreement would become void and the original ruling would go into effect."

My throat clenched, hearing the words. My skin got cold and clammy. My eyes bore holes into the back of his head, but I couldn't see his face. I needed to see his face, but nothing right now would allow it.

She paused briefly, gathering her thoughts. "As of right now, the sheriff's office is still sorting through the details of the incident."

"Your Honor." The man stood up again. "You can't brush this under the rug like it was some minor tea party. It's a very clear violation of the agreement with potential other charges. There was an actual gun fight, causing a woman to be shot. The other man had enough meth in his truck for a distribution charge. My office is currently looking into this as a drug deal gone bad."

The noise in the room picked up with chatter as people took in the allegation and my hope trickled right out of my skin like the grains of sand in an hourglass. His mom reached over, grabbing my hand, squeezing it tight within her fingers.

"I know for a fact that wasn't the circumstances involving the incident at *my* kennel. And that your office will get caught up on the real facts soon. But for now, we are here to address the original issue." She turned her attention to Wyatt. "Mr. Carter, did you read the rules that pertained to our agreement when you signed the papers?"

"Yes, ma'am." His deep voice echoed in the courtroom. Everything between them seemed so formal and unreal.

"Did you break the rules that pertained to our agreement?"

His lawyer tried to stop Wyatt, but he answered anyway. "Yes, ma'am."

The guilt weighted down my heart, making it hard to breathe. I didn't know where she was going with this line of questioning, but none of it felt good. The noise behind me got a little louder. Judge Sweetwater turned to address the whole room.

"Well, the original agreement was for five years in my custody at the kennel. Mr. Carter has served half of that time. I am proposing an amendment to our agreement if both parties will agree. I propose taking the current time served and counting that toward the original prison sentence."

"You are not going to just let him walk out of here." The blond man jumped up from his seat before she could continue. "My son is stuck in that damn chair over there. His organs are rotting. He can't even use the bathroom on his own. There's no way in hell I am going to agree for Wyatt Carter to just *walk* out of here."

Marcus slumped a little in his wheelchair, casting his eyes down at the floor. And then a frenzy broke out—starting with the man I assumed to be Fred Tucker—as he shouted louder, pointing his finger at the defense table.

Wyatt's dad jumped up and yelled across the aisle. His mom grabbed his dad, trying to force him back down in the seat. Some man in the back started a commotion that got several more people fired up, yelling about bankruptcy and the fire. This just caused Wyatt's dad to go ballistic. Spit flew from his mouth as he launched an attack at the people talking behind us.

My stomach turned over several times, and I focused on the back of the familiar head in front of me. Wyatt never turned around to face the people who were coming completely unglued about his fate. My heart ached for him. They really did hate him. And his father really did fight tooth and nail for his son.

I heard the banging amidst the chaos. The rap of the gavel beat against the wood until it was the only sound left in the room.

"You people have lost your damn minds." She looked pointedly at Marcus's dad. "When is it going to be enough? You want me to give you a crowbar so you can break his damn knees in front of everyone? Would that finally make you happy? Just sit down, Fred Tucker."

She turned her attention to the man next to him. "Hollings. You're the damn DA. Keep him quiet, or both of you will be staying here tonight for contempt." She took a deep breath, trying to calm the anger in her voice. "Now as I was saying. Mr. Carter has admitted to breaking the rules of the agreement. Therefore, our contract is void and the original ruling goes into effect, which is thirty months. I propose for his time at the kennel to count toward his original sentence. Half the time served at the kennel, leaving half the original sentence. Thus, Wyatt Carter's sentence will be amended to fifteen months with eligibility for parole at twelve."

A flash of sadness echoed in her eyes as she stated the terms. I'm sure this pained Diana. Not only did she put herself on the line for Wyatt, but she'd become his caretaker the last few years. She had tried to help him, save him, and keep him out of actual prison. And in one evening of complete stupidity, I'd brought down the whole house of cards.

She stared at Wyatt for a moment before turning her gaze to the prosecution. "I can give you a thirty-minute recess to discuss."

Wyatt leaned over and whispered something to his lawyer. The man nodded his head before looking at the judge. "Your Honor, my client doesn't need a recess. He would like to accept the offer."

I heard the painful cry come from his mom. The room spun slightly as the words sunk into my heart. I couldn't stop the wild thoughts of Wyatt locked away alone in a cell. What would prison do to him? What if the dark clouds inside his mind suffocated the life out of him? Or maybe something even worse. Maybe he wouldn't be alone. Maybe he would be tossed inside with a man who had stabbed a whole family in a cabin in the woods.

My lips were numb, and I wanted to scream no, but I guess

there really wasn't another alternative. Actually, the alternative was for much longer if the prosecution didn't agree to the proposal.

My eyes glossed over as I looked in the direction of Fred Tucker. Maybe the words of Judge Sweetwater had finally made a difference in him. The DA whispered frantically with the mayor. He glanced over his shoulder a few times, looking at his son.

I felt sorry for Marcus. This must be so incredibly hard for him, torn between his family and his friend. Marcus spoke to his father too low for me to hear, but I saw the way he pleaded with his eyes, begging him to let this go. And finally, his father nodded back in agreement.

The DA stood up and faced Judge Sweetwater. "Mayor Fred Tucker has been the voice of the people affected by the circumstances of this case. And we both agree to the new terms."

Diana nodded her head, looking at Wyatt. She didn't say anything for a moment as her lips pursed into an expression I couldn't read. "Mr. Carter, do you understand what is about to happen?"

"Yes, ma'am."

"Okay." She nodded her head. "I will give you a few minutes to talk to your family. And for everyone else." Her eyes drifted across the courtroom before settling on Fred Tucker. "When he gets out, this is over. It's time for everyone to get back to living."

Her gavel echoed in the courtroom. The stillness filled with the low chatter of the people behind us. It got louder, consuming my head as I tried to process what had just happened. The air seemed heavy as I pulled in breath after breath.

I stayed in my seat, watching Wyatt be escorted toward the little brown wall separating us from him. Wyatt's father got up first. He went over to his son. They talked for a few moments. Wyatt nodded along to whatever words transpired between them—maybe words of promises or encouragement. I wasn't sure, but it all came across civil as he listened intently to his father. And toward the end, the large man reached forward, engulfing his son in a huge embrace.

I swallowed the lump in my throat. The older man let go, making room for his mother. I looked at the floor. This exchange wasn't something I wanted to witness. I heard Willa get up from her seat. Scooting over to the edge, I caught a glimpse of her long brown hair as she flung herself around his shoulders.

I closed my eyes, preparing myself for the moment. And for a brief second, I wished for this to be one of his nightmares. That maybe I had been pulled along into his vivid dream sequence. I wished to wake up in his bed. I wished for him to pull me into his arms, telling me it was only a dream—a nasty and terrible nightmare.

"It's your turn," Willa whispered next to me.

My eyes abruptly opened, seeing him just a few feet away with one very important brown wall separating us. I walked toward Wyatt as the sound of the courtroom faded away. I reached his side, seeing the smile on his face as he flashed those dimples. They usually made a spark sizzle in my chest, but this time they just made me want to cry.

"Are you okay?" I whispered.

He nodded, never taking his eyes off me. "I'm okay."

"I tried to come see you, but they wouldn't let me."

Wyatt cupped the sides of my face. "You look beautiful, Emma."

I tried to smile at his compliment. This morning, I had done my best to look nice just for him. I curled my hair and put on a long-sleeved flowery dress with leggings and my brown boots. I had worked hard on my eye makeup, which was currently smudged all around my face.

"Wyatt, I'm so sorry." I tried so very hard to hold it together, but nothing worked. I sniffed, feeling the wetness run off my lashes. "I-I'm sorry. I caused all of this."

"No, you didn't."

"But you are going to prison. Actual *real* prison. What if something happens to you? I just wanted to help you and now look what I've done." I choked on the words, making the rest come out as mumbled. "I-I should have just l-left you alone."

"Emmy baby, don't cry." He wiped the tears off with his thumb. "You saved me, from myself. I was rotting away out there. And you found me. You convinced me I was worth saving." His lips got close to mine. "And you loved me. Remember? You loved the good and the bad. And because of that love, I'm going to be okay in there. So don't worry."

"How am I supposed to not worry about you?" I sniffled.

"Just try, okay? I don't want you sitting around, waiting for me to get out. Keep living, and I will see you when it's over."

I nodded. "And I'll come see you every week. It will be just like coming out to the kennel, just—"

"No, Emma." His gruff voice cut on the words as the pain flashed in his eyes. "I don't want to see you there."

"You don't want to see me?" My heart crunched like a wad of aluminum foil before it's tossed in the trash.

"I love you. But I can't bring myself to see you there. You are so sweet and innocent and everything that is good about my life. You don't belong in a place like that. But it's going to be okay. I won't stop loving you. And I hope you won't stop loving me." His voice cracked on the words. "But I would understand if you did."

"How could you even say that?" I pleaded.

"I just wanted to give you an out."

"There's no *out*, Wyatt. I love you so much." My hand touched his chest. "I love who you are in *here*. Nothing will stop that. No matter what happens in there. Remember that."

"You are everything to me." The words whispered like a breath across my lips before he kissed me. It was hard and full of emotion as we both knew it would be our last kiss for a very long time. We struggled to get closer, but the wall kept us apart. And finally when I didn't have a breath left in me, he lifted his mouth from mine.

"I have to go now." His smile was heartbreaking. "But I will be thinking of you. Every day and every minute until I see you on the other side."

We stared at each other for a moment, neither of us willing to mutter an actual goodbye. Those words had always seemed so final for us—whether it was for twenty-four hours, two days, or twelve months.

My heart struggled to beat. In the hazy fog, I turned around first. I couldn't bear to see them put the cuffs on again. I couldn't bear to see him walk away. So I turned around. I let him watch me walk away—one last time.

Several people flashed me curious glances, having witnessed our final moments together. Several others fought back the urge to fling a few insults at me for being involved with the boy who burned down that dang town. But I didn't care. Not that I ever did when it came to Wyatt. I believed with all my heart that he deserved a second chance at life and I planned to give it to him.

I stepped outside the courthouse. The clouds were as dark as my mood. And then I saw my sister. She was waiting by my car with her arm in the sling. The doctor said she had to wear the contraption for a few weeks until the muscles healed. Her little blue wool hat was sitting crooked on her stringy blonde hair, making Blaire seem younger than twenty-one.

"You're not supposed to be driving. How did you get here?"

"Mom dropped me off a few minutes ago. I thought maybe you could use some company." Her sympathy was genuine, which seemed so strange. But I was too numb to question it.

"They are sending him to prison for a year." A tear fell down my cheek as I said the words.

"I know. I heard people talking. These jerks *really* don't like him." She shook her head. "Too bad. They are really missing out.

Wyatt would make one badass hunting guide."

I smiled at her attempt to cheer me up. She walked over to the passenger's side of my car. We both climbed inside the cab, but I didn't even start the engine. I wasn't sure how to continue or where to continue. Should I just drive home? Sit on my couch? Eat dinner? Try to have Thanksgiving tomorrow? Go back to classes next week? I didn't know how to carry on, knowing Wyatt would be alone in a cell.

I felt a panic attack. I couldn't breathe, feeling my muscles clench tight in my chest. My heart beat rapid as I pictured his face. His sad face. His sweet face. His lonely face. I tried to swallow, but the spit wouldn't go down my throat.

Closing my eyes for a moment, I tried to block out the image but nothing worked. I looked over at Blaire. She was on her phone, trying to text one-handed. And a thought appeared out of nowhere. That very thought caused the panic to calm down just a bit.

"Is that Matt?" I whispered.

Her eyes cut over in my direction. "Yeah."

"Is he in Norman right now?"

"Yeah. Why?" She paused, giving me a skeptical glare.

"Tell him to go to Bricktown. We will be at the Starbucks by the movie theater in about forty minutes."

"Whoa! Just wait a minute," she gasped.

"Just tell him that, Blaire. I want to take you to meet Matt. I *need* to do this," I pleaded with my sister. "One of us should get a happy ending today."

She stared at me, contemplating my words until finally nodding her head. Blaire typed across the little screen. Her terrified eyes looked back up at me. "He said yes."

"Good." I wiped another tear off my cheek before starting the engine. Everything still hurt, but helping my sister made the clouds not so gray.

We didn't speak on the drive down the interstate. She periodically picked up her phone, glaring at it like she planned to type some apologetic message to back out of the meeting. But each time, my sister grumbled under her breath, slamming the phone back down in her lap.

Blaire's eccentric antics kept my sanity in check. This was better than just driving home. This was better than sitting on the couch, trying not to picture him alone. This was better than thinking about Wyatt.

When we reached Starbucks, I had to practically drag my sister from the car. "I can't, Emma. What about this thing on my arm?"

"It's a good conversation topic." I felt a brief grin on my lips. As we walked in the door, I recognized Matt immediately at the table next to the register. I pulled her along until we reached him. He got up and greeted us shyly. Matt didn't look at me. He only looked at Blaire.

Excusing myself, I drifted away out of the picture and placed an order at the counter. I took a seat toward the back of the store, holding a latte with a dash of cinnamon. Inhaling a deep breath, the smell filled my nose with sweetness. I took a sip, letting the hot liquid run over my swollen throat.

My sister glanced over in my direction a few times. I smiled at her. They seemed to be hitting it off. After all her terror-filled moments of dread, she was doing just fine with Matt. They were in the beginning stages of their friendship or relationship or whatever my sister decided to call it.

In the midst of the broken pieces of my heart, I felt a surge of happiness. And something clicked. I would survive. We all would survive. Even Wyatt.

Part IV

Wyatt and Emma's Epilogue

CHAPTER 37

Emma

THE HOLIDAYS CAME AND WENT AS THE MONTHS PASSED WITH a blur. I never saw Wyatt or even heard his gruff voice through the phone. I wrote him letters, but he never wrote back.

The lack of communication was painful, but I understood. He needed this time to help reconcile some demons inside of him. And I knew it was difficult for him to share his daily world. The very thought made my gut clench up in fear. I was afraid for him. I was afraid for his safety. I was afraid for him being alone.

I would do anything to touch him. So I touched him in the only way I knew he could feel. I kept writing. He needed me right now more than I needed him. I knew Wyatt kept my letters. I knew they were tattered on the edges from where he held them tight. I knew because Diana told me.

Even though Wyatt and I didn't speak directly, she kept me updated on him. Her emails always ended with something like, "The kid's hanging in there, and he said to let you know that he's okay and he loves you."

At first I cried, seeing his little messages come from Diana. But as the months passed, they eventually made me smile. I'd never pegged him as a guy who wrote his deep thoughts down on paper. It must have pained him to say those words to Diana's face so that she could pass them along to me.

As for the incident at the kennel, everything was eventually settled. Wyatt didn't have any extra time tacked onto his sentence. However, Kurt received ten years for drug charges. And Diana was allowed to give a guy on parole the job as caretaker of the kennel.

After twenty-two years of being joined in the womb and in life, my sister and I finally went our separate ways. I moved out in the spring after getting into a nursing program in Tulsa. It was a strange day for both of us. Lots of awkward shoulder shrugs from Blaire. Lots of body-crunching hugs from me. Lots of tears from my mom. Tulsa wasn't that far away, but she acted like it was at least three states. And I promised them both I wouldn't talk to strangers.

I rented a one-bedroom old house with a fenced-in backyard full of trees. The fence was a necessity since Charlie came with me. We didn't have much in our tiny house, but I felt older and wiser. I was no longer living on the fringe of where I was supposed to be in life. I was finally on the right path, going in the right direction.

About a month after I moved into the house, I got a call from Diana. Things were going pretty well with her new kennel tenant with one exception: Cye. After Wyatt and I had disappeared, the poor dog had slowly regressed. He wouldn't allow the new guy to touch him and he eventually disappeared into the back corner of the pen. Diana asked if maybe I had time to visit him.

The next Saturday, I made a trip back down that long, dusty road. It was strange driving to the place, knowing Wyatt was no longer waiting at the end of the grass path. I parked outside, seeing the same old trailer, remembering all the times I'd stood on the steps—sometimes yelling angry words and sometimes breathless as Wyatt kissed me against the old door.

The new guy was nice, but this time, I didn't ask questions. Going inside the kennel, I grabbed a leash from the hook on the wall. As I walked down the aisle, I saw the familiar faces, pressing against the gates along with a few new ones. I pulled a dog bone from my pocket as I reached his pen.

Cye was hunched down in the back corner. His sad, lone eye caught mine, yet the dog didn't move an inch. Opening the gate, I went inside, crawling slowly on my hands and knees. I placed a bone a few feet from the poor dog. He stared at me. And my heart broke.

Very slowly, he inched forward, taking the bone between his teeth. I scratched behind his ears, feeling the familiar dents in his skull. The dog eventually rolled over on his back, letting me pet his fuzzy belly. I clipped the leash on his collar and he snapped to his feet. After I'd received the call from Diana, I knew there was only one option. I had to take Cye with me.

We left through the gate and down the aisle and out to my car. Placing him in the backseat, I shut the door and took one more look at the kennel. The memories were fresh. They were painful. But that wasn't the part that pulled at my heart.

Before I could stop myself, I went back inside, taking another leash from the hooks. Her face was still pressed against the gate from where I'd left her. I knew she was his favorite. I knew that toothless pit bull must have waited every day trying to figure out why Wyatt had abandoned her. Lola licked my hands as I fastened the leash to her collar. My house would be busting at the seams with dogs, but I knew I couldn't leave her here.

It was a peaceful drive back down the dirt road with Cye and Lola in the backseat. I returned to our house. I had always considered it *our* house, even when I signed the lease with just my name.

I wanted Wyatt to eventually come home to this place.

I missed him. Some days, I missed him more than others, but I never missed him less. And some days I still cried as his presence hovered just beyond my reach. But I had Charlie and now Cye and Lola to keep me company. Even with the ache in my heart, I was doing okay.

It didn't take long for the new dogs to get settled into my routine of school and work. I installed a doggy door for the long days I worked at a new nursing home. But I spent most of my evenings in the living room with Cye draped across my feet, and Charlie in my lap with Lola under my arm. The three dogs and I would cuddle up on the couch, reading a book out loud—waiting for Wyatt to come back to us.

That's another thing that came with me from the kennel. The day I moved in, Diana had arrived out of the blue in her big truck, hauling his bookcase and several boxes. She had helped me set it up on one side of the living room.

I loved the feel of having that piece of Wyatt in this place. I loved knowing that he'd read each and every one of those stories. Every time I looked at that colorful shelf of books, I heard his deep voice, drifting out across the moonlit kennel.

I know that place had been considered his confinement. But for me, I had good memories of being with him at the kennel. I had wonderful memories because that was the place where I fell in love with Wyatt. It was the crazy and unusual beginning of our story, but I knew it wouldn't be the end.

CHAPTER 38

Wyatt

PRISON WASN'T EASY. I WON'T LIE AND SUGARCOAT IT WITH A bunch of colorful shit. Those days were hard, and the nights just about wrecked me. I was alone. But it was a different kind of alone than at the kennel. I never felt more isolated in my life despite the fact I was surrounded by hundreds of men. Some were better than me and some were much worse. But none of that really mattered on the inside of the razor walls because all of us had ended up in the same damn place: our new home of suffocation and redemption.

My chest always felt tight. The claustrophobia festered inside my lungs, making me restless. Somewhere in my gut, I thought prison would alleviate some of my guilt. Maybe if I finally served my time. Maybe if I finally sat in the exact spot Fred Tucker had wanted me to be all these years, then I would eventually lose some of the boulders shackled to my feet. But none of that happened. I was still just as twisted with guilt as the day I entered through the door.

I think the real answer rested with the ideas I'd shared with

Emma. Prison was my punishment, not my salvation. That part would come once I was on the other side. Redemption would be determined by the person I became out there in the world. At least that's how I imagined Emma saying it to me.

My beautiful Emma. I missed her. I missed her skin. Her lips. Her annoying questions that made me think clearer. I missed the one piece of my life that had leveled out the bad. I missed the part that made me feel like I was worth saving.

That girl had swallowed me with her big heart. She had wrapped that love around me until I felt her in my mind and my thoughts. She had consumed me, making the darkness disappear. She had made everything brighter, softer, and sweeter. She had made me feel alive again.

I missed Emma so damn bad. I thought telling her goodbye in the courthouse would have been the worst part. It wasn't even a sliver of the pain I'd felt the days and months that followed. The agony of our separation felt like a knife right in my heart, twisting and stabbing, around and around in my chest. Each night in my cold bed, I tried to fall asleep with a fucking knife jammed down in my heart. It hurt like hell.

But I couldn't show my pain. And I damn sure couldn't show my fear. I just had to learn to deal with the emotions and keep my head down. Day after day, I trudged along, not making eye contact. It was my way of trying to survive. But that wasn't always good enough. Every so often, survival required actual fists and bloody faces and broken fingers.

But in my darkest moments, I still found the strength to endure. And that strength came in the form of her letters that arrived each week. Emma told me about her life. She made sure I knew everything that was happening while I was gone. And sometimes she penned sappy lines I could only read at night when no one else would see the tears run down my cheeks.

I loved her with everything in me. I loved her enough to

make her stay away. It was so damn hard. I was alone, and it was a daily struggle just to stay afloat. Sometimes in my depressing pain, I almost asked Diana to bring Emma. I just needed to see a glimpse. I just needed a little taste of her lips. But I never gave in to my weakness. Seeing her beautiful face would just make the ugliness around me a darker shade of black.

So I kept trudging along, reminding myself this sentence was only for a year. I could survive three hundred sixty-five days behind bars if Marcus could survive the rest of his life in a wheelchair. I could survive this time without Emma if Willa could live every day in fear of having another attack.

I could do this. I *would* do this for them. In some strange twist of fate, I had been the only person not permanently destroyed by the accident. It wasn't fair. Nothing would ever make it fair. But when I finally left this place, I would do everything in my power to be a better person. I would be someone worthy of this second chance.

CHAPTER 39

Wyatt

THREE HUNDRED AND TWO DAYS LATER, I WALKED OUT THE door on early release, feeling the sunshine on my skin.

"Good to see you, son."

I stared at my dad for a moment before giving him a tired smile. "Good to see you too."

Getting in my father's truck, we got on the highway for the drive to my parent's house. He talked while I listened. The man had visited me every week over the course of my incarceration. And now our relationship was different.

I can't say every grain of it was perfect, but I respected the man. After he had lost his job as police chief, my family moved to Stillwater. The town was a little bigger than Gibbs, and he had gone back to being just a police officer. His loss of command had been another causality of my actions.

No one ever thinks about the aftereffects. When a rock pings a windshield, it doesn't create a big hole that brings down the glass. It's the rings radiating out from the initial impact. My actions had cracked across my whole family, especially my father. It had brought us all down, as they were forced to move away while I'd turned my back on them out of shame and grief.

But now it was different. We had repaired some of that damage. My father wasn't a commanding asshole, and I wasn't a stupid jackass.

My father parked at their new house. It was my first time to see the place. I gazed at the unfamiliar front porch. While I was away, my family had moved from the only home Willa and I had known as kids. Seeing the smaller house, I felt the damn guilt hit me right in the gut.

"You coming?" his gruff voice asked.

"Yeah." I took a deep breath, shaking off the past. "Hey, Dad?"

"Yes?"

"Thank you." The emotions made my throat ache. "For not giving up on me. I'm sorry that it . . . um . . . that I—"

My dad hugged me across the console of his truck, cutting off my words. I truly was sorry that I'd cost him so much of his life and career. He held onto me for a moment.

"I'm sorry about Willa," I whispered.

He let go, looking me right in the eye as a tear fell down his cheek. "I know."

I swallowed the lump in my throat. This part was the hardest. I had finally said it to him. I had finally addressed the awful cloud that had hung over our entire family. "Why didn't you hate me?"

"You're my kid. And I don't love one of you less than the other. I hate what you did. And I hate that you hurt Willa. But I still love you too. You're my son. Always will be. And you fight for your kids. Even when they don't want you to."

I couldn't stop the tears from falling down my cheeks. He hugged me again. I was crying damn tears as my dad held onto me.

After a few minutes, he let go. "We better go inside before

the girls come out here."

"Okay." I wiped my face against my sleeve.

Climbing out of the cab, I surveyed the street. The warm September air made beads of sweat form on my forehead. My mom came out the front door with Willa running at a dead sprint behind her. My sister latched herself around my neck in a death grip.

"Oh my gosh. You're here. Like, *really* here," she squealed.

I smiled at her, hugging her back. My mom waited until Willa got through mauling me before getting a turn. She cried. Maybe she thought this day would never happen.

I spent the evening with them. I didn't talk much and I think it made my family slightly nervous. My mom wanted my return to be perfect while I tried to wrap my head around everything seeming so normal. It was hard when I didn't feel *normal* on the inside.

My emotions were a little numb after being away for three and a half years. Between my time at the kennel and then prison, I'd forgotten what it felt like to have complete freedom.

After the first week, I contacted Diana for the address of a certain house in Tulsa. Part of me had wanted to run straight to her the moment I was free. But I knew my family deserved some time with the prodigal son. And I enjoyed spending time with my parents and Willa. We played games and had dinner and watched movies late into the night until I fell asleep on the couch.

And then Willa had her first attack while I was at home. I stood there terrified while my mom acted like it was no big deal. I guess her episodes had gradually become part of their normal life. After it was over, I locked myself in the bathroom, crying so hard my chest physically hurt. The past would always be right in front of me. But I knew they had moved on and accepted it. I must too.

I found Willa lying on her bed with Gus. "Hey."

She opened her eyes. "Hey."

The fatigue was visible in her smile. The seizures had always worn her out, making Willa sleep for hours after an episode. I lay down beside her on the bed. "You care if I hang out here for a while?"

"I think Emma might care if you stayed with us too long," she teased.

"I meant in *here* with you, dork." I let out a deep breath. It was hard to act normal with her, knowing I was the reason she was like this, but I needed to try for her sake.

"As long as I never hear you say I'm sorry again."

The emotions got tight in my chest. "Okay."

"And you better go see Emma soon. I don't want you messing that up. I like her a lot, Wyatt."

"Well, I love her."

She laughed faintly. "I know. And that makes me happy because I want you to be happy."

Those words were hard for me to hear, but I didn't argue. We stared at the ceiling, not speaking as she rested. Our relationship was so different now than when we had been kids. Adult issues and adult mistakes.

"I've been emailing with a doctor in Boston."

"You have?" I glanced over at Willa, seeing her eyes still closed.

"Yeah. He thinks there's a good shot at fixing me with surgery."

Shit! My stomach tightened at the layered meaning of her words. Part of me wanted to jump up and down. But part of me knew there must be some risk or another doctor would have suggested surgery already.

"I'm gonna do it, Wyatt. I'm not sure when it's going to happen, but I've already made up my mind so don't try to guilt me into backing out."

"I won't." My throat felt raw as I swallowed back the words I wanted to say. "I will support whatever you decide to do."

"Thank you."

I thought about my sister. She was in charge of her own health at this point. Willa had turned nineteen a couple of months ago. And she lived every day in that body. If she wanted to try to fix the damage, I didn't think any of us should stop her.

My eyes closed as the afternoon sun drifted through the window. And then as I was falling asleep, I heard my sister whisper, "I visit him for you."

"Who?"

"Trevor. Mom takes me out there sometimes, and I leave flowers. I figured no one else would visit him."

Her news made me both sad and happy. "Thank you."

And then I asked the question that had tumbled around in my head for quite some time. "Is that the only reason you visit him?"

She didn't answer immediately as I searched my memory from the night of the accident. Willa had been sitting in the chair *with* Trevor. She had been sitting in his lap. That part had set me on fire when I'd first seen them on the back porch. But afterward, when I'd had plenty of time to mull over all those thoughts, that scene had never quite made sense. Why was Willa sitting in Trevor's lap?

"I don't know what you mean, Wyatt?"

The sadness in her voice stopped me from asking the question again. She had confirmed my suspicions. I had my answer, but not the one I'd really wanted to hear. But I guess that was okay. Neither of us could change the past at this point. We all would have chosen differently that night. *Would have? Could have?* Those did absolutely nothing. It was time to move forward.

"Nothing. Just get some rest. I'll stay in here with you."

My sister fell asleep while I stared at the ceiling. I had a lot of questions, but some questions should just stay unanswered.

Letting out a deep breath, some of the weight lifted off my

shoulders. I felt calmer than I had in years. Things were better with my family, and I was finally mending some of the broken pieces of my life.

When I finally pulled my bike out of the garage, they each hugged me goodbye. My family understood my need to be somewhere else—*with* someone else. Even though they didn't say it, I think everyone knew who was responsible for changing me. For pulling me out of the gutter.

As I drove down the highway, I noticed the red and orange leaves changing on the trees. I felt the warm breeze touching my face. I savored every piece of this freedom.

It didn't take long to find the little house. Knocking several times, I waited nervously on the porch. The sound of dogs echoed from behind the old wood door, but Emma never answered. I finally sat down on the cement, leaning back against the house. It reminded me of all the times I had waited for her to show up at the kennel, except this time I would be surprising Emma. A smile spread across my face. I had made Diana promise not to tell her about my release.

Several hours passed as I waited on the porch. The sun fell slightly in the sky, making an orange glow across the clouds. I felt so damn nervous. I shouldn't be nervous, but telling myself not to be nervous didn't make me any less fucking nervous.

Out of the corner of my eye, I saw her little white car pull into the driveway. I stood up, wiping my palms across the legs of my jeans. Walking to the edge of the porch, I smiled, seeing her struggle with two brown sacks of groceries. Her blonde hair fell in soft curls against her flowery dress. She was just as beautiful as I'd remembered.

"Here, let me help you," I said, going toward her.

Hearing my voice, Emma looked up as the bags crashed to

the ground. Apples rolled across the cement. She didn't move as her eyes watered up. I closed the gap, pulling her to my chest.

"Is this real?" she whispered against my T-shirt.

"Yes." My fingers traced lightly over her back as she buried her tears in my chest. "Don't cry," I whispered.

"Happy tears." She sniffed.

"Let me get your stuff, and you can show me the house." I felt her head nod against my chest, but her arms didn't let go. "It's okay. I'm not going anywhere. You can let go for a minute."

Emma reluctantly released her grip and backed away. I scooped her groceries back into the sack, minus a few apples. "You're early? Why didn't you tell me that you were getting out early?"

"I wasn't sure it was going to happen. And I needed some time with my parents and Willa. And if you knew I was out, then I would just want to rush here."

"You stayed with them?" Her eyes grew brighter as we walked back to the front door.

"Yeah. It was good." I smiled.

"Good." She wiped another tear off her cheek. I held the bags in my arms as she unlocked the door. I don't know why I'd gotten nervous seeing Emma. It felt the same even though it was almost a year later in a different city. She felt the same and smelled the same. And in just a few minutes, I knew everything was going to be okay.

"The kitchen is to the right." Charlie lunged at Emma the moment the door opened, followed by Lola.

I went into the house, placing the sacks on the counter. It wasn't a very big place, but it seemed perfect for her. A square body almost tripped me. Lola went crazy as I petted the old girl. And out of the shadows, Cye made his way cautiously into the kitchen like he wasn't sure if I was real either. I approached him slowly, running my hands over his battered head.

"I guess you didn't forget me," I said as the dog rolled over on the tile. I rubbed his exposed stomach.

Glancing up at Emma, I felt a sudden catch in my chest. She still seemed a little shell-shocked from my sudden reappearance. I felt protective of her. Something I'd struggled with at the kennel. But here, it was different. I could finally take care of her. Be the person Emma deserved to have in her life. I got up from the floor and went over to her. My hands circled her waist, pulling her little body close to me. She felt so real, so warm and full of love as her eyes held on to mine.

I kissed her. And then she melted against me. My tongue touched her mouth. I had spent many lonely nights remembering the taste of her cinnamon lips. But tonight, she felt softer and sweeter than I'd remembered. I couldn't get enough. My fingers found their way down to her bare thighs. I traced over her soft skin before slipping under the fabric, touching her solid lace panties. My palms cupped each butt cheek as I pushed her tighter into my hips, making everything in me light on fire.

I had missed the feel of her. I had missed the way she pressed against me, begging me to be inside of her. That girl made everything in my head disappear except for the need to hear her soft moans as I pushed her body over the edge. And I needed it right now. I had planned on dinner and maybe some talking first, but all of that could wait.

"Show me the rest of the house," I whispered against her lips.

"Huh, um . . . what?" She seemed confused, and then her cheeks got a little pink. Emma peeled herself away from me. Taking my hand, she pulled me through the living room. "Bookshelf." She pointed over by the wall. As I scanned the familiar titles, a warm feeling caught me in the chest. "Couch," she muttered as I followed behind her. Going into the tiny hallway, she nodded at the closed door. "Bathroom."

And then we reached our destination. I had never seen her bedroom. My eyes drifted across the dresser and yellow bedspread before going back to the girl who had haunted my dreams. She took the final few steps, lying down across the brightly colored bed. It suited her. All cheery and warm. All Emma.

I unfastened my belt and tugged the zipper, letting my jeans fall down to my ankles. My fingers ran up her soft thighs, tugging the edge of those lacy panties. They moved smoothly down to her ankles. Tossing them to the floor, I climbed on top of Emma. I kissed her softly, running my tongue against hers. As I settled between her legs, the flowery dress bunched up around our hips. I wanted her like this. I wanted her in that beautiful dress on that yellow bedspread like the sun was shining all around her. She looked so innocent and beautiful.

"Look at me, Emmy." Her eyes held onto mine as I pushed deep inside her. The real Emma was more incredible than all the memories. As I moved inside her sweet, warm body, she whispered, "I love you," over and over against my neck. I got lost in her kisses. I got lost in the way she wrapped herself around me. As my past slowly disappeared, I got lost in my future. I got lost in Emma.

CHAPTER 40

Emma

WYATT HAD COME HOME. I COULD BARELY BREATHE FROM the flutters of excitement overtaking every emotion. We spent the next day basically in my bed. Our bed. He was staying. Diana had made arrangements for Wyatt to work at a dog shelter in Tulsa until the terms of his parole were completed. He was *staying* with me. We were *staying* together.

Every moment felt like a new beginning. He was different. He *felt* different. Lighter. Younger. We ventured out to a movie theater. We had dinner at a restaurant. According to Wyatt, that night was technically our first date. And then a few days later, he took me dancing. I learned something new about Wyatt Carter. He was *really* good at dancing, all sweet and sexy as he guided me across the floor.

I loved spending time with him. And I loved him. I didn't think it was possible to love him more than I had a year ago. But I did. I loved *that* Wyatt and I loved *this* Wyatt, the one who woke every morning with a giant smile spread across his lips.

And I loved walking outside of the little house, seeing the

familiar silver and black bike parked in the driveway. It was funny. Every time I saw Priscilla, I thought about Mr. Hughes.

My old neighbor and I still exchanged letters. I had even mailed him a picture of me sitting right on the back of Priscilla. And in return, Mr. Hughes had sent a weathered photo of a familiar, younger man, sitting astride the very same motorcycle on the California coast.

Wyatt and I road everywhere together while the weather was still warm. We visited his family. And he finally met mine. My father gave him a leery stare at first, but he had a private talk with Wyatt, which seemed to settle his nerves. I didn't know the words that transpired between them, and probably never would. However, the whole family eventually warmed up to the idea of Wyatt. How could they not? He loved me and would break every bone in his body before ever hurting me.

Everything seemed surreal as our future plans gradually came to light. Wyatt talked about all the ideas he had for us. For him. And I knew every one of those ideas tied back to something that provided redemption to his soul.

And then one afternoon, I came home from work and found Wyatt on the phone with Diana. His face was tight with emotion as he spoke to her. "I promise. I'm okay. I need to do this."

He listened as she talked, nodding his head a few times. "Okay. I'll see you tomorrow."

After they hung up, Wyatt came back into the living room. He wrapped his arms tight around me, clutching me against his chest.

"What's wrong?"

He buried his nose into my hair, pressing his lips gently against my neck. "I called Diana."

"I figured out that part."

"I've been thinking about what I said to you last year. How I want to make this better. I told Diana that I would like to get a group together to talk to some of the high schools in the area. Like a panel thing. I . . . um . . . I'm going to tell my story."

My thoughts spun back to all the times I had begged him to share his story, to share the piece that had twisted him up so tight. And now, he was willing to share that story with strangers in an effort to right his wrongs. I swallowed the lump in my throat. "Are you ready to do that yet?"

"I doubt that I will ever be ready."

"I know," I whispered.

He held me tighter, letting out a deep breath. "But I need to do it, whether I'm ready or not. And I won't hold anything back or sugarcoat the truth. If it stops just one person, then it's worth exploiting my sins to the world."

My heart ached for him. I knew this was important to Wyatt. "You can do this."

"Only because of you, Emma. You make me feel like I can do anything."

We stayed cuddled up on the couch as Cye slept on the floor in front of us. Wyatt kissed the back of my neck and whispered, "There's something else I want to do."

"What?"

"I've been thinking about a contract you signed last year."

"A contract?" I turned around in his arms, giving Wyatt a funny look.

"Something about Emma Sawyer jumping out of a plane with Wyatt Carter."

My eyes got a little big. "Oh, *that* contract."

"I've been looking into it. You can go or just watch." He pressed his lips to mine, kissing me softly. "I was kidding about the contract."

I shook my head. "No, I want to jump."

"You sure?" His eyes teased me with the challenge.

"I signed the contract. I'm going." My sister was right. It was just a matter of time before my stupid decisions would get me killed.

A few days later, I climbed on the back of Priscilla, wrapping my arms around Wyatt. We took off toward the sky-diving place outside of town. I loved riding with him, holding on tight with my body pressed snug against his shoulders, feeling my hair swirl around in the cool November air.

The training class lasted most of the morning. With each practice session, I questioned my sanity. But he seemed so alive, so excited like the bricks were falling off his shoulders with every smile.

Before we got on the plane, Wyatt pulled something from his pocket and handed it to me. I studied the little photo of three boys about twelve years old. They were sitting on a bench, in their football pads with the evening sunshine setting in the background. He had been just as cute at twelve as he was at twenty-three. And I knew without asking, the other two were Marcus and Trevor.

I handed Wyatt the photo back. He slipped it inside the pocket of his faded jeans before fastening the harness around his body. Suddenly, I understood why this was so important. He was jumping for them; a memorial to the *three* boys who no longer existed. My throat felt tight as I fought back the tears. I knew this would never truly be over for Wyatt, but somehow, he had finally learned to move forward and to live with it.

As we reached the final altitude, we watched the other couple in the class go first. And then it was our turn. We got close to the edge. The wind howled outside the door. My stomach flip-flopped at the prospect of launching myself out into the open air.

But somewhere inside, I got that feeling, the one that always filled my senses as I reached that pivotal point when running. The mind-blowing rush that transcended into a beautiful release.

I knew without a shadow of a doubt, this would be fifty times greater. I got a little giddy and laughed. Turning to face Wyatt, our eyes locked in a burning stare full of excitement.

"I love you," he yelled. I barely heard him over the sounds of the engines and blowing wind. He flashed a big smile, letting those dimples settle deep on the corners of his cheeks. "See you on the other side."

Wyatt and the instructor jumped tandem out the door. I watched him fall through the open sky with that picture buried in his pocket. A deep rush of adrenaline shot through my skin, and I couldn't wait to go with him. My instructor had us pause for a few moments, and then I jumped too.

As the air hit my face, the tingles went from my head to my toes. It was the most incredible feeling. I saw Wyatt's parachute open below us. I smiled, seeing him float away in the breeze. He was finally free. And I knew in that moment, everything in our lives would be okay.

If this were a movie,
the credits would roll and a song would play.
And if so, it would be this one.

"You'll Be Okay"
Performed by A GREAT BIG WORLD

Look it up. Give it a listen while picturing Wyatt and Emma falling through the clouds, seeing their red parachutes open as they float over the world together.

ACKNOWLEDGMENTS

Thank you for reading *Waiting for Wyatt.* I wanted to write a book about rescue dogs and then I built the human story around it. I hope you enjoyed both the animal and human side of the novel.

I also would like to thank all the readers who took a chance on *The Mason List.* It was not a perfect story, but you loved it anyway. You told friends and promoted it on social media. You wrote reviews and featured it on blogs. And you sent personal messages and comments, letting me know how much the story meant to you. Thank you!

And the bloggers. You embraced a new author and shared the story with your followers. Your passion and devotion make the indie book world possible. I am very grateful for everything that you do. Please know that I try to read every single review and social media post. It's been fun getting to know so many of you. Thank you so much for your support!

And thank you to Aestas Cross for being the first blogger who was ecstatic about *The Mason List* before it was even released. You are just as fun and nice in person as you are online.

My new author friends. You have been supportive, letting me ask tons of questions and sharing my books with your friends and followers. Thank you for being so nice and welcoming!

My amazing agent Kimberly Brower. Thank you for helping me navigate the world of publishing. And thank you for taking a chance on me.

My wonderful foreign agents Flavia and Meire. You are incredibly sweet ladies.

My awesome beta readers who put up with my insanity while writing *Waiting for Wyatt.* Some of you read it chapter by chapter, some part by part, and some at the frantic end. Your input and encouragement helped me finish the story. Kelli Boland, Jenny

Sager, Trisha Rai, Brittney Lam, Patty Tate, Lisa Worth, Robyn Cowley, Bonnie Polak, Rachel Alexander, Olya Clark, and Kimberly Brower.

My awesome and amazing editor Shayla at Curiouser Editing. You cleaned up my weird grammar and made-up words. You went above and beyond. You polished the story and made it shine. Thank you for all your help and encouragement.

My sweet husband John. You put up with my spastic episodes at the end of *Wyatt*'s edits when I couldn't remember the day of the week. You are my biggest fan. You have believed from the beginning that I could be a writer. Love you.

And I thank God for second chances. None of us are perfect, but grace still exists. "Be kind and compassionate to one another, forgiving one another, just as God forgives you." (Ephesians 4:32)

ABOUT THE AUTHOR

SD Hendrickson received a Bachelor's of Science in Journalism and Public Relations from Oklahoma State University. She lives in Tulsa with her husband and two schnauzers. Currently, her days are spent teaching computer software to oil and gas companies. The Mason List was her first novel and it was a 2015 Goodreads Choice Award Semi-Finalist for Best Debut Author.

Visit www.sdhendrickson.com for more information on upcoming projects or follow on Facebook (www.facebook.com/sdhendrickson) and Instagram (www.instagram.com/sd_hendrickson/).

Made in the USA
San Bernardino, CA
26 February 2016